P9-DMT-143

Praise for

JEANETTE
BAKER

RITA® Award-winning author of *Nell*

"Baker is a fantastic writer with talent to spare...
a storyteller, plain and simple..."
—*Amazon.com*

"Delivered with thoughtful exposition and flawless
writing...a provocative book."
Publishers Weekly on *Blood Roses*

"Baker is a forceful writer of character and conflict."
—*Publishers Weekly* on *Nell*

"It grips the reader from first page to last."
—*Diana Gabaldon, author of the
Outlander series, on *Irish Lady*

Also by JEANETTE BAKER

CHESAPEAKE TIDE
THE DELANEY WOMAN
BLOOD ROSES

Watch for the next book by
JEANETTE BAKER
Coming June 2006

JEANETTE
BAKER

A Delicate Finish

MIRA®

If you purchased this book without a cover you should be aware that this book is stolen property. It was reported as "unsold and destroyed" to the publisher, and neither the author nor the publisher has received any payment for this "stripped book."

ISBN 0-7783-2182-7

A DELICATE FINISH

Copyright © 2005 by Jeanette Baker.

All rights reserved. Except for use in any review, the reproduction or utilization of this work in whole or in part in any form by any electronic, mechanical or other means, now known or hereafter invented, including xerography, photocopying and recording, or in any information storage or retrieval system, is forbidden without the written permission of the publisher, MIRA Books, 225 Duncan Mill Road, Don Mills, Ontario, Canada M3B 3K9.

All characters in this book have no existence outside the imagination of the author and have no relation whatsoever to anyone bearing the same name or names. They are not even distantly inspired by any individual known or unknown to the author, and all incidents are pure invention.

MIRA and the Star Colophon are trademarks used under license and registered in Australia, New Zealand, Philippines, United States Patent and Trademark Office and in other countries.

www.MIRABooks.com

Printed in U.S.A.

ACKNOWLEDGMENTS

I would like to thank everyone at Clos Pepe Vineyard and Winery who educated me in the "business of wine making." Their detailed and fascinating descriptions of Pinot Noir and Chardonnay grapes from vine to table were invaluable. I could not have managed this book without them.

Clos Pepe is a family-owned operation set in the heart of Santa Barbara County, Southern California's fledgling wine country. Of Clos Pepe's twenty-eight vine-planted acres, twenty-four grow Pinot Noir grapes and four grow Chardonnay. Each year the winery produces tiny quantities, between eight and fifteen barrels, of exquisite Estate Pinot Noir and about four barrels of equally fine Chardonnay, aged without the use of new oak. I was particularly impressed with their reluctance to use pesticides, and modeled my fictional DeAngelo Vineyard on theirs.

I would also like to thank my long-suffering friends and fellow writers, Patricia Perry and Jean Stewart, who frequently left their own work on back burners to painstakingly go over mine; my agent, Loretta Barrett, a constant and enthusiastic supporter of my goals; Valerie Gray, my editor at MIRA Books, for her lovely sense of humor and her belief in building authors; my husband, Stephen Farrell, because he reads every word I write and tirelessly explains the ever-unfolding mysteries of the computer; and a very special thank-you to June Quirk, a kind and generous lady, who fed and housed me from September through June while I wrote this book.

AUTHOR'S NOTE

DeAngelo Vineyards is a hundred-year-old fictional estate winery and vineyard set in the Santa Ynez Valley in Southern California. In reality, grape growing is only about forty years old in Santa Barbara County and, at the time this book was written, there were only two estate vineyards, Firestone and Fess Parker. The Santa Ynez River Watershed supports three reservoirs and three dams built between 1920 and 1952. None of the reservoirs is operated on a safe-yield basis, and therefore reservoir water users rely on other sources to meet demands at times when the reservoir cannot deliver. Cachuma Reservoir is the major water supply source for the towns of Santa Ynez, Los Olivos, Ballard and Solvang. Because it is not enough, remaining demand is met through surface and groundwater extractions. Vintners are dependent upon underground wells. Capturing a water supply is a continual problem in Southern California. Earthquakes are also common. However, it is highly unlikely that a crack in the dam would produce a significant change in the water table.

Jeanette

One

Francesca DeAngelo wasn't a praying kind of woman. She had her own personal arrangement with God. It went like this: she wouldn't ask for anything unless it was absolutely necessary but, when she did, He better damn well come through. Over the years this had worked for her quite well, with one major exception.

She climbed down from the tractor seat, walked back to where the spray rig was connected and bent down to examine the attachment. Pulling off her gloves, she wiped the nozzle free of wet sulfur. Then she clambered back up into the cab and, holding her breath, tried turning over the engine.

"Please, please, don't die on me now," she muttered. The motor coughed back into life and once again the bulky machine rolled forward. Maneuvering the vehicle between rows of Syrah vines, she looked back over her shoulder hoping to see a dusty cloud of sulfur pouring from the rig. Nothing. The machine was still jammed.

Setting her teeth, she turned off the engine and climbed down to check the nozzle once again. Everything looked normal, everything except that it wasn't working. Pushing her protective goggles to the top of her head, she gazed out over the burlap-dry hills on one side of the valley and the lush green grapevines on the other, tilted her head back to consider the position of the sun and swore like a field hand. When things went south, they went with a vengeance. She kept her voice low, a habit she'd acquired around her son, Nicholas. He was eight years old and a sponge for four-letter words.

It was late spring in Santa Barbara County. The valley between the San Rafael and Santa Ynez Mountains where the twelve-hundred-acre DeAngelo Vineyards nestled was still damp and misty even though it was high noon, perfect mildew weather. Francesca had absolutely no liquid assets to repair her rig, a grape grower's only defense against crop-destroying mildew. The weather had simply not cooperated. Because of a cool spring aided by the La Niña weather pattern, the vineyard would produce a thinner crop of Chardonnay this year and an even thinner crop of Syrah. Those annoyances she could manage. Every vintner faced weather conditions and mechanical problems. A short summer meant adding sugar to the wine. A long one meant an early harvest. A broken spray rig or linchpin meant paying interest to the bank until the profits rolled in. It all went with the territory. This was not one of those times when divine intervention was necessary. This was no more than an ordinary setback.

What Francesca couldn't think about without a serious knotting of her stomach was the county's newest adversary, Grape Growers Incorporated, the Wal-Mart of the wine industry, building a world-class winery in her valley. GGI meant bankruptcy for family vineyards. DeAngelo Winery, with its vines stitched into gently sloping hillsides and its flatlands with excellent drainage, would be among the first to fall. A weak harvest wouldn't help matters. Unless the spray rig was repaired quickly, mildew would form and she would lose three-fourths of her grapes. Then she would be in serious trouble.

Francesca would never call herself bitter. Her lip curled. Bitterness followed in the wake of disappointment and disappointment came when expectations didn't materialize. She'd given up on expectations long ago. She barely remembered what it was like to want something so badly she could think of nothing else, the time when she'd first negotiated with God, promising that if He granted her this one and only wish, she would never ask for anything else again. God listened and, very soon after, Jake Harris asked her to marry him.

Seven years later, Jake gave up on her, the marriage, the vines, their six-year-old son, Nicholas, and took a position as winemaker for a vineyard in Napa County. She still couldn't pinpoint exactly when the relationship began to sour. It had happened suddenly, without warning. One minute they were happy and the next they weren't. They'd had a fight, not a major one, certainly not the worst they'd ever had, but for some reason it was the most important one.

Jake had packed up his suitcase while she'd gone into town for fried-chicken strips, his favorite, to appease him. "It just isn't working," he said calmly, before walking out into the rainy night. He forgot the chicken strips, or maybe he hadn't really wanted them in the first place. Maybe it was just an excuse to get her out of the house so he could gather his belongings and leave.

She remembered the odd timbre of his voice and the way the back of his head glowed like a silver orb in the rainy night and the way her ribs ached because she thought about him so much. Mostly she remembered the chicken strips rising into her throat and filling her mouth before she vomited the contents of her stomach into the toilet.

In the blink of an eye, she'd gone from Francie Harris, wife, mother and half of a successful wine-making pair, to Francesca DeAngelo, single-parent vintner struggling to make do.

As far as Francesca was concerned, God owed her. He broke their bargain, freeing her to resume asking for favors once again. After all, a marriage should be worth quite a few favors. At first she prayed for a successful harvest and enough income to pay the help and her bills. Later, she added a few more items to her list, items like the evolution of the perfect grape to add to her Pinot Noir blend or enough profit from the year's harvest to pay off her bank loan for the new winery. Lately, she'd prayed for the demise of Grape Growers Incorporated. She wouldn't pray for the broken spray rig. It was too far down on the list. She would figure out something else.

The familiar ring of the lunch bell brought with it a new set of problems. Julianne, her mother-in-law, would have to be told about the faulty rig. She would wonder why the spraying had stopped. And, as usual, she would step in with the offer of a loan. If Francesca didn't accept, the tension in the house would be thick as the unfiltered must from her red grapes.

She sighed and turned toward home. It wasn't that she didn't appreciate her mother-in-law. The problem was that Julianne's generosity had created a debt Francesca couldn't possibly repay. She walked down the hill between leafy vines that soon would be thick with plump Chardonnay grapes. Her footsteps slowed as she reached the porch. She heard Nick's chattering and his grandmother's bubbly return laughter. Francesca's resolution faltered. She was ashamed of herself. Where would Nick be without Julianne? Where would anyone be without her?

Intent on her thoughts, she almost didn't recognize the truck parked in the gravel driveway. When she did, her charitable thoughts vanished and she struggled with her temper. Living with Julianne required tolerating her son. Other ex-wives stood in their doorways, sentinels barring their personal lives from the men who no longer had key privileges, smiling benignly, waving goodbye to their children on alternate weekends. Not Francesca. Jake Harris not only had key privileges, he knew every intimate detail of her refrigerator and her medicine cabinets. She didn't like it, but she couldn't exactly tell Julianne that her own son wasn't allowed to visit, not when the woman had bailed her out of more than one harrowing situation.

A whirl of brown limbs and blond hair shot out the screen door, nearly knocking her down. Francesca reached out and grabbed the back of her son's T-shirt.

"Not so fast, young man. Where are you going? It's lunchtime."

"Gran told me to tell Danny and Cyril to come right away. Dad's here and lunch is ready."

Francesca released her hold on the shirt. "Is he staying for lunch?"

"Uh-huh." Nick smiled happily. "Then he's taking me fishing. I gotta go, Mom."

"Cyril and Danny heard the bell," Francesca said. "They'll come if they want food."

Nick was down the porch and across the lawn before she'd finished the first sentence.

For the second time in just as many minutes, Francesca felt like cursing. It wasn't right that she felt so uncomfortable in her own home. She opened the screen door and stepped inside, glancing into the hall mirror. Her reflection lowered her spirits even more. She was definitely at a disadvantage. For reasons she refused to analyze, she didn't want Jake to see her looking workstained, dusty and stinking of sulfur, never mind that he'd seen her this way every day for seven years. She would have walked quickly past the kitchen and run up the stairs to her room, but Julianne spied her before she reached the landing.

"Frances," her mother-in-law called from the bottom of the staircase. "I was worried that you wouldn't take a break. Thank goodness you're sensible." Her voice changed. It was brighter, more artificial. "Jake's here."

Slowly Francesca turned and walked back down the stairs, following Julianne into the large, sunlit kitchen.

Her ex-husband sat at the table holding a mug of coffee in his left hand. His right arm was tied in a sling.

Although his face was paler than usual, the blue eyes and thick, corn-colored hair were the same. Francesca's stomach tightened.

"Hello, Frances," he said coolly.

She nodded. "It looks like you had an accident."

He shifted and she saw that his leg from the knee down was cased in plaster. "My God," she said involuntarily. "What did you do to yourself?"

"The brake cable on the tractor broke," he said briefly. "I was behind it. I hope you don't mind that I dropped by without calling first."

"I invited him for lunch," Julianne said. "I said you wouldn't mind, Frances."

"This is your house, too," replied Francesca quickly. "You don't need to ask me when you want to invite someone for a meal. I'll just go upstairs and change."

"Change?" Julianne's forehead wrinkled. "Are you done for the day?"

"The spray rig's jammed. Nothing's coming out. I'll have Cyril check it out, but I think we need a new one."

"Won't that be expensive?"

"I'll look at it," Jake volunteered. "Maybe I can jimmy something to get you through this spraying."

"Don't worry," Francesca said breezily. She would not discuss money in front of Jake. "I've got it covered. Don't wait lunch on me. I may be a while."

Once she was safely upstairs with the door of her room closed and locked behind her, Francesca turned on the bathroom shower and stripped off her clothes. Not until she was under the warm spray did she allow the gamut of emotions that Jake Harris inevitably called up to wash over her. Her heart still raced and her breath came too quickly, but she was safe behind locked doors and the comforting heat and deafening stream of water from the showerhead.

She'd always believed that pain had its own statute of limitations. Two years was long enough to recover from a divorce. All the books said so and there weren't many she hadn't read. By now she should be happily dating and on the road to a new and better romantic relationship. Why then did the mere sound of Jake's voice on the telephone bring on the air-light feeling in her stomach that she associated with childhood nightmares and oral reports and, when she was very small, losing her mother in crowded places?

Francesca rinsed the shampoo from her hair and applied a healthy handful of conditioner, working it from roots to ends. She eyed her razor, ran her hand up and down her legs and decided against shaving. Then she rinsed herself clean and stepped out of the shower. Wrapping her hair in one towel, her body in another, she pulled out her makeup bag and sat down on the floor in front of the full-length mirror.

"Mom?" Nick pounded on the door. "Gran wants to know if you're eating with us."

Francesca frowned at herself in the mirror. Was that line between her eyebrows new? "No, I'm not."

"Why?"

She relaxed her forehead and sighed with relief. The line was gone. "I'm going to the bank. I'll get something on the way."

"Dad's here."

"I know, Nick. I've already spoken to him."

"We're going fishing. Do you want to come?"

"I can't," she said patiently. "I'm working."

"You said you were going to the bank."

Francesca sighed, stood and crossed the room to open the door. She pulled Nick into her arms, regretting, not for the first time, the loss of his baby roundness. At eight years old he was all jutting angles and flat planes, with legs and arms so shadow-blade thin she wondered how they could support him.

"Going to the bank is working, Nick," she said, bending to bury her face in the warm sweatiness of his neck. "Now, go make your grandmother happy and eat lunch. Don't be too hard on your dad. He's already broken enough bones."

Nick pulled away and studied her seriously. His eyes were like hers, a warm velvety brown, but everything else came from Jake. "How come you don't go anywhere with us anymore?"

Francesca's heart ached. "Oh, Nick. You know that Dad and I are divorced."

"Don't you like Dad anymore?"

For a minute she said nothing, mentally wishing for Jake Harris a long and uncomfortable recovery. Then she shook her head. "It isn't going to be like it was, Nick. I'm so sorry."

"Dad still likes you. He asked if you wanted to come."

"Maybe some other time," she said, forcing a smile. "Today, I really have to get to the bank." She touched his cheek with her finger. "Kiss me goodbye and catch lots of fish."

Obediently he pecked her cheek.

"See you later." She watched him skim down the stairs and disappear around the landing.

Her smile faded. She closed the door and with shaking hands locked it again. Damn Jake Harris. How dare he make it seem as if she was the uncooperative one, the one who didn't want to be a family. She'd handpick every grape herself before she'd go anywhere with him again.

She was angry. According to the therapist and support group she'd joined after Jake left, anger was good. Hurt was the first stage. Anger was the second. Healing didn't happen until all stages were experienced. She didn't remember how many there were or even what they were, but Francesca certainly hoped it didn't take two years per stage. If so, she could kiss goodbye the idea of finding happiness with anyone else, unless it was all right to meet someone before finishing all the stages. She would ask the group the next time they met.

Francesca pulled a comb absently through her hair. It was thick and roan-colored and in the sunlight it glowed like a nimbus around her head. But it was absolutely straight and nothing would bring out even a hint of curl. In high school she'd tried everything, from damaging perms to heat rollers, all without success. Finally, Julianne, who was as handy with a pair of scissors as she'd been with a spatula, threw up her hands. "Your hair is your hair, Francie. Texture is one of the few things that can't be changed. Live with it or buy a wig."

So, Francesca lived with it and in the process, found that she didn't mind it as much as she thought she did. It was the perfect hair for a low-maintenance woman. During the day she would pull it back into a ponytail or braid. On special occasions she would twist it into a knot at the back of her head. Hair was a lot like the passing of seasons. After a while, you simply adjusted to whatever the day or the weather brought.

The warmth of the hair dryer soothed her. She looked longingly at the bed. It was after one and she'd been up since before dawn. Mustering her willpower, she pulled her shiny-smooth hair into a barrette, applied a light dusting of powder, enough to cover the freckles on her nose, eye shadow, mascara and her favorite lipstick, tea coral. She looked at her reflection in the mirror and smiled. Not bad. Surely Marvin Roach, the bank manager, would be impressed. She didn't primp for just anyone. Pulling a beige linen wrap skirt and sleeveless white blouse from the closet, she dug through the shoe rack for her strappy, low-heeled sandals and dressed quickly.

Quietly, she opened the door and listened. Silence from the kitchen. Tiptoeing down the stairs, she still heard nothing. Relieved that she'd escaped another encounter with Jake, she eased open the door, just in case, and peaked outside.

"They're gone," Julianne said from behind her.

Francesca jumped guiltily.

"You know, Francesca, you don't have to walk around here like a scared rabbit when Jake comes for Nick. He won't bite, you know," the older woman said. "He's really a very nice guy. Just because the two of you didn't make it as a married couple doesn't mean you can't be civil to each other. The two of you share a child, after all."

"We *are* civil to each other." She ignored the part about Jake's being a nice guy. Julianne was his mother. What else would she think?

Julianne crossed her arms, every muscle in her petite form stiff with the toll of her words. "You can't exchange more than two sentences before you're running away to wherever else you say you need to go."

The unfairness of the accusation lit a fuse that had long been simmering. Rage surged through Francesca, bringing on a display of temper. Her words were bitter, chosen to wound. "Please, remember, Julianne," she said icily, "that I'm not the one who did the running away. You're not my mother. Maybe you should have this discussion with your son."

The older woman's cheeks flamed. Her mouth opened. "No, I'm not your mother, Frances, but if I were—" She stopped abruptly, thought a minute and then turned on her heel and walked quickly back into the house.

Francesca climbed blindly into the nearest vehicle, her foreman's Jeep, turned the keys that were already in the ignition and sped east on Highway 154 toward the town of Santa Ynez.

Two

Julianne Harris moved mechanically through her state-of-the-art kitchen, gathering cake pans, spatulas, wooden spoons and ingredients, eggs and cream from the refrigerator, cake flour and sugar from the bins, baking powder and salt from the cupboards, lemons and sweet potatoes from the large, overflowing bowls on the center island, a grater, two stainless-steel bowls, her mixer and the double boiler from the cabinets. She was contracted for a fiftieth birthday party for a dozen guests. The theme was an English tea. Pasties, delicate meat pies, were already simmering in the standard ovens. The cakes could be made ahead as well as some of the sandwich fillings. She would bake the scones and assemble the perishables, cream cheese and cucumbers, chicken salads, lettuce roll-ups, salmon and shrimp wheels, lemon curd, cream-cheese frosting and raspberry sauce tomorrow morning. Now she would concentrate on her lemon, apple and chocolate-espresso cakes. She would not think about Francesca or Jake and the mess they had made of their personal lives, even if that mess included her beloved Nicholas, the love of her life, her pride and joy, her only grandchild.

Julianne loved children. She had three of her own, a son and two daughters. The regret of her life was the wide geographical spread of her offspring. The girls, Maggie and Kinley Rose, had high-powered careers that led them to childless lives in New York and London, respectively. Only Jake, her oldest, remained nearby to carry on the family tradition of working the vines. With his degree in enology and his choice of bride, lovely, long-limbed Francesca DeAngelo, a woman who not only shared his Basque ethnicity, hers on her father's side, Jake's on his mother's, but also his passion for producing wine and his desire for a large family, Julianne believed her son and daughter-in-law would give her grandchildren to indulge.

To her delight, Francesca was pregnant almost immediately. A year after the wedding she gave birth to Nick, a bright-eyed happy baby, the image of Jake except for his brown eyes. Julianne adored him. She was widowed by then, an empty nester struggling to establish her catering business in town. It didn't take much to convince her to move her business back to the big DeAngelo house and help out with Nick while Jake and Francesca worked the vineyard. The arrangement suited everyone for a while.

Normally Julianne would have cautioned against an early marriage. Jake and Francesca were barely twenty when they announced their engagement and plans to marry six months later. But there was something about the way they interacted that stopped her words. They were so in love, they had so much in common and they'd known each other since kindergarten. A marriage with that much going for it had to work, Julianne had rationalized.

It *had* worked, for a while, until Francesca's father succumbed to pancreatic cancer. He went quickly. Her older brother had long since disappeared into the alternative lifestyle San Francisco offered. He was never spoken of, disowned, gone the way of Francesca's mother who had left the family shortly after her daughter's sixth birthday. Julianne had been Francie's role model and confidante since before the child could walk steadily.

Julianne saw the Santa Ynez Valley for the first time thirty years ago in early October, after the harvest. Rows and rows of bare splintery grapevines stood in stark relief against a backdrop of golden hills covered in wild mustard and bathed by afternoon sunlight. Carl, her husband and childhood sweetheart, had been hired on as manager of the DeAngelo Vineyards. Julianne and Carl were Orange County bred, the children of farmers, born and raised in the rural shrub lands of the Irvine Ranch.

It was love at first sight for the young woman who carried the Mediterranean genes of her pastoral ancestors. But it was Carl who knew the land. It was Carl who'd predicted that the odd arrangement of east and west mountains standing perpendicular to the ocean would bring hot days and cold nights and a long growing season, perfect for lushly flavored grapes and unique wines. It was Carl who'd instilled a passion for the vines in his son as well as in Frank DeAngelo's daughter, a child well aware that she could never become what her own father valued most of all, a son to raise up in the family tradition.

Julianne felt sorry for the little girl, all big eyes and long legs with hair and skin the color of aged oak. Whether Frank DeAngelo liked it or not, Francesca would take over the vineyard. She should know the sacrifices needed to keep it running properly.

Something happened to the girl after her father's death. Julianne couldn't explain it, but it seemed that Francesca lost her softness. Determined to succeed in a man's world, she worked relentlessly to stand out as a vintner. Her wines were good. Julianne wouldn't argue that. But her methods were brutal.

At first, Jake tried reasoning with her. When that didn't work, he simply disagreed and made decisions on his own, both of which incited Francesca into a fury never before seen in the sweet-tempered child and young bride, a fury of such intensity it could only have been inherited from the long-lost Lisa DeAngelo. Thank God that was all Francesca had of her mother.

Julianne rubbed her arms. Thoughts of Lisa never failed to raise the goose bumps on her flesh. The pain of all that had passed between the two of them in those early years had faded to a dull ache, whitewashed, but not forgotten, certainly not forgiven. Never forgiven. Lisa was evil, without conscience. But she was gone and Francesca, hard-edged, softhearted Francesca, was her father's daughter, even down to her brown eyes.

Jake, too, was like his father, a man with a slow smile, an easy touch and a stubborn streak so unparalleled it was legendary. But he was smarter than Carl and he refused to play second fiddle to Francesca.

Julianne wouldn't allow a word to be said against Carl Harris, but the truth was, she hadn't married her intellectual equal. To keep the marriage intact, she'd had to assuage Carl's ego. She often wondered what was wrong with her that she couldn't manage her husband the way other women did, women who scrimped and saved their "egg money" for a rainy day, little by little amassing a small fortune and investing wisely so that when they were alone, they had a comfortable nest egg. She was a straightforward kind of woman, the kind who stood up and told the truth and took her lumps. But with Carl, she caved in, handing over her paycheck, allowing him to pay the bills and make the investments. They never did own their share of the valley, never managed to save enough for their own vineyard. Carl was always an employee and, until he died, so was Julianne. He was gone less than three months when she made her move, giving up her secure teaching job and striking out on her own. Not for one minute had she regretted it.

Julianne didn't realize how serious her son's rift with his wife was until it was too late. She remembered it as if it were yesterday. It was early evening and a rare summer rain had flooded the driveway. Without a single word of warning, Jake had knocked on her bedroom door to tell her he was leaving. "Where's Frances?" she had asked.

"Picking up takeout for dinner."

"Surely you'll wait until she gets back?" said his mother, aghast at the callous behavior of her only son. "You can't just leave without saying goodbye."

"If I wait, I won't leave," he explained tersely, running his hands through his hair. "I don't want to fight in front of Nick."

Nick. She'd nearly forgotten Nick. "Where is Nick?"

"With Francie."

"You can't do this, Jake," Julianne had begged. "You can't simply take off when your wife isn't home. You have to talk this through, come to an understanding."

He'd laughed bitterly. "An understanding? *With Francesca?* You've got to be kidding."

"Don't be sarcastic."

"Don't *you* be ridiculous. You've heard us. You know what she's like."

"Her father died, Jake. She's having a hard time."

"Frank died a year ago, Ma. If anything, she's getting worse."

Julianne drew herself up to her full height of five foot three inches. "This is a coward's action, son. I didn't raise you to run away from conflict. I'll take Nicholas out while you talk to Frances. At least tell her you're leaving. Don't run off into the night. She's your wife. She deserves more from you than that."

"You have no idea what she deserves and, because of the way you raised me, I'm not going to give you the specifics. Besides, she'll know why I've gone." He turned to leave.

"Where will you go?"

"I don't know," he said.

"Jake." Her voice cracked.

He looked back at her.

Julianne held out her arms.

He hesitated briefly, then pulled her close, kissed her

fiercely and disappeared down the stairs. Francesca and Nick pulled up in the car just as Jake was leaving. Julianne hadn't witnessed their final scene. She'd rushed out to rescue Nick, leading him to her bedroom at the back of the house using a fabricated excuse she could no longer remember.

That was two years ago. It wasn't always easy living with Francesca, but Nick needed his grandmother and Julianne swore she would crawl the distance between Sacramento and San Diego on her bare knees rather than cause him any more pain. Besides, with Jake gone, Francesca's temper had cooled. She didn't smile as much as she had before, but she was rarely angry and Julianne had to admit that she was a marvelous mother. She sighed. Perhaps certain people really did bring out the worst in each other. Still, two years had gone by and neither Jake nor Francesca had shown the slightest interest in anyone else.

Turning the electric mixer to the medium setting, Julianne cracked four eggs, separated the whites and dropped the yolks into the bowl, added sugar and waited until the mix was thick and yellow. Then she sifted in flour, baking powder, a pinch of salt and the squeezed juice and zest of three lemons. She stirred until the batter was barely moistened and then folded in a bowl of stiffly beaten egg whites.

Humming to herself, she spooned the lemon batter into a bundt pan, slid it into a preheated convection oven and reached for the grater and a bar of bittersweet chocolate. Cooking soothed her. Here, in the kitchen she'd designed, Julianne had created her own niche. Most of her family and many of her friends thought she was crazy to give up the security of her job and pension. But after twenty years, teaching elementary school was no longer a challenge. It seemed to Julianne that she was reporting to parents, filling out forms and handling discipline problems more than she was teaching. It was time to move on, time to start something of her own. She had always loved to bake, not so much after a long day in the classroom, but on weekends and vacations. She'd gained a reputation for her cakes and cookies. Her children bragged about her quick, delicious meals. But would she enjoy it as much when the food went out the door to be enjoyed by someone else's family? There was only one way to find out.

Julianne cashed out her pension, sold her home, paid down the second mortgage on the old Victorian manor house Frank DeAngelo had willed his daughter when she married and moved in with Jake and Francesca. She started out slowly, biding her time. Gradually the orders grew. Julianne knew her limits. At first, serving was not part of her contract. Sometimes she would deliver, but usually every order was picked up on location with complete instructions for reheating and assembling.

Two years later, she'd put away enough to streamline and remodel the DeAngelo kitchen, and when Frank died she'd paid off a few of the vineyard's bills, a thank-you for the years she'd lived with her son and daughter-in-law, both of whom believed in her and required nothing back. She'd helped with Nicholas but she would have done that anyway. She thought of relocating when Jake left, but Francesca wouldn't hear of it. The arrangement was uncomfortable for a bit, but that was over now, with the exception of when Jake came for an extended visit.

She surveyed her work. Something was missing, something that would soothe her spirits and bring her a sense of true accomplishment, something the ladies at the tea party would drool over and make them forget their high-protein diets. Julianne could never quite warm up to a woman who ate only protein. No one ever expanded from indulging in a slice of cake or a cookie now and then.

She thought for several minutes and then smiled. Inspiration hit. Chocolate-toffee cookies! That was it. As she worked the chocolate over the teeth of the grater and pounded the toffee bars into casual chunks, the tension in her shoulders eased. No one tasted her chocolate-toffee cookies without moaning in delight. They were rich and gooey with just the right blend of sweet chocolate, buttery toffee and walnuts. As she worked, her priorities settled into place. Nick was with his father and Francesca could be dealt with later. Julianne would brew a pot of her naturally sweetened cinnamon tea, the kind Frances liked, and the two would curl up on the old couch in the sitting room and clear the air. Jake needed a few weeks of well-deserved rest, and with a broken bone and an arm and leg out of commission, he needed tender loving care. Who else was going to give it to him but his mother? Like it or not, Francie would have to accept it.

Francesca blinked back tears and rubbed the corner of each eye with tissue. And still they came, welling up until she could barely see, spilling over and down her cheeks, leaving a salty taste on her lips. Furious at her loss of control, she gave up, reached into her purse for her sunglasses, pushed them up over her nose and ignored the tracks forming on her cheeks. Normally, she wasn't at all emotional. Jake brought this on. Just when she thought she was managing, he would show up and tear her apart all over again. What hurt the most, other than his completely unforeseen defection, was the way Julianne stuck up for him, as if Francesca had left *him* instead of the other way around.

His timing was perfect. She'd been at an all-time low, with her father's death barely behind her and a mountain of debt she'd known nothing about, all because Frank DeAngelo never believed Francesca was up to the task of running a vineyard and winery. She knew how to grow grapes, thanks to Carl Harris, but the day-to-day operation of the vineyard was unfamiliar territory. She had to learn on her own, which meant late hours and enough frustration to drive anyone insane. Jake never understood the pressure she was under. Sometimes, she was too exhausted to try and explain it to him, but most of all, she didn't want to burden him. He'd been attracted to her because she was smart and competent. She wanted to live up to his expectations. In the end, her reluctance to confide in him backfired.

She sighed. There was no point in dwelling on lost causes. It only made her miserable all over again.

As the highway opened, Francesca relaxed, caught up in the subtle colors of the landscape, butterscotch hills, golden savannah grasses, olive trees, yellow mustard, majestic white oaks, darkly crowned, their twisted limbs a canopy for birds, horses, cattle and an occasional hiker, all part of the giant watershed bound by the San Rafael and Santa Ynez Mountains rolling to the sea beneath a blister-blue sky. This was California, the real California, originally inhabited by native Chumash, explored by Catholic monks, settled by Spanish nobles and Mexican patriots, exploited by Americans seeking gold and finally, planted and tilled by waves of immigrants from every third world country on the planet, among them the DeAngelos, her own ancestors. Francesca found it laughable that legislators in Sacramento routinely tried to curb the flow of illegals into California. Most elected officials weren't more than two generations away from their own illegal-immigrant roots.

The sun-kissed hill country revived her spirits just as the river brought life to the valley, depositing fertile sediment from the mountains, nourishing America's breadbasket, a land rich as Eden. A single red-tailed hawk circled overhead and settled on a telephone pole. A swaybacked horse munched dry grass behind a white, split-rail fence. The two-lane highway stretched ahead, curving smoothly, effortlessly, under the tires of her Jeep Cherokee. The township of Santa Inez, renamed the Spanish *Ynez,* founded in 1882, lay just ahead.

Francesca crossed the city limits and eased up on the gas pedal. She was a fan of old TV westerns, *Gunsmoke* and *Rawhide*, and the town never failed to thrill her. Along the boardwalk and old-fashioned storefront facades, fine bistros and chic California eateries nestled inconspicuously among barbecue and steak restaurants. The town's flower shop and museum, crafts galleries, lovely eighteenth-century mission, homey Main Street with parking at a diagonal and fledgling backyard wineries were all within an hour's drive from the ocean. Santa Ynez had a bit of everything for everyone. Francesca was born and raised in this valley. Except for a brief stint at the University of California at Davis, her entire experience was the rich farmland sandwiched between two mountain ranges. She had good cause to be biased. In her opinion, the Santa Ynez Valley had it over Santa Barbara by a long shot. It wasn't nearly as crowded. Housing was affordable. People were friendlier and it was every bit as beautiful.

She turned down Edison Street and maneuvered the Jeep into an empty parking spot near the Santa Barbara Bank and Trust. Checking her hair and makeup, she repaired the damage to her cheeks, applied more lipstick, pasted a smile on her face and mentally rehearsed the speech that would convince Marvin Roach that she needed yet another loan to tide her over until her grapes were harvested.

"You don't have an appointment, Francesca," the bank manager's secretary informed her.

"I know that, Millie. My spray rig's jammed. I need another one or mold will set in on the vines. This is an emergency."

The woman fluttered her lashes, thick with mascara. "It pays to save for a rainy day."

Francesca smiled sweetly. "Please tell Marvin I'm here. Why don't we let him decide if he has a spare minute or two."

Millie Robbins shrugged and picked up the phone. "Francesca Harris is here to see you, Mr. Roach. I told her you were booked today but she—"

Two spots of color appeared on the woman's cheeks.

"I see," she said briefly. "I'll tell her." Carefully, she replaced the phone. Then she opened the top drawer of her desk and spent several minutes arranging the contents. Finally, she looked up and met Francesca's amused glance. "He's just about ready to go for lunch. He wants to know if you're free."

"I'm free." Francesca hitched the strap of her purse over her shoulder and walked toward his office. "I'll tell him myself."

Knocking briefly, she opened the door of Marvin's office without waiting for an invitation. She closed the door behind her and leaned against it, arms crossed against her chest.

Marvin, a large, unkempt, middle-aged gentleman with merry eyes and a head of iron-gray hair, had a mind that belied his careless appearance. He grinned at her and pulled on his coat. "I was thinking of Los Olivos. Is that okay with you?"

"I never subsidize the competition. Besides, I have to get back. What about the diner?"

Marvin looked disappointed. "I don't know how you can live with Julianne's cooking every day and then make do with food from the diner. "

"I don't think about it," Francesca replied, "and I'm not very hungry."

He took her arm and ushered her out of the office, nodding at Millie Robbins. "Hold my calls, Millie. I'll be back in an hour and my cell phone will be turned off."

Millie sniffed audibly but she said nothing.

"I'm assuming this isn't a social call," Marvin said to Francesca, "but let's wait until we order before I hear the details."

"Why don't you fire your secretary?" Francesca asked. "She scares everyone away."

Again, Marvin grinned. "That's the point. Only hardened borrowers like yourself aren't intimidated." He pushed opened the door of the Red Barn Inn and led Francesca to a booth by the window.

"I thought the whole point of a bank," she said, sliding in across from him, "was to finance people's loans, collect interest and invest money. What kind of businessman scares away his investors?"

He laughed. "Don't take this wrong, Francie, but you're hardly the type of client a bank profits from. Millie smiles at the right people."

"That's insulting. My family has been doing business with your bank for years."

He drained his water glass. "I know. That's the reason I put up with you. Decide what you want and then we'll talk."

Francesca's dark eyes narrowed. She leaned forward and lowered her voice. "Admit it. You put up with me because of Julianne."

Marvin nodded. "I won't deny it."

"Give it up, Marvin. She's not going to bite. If she hasn't already, she never will."

"Stranger things have happened."

Francesca sighed and smiled at the waitress who'd appeared at their table. "Hi, Shirley. I'll have the chicken salad and an iced tea."

"You got it, honey." She smiled at Marvin. "What'll you have, Marv?"

"Pot roast with mashed potatoes, apple pie and coffee."

"Too high on the cholesterol," she said flatly. "I'll bring you a grilled chicken breast with vegetables, and if it's gotta be coffee, you'll have decaf. It'll be here in a jiffy."

Marvin groaned. "All I eat anymore is chicken, vegetables and egg whites."

Francesca laughed. "I don't believe it. If that were true you'd be a hundred pounds lighter."

"Are you suggesting that I'm fat?" He looked offended.

"I'm suggesting that you should be grateful you have friends who care whether you live or die."

He sighed. "All right. What's this about, Francie?"

"My spray rig's jammed. The last time it happened, Herb told me not to bother bringing it in again. It's twenty years old. I need a new one and I need it fast."

"You're already in quite a bit of debt," he reminded her. "I don't know if I can get any more money for you past the committee."

"You know I'm good for it. The harvest will pay my debt and then some."

"Things have changed."

"How?" she demanded.

"GGI is here. Several wineries have folded. There's no guarantee that yours won't go the same way. We have to protect our interests."

"I'll never sell the vineyard, Marvin. It's been in my family for more than a hundred years."

He looked at her pityingly. "You may not have a choice, Francie. People depend on you. You have to think of Nick. If they make you a strong enough offer, I'd go for it."

Francesca's stomach churned. She sipped her water. "If I sell the vineyard, all loans would automatically be paid, wouldn't they?"

He nodded.

"Then you have nothing to worry about. You'll be paid when I harvest the grapes or when I sell. Either way I'm covered."

"How much do you need?"

"Thirty thousand."

He frowned. "That's a mighty expensive spray rig. May I make a suggestion?"

"Go ahead."

"You're wedded to producing without pesticides. That's bringing you three tons of grapes per acre. If you'd consider an alternative, you'd get twelve tons per acre. Your financial worries would be over."

"No, thank you."

He shook his head. "Why thirty thousand?"

A tide of red rose in her cheeks. She lifted her chin. "I don't want to come back for more later."

He nodded. "I'll bring it to the committee."

"I'm in a time crunch, Marvin. If they approve, when do you think I can have the money?"

"Tomorrow afternoon."

Relieved, Francesca leaned her head back against the vinyl of the booth. She knew that Marvin was the committee. If he agreed, they agreed with him. Her spray rig was a done deal. Now, if GGI would suddenly go bankrupt, and if Jake would disappear from the face of the earth, she would consider her life to be on the up-swing.

Three

Mitchell Gillette flipped his cell phone shut, glanced at his watch and frowned. So far the day had been wasted. He hadn't found a place to live nor had he found a horse that satisfied Sarah. Of course, nothing he did ever satisfied Sarah. He was beginning to think that short of resurrecting the girl's mother, his late ex-wife, from the dead, whatever he suggested was doomed to failure.

He looked across the table at his daughter. She was listlessly stirring her chocolate malt with a straw. At fifteen, Sarah was all arms and long legs and silver braces. She was also an impossible conversationalist. "Aren't you hungry, Sarah?" he asked.

She shrugged.

"You can choose something else from the menu if you like."

"Won't that be a waste of money? Mom was always worried about money."

Mitch gritted his teeth. There had been no reason for

Susan Gillette to pinch pennies. Not only was his spousal and child support more than adequate, but she was an heiress in her own right. Wisely, he refrained from voicing his comments. "I'm more concerned that you eat something," was all he said.

"I never eat much."

That was obvious, but in the interests of preserving the peace, once again he refrained from commenting.

"I miss Mom."

Immediately he was ashamed. She was fifteen years old and she had lost her mother less than a month ago. Under the circumstances, she was holding up quite well, better than Drew, her twin brother, who'd refused to accompany them on this expedition. His voice gentled. "I know you do, honey. I wish there was something more I could do."

She fixed her large blue eyes on his face. "I'm surprised you've taken us on. I didn't think you would. I mean, you weren't around all that much and you don't seem too comfortable around kids."

He had to give her points for honesty. It was all too true. Mitch cleared his throat, again deciding to preserve the peace. At this rate he'd be a candidate for the Nobel Prize. "I'll do everything I can to make it up to you and Drew."

She nodded, apparently satisfied. "Do we have any more appointments today?"

"A lady just west of here has a horse for sale, a thoroughbred. Are you willing to look at one more?"

Her eyes brightened. "If you are."

The last thing Mitch Gillette, vice president of Grape Growers Incorporated, wanted was to muck around in a horse stable, but he would have done a great deal worse to bring that look of interest to his daughter's face. "All right. Let's go."

Sarah followed him to the cash register where he took his place in line. A tall woman with striking bone structure stood in front of him holding a glass of water in her hand. She had taken a sip and was handing it to the waitress behind the counter when a small boy lost the helium balloon tied around his wrist. Without looking, he charged into her, knocking the glass out of her hand. It shattered on the tile floor, spraying glass fragments and water over Mitch's shirt and the fly of his trousers.

Francesca, waiting for Marvin to return from the rest room, turned quickly. "I'm terribly sorry," she apologized to Mitch. "Are you all right?"

Mitch removed a splinter of glass from his thumb and watched a bubble of blood form where it had lodged. His lips were thin and tight, but his voice was level, a testimonial to his years in the GGI boardroom. "No permanent damage." He nodded at the boy, sobbing over the loss of his balloon, now hovering at the highest point on the ceiling. "I imagine he belongs to someone, although I don't blame the person for not claiming him." He dropped two twenty-dollar bills on the counter and nodded at the waitress. "Keep the change."

Francesca's eyes widened. She watched him walk out of the restaurant with a very thin teenage girl. "Poor child," she muttered. "I wonder what her life is like." Then she knelt on the floor beside the little boy. "Don't cry, honey," she said, checking his hands and bare legs for cuts. "Someone will get your balloon."

The busboy knelt on the floor with a dustpan and broom. Shirley hurried forward and corralled the child. "I think he belongs to one of the two women having lunch in the back. I'll take him."

Marvin Roach emerged from the rest room and stepped gingerly around the glass. "Did I miss something?" he asked.

Francesca shook her head. "Just an obnoxious man, a screaming child and a runaway balloon." She pointed at the ceiling.

"Good Lord."

Francesca laughed. "Walk me back to my car and be grateful you're childless."

"I am," he said reverently. "Every day."

Mitch Gillette drove west on Highway 154 past the glider port and airstrip, past the Shetland-pony farm and the equestrian center, past rolling-hilled ranches dotted with long-legged horses grazing on yellow grass, past wineries he'd never heard of and others he had. He almost missed the sign. Easing his foot off the gas, he drove down a beaten dirt road lined on either side by olive trees leaning into each other, forming a leafy canopy of green. Fields of purple lavender and Mexican sage perfumed the air. In the distance an eagle descended gracefully over a hill of young Riesling vines. Rows of Sangiovese spilled into a pasture of lupine where a herd of cattle munched sleepily. He was mindful of the words he'd read in *Spectator,* the guru of wine periodicals. *"Wine and horses. Horses and wine. The two overlap in a harmonious symphony of sensory sensation against golden hills and verdant vines in California's central wine country."*

A flutter of anticipation rose in his chest. He was nearing one of the few estate vineyards in the area. An open wrought-iron gate flanked by brick pilings loomed ahead. The name *DeAngelo Vineyards* had been worked skillfully into the iron.

Mitch continued through the gate, up the long dirt road, through the leafy arched trellis into the gravel driveway and turned off the engine. For a long minute he looked at the house. Then he breathed deeply. Three stories of pristine white wood, trimmed in green, rose up before him. On the wraparound porch, rattan furniture was comfortably arranged and every windowpane sparkled.

"Nice house," said Sarah. She unbuckled her seat belt and followed him up the slate steps.

Julianne was elbow deep in cake flour and didn't hear the doorbell. When she did, she considered the time it would take to wash away the evidence of her trade and dry her hands thoroughly and decided against cleaning up. Whoever it was would be long gone before she answered the door. Grabbing a towel to protect the wood floors, she dashed out of the kitchen and down the hallway. As it was, the two were nearly down the porch steps before she opened the door. "Don't go," she said quickly, and then, "May I help you?"

At the sound of her voice, Mitch Gillette turned back. His first sensation was that of pleasure. For some inexplicable reason, he was pleased to see this woman, small-boned, dark-haired, with startling blue eyes and the loveliest smile he had ever seen. She was dusted from head to foot in white powder. He smiled back and held up a current copy of *Horse and Rider* magazine.

"I'm here about your ad. I called this morning. Is the horse still available?"

"It's not my horse," said Julianne. "My daughter-in-law placed the ad. Fairy Light is her horse."

"May we see her?"

Julianne shook her head. "She's out in the pasture right now and I'm afraid I don't know very much about horses. I wouldn't be able to answer your questions, but Francesca should be back soon. Would you like to come inside and wait? I have cake and a pitcher of fresh lemonade."

Mitch wanted nothing more than to follow this woman with the delightful smile and the lovely crinkles around her eyes into her kitchen. But there was Sarah to consider. He hesitated.

Julianne smiled again. This time she addressed the girl. "I'm Julianne Harris. Fairy Light really is a beautiful animal and very gentle. It would be a shame for you to leave without seeing her."

Sarah came to life. "I'm not much of a cake eater."

"No problem. There are other options. You can pick and choose for yourself." She wiped her hand on the towel. "Please, come in."

Mitch found himself inside the kind of home he hadn't believed existed anymore. A large Victorian with original wood floors and beveled mirrors, it had the look of being cared for, as if generations of children had grown up in these rooms, boldly colored with moldings and classic carpets and long old-fashioned French windows opening out to allow a spectacular view of sunlit hills covered in healthy grapevines.

"Have you lived here long?" he asked, shortening his stride to match hers.

"Ten years," she said. "This is my daughter-in-law's family home. The house was built more than a hundred years ago by the original Frank DeAngelo. Now it belongs to his great-granddaughter, Francesca." She led them around the kitchen, filled with appetizing smells, into a small sitting room furnished with two matching love seats, a coffee table and another long window with a view of the hills. She motioned toward the couches. "Please sit down. I'll bring out the lemonade and a tray."

Mitch chose the couch facing the window and sat down. "I'll enjoy your view. The lemonade sounds wonderful, but don't worry about feeding us. We've just eaten."

Julianne smiled and spoke to Sarah. "Would you like to come with me and see if anything appeals to you?"

Sarah nodded and followed her into the kitchen. She stopped at the entrance and gasped. Every available foot of counter space was filled with desserts. "Are you having a party?"

"It's not my party. I'm a caterer. It's my business. But I'm sure I can spare something for you and your dad."

"It looks great. Really, it does," the girl stammered, "but I'm full from lunch."

Julianne was already assembling a plate with two huge chocolate cookies and two slices of lemon-colored cake. The girl could use a few calories. "Take this back to your dad. I'll join you in a minute with the lemonade."

Sarah carried the dessert plate in one hand and two smaller plates and forks in another. Julianne followed with glasses and a pitcher of lemonade. "Here you are," she said. "Just in case you're in the mood for something sweet."

"You should see the kitchen, Dad," the girl said. "She has desserts coming out of the woodwork."

"I'm in the catering business," Julianne explained.

"That must keep you busy."

"Very."

He watched her pour the lemonade. She wasn't as young as he'd first thought, somewhere in her mid-forties, a woman who kept herself in very good shape. The laugh lines around her eyes gave her away. There was something else about her, a careful quality about her speech, a formal tone to her words. She intrigued him.

"You didn't tell me your names," she said.

Mitch was embarrassed. He didn't often make social gaffes. "Excuse me. I'm Mitchell Gillette and this is my daughter, Sarah. We're new to the area."

Julianne looked surprised. "You're from around here?" She handed him a plate with a cookie and a slice of cake.

"Not yet, but we're looking. We drove down from the Bay Area and stayed at the Santa Ynez Inn last night. I'm sure we'll find something soon. We have to."

"Why is that?"

"My job is here. I live in Tiburon, near San Francisco. That's an impossible commute." For the sake of good manners, he bit into the cookie. A look of surprise came over his face. He took another bite and then another.

Meanwhile, Sarah picked up her fork and cut into the lemon cake. Delicately she lifted the cake-filled fork to her lips and nibbled at it. "Wow!" Down went the fork again for a bigger bite, again and again, until the slice was gone. Then she went for the cookie. "I've never tasted anything like this," she said. "What's in it?"

"Which one?"

"Both."

"The cookies are made with crushed toffee bars, semisweet chocolate and nuts. The cake tastes the way it does because I use fresh lemon."

"I suppose nothing you make is from a box," the girl ventured.

"Not much," Julianne admitted. "I'll give you the recipes if you like."

"You mean your recipes aren't guarded secrets?" Mitch teased.

Julianne laughed. He noticed that she laughed a lot.

"Of course not," she said. "I'm flattered when someone wants to re-create my food."

A voice called out from the hallway. "I'm home, Jules. Whatever you're baking smells delicious."

"Back here," Julianne called out. "We have company."

A long-legged woman with dark eyes and creamy skin walked into the sitting room. Mitch experienced a jolt of recognition. *The woman from the diner.* Apparently, she remembered him, too. Her smile faded.

He stood and held out his hand, hoping to correct his first impression. "I'm Mitchell Gillette. This is my daughter, Sarah. We're here from San Francisco to look at your horse, Fairy Light."

Francesca didn't smile. She shook his hand briefly. "I'm Francesca DeAngelo. Fairy Light is outside today.

We'll have to track her down. How well does Sarah ride?"

"Why don't you ask her?" Mitch replied coolly.

Francesca's eyes narrowed. "All right. Are you a competent rider, Sarah?"

The girl leaned forward, her elbows on her knees. "I think so. I've ridden horses since I was seven and I'm fifteen now. I had my own quarter horse until two years ago when I had to sell her. My mom—" Her voice broke.

Mitch rested a hand on his daughter's knee.

Francesca's eyes met Julianne's in a silent question. Julianne shrugged discreetly.

"Sarah and her brother lost their mother three weeks ago," Mitch explained.

"Oh, no," Julianne cried. Involuntarily her hand reached out toward Sarah.

Francesca's voice changed completely. "I'm so sorry. I'll change my clothes and take you to see the horse."

"How old is your brother, Sarah?" Julianne asked when it was clear that Sarah had regained control of herself.

"Drew and I are twins. He didn't want to come today," she volunteered. "He's upset about the move."

"It's hard to leave your home and friends when you're fifteen," Julianne agreed. "However, it's rarely as terrible as you imagine it will be. Life turns out to be school and friends and homework and, before you know it, you're settled in."

Mitch wasn't feeling like himself at all. He had the insane desire to curl up with his head in this woman's lap, listen to her sensible wisdom and her warm laugh, eat her cake and drink her lemonade until the world righted itself again. He wanted his life back, the life he had before GGI decided they wanted to grow grapes in Santa Barbara County and Mitch was to be their pioneer. He wanted the bright lights and smoky pubs and warm restaurants and fog-shrouded streets of San Francisco. He wanted his freedom and the predictable organized existence he'd created for himself before Susan died and left him with two children he didn't know and would never understand. He wanted to be far away from the censorious judgment he'd seen in Francesca DeAngelo's eyes. Mitch wasn't used to women who disapproved of him, and somehow he knew the young woman was not impressed with his credentials.

He wasn't aware that Julianne had asked a question until the silence had stretched out for several seconds. "I'm sorry," he said, embarrassed again. "What did you say?"

"I asked what line of work you're in."

"Grapes," he said briefly, hoping she would leave it at that.

"As in growing or producing wine or both?"

Thanks to Francesca, he was spared the necessity of answering. She was back in the room, this time dressed in jeans, boots and a blue work shirt.

"Would you like to come with us, Julianne?" she asked.

"No thanks. I have plenty to do here and I wouldn't be much help anyway."

Mitch was disappointed, but he rose to the occasion. "It was very nice meeting you, Mrs. Harris. Do you have a business card? I can always use a good caterer."

Francesca looked surprised. "San Francisco is a long way to go for catering."

"We're going to live here," Sarah said. "Dad's company is transferring him."

"What business are you in, Mr. Gillette?"

It was the same question Julianne had asked, but from her daughter-in-law it took on another meaning. "I'm in the business of grapes, Ms. DeAngelo." He drew a deep breath. He'd known this would be difficult. "I work for Grape Growers Incorporated."

The icy blankness of the younger woman's face didn't disturb him nearly as much as Julianne's obvious disappointment. The silence was difficult.

Finally, Francesca broke it. "Are you aware that your cause might be a lost one, Mr. Gillette?"

"I'm here for a horse, Ms. DeAngelo."

She looked at him, judging once again. Then she looked at Sarah and her face cleared. "My car is outside. We'll drive together."

Francesca maintained a continuous flow of conversation until they reached their destination, a paddock several miles from the house where three horses munched on yellow grass behind a white rail fence.

"Fairy Light is the red one in the middle," she said, always addressing her comments directly to Sarah.

"She's beautiful," the girl breathed. "Why are you selling her?"

A look of pain flitted across Francesca's features. "She's worth too much to keep her," she explained. "She's not fast enough to race and I don't have the time to show her."

"How old is she?"

"Four. She's beautifully trained and very manageable, if you know what you're doing."

"How much is she?"

"I'll talk that over with your dad. Meanwhile, if you're interested, you can ride her."

The girl's eyes were like stars. "Can I, Dad?"

He smiled at his daughter. "That's why we're here."

"I assume you don't know very much about horses," Francesca began.

He cut her off. "I know nothing about horses. What I assume is that you'll tell me whether or not this is a horse for a fifteen-year-old girl and that your price is a fair one."

"My price is fair for a horse like Fairy Light," Francesca said carefully. "Whether she's the one for Sarah, I won't know until I see her ride. This horse won't cooperate with a hesitant rider."

"There's one more thing."

Francesca tilted her head back. He was a tall man, taller than Jake and thin like his daughter, with dark, gray-peppered hair and light eyes. His skin was unlined, making it difficult for her to tell how old he was. "What is it?"

"If I buy her, I'll need a place to board her until we relocate. It makes no sense to move her up North and then back down here again. Also, Sarah will need lessons. She's a good rider, but the whole point of buying a horse is to give her a hobby where she can be challenged and excel. I want her to have something to think about besides—" He stopped.

"Fairy Light can stay here, but I'll have to charge

you, Mr. Gillette," Francesca said matter-of-factly. "Horses take food and care. They're expensive."

"I understand."

She couldn't stop herself, even though it was none of her business. "What about your son? Is he interested in horses?"

"I'm afraid not. Drew will have a harder time settling in. He's a city boy." *Like his father,* he added silently.

Less than an hour later the transaction was completed. Francesca was satisfied that Sarah Gillette had enough knowledge to ride Fairy Light without doing damage to herself or the horse. The check she had in her pocket would more than pay for the new spray rig. The lessons she'd promised the girl wouldn't start until the Gillettes had moved to Santa Ynez. She wasn't happy about GGI's presence in the county, but she had expected it. They didn't have water rights and until they did, their plan for a world-class wine-production center was no more than a dream.

Francesca was more than pleased with her afternoon. Now, if Jake would have already gone home by the time she walked through the front door, her satisfaction would be running at a serious high.

Four

Julianne was brushing the last of the glaze on the top of her walnut rum cake when Francesca breezed into the kitchen, the tension of the morning forgotten.

"He gave me twice my asking price," she said. "I won't need the bank loan after all." She swiped a finger along the inside of the bowl of sugary glaze and stuck it in her mouth. "Yum. This is delicious. It'll be wasted on Mildred Harrington's geriatrics party."

"It's her fiftieth birthday, Francie. Don't forget who you're talking to." Julianne's fiftieth birthday had passed last month.

Francesca sucked the last drop of glaze from her finger. "You'll never be fifty, Jules. Men are still throwing their phone numbers at you."

"Name one."

"Marvin Roach."

Julianne groaned.

"Okay. Maybe he's not your type. But you wouldn't have noticed that he's interested unless I told you."

"That isn't true."

"Yes, it is. You didn't even notice the way that man was looking at you today."

"What man?"

"Mitchell Gillette."

Julianne's horrified expression spoke volumes. "Francesca DeAngelo! Shame on you. He's years younger than I am, he has teenage children and, even if neither of those were true, he's the vice president of Grape Growers Incorporated. You can't think I'd consider someone like him, even if I was in the market, which I'm not."

"Calm down." Francesca looked around for another bowl she could lick clean. "I wasn't suggesting you go out with him. I was simply pointing out that you're a young, attractive woman who shouldn't be hiding her charms behind an apron and a mixing bowl."

"I don't wear aprons and this mixing bowl brings quite a bit of income into the family coffers," Julianne reminded her.

"I know that and I'm grateful, but..." Francesca hesitated.

"But?" Julianne prompted her.

"You've been a widow for a long time. Don't you want to get married again?"

Julianne leaned against the counter, gripping the mixing bowl in one hand, the wooden spoon in the other, a thoughtful expression on her face. Francesca wondered, not for the first time, if her mother-in-law knew just how unusual she was.

Julianne Changala Harris combined the best qualities of her Basque ancestors. She had the olive skin, dark hair and silver-blue eyes typical of the people who had once populated the Pyrenees and claimed all of France, Spain and Italy as their homeland. High cheekbones, a square chin, a tilted nose and a small overbite brought a youthful, gamine quality to her features. She was naturally petite and did nothing more than walk occasionally to maintain her weight. Yet despite her many attributes she never dated and seemed more than content to occupy her time with her cooking, her family, her books and a few choice friends.

"Well?" Francesca prompted her. "Don't you?"

"I don't think so," she said with finality. "What would be the point? I'm happy the way things are."

"You're still young. Don't you think about growing old with someone?"

"I have you and Nick and Jake."

Francesca sighed. "For the time being. Nick will grow up and leave and—" She stopped.

"You don't have to warn me, Francie. It's all right. I know you'll marry again and so will Jake. I'm prepared for it, actually. I've even thought of what to do with the business."

The timer went off. Julianne pulled a pan of pastry puffs from the convection oven. "I've put some money aside and, hopefully, whomever you choose will have enough wherewithal to buy out my interest in the house."

Francesca's eyes were wide and accusing. "You'd actually consider leaving us?"

Julianne smiled. "I don't think your future husband will want to live with your ex-mother-in-law. That would be hard for any man to take."

"I haven't even met anyone yet," Francesca protested.

"It doesn't hurt to plan ahead."

The timer and the intensity of their conversation muted Jake's arrival. He stood in the doorway. "Smells delicious," he said. "Who's planning ahead?"

"I am," his mother replied. "I'll need somewhere to go when Francesca marries again."

It was a full minute before Julianne removed the remaining pastry puffs to a cooling rack and turned to look at her son. His expression hadn't changed, but his skin had gone pale. All at once, Julianne understood what she had long suspected and her heart broke.

He forced a smile, a painful stretching of skin across teeth. "So, when is the happy day?"

"It isn't," Francesca said. "We were speaking hypothetically."

Slowly, like a developing photograph, Jake's color returned. He lifted one of his crutches, pointing to the tray of cookies. "I could use one of those."

Julianne reached for a cookie and pulled out a chair from the long wooden table. "Sit down and eat. You look tired."

Carefully, Jake eased himself into the chair. Leaning his crutches against the table, he bit into the cookie. Pure pleasure lit up his face. "You have no idea how much I miss your cookies."

Francesca could feel the anger boil up in her chest. He didn't deserve Julianne's cookies. He deserved to be miserable for the rest of his life for what he'd done to their family. She clenched her hands, fighting to control herself. "Where's Nick?"

"He'll be along in a minute." Jake glanced at his mother and then at Francesca. "Did you have any luck at the bank?"

She didn't bother to ask how he knew. "Yes," she said briefly, "but circumstances have changed. I won't need the loan after all."

"I'm glad to hear it."

She looked at him pointedly. "It's getting late. Shouldn't you be on your way home?"

Once again his eyes met his mother's in a mute appeal.

Julianne stepped in. From across the room her voice, though not at all loud, was clear and deliberate. "Jake will be staying with us for a while, until the cast is off his leg. It's awkward for him to get up and down the stairs. Besides, he's due for some vacation time."

"Are you saying he'll be living here with us?" Francesca refused to believe what she was hearing.

"For a while." Julianne's eyes were level on her daughter-in-law's face, daring her to say otherwise, reminding her, silently, that the second mortgage and a good share of the maintenance for the house over the last ten years had come directly from her.

"How long is a while?" Francesca asked stiffly.

Jake spoke up. "Maybe this isn't such a good idea."

"Nonsense." Julianne was firm. "You're living in a second-floor apartment. Every time you answer the door or go shopping for food, you have to negotiate the stairs. The effort isn't worth it. If I know you, you won't bother to eat. Besides, it will be good for Nick to have you here. Frances is an adult. She'll manage. There's no reason why the two of you can't be civil to each other for a few weeks."

"It might be more than a few weeks," muttered Jake.

"I'm always civil," replied Francesca. "What I don't understand is why Jake would want to come back here at all. He was in a desperate hurry to leave two years ago."

"I'm not moving in, Frances," he said wearily. "I just need some help for a short time."

"You look like you're handling your handicap quite well. You drove your car all the way from Napa and you took Nick fishing."

"I'm not helpless. But the day-to-day routine is strenuous. Everything takes four times as long. I don't intend to be a burden. I'll help out wherever I can."

"If you can't work your own vineyard, how can you work mine?" She stood there, scornful, self-righteous, long, dark hair falling on tanned shoulders.

Jake swallowed, wondering, not for the first time, how someone so smart and so beautiful could have the killer instincts of a barracuda. He chose his words carefully. "You're already in budburst. The season will be short down here. I can help with the suckering and shoot positioning. I may not be fast but, if I remember correctly, every pair of hands is usually welcome this time of year."

He was right about her needing help, but he was hardly in any condition to tear off water shoots. She was silent, thoughtful. Finally she spoke. "Suckering requires too much stooping and pulling. Besides, we need twenty-four-inch vines before we do any shoot positioning. You won't be here long enough for that." She looked at Julianne. "Will he?"

"Probably not," she replied. "However, the offer was made graciously. It deserves a gracious thank-you."

Francesca flushed, embarrassed. Julianne always managed to put her in her place. "I apologize," she said stiffly. "As far as helping out, let's just see how things go."

"Meaning you hope I'll be long gone before you need me."

She ignored his comment and changed the subject. "Nick will be happy you're here. He misses you."

"I miss him, too."

She opened her mouth to remind him, once again, that he was the one who'd decided on separate living arrangements, then decided against it. She did not want to argue in front of Julianne.

Turning her back, Francesca rinsed her hands in the sink and passed them over a dish towel hanging over the sink. "You know your way around. Make yourself comfortable." She looked at Julianne. "I ate a late lunch. I'd like to order the spray rig and go over the books. Don't worry about dinner for me."

Julianne's lips twitched. "I'll leave any leftovers in the refrigerator in case you get hungry later. I've put Jake in the downstairs guest room."

There was no mistaking the look of relief on Francesca's face. The guest room on the other side of the house had its own bathroom and entrance. Other than an occasional meal, she wouldn't have to see him at all.

Mitch drove past the sign welcoming visitors to the elite harbor town of Tiburon with a sigh of relief. The drive had been long and awkward, a sad state of affairs for a father and daughter, but true nevertheless. Turning on Edison Street, he slowed to accommodate the tourists that inevitably crowded the picturesque bayside town where he chose to live. Hugging the side of the street, he turned left on to Paradise Road and made his way up the hill toward home. Even before he pushed the button on the garage-door opener, he could hear the loud pounding of the modern age's definition of music. He drove into the garage. Drew was home and, as usual, he had eschewed his father's request to use headphones.

Sarah looked at him nervously. "I guess Drew's home."

"I guess he is."

"Maybe he didn't expect us this early," she offered.

"I'm sure he didn't."

Sarah drew a deep breath. "Are you mad?"

Mitch frowned. "Do I look like I'm mad?"

She nodded.

He rubbed the spot between his eyebrows. "I'm not. I don't like Drew's music, but I suppose my parents didn't like mine either. Drew thought he'd be alone. How can I be mad?"

Sarah relaxed. "Mom didn't like his music either. She wouldn't let him listen to it. He did anyway, but not in the house."

Mitch had a new appreciation for Susan. He was about to ask Sarah how her mother had managed to get Drew to do what she asked, when the side door leading to the house opened and a young girl, pierced in every conceivable orifice, stepped out. Her eyes widened for an instant but, recovering quickly, she waved, sauntered to the refrigerator Mitch kept in the garage, helped herself to two cans of soda and walked back inside.

"Who is that?" Mitch asked.

Sarah shook her head. "I don't know many people here in Tiburon yet."

"Did your mother allow him to have a girl in the house when she wasn't home?"

"I don't think it ever came up. Drew is..." She hesitated.

"Go on."

"He's different here. He didn't want to move."

"I know." Mitch sighed and looked at his daughter. "What about you, Sarah? How are you doing? I don't think you wanted to move either."

She shrugged. "There wasn't anything else to do," she said dully. "Mom's dying was the worst. Nothing else really mattered after that."

"Did you know she was sick?"

"Not that sick. I guess she wanted to keep it from us."

"I wish I'd known." It was a safe and false sentiment. Mitch felt it the instant he said it. What could he have done even if he had known?

Sarah kept silent.

Mitch tried again. "I need some help here, Sarah. I don't want Drew to think it's okay to have a girl in the house when I'm not home, but I don't want to make a big deal of it. After all, we're moving. She'll be irrelevant in a matter of months."

"*Months* is a long time, Dad. She could be pregnant by then."

Mitch blinked. Matter-of-fact reality doled out by a child impervious to shock. "I'll keep that in mind," he said dryly and opened the car door. "Let's go inside."

The house was blessedly silent when Mitch walked inside and up the stairs. The guest room, now Drew's bedroom, was the first on the left. The door was closed. Mitch knocked. "Drew, we're home."

"Hi."

The monosyllabic response lit the fuse on Mitch's anger. He turned the knob. The door was locked. "Open the door, Drew," he ordered.

Seconds passed. Mitch fought his rising temper. Finally, he heard movement on the other side of the door. The latch clicked, the knob turned and Drew opened the door a crack. He glanced at his father and then looked at the floor. The whites of the boy's eyes were bloodshot and his lids were swollen half shut.

Mitch pushed open the door. Candy wrappers, Coke cans and empty bags of potato chips littered the floor, and the sweet weedy smell he hadn't forgotten from his college days hung in the air. He motioned to the girl half sitting, half lying on the bed. "I think you'd better go home."

She slid off the bed into a standing position, a look of relief on her face, and then passed through the door and down the stairs without saying a word.

Drew continued to stare at the floor.

"Give me the marijuana."

"I don't have any more."

"Where is it?"

"She took it."

"You will never bring drugs into my house again. Do you understand?"

The boy shrugged.

"Answer me when I speak to you."

"Whatever."

"I don't want you bringing anyone home again without permission either."

Again, the nebulous shrug.

"Are you listening to me, Drew?"

"I'm listening."

"I won't tolerate defiance. I'm not your mother."

"That's an understatement," the boy muttered.

Mitch's hands clenched. He wanted to wipe the blank smirk off his spoiled adolescent face. "What did you say?"

"It doesn't matter." Drew's voice cracked. "Nothing matters anymore." He threw himself down on the bed and buried his head in his arms. "You can do anything you want to me," he said, the words muffled in the folds of his shirt. "It just doesn't matter."

Mitch stared down at the lanky form of his only son, wondering if there was anything he could do to repair the rift between them. Deciding he needed a strategy that would take more than a minute to formulate, he backed out of the room and closed the door. His hands shook.

Sarah stood at the top of the stairs, her eyes huge. He'd forgotten her. "Did you know that Drew was experimenting with drugs?"

She opened her mouth, hesitated and closed it again. Then she shook her head.

"What is it, Sarah? If you don't tell me, I can't help him. Does Drew have a drug problem?"

"He never did before," she said defensively. "It isn't going to help him if you act like you don't like him."

Mitch reared back as if she'd slapped him. "Of course I like him," he exploded. "I love him. He's my son. How am I supposed to react when I see that my fifteen-year-old son is locked in his room with a girl and they're both loaded?"

Sarah changed the subject. "Speaking of the girl, you shouldn't have let her go home."

"Why not?"

Sarah sighed. Did she have to explain everything? Was he really as dense as he seemed? "Mom would have called her parents," she explained.

Mitch's face froze. She was right. How long did it take before one was qualified to be a parent? When did the right instincts kick in? He had always been a high achiever, reaching the top of his class and his field relatively quickly. Why was this particular and most important learning curve so difficult for him?

Five

Objectively, Mitch knew that Francesca DeAngelo was beautiful, in the long-legged, earthy way of an Aldo Luongo painting. He wondered why he wasn't the slightest bit attracted to her. Maybe it had to do with her age. On rare occasions, he'd seen younger women socially, but usually he preferred them over forty. Women who remembered and had opinions on the same important societal and historical moments he did were simply more interesting. However, that didn't stop him from admiring a pretty face. Francesca DeAngelo, unadorned by makeup, her hair pulled back into one of those elastic things women wore, was undeniably one of the prettiest faces he'd seen in a long time, but Mitch was not admiring her. More than likely it was her demeanor rather than her youth that put him off. She wasn't at all friendly, or even accommodating.

He rested his hand on Sarah's shoulder and spoke to Francesca. "Are you sure you don't mind if I leave her with you until noon? I'd like to take my son to look at a house."

She waved her hand airily. "Not at all. I can't imagine why you'd want to stay. You'd only be in the way."

Mitch stared at her in amazement. Rudeness was an attitude he didn't tolerate easily and he was sure he'd never experienced anyone as rude as this young woman with her lovely face and her razor-sharp tongue. Interestingly, she seemed oblivious to her offensive behavior. He hoped it wouldn't rub off on Sarah. One teenager with attitude was enough. He hugged his daughter briefly. "I'll be back in two hours, honey. Have fun."

She barely acknowledged his departure, completely focused on the red horse, Fairy Light.

Mitch made his way up the path from the barn, across the circular driveway to the back of the house. Against his better judgment, he'd left Drew with Julianne while he walked Sarah to the stables. Julianne had insisted. He only hoped his son hadn't destroyed all possibility of friendship between the two families, especially since they would, more than likely, be neighbors. He knocked on the door, waited a minute and walked in. "Hello," he said. "I'm back."

"We're in the kitchen," Julianne called out.

He found them sitting on stools in front of the large island, Julianne on one side, Drew on the other. She held a pencil poised over a pad of paper. A glass of water and four plates, each with a fork and a piece of cake, sat in front of the boy. Two of the pieces had already been sampled.

"I'm thinking about accepting a regular client, a local hotel," Julianne said. "They want two cakes a week."

"That clarifies everything," said Mitch, completely baffled. He leaned against the counter and crossed his arms.

Julianne laughed.

Once again, Mitch wanted to do whatever he had done to make her laugh again.

"Drew is helping me decide which cake should be a standard every week and which I should alternate," she explained.

"It sounds like quite a responsibility," Mitch replied. "I hope he's up to the task."

Her eyes twinkled. "Oh, I'm sure he is. Who better than a teenage boy?" She smiled at Drew. "Well? Which one will it be?"

Drew swallowed the last of his bites and thought a minute. "The chocolate-mocha," he pronounced.

Mitch laughed. "Why am I surprised?"

Julianne nodded, completely serious. "Okay. Why the chocolate?"

The boy's forehead wrinkled. "Well, chocolate is a popular flavor. Most people like it for any occasion. Plus, you'll always be able to find the stuff it takes to make a chocolate cake. I like the strawberry-cream and the lemon-blueberry, too, but fruit is seasonal, isn't it?"

Julianne smiled. "I never thought of that. Fruit isn't exactly seasonal here in California, but it's hard to find sweet berries in winter without paying more than I want to. It would also raise the price of the cakes. You're absolutely right, Drew. Chocolate will be my standard and I'll alternate the others depending on the season. I knew you'd be the one to ask the minute I saw you."

Drew grinned. "You would have figured it out, but

maybe not for a while. My reward will be a piece of cake anytime I want."

To Mitch's delight, Julianne laughed again. "You're on," she said.

Mitch couldn't believe it. His surly, difficult son was actually communicating and doing it with charm and intelligence. The woman was a witch, a good witch. Once again he didn't want to leave this warm, sunlit kitchen with its wonderful smells and copper pots and sweeping views of burlap hills. Most of all he didn't want to leave Julianne. Her contagious laugh and the knack she had for saying just the right thing to make a teenage boy feel important was balm to his spirits.

Reluctantly, he left his hostess and drove north with his son.

Mitch had looked at a number of houses since his first visit to the valley two months ago, but none had satisfied him. He couldn't have put into words what he was looking for. It was an ideal, not easily described, but he knew he would recognize it when he found it. Without a great deal of enthusiasm he negotiated the twisting road into the hills, shaded by giant oaks and peeling eucalyptus, crossing the stone bridge with the creek below.

When he first set eyes on the house, he rubbed his eyes, blinked and rubbed them again. Then, with pounding heart, he pulled into the courtyard and climbed out of the car to explore.

The rambling structure was perfect, more than he'd hoped to find, an old Spanish hacienda with tile floors, original moldings, oddly shaped bedrooms and old-fashioned windows. It was a house with charm, a house for raising a family.

The real estate agent had given him a map, confident that no sale would occur, that this would be a morning wasted. Wealthy, confident businessmen from the city who owned property in Tiburon would not be interested in a ramshackle stone house surrounded by leaning oak and eucalyptus, enclosing a courtyard wild with red bougainvillea, a defunct winery on one side and a mountain on the other. He had no idea that Mitchell Gillette would walk up the creaking stairs, rest his eyes on the shrouded furniture, finger the faded drapes covering the long windows, explore the spidery, bat-filled caves of the winery dug into the mountain and feel a tug, a definite pull from a bygone age. He didn't know that Mitch's dream was to grow grapes, the kind of grapes that would not survive anywhere but in the hot days and cold misty nights of perpendicular mountains, grapes that would produce a Pinot Noir unlike any other in the world.

Drew was less than impressed. At first he'd refused to leave the car, but when his father didn't return after thirty minutes, boredom overcame his desire to prove a point. He climbed out of the car and walked through the copse of eucalyptus, under the canopy of oak toward the gurgle of a stream. He would never be happy away from the city. Tiburon, where his father lived, was a barely acceptable alternative, a ferry's ride across the bay from everything familiar, everything he wanted back again.

His dragging feet disturbed the dry soil. The dusty nimbus rose into the air around his face. He sneezed and wiped his nose on his sleeve. It was hot and dry, nothing like San Francisco, and he'd worn the wrong clothes. The idea of starting school in this place was an unimaginable horror he couldn't think about, not without the dulling help of the weed that, lately, had become more than recreational.

Drew couldn't think about tomorrow. It was enough just to make it through the present. When the sun set, signaling the end of another day, he sighed with relief, another one down. Night meant nothing more was expected of him. He could disappear into his room, turn on the television or his CD player and bury himself in a world that required no response.

He found the stream behind a tangle of wild vines, thick with cane and buzzing with insects. Collapsing on the bank, he pulled off his shoes and stuck his feet in the water all the way to his shins, careless of the dragging cuffs of his jeans. Pulling a pack of cigarettes and matches from one pocket, and a cell phone from the other, he lit up, inhaled and looked at the face of the phone. No reception. Frustrated, he jammed the phone back into his pocket, leaned his head against the trunk of a three-hundred-year-old oak and closed his eyes.

Drew didn't think he'd ever hated anyone as much as he hated his father. Three months ago his world had irrevocably changed. Until then he could pretend his mother would get better. Her days spent in bed, the radiation treatments, her loss of hair and weight, the color of her skin, a frightening gray-green, he ignored. It wasn't until she actually stopped breathing that reality struck. She was dead and, except for Sarah, he was alone in the world. Drew didn't really consider his father. He was an absorbed stranger, decent enough, but involved in other things. Drew couldn't remember the last time he and Sarah had spent the night with him before their mother died. He hadn't thought beyond the funeral and making it through the end of the semester. Even the presence of his father in the house that breathed and smelled of his mother didn't faze him. It wasn't until the school semester ended and Mitch said the house had been sold and Drew and Sarah would be moving with him to Tiburon did he realize what losing his mother really meant. Because she had died, he'd lost it all, his home, his friends, his world as he knew it, all the comfortable routines cultivated over the span of his lifetime. He hated Tiburon. He hated his father and he hated this nowhere place Mitch was probably planning to buy without even asking what he and Sarah thought about it.

Drew buried the butt of his cigarette, unwrapped a stick of gum, stuck it in his mouth and stood. His feet were numb. Where was Mitch anyway? How long did it take to look at a house? Just then he heard his name. His father was calling him. Slowly, taking his time, Drew pulled on his shoes, climbed up the embankment and walked back toward the house.

Mitch leaned against the car and frowned. The euphoria of finding the house was fading, replaced first by annoyance and then worry. Where was Drew? He checked his watch. Sarah's lesson would be over in ten minutes. There was no way he could make it back in time and his cell phone had no reception to warn Francesca that he would be running late. Then he saw him. Relief, so strong the words stuck in his throat, flooded through him.

Drew spoke first. "Are we done here?"

Mitch nodded. "I think so. What do you think of the place?"

Drew shrugged and opened the car door. "It doesn't matter what I think as long as you like it."

Mitch climbed in beside his son and backed out of the courtyard. "Is that the way it seems to you?"

Again Drew shrugged.

"It matters very much to me what you and Sarah think."

Drew didn't answer.

"I'm being transferred down here to oversee this project. It's my job. You do see that, don't you?"

"I said it doesn't matter."

"You could try to be agreeable."

Drew stared out the window. If only he could just make this all go away.

"Drew? Are you listening?"

He nodded.

Mitch gritted his teeth and drove on, hoping Francesca wouldn't be too angry over the time.

Francesca ran her hand over Fairy Light's flanks, replaced the brush she used for rubbing her down and locked the door of the paddock. She smiled at Sarah. "I'm impressed. You really don't need riding lessons."

"Don't tell that to my dad," Sarah warned her.

"Why not?"

"He won't let me ride alone."

Francesca laughed. "You can't take lessons forever."

"If he thinks I've learned a lot, he'll change his mind."

Francesca looked beyond Sarah to the swirl of dust on the road. "I wonder where he is."

Sarah glanced at her watch anxiously. "He's never late. Something must have happened."

"Maybe I'll have to adopt you," Francesca teased her.

Sarah grinned. "That wouldn't be so bad." She looked around. "I like it here."

The dust cleared and they watched the sleek, silver-gray Infiniti pull up beside them.

Mitch stepped out of the car. "I'm sorry about the delay." He smiled at Sarah. "We found a house."

Sarah swallowed. "Where?"

"Up in the hills. It needs work, but it's big enough and it has a winery."

Francesca's eyes widened. "Are you planning to grow grapes?"

Mitch's smile faded. "I'm going to try."

She folded her arms and leaned against the rail fence, one hip jutting out aggressively. "Isn't that a conflict of interest on your part?"

"In what way?"

"You work for GGI. Isn't your job description to buy up all the choice vineyards in the area for the purpose of creating an all-purpose coastal winery?"

"GGI is buying land for a winery," he agreed. "However, we aren't in the business of bankrupting small vineyards. We offer market-value price and we buy only when the seller is completely satisfied."

Francesca's lovely mouth turned down. "How noble of you. Do you honestly think the rest of us can make a living when GGI comes in and offers nonunion wages to employees and rock-bottom prices to customers who don't know a good wine from a bad?"

"That isn't my problem."

Francesca's hands clenched and a thin white line appeared around her lips. "If you intend to live in this community, Mr. Gillette, it had better become your problem. Your children will be attending school here. You'll need to shop in our stores. The fire department relies on volunteers. Since I've never heard of you before, I assume you're a novice at growing grapes and producing wine. Where will you go when you need advice or, God forbid, help if the weather isn't right or a virus takes most of your vines? We work together here, and unless you want to isolate yourself completely, you'll have to fit in."

Her words were delivered calmly, with only the slightest hint of passion. Because of her logic and lack of temper, Mitch was impressed. Francesca was intelligent. He wanted to appease her. "I'm interested in experimental enology," he explained. "I won't be marketing wine commercially. My job is to establish a winery here, not put people out of business. Whatever GGI does, it will be with that in mind."

"Do you think I don't read, Mr. Gillette? Do you think people don't talk to each other? Your company has a reputation. I don't see that your behavior here has been any different than in Paso Robles or Sonoma."

That stung. He had not been in charge of those operations. "You didn't mention Napa," he said softly. He was proud of Napa.

"Napa has been established for a hundred years," she said contemptuously. "You can't hurt the connoisseurs who produce hundred-dollar bottles of wine. As for the others, Mondavi and Gallo already have a monopoly on cheap wine. You're just one more winery in Napa. Here, it's different. We're struggling to be taken seriously. For the first time our wines have world markets. You'll offer wine at half the price. It won't be as good, but most of our clientele don't know that. We'll be obsolete in five years."

"You're painting a dire picture."

"I'm a realist."

Something didn't fit. "I'm curious, Ms. DeAngelo. If this is a done deal, why aren't you selling out? GGI has made you a generous offer."

Francesca shook her head. "You've misunderstood. I didn't say it was a done deal. You can tear up the ground and plant your vines and build your monster vineyard, but unless you have water, that's as far as you'll go."

"What makes you think GGI won't get water rights?"

"Because I'm on the council."

Mitch recognized when he was bested. But it was by no means a permanent dilemma. He held out his hand. "What do I owe you for the lesson, Ms. DeAngelo, and when can we schedule another one?"

"Touché," she said softly, tilting her head to one side. She did not take his hand. "Under different circumstances, I might have liked you."

"I'll have to work on that, won't I?"

She shook her head. "My price is too high."

He grinned. "Sometimes it's not about money."

"Who said money had anything to do with it?"

His grin faded. "I don't want to make enemies among the vintners. I could use your help. Is it possible for us to compromise?"

"I don't think so," she said slowly. "Everything you stand for, I'm against. But, if you'd like me to explain why, I'll be happy to do so."

"When?"

She nodded at Sarah and then at the car. "You're tied up right now. Tell me when you're down here again, and we'll work something out."

"It's a deal." He held out his hand again and this time she took it. "I'm afraid you're not to be rid of us so quickly," he said. "Julianne invited us for dinner. I've accepted, but if you'd rather have us leave, we will."

There was nothing else Francesca wanted more, and if Mitch Gillette had been alone she would have told him so. But he wasn't alone. She smiled brilliantly. "Don't be ridiculous. Of course you'll stay."

Six

Jake Harris was attempting to walk the rows of DeAngelo Vineyards's award-winning Syrah grapes by positioning one crutch in front of him, balancing on his good leg, then stabilizing the other crutch and swinging the bad leg over. It was an arduous task. Sweat rolled off his forehead. Fifteen minutes had passed and he hadn't covered more than a few yards. At this rate he'd be here until midnight. He stopped, wiped his forehead with the sleeve of his shirt and cursed. Breaking a leg at twelve meant three weeks of misery. Breaking one at thirty was another story altogether.

A stone's throw ahead, eight-year-old Nick waited patiently. He refrained from reminding his father that Francesca had banned four-letter words from the fields and the winery. Pitching his voice after the optimistic boom of his soccer coach, he spoke encouragingly. "You can make it, Dad. You're doing a good job. It isn't too much farther."

In spite of his discomfort, Jake laughed. "I'm done,

kiddo. Sorry to disappoint you, but walking in the dirt is a lot harder than crossing a parking lot on these things." He waved one crutch in the air.

Nick walked back to where his father stood, sat down between the vines and crossed his brown, spider-thin legs. "You're gonna get better, right?"

Jake nodded. "No doubt about it."

"I wanted to show you the section that Mom gave me. I've done it all myself, even the grafting. She showed me how."

"I know, Nick. I'm sorry, but all isn't lost. We'll take the four-wheel in tomorrow as far as we can. I'll be able to make it from there."

Nick nodded, satisfied. "It's nice having you here again."

Jake ruffled his son's hair. "It's good to be with you wherever you are."

"How long will you stay?"

"Just a few weeks more, until the cast comes off my leg."

"Why don't you ask Mom if you can stay longer?"

There was a great deal he wanted to say, but Jake didn't know how honest to be with an eight-year-old. He hesitated, starting slowly. "I know you were still a little guy when I left, but do you remember the way it was when I lived here?"

Nick nodded.

"Your mom and I didn't get along all that well. We argued all the time."

Nick's brown eyes, so like Francesca's, were wide and curious. "What did you argue about?"

Jake laughed bitterly. "Everything from how to run

the vineyard to what to have for dinner." There was more, but the subject was hardly one for a child's ears. "It wasn't *what* we said that was important, Nick. It was why we said it."

"Why did you say it?"

Jake thought a minute. "I don't know," he said at last. "I guess I didn't feel very important. Nothing I said or did was right."

Nick was fidgeting, sweeping the dirt around him into little mounds. "Are you happier now?"

Jake was about to say he was. He opened his mouth to speak and made the mistake of meeting his son's pure, unflinching gaze. The boy deserved the truth, no matter how difficult it was to admit. "The thing is, Nick, I'm not really very happy at all. I miss you. I miss your grandmother and I miss your mom. I love it here. It's home."

"Why don't you come back?"

Jake stretched out his good leg and massaged the knee of his other one above the cast. "Some things," he said, "can't be taken back. When I left, it made your mom mad. She's not so mad anymore, but she doesn't want me to come back. Do you understand?"

"Yes." The word was definite, spoken with surety. Nick had always been like that, even as a baby. No half-hearted *yeah* or *I think so,* always a distinct *yes.* He was like Francesca. She answered questions without disclaimers, leaving no one guessing where she stood on a matter. *Opinionated* wasn't a strong enough word to describe her. At first Jake had approved of and even admired her decisiveness, until he realized that it came with an inflexibility so rigid and controlling that he couldn't breathe. At DeAngelo Vineyards, *her* way was the right way. And it wasn't only the vineyard. She'd dominated every aspect of their lives, from the grocery store to the checkbook to their bedroom. Jake had felt strangled. It was either leave or give up every part of himself and suffocate. He chose to leave.

But lately he'd questioned his decision. After his initial relief, he realized he wasn't any happier than before. Apparently, according to Julianne, neither was Francesca. Happiness was important to Jake, unlike Francesca who believed it was enough to be reasonably content. Jake wanted no part of reasonable or content. He wanted bells and whistles. He wanted spontaneity and delirious hilarity. He wanted fun and giddiness and the shortness of breath that came with watching his wife come out of the bathroom after she'd dried her hair and it floated down her back and across her shoulders like a curtain of dark amber. He wanted to appreciate her and be appreciated in return. He wanted it the way it was before Frank DeAngelo died and his daughter thought she had to prove to everyone in the valley that she was every bit the vintner he was.

Jake thought the situation was worth exploring. But, so far, Francesca had made it very clear that she wasn't interested in rehashing what might have been. He was determined to respect her wishes. Jake knew he'd hurt her badly. When she was full of questions, he wasn't willing to talk. Now he was ready and she wanted no part of him. It was a frustrating situation, but turnabout was fair play. The thing was, he didn't believe he'd ever meet anyone he could love half as much as he'd loved Francesca DeAngelo before it all went sour. It was a lowering thought to realize that the best he would ever have, the most he would ever feel, was all behind him.

Nick's penetrating stare leveled him. He shouldn't be having this conversation with an eight-year-old, even a very special eight-year-old. He pulled himself together. "We should probably get back. Your grandma puts a lot of effort into her meals. She wouldn't want us to be late."

"I think we're having company," Nick pronounced. He stood and dusted off the back of his shorts.

"Who is it?"

"Some girl who bought Fairy Light. Mom is giving her riding lessons. Gran invited her dad, too."

"All the more reason not to be late."

They walked back to the house. Nick danced around his father, first in front and then behind him, bending to pick up bugs and inspect pebbles, which he either tossed aside or stuffed into his pocket. It was pure pleasure to have Nick beside him, comfortable, chattering about whatever was on his mind. Never, in his wildest dreams, had he imagined having his son grow up without him.

A silver-gray Infiniti was parked in front of the house. Jake nodded approvingly. "The guy's got great taste in cars."

"I like yours," Nick said loyally.

"Thanks, pal, but I wouldn't mind trading up. Who is this guy that Gran invited?"

"He's Sarah's dad. I think they're moving here, but I wasn't really listening." He brightened. "I'll race you to the porch. If I win we'll rent a movie tonight."

"It's hardly a fair competition," Jake protested.

Nick thought a minute. "I'll give you a head start."

"How much of a head start?"

"I'll go all the way back to the end of the grass."

Jake considered it. "Which movie?"

"Nemo."

"You've seen it a dozen times."

"Don't you like it?"

"I liked it the first three times I saw it with you. Let's try something else," Jake suggested.

"If I win, it's *Nemo*. If you win, it's something else."

"Why don't we do something else?"

"Like what?"

"We can play chess or Scrabble, or we can read a book."

Nick's forehead wrinkled. He was thinking seriously. "Okay," he said. "If I win, we do what I want. If you win, we do what you want."

"It's a deal." He held out his hand. Nick shook it before heading back to where the lawn started.

"Ready, Dad?" he shouted.

Jake balanced on his good leg. "Ready."

"On your mark."

Jake leaned forward.

"Get set, go!" the boy shouted and shot forward, his long legs covering the ground like a deer. He reached the porch a full five seconds ahead of his father.

Julianne opened the door. "What's going on here?"

"I won the race." Nick flung his arms around his grandmother's waist. "Now Dad has to watch *Nemo* with me."

Julianne's lips twitched. "Again?"

"Again," Jake groaned.

"What possessed you to think you could actually beat him?" she asked. "I mean, look at you."

"Madness."

Julianne laughed. "You're pathetic. He can talk you into anything." She moved aside. "Come in and wash your hands. Dinner's almost ready."

"Who's our guest?" asked Jake under his breath.

"The vice president of GGI and his children, a boy and a girl."

Jake's eyes narrowed. "You're kidding? Francie wouldn't let him within ten miles of this place."

Julianne shrugged her shoulders. "Obviously, he's very persuasive."

"No one's that persuasive."

"See for yourself. We're eating in the dining room tonight."

"No cocktails in the living room?"

Julianne shook her head. "Frances isn't that far gone."

Jake took his time cleaning up. By the time he hobbled into the dining room, everyone was already seated. "Sorry, I'm late," he apologized. "I'm at a disadvantage."

Mitch stood and extended his hand. "I'm Mitch Gillette, and these other strangers are my children, Sarah and Drew. It looks like you've had a bad time."

Jake grinned and shook the older man's hand. "I'm Jake Harris and I've had better days." He took the chair opposite Francesca.

"Sarah is taking riding lessons from Francesca," Julianne explained and smiled at the girl while she began passing around the serving bowls. "How is it going?"

"It's great," replied Sarah. "I love Fairy Light."

"Francie loves her, too," said Jake. "I remember the first day we brought her home."

"That was a long time ago," replied Francesca hurriedly. "I'm glad she'll have a good home with Sarah."

"How about you, Drew? Do you like horses?" Jake asked.

"No," the boy said shortly.

Francesca buttered her roll carefully. "Tell us about your job, Mr. Gillette. Exactly what is it that you do at GGI?"

"I buy land, then arrange for the building and operation of the plant after the land has been acquired," he said pleasantly. He heaped his plate with mashed potatoes and salad. "What I'm really interested in is producing a top-notch Pinot Noir."

Jake's eyebrows rose. "Pinot Noir grapes aren't as marketable as Chardonnay, Merlot or even Cabernet. I would have thought GGI would be interested in whatever made the most money."

"This has nothing to do with GGI. I plan to start my own vineyard and winery."

The silence around the table was palpable. Forks halted halfway to mouths as six pairs of eyes stared at him.

Francesca was the first to speak. "You're really serious. I didn't believe you."

"Yes, I am."

"Where?" Julianne and Jake spoke at the same time.

"I've found sixty acres thirty minutes north of here. The property has a cave and a winery. I notified my real estate agent earlier today. The offer was accepted."

Julianne's eyes were narrow and slightly slanted. Cat eyes. "You bought the Vandenburg estate?"

"Yes, I did."

Sarah gasped. "You're kidding? You already bought it without even showing it to me?"

"Drew saw it," her father pointed out. "Besides, I want to make some changes. Not a great deal, but enough so you'll like the house right away."

"Pinot Noir grapes don't grow as well here as they do farther west," Jake pointed out. "You might consider other varieties."

Mitch lifted his glass and considered the wine. It was a rich, clear ruby with hints of black currant and cassis, obviously an estate wine and a good one. More than likely the two bottles on the table sold for a hundred dollars each, retail. "Such as?" he asked politely.

Jake shrugged. "You name it. Cabernet, Merlot, Syrah, even Semillon. Syrah is our specialty here in the valley. As for whites, you might try Riesling or Viogier if you don't want to compete with a Chardonnay."

"I have nothing against Chardonnay," replied Mitch. "The thing is, I've got my heart set on Pinot Noir. If you have any tips in that area, I'll be happy to hear them."

"Why Pinot Noir?" Francesca asked, interested in spite of herself.

"I think of it as a challenge," Mitch explained. "I've tasted all the varieties available in this valley. They're all very good. In fact, they're as good as Napa and most of Europe. What I haven't tasted is an outstanding Pinot Noir."

"Pinot Noir grapes need a climate colder and mistier than this one," Francesca explained.

"You grow them," Mitch pointed out.

Francesca smiled ruefully and once again he was reminded that she was unusually lovely.

"We don't make any money on them," she confessed. "Once in a while, we have a very cold growing season and an excellent Pinot Noir harvest. But not very often. If you want really good Pinot Noir, you should settle closer to the coast."

"But that isn't where GGI wants me."

Her smile faded. "For a minute I'd forgotten you were a company man."

He laughed, disarming them all. "I'm taking that as the highest compliment. Thank you, Francesca."

Julianne changed the subject. "When will you move in?"

"When the house is ready to be lived in. I'll have to meet with contractors and see if we can come up with a schedule. Until then, I'll commute."

Jake whistled. "That's quite a commute."

"You sound like a man who speaks from experience."

"I've been living in Napa for about two years now," Jake said. "I make it down here about every other week to see Nick."

Francesca interrupted him. "I'm sure Mr. Gillette isn't interested in our personal history, Jake."

Jake wiped his mouth with his napkin. "I was answering an implied question, Francesca. It isn't unusual to tell someone where you live."

This time Mitch jumped in, alleviating the tension. "The wine is excellent. It's perfect with the pork. May I ask how it's done?"

"The meat or the wine?" Julianne asked.

"Both."

"The wine is a '98 Syrah," she began. "The grapes are three different kinds and estate grown, as you can see by the label. They're aged for eighteen months in sixty-five percent French oak and thirty-five percent American-oak barrels. This particular case has been aging in bottles for about four years. As for the pork— garlic, white pepper and plum sauce are my secrets."

Mitch was intrigued. "I didn't realize you knew wine as well as food."

"My husband was a winemaker. I've lived here since I was barely out of my teens. I would've had to be deaf and blind not to learn the trade inside and out."

Mitch was beginning to form a hazy idea of the family dynamics here at the table.

Sarah spoke to Francesca. "Why does Jake live in Napa if you're here?"

"We're divorced," Francesca said bluntly.

The girl looked surprised. "You're awfully friendly for a divorced couple."

"Jesus Christ," Drew muttered. "Shut up, Sarah."

"No. I mean it." Sarah appealed to her father. "You never ate dinner with Mom and us when you were divorced."

"I can't remember ever being invited."

Julianne pushed back her chair. "Jake is my son. I invited him," she explained. "Now, is anyone ready for dessert?"

"Is it chocolate?" Drew asked.

"I think I can scrounge up some chocolate," she said. "I'll be right back."

Mitch rose. "I'll help you." He followed her into the kitchen and watched as she assembled plates, more napkins and forks.

"The coffeepot's over there behind the cups" she said. "If you don't mind carrying them out, I'll bring the dessert."

He looked appreciatively at the gooey chocolate bubbling out of what looked like pieces of chocolate cake.

"It's called chocolate bread pudding," she said, guessing his question. "It's Nick's favorite."

"Is that why you stay here? Because of Nick?"

She frowned. "Why wouldn't I stay? This is my home."

"Even though your son is no longer married to Francesca?"

"Even more so." Deftly, she spooned servings of pudding-cake onto seven plates. "When Francie's father died, she needed help with some debt. I paid it down. She's done wonderful things with the winery. I support her every step of the way."

"What about Jake?"

Julianne sighed. "Now, that situation breaks my heart. I don't think I've ever seen two young people so much in love with each other." She smiled sadly. "I guess it proves there's more to the equation than love."

She rinsed off the spoon and left it in the sink. Then she faced him, hands on her hips. "Next time it's your turn to be interrogated."

"Is that what you think I'm doing? Interrogating you?"

"What else?"

"Do you mind?"

"That depends on what you do with the information."

"What if it's pure curiosity?"

Julianne nodded. "That's acceptable as long as you return the favor."

He picked up two plates. "On one condition."

She tilted her head. Her eyes were very blue. "What's that?"

"That I provide dinner."

She looked surprised. "Do you cook, Mitch?"

"No, but I'm a connoisseur of fine restaurants. Will you have dinner with me?"

She hesitated. "Does it have to be a date?"

"I think so, if it's all right with you."

"How old are you?"

"Forty-five."

Julianne breathed in. "I'm fifty."

"Is that a problem?"

"I don't know," she said, releasing her breath. "May I think about it?"

"My escrow closes in four weeks. I'll be here permanently. Will that be long enough?"

She laughed. "You are persistent. Four weeks will be fine."

Seven

Francesca closed the book and tucked the covers around Nick. His eyes were still bright and clear and a long way from sleep. "You're usually snoring by now," she teased him. "What's going on?"

"I don't snore."

"How do you know?"

"I would hear it."

Recognizing where the conversation was going and why, she refused to get caught up in a debate. "What's going on?" she asked instead.

He shrugged. "I'm just not tired."

"It's ten o'clock."

"I know."

She smoothed the silky hair away from his forehead. "Is something bothering you, Nick?"

"I think Dad wants to come home."

The words pierced her skin like tiny splinters. She forced herself to react calmly. "Why do you think that?"

Again Nick shrugged.

"Did he tell you he wanted to come home?" she pressed him.

"He said he misses us."

She swallowed and spoke softly. "I'm sure he does miss us, Nick. We miss him, too, but that doesn't mean he wants to live here again. People miss each other all the time." Francesca lifted his chin and looked at him. "Can you see that?"

Nick sighed and turned over. "Yes," he said. "But this is different."

Her eyes burned. She couldn't talk about this now. Leaning over, she kissed his cheek. "Good night, sweetheart."

He burrowed down into the sheets and closed his eyes.

Francesca hovered on the landing, undecided as to whether she should offer to help Julianne with the dishes and take a chance on running into Jake, or go straight to her room. Her better half prevailed. She walked into the kitchen just in time to dry the wine goblets and serving bowls. "I'll clean what's left," she offered, picking up a dish towel.

"You've worked all day, Francie," her mother-in-law said. "I don't mind."

"And I suppose you've been lying around eating chocolates and watching television?"

Julianne laughed her lovely laugh. "You win. I am tired."

In companionable silence the two women finished the last of the dishes and wiped down the counters. Francesca broke the silence. "He's nice, isn't he?"

"Who?"

"Mitch Gillette."

"Very nice."

"It's going to make it all that much harder," Francesca observed. "If only he didn't work for GGI."

Julianne nodded.

"He doesn't have a prayer of succeeding."

"I don't know about that."

Francesca raised her eyebrows. "He's unfamiliar with the soil. He won't find a decent winemaker and he won't get any help because of his credentials. It's a recipe for disaster."

Julianne folded the towels and hung them over the sink. "On the other hand, he doesn't need to make a profit any time soon. You heard him. He's experimenting with blends. It doesn't sound like he's going commercial. He can take as long as he wants." She sighed. "Who knows? He might be here longer than we are."

"He doesn't have water rights."

"He'll get them soon enough."

Francesca folded her arms and leaned back against the counter. "That remains to be seen."

"Don't tell me you're going to use your influence to refuse him water rights. I know you better than that. The minute he said he wanted to experiment with Pinot Noir grapes, he had you."

"I wouldn't influence anyone to refuse *him*," Francesca stated bluntly. "But I have no problem with doing it to GGI."

Francesca's stubborn streak was blinding her. Julianne spoke gently, keeping her eyes on her daughter-in-law's face. "It's only a matter of time, love. You know that. The small vintners will have to offer something GGI doesn't if they're to survive. I'd be thinking about that right now instead of burying my head in the sand."

"Whose side are you on?"

"Yours," Julianne said immediately. "Always. Now, I'm going upstairs." She blew Francesca a kiss and left the room.

Francesca poured herself another cup of coffee and carried it outside to the porch. She sat down in the glider and stared at the hills, black against a star-bright sky. She was terrified of losing the vineyard. What else did she have besides Nick and Julianne? What else was she qualified to do? It was unthinkable. She knew nothing but wine.

Jake's voice interrupted her thoughts. "Are you in the mood for company or would you prefer to be alone?"

Francesca stiffened. She didn't want him beside her. That would be too much. She nodded at the chair opposite the swing. "Have a seat. It's your mother's porch, too. I'll go inside."

Jake sat down, leaning his crutches against the house. "Does it always have to be like this, Francie? Can't we have a normal conversation?"

She thought a minute. "I don't think so."

"Why not?"

"Well, it's like this." Ignoring her coffee, she leaned forward, her long braid swinging over her shoulder. "You deserted me. You walked out after my father died, leaving me with a vineyard to harvest, a mountain of debt and a six-year-old child. That was bad enough. But the worst part, the unforgivable part, is that never once did you explain why, nor did you give me a chance to remedy whatever was bothering you. I think that merits a good deal of resentment on my part. What amazes me is why you're surprised that I won't give you the time of day."

"You're serious!" he said incredulously.

"Yes."

"We fought like cats and dogs for the entire year after Frank died. I tried talking to you. Hell, I tried everything. You weren't interested in what I had to say. You were my wife, Francie, but I felt like yesterday's leftover catch. Nothing I did was right. You made it perfectly clear this was your vineyard and you made the decisions."

Francesca looked at the sky. "I can't believe this."

His mouth twisted. "Believe it."

"I needed you."

"You had a sorry way of showing it."

"I was going through a lot, Jake. Surely you can see that."

"What I saw was a woman who wanted to run the entire show, a woman who had no respect for her husband. What kind of man would I be if I let that happen? I didn't want Nick to grow up thinking we were normal."

He almost had her. He would have had her until his last remark. "No. You'd rather Nick have an absentee father he sees only four days a month."

"When did you get to be so bitter?"

She stood, slim and straight and furious. "When I brought back chicken strips for my husband's dinner just in time to watch him carry out his suitcases." She stepped over his plastered leg. "You've been here for quite a while. How much longer do you plan to stay?"

"Are you throwing me out?"

She ignored his question. "Good night, Jake."

Jake lifted his hand in a mock military salute. "Aye, aye, sir."

Upstairs in her bathroom, Francesca placed both hands on the basin of the sink and leaned close to the mirror. She felt fragile, unsteady, as if her skin had been peeled back and all her nerves exposed. Her eyes were dark and unfocused, the pupils filling up the brown of her irises. Her cheeks were attractively flushed. Rage had its advantages. The involuntary shaking began in her knees and moved upward.

Concentrating, she turned on the faucet, waited until the water felt warm to the touch and splashed it over her face. She pulled a towel from the rack, patted her forehead and cheeks, walked back into the bedroom and threw herself facedown on the bed. She hated him. In fact, she was quite sure she'd never hated anyone as much in her entire life. He didn't deserve her. He didn't deserve Julianne and he certainly didn't deserve Nick. What Jake deserved was to sit broken and alone in an upstairs apartment with no one to wait on him.

Julianne had indulged him. It wasn't all that unusual. Jake was her only son. But that didn't mean Francesca had to put up with him, not anymore. She buried her head in her arms. The irony was there had been a time when she wanted nothing more in the world than to put up with Jake Harris forever.

She'd known him for a long time. Everyone knew each other in the small-town atmosphere of the Santa Ynez Valley in those early days when central valley grapes were just becoming reputable. But it wasn't until the spring of her second year at UC Davis that she really saw him for the first time. She was climbing the slope of a greenbelt on her way to class when she looked up, suddenly self-conscious. He stood there, motionless, backpack slung over his shoulder, a smile on his face, shiny gilt-colored hair falling over his forehead. Walking back down to meet her, he held out his hand to pull her up beside him.

Why Jake Harris, a boy she'd skinny-dipped in the creek with until she was eleven years old, should suddenly tie up her tongue, she couldn't imagine. But that was the way it started. They were perfectly matched, everyone said. Even his Viking good looks were a complement to her olive skin, dark hair and eyes. For the entire two years before and after they married, she couldn't remember an unpleasant word or even a misunderstanding between them. Life was blissful. When Nick came along, it seemed to Francesca that no one had ever been more blessed. At night, curled up with Jake against her back, she smiled in her sleep. Each year was better than the one before. When had it all changed?

The answer came on the wake of the question. When her father died. She understood the yoke of responsibility for the first time. Keeping up the vineyard and the winery required eighteen-hour days. She woke before five and was out in the field before the sun rose over the hills, and she fell into bed at night well after midnight, spent and numb. Jake disagreed with her on nearly everything. After a while, she couldn't bear the arguing and she stopped telling him her plans. He didn't understand her need to keep DeAngelo Vineyards the way her father had kept it and his father before him. She wanted her grapes grown in organic fields. She wanted her son to grow up without the taint of poison searing his lungs.

Jake didn't agree. He talked with other vintners and took classes and dusted off his chemistry books. He toured pesticide companies and asked questions. Convinced that the vineyard could produce a greater yield safely, he tried to wear her down with statistics and spreadsheets and flowcharts. More and more her temper flared, forcing a chasm between them. Angry words were hurled back and forth, words that could never be taken back. Icy silences followed the shouting. They shared a bed awkwardly, lying stiffly in mummy-like poses until exhaustion claimed them. Jake usually fell asleep first, and when Francesca heard his breathing deepen, she relaxed and fell asleep on her stomach, careful to keep her hands tucked beneath her thighs, careful not to roll over and touch him. She couldn't remember the last time they'd made love. Not that it mattered. She was too exhausted to remember what desire felt like.

Francesca burrowed her head in the quilt. Looking back, it was quite clear to her now, when she closely examined the events that led up to Jake's departure. She had simply been too tired and too consumed with the vineyard to see what should have been obvious. But what could she have done differently, even if she'd known?

Frank DeAngelo had been a legend in the Santa Ynez Valley. Even though Francesca was his daughter, no one had believed a woman could fill his shoes. She'd worked her tail off to prove them wrong. DeAngelo Vineyards was as productive as it had been when her father signed the checks. And the winery was hers. She and Jake had started it together. When he left for Napa, he'd left it to her. It was productive now, but it hadn't been easy.

If only Jake had waited. *If only she'd allowed him an equal partnership,* a tiny voice in her head chimed in. Why hadn't she? The question loomed in her mind without an answer. Francesca had never been one to delegate easily. Even in school she'd preferred individual projects over group ones. *If you want something done right, do it yourself,* her father would say, and Francesca agreed.

In the end, her preference had cost her a husband. Jake was proud, too proud to be squeezed out of the important decisions, too proud to have his ideas tossed aside, too proud to be supported by his wife's family vineyard.

Francesca pulled the edge of the comforter over her body and turned around twice until she was rolled up like a sausage. If only she could sleep in tomorrow. If only someone else would manage the sugar testing and the harvesting. If only Mitchell Gillette would announce GGI was taking their conglomerate elsewhere, never to return. If only she was Frank DeAngelo's daughter again with someone else to share her worries.

If only she could start all over again with Jake. This time she would get it right. This time he would realize leaving wasn't the answer. None of those *if onlys* were likely to happen anytime soon. The most she could hope for was to keep her vineyard solvent. Maybe, if she kept her fingers crossed, and if she ever had a spare moment, she might fall in love again.

She stared at the light. If she reached far enough across the bed, she could just about turn it off. Her arms were aching and weary from pruning the shoots. Moving, even inches, was the last thing she wanted to do. To hell with the light. It could stay on all night for all she cared.

Slowly, Francesca's eyelids fell. She would rest a while, no more than ten minutes. Ten minutes wouldn't hurt. In less than a minute she was asleep. She slept through the twelve chimes of the grandfather clock signaling midnight, nor did she wake when Julianne, seeing a crack of light beneath her bedroom door, opened it and turned her lamp off. Not until the rooster crowed at six the following morning did she wake cramped, bleary-eyed and thoroughly unprepared for the day ahead.

Eight

Francesca poured coffee into her travel mug, decided against milk and sugar, twisted down the top and headed for the door.

"Whoa." Julianne's voice stopped her in midstride. "Where are you going?"

"Where do you think? It's time to test the grapes for sugar content."

"Already?"

"Time flies when you're having fun."

Julianne ignored her sarcasm. "How about some breakfast, Francie? You'll be dead on your feet with nothing in your stomach but that huge cup of coffee. The caffeine alone will make you too shaky to function."

"I need caffeine. I didn't sleep well last night."

"Why not wait for Nick," Julianne urged. "He'll be up soon and it's good for him to see you eat breakfast. That way he'll eat some, too. He's so thin I wonder how his legs support him."

Francesca shrugged into her jacket and zipped it to her chin. Then she grabbed her notepad with one hand and her coffee and cell phone with the other and wrestled with the doorknob. "If I wait for Nick I'll never get out of here, and there aren't enough hours as it is. Jake can eat with him." She added under her breath, "That way he'll be good for something other than to annoy me." She spoke up again. "I'll call you if I can't make it back for dinner."

Julianne hesitated.

Francesca, sensitive to her mother-in-law's expressive face, frowned. "What is it?"

Julianne's words burst out quickly on a breath of air. "The three of you will be on your own tonight. I won't be home for dinner."

"Why not?"

"I'm going out."

Francesca's face lit up and she leaned against the door. "You're wicked, Julianne. How dare you drop that bit of information when you know I can't stay."

"Am I tempting you?"

"Even more than your waffles, but I really am in a bind. Tell me the highlights."

"They're muffins not waffles. What do you want to know?"

Francesca's eyes crinkled. "Who is he, of course?"

"How do you know I'm going out with a man?"

"C'mon, Julianne. Come clean. Who is he?"

You won't like it, Francie."

"I will. I promise, no matter who he is."

Julianne drew a deep breath. "Mitch Gillette."

"Wow!" Francesca's mouth formed a perfect circle. "You are truly amazing, a secret weapon in disguise."

Julianne's eyes narrowed suspiciously. "Meaning what?"

"You've met the man twice and he's already caught."

"He isn't caught at all," Julianne protested. "And it's three times. I've met him three times. He's called twice since he had dinner here, but it isn't like that."

"Of course not."

"You're teasing me."

"Would I do that?"

"Yes, you would. You're terrible. I can't explain it, Francie, but it isn't a date. After all, he just lost his wife. He and the children are down here now."

"All right. I'll bite. Where is he taking you?"

"To see his house. He's cooking." She turned off the stove and pulled out a tray of muffins. "Can you believe it? Someone's actually cooking for me."

Francesca's smile disappeared and she looked thoughtful. "We don't ever give you a break, do we? You run your catering business and do all our cooking and cleaning, too."

"I love doing it. It's my contribution."

"Everyone gets a break, Julianne. Everyone, except you. I'm ashamed of myself. I never even considered it."

"Don't consider it. I'm getting my break tonight."

Impulsively, Francesca reached out and hugged her mother-in-law without losing any of her belongings. "Be careful, Julianne," she warned. "He seems nice enough but we don't know very much about him."

Julianne nodded. She'd said enough, but her cheeks were very pink. "Please, Francie. Eat a muffin."

Relenting, Francesca accepted Julianne's offering and hurried out the door.

* * *

Francesca set the brake on the rise of the slope and climbed out of the Jeep. She had wasted precious time in the kitchen. Already light poured over the hills, bringing color to the land, to tree and shrub, olive and spruce, eucalyptus and oak, pear cactus and lavender. Mountains, their peaks swaddled in backlit clouds, dark in the distance and light in front, teamed with life from recent rains. Below the rise, vines, spaced five feet apart, grew in traditional rows surrounded by lavender and Mexican sage. Swarms of ladybugs billowed like red parachutes above the blooming Grenache and Mourvedre clusters. To the north, toward Los Olivos, Syrah and Cinsault grew beside each other, their delicate leaves twisting together in Medusa-like tangles and, just above them, planted in formation to catch ocean breezes from the west and the fog banks blanketing the mountains parallel to the sea, were her pride and joy, her Pinot Noir vines complete with reflectors to scare the birds. This was the first year DeAngelo Vineyards would produce really top-notch Pinot Noir. God willing, there would be a next year.

She grabbed a bucket from the passenger seat and walked six rows into the vineyard. Then she walked six plants in, lifted the bird net and picked the sixth cluster from an immature Chardonnay vine, repeating the pattern until she'd worked her way down to the end of the row. Then she would begin on the next row until she'd collected fifteen pounds of fruit.

Gently she cupped a pale green cluster and snapped it from its stem. The grapes had to have a perfect balance of sugars and acids. If she waited too long, they would be too sweet and lacking in acid, resulting in a flabby, amorphous wine. Fruit had to be tested weekly, sometimes daily. After the fruit was photographed, it was destemmed, crushed and allowed to soak in its skins for thirty minutes or so. This allowed phenolics from the skins to soak up the juice before a hydrometer measured sugar and a pH meter checked acidity.

The grapes were still young, but the color and shape were perfect. They would ripen quickly. If the sugar-and-acid combination turned out to be right, Francesca predicted that the harvest would begin soon, maybe as soon as three weeks. A third of the vines still needed hoeing, but the cover crop was coming along well, bell beans, Oriental radish and California poppies to attract insects, crimson clover and purple vetch for nitrogen, annual rye and barley for erosion control. Not an herbicide or seed sterilant in the bunch. Francesca was proud of her policies. She had occasional doubts, but harvesting a pesticide-free crop wasn't one of them, despite Jake's arguments to the contrary.

At DeAngelo Vineyards, producing wine had never been about volume or profit. It was always about good wine. Frank DeAngelo had insisted on pruning back three-fourths of all dormant vines, retaining only the strongest sun vines. By reducing the yield from six tons per acre to three, he'd produced superior grapes with intense varietal characteristics. Francesca, desperate to prove herself her father's daughter, refused to consider anything less. *Wine Spectator,* the magazine that could make or break a vineyard, had been highly complimentary about her methods. People wanted wines made from organic grapes. A thought occurred to her. Maybe Julianne was right. Maybe the only way to beat GGI was to offer something they couldn't, something DeAngelo Winery already produced, a pesticide-free product. Immediately she felt better. The future looked less ominous.

She moved on to the Pinot Noir vines. The clusters were tiny, velvety and lustrous, dark purple against a background of gray fog. These specialty grapes needed to ripen on the vine a bit longer than Chardonnay clusters. Brix, sugar and acidity levels were only the beginning. The test of a perfect Pinot Noir harvest depended upon an educated palate, a rich, ripe, delicious fruit with dark seeds. Francesca, according to plan, tested her sixth cluster from the sixth vine from the sixth row, moving steadily until she'd finished. She shivered with excitement. They were close to perfect. She was sure of it. Still, another opinion wouldn't hurt. She needed Jake. He had a sixth sense about grapes. Normally, pride would have prevented her from asking him for anything, but this was too important. For this, her precious Pinot Noir yield, she could bend.

At a loss, Julianne stood in front of her closet. What did a woman invited to a man's home, for a dinner that was not a date, wear? She pushed aside her three *dressy* dresses. They seemed pretentious. She did not want to appear as if the evening and the invitation were more than they were.

It was late August and Mitch had said something about a barbecue, but shorts weren't appropriate either. Julianne did not want to look as if she'd gone to any trouble. Perhaps a summer shift? That was it. She pulled out a white eyelet dress with straps that crisscrossed her back and bared her shoulders. White was good against her skin. It was simple and comfortable and, most important of all, not too much. White sandals and a short cardigan sweater completed her outfit. She wouldn't even bother to change her purse, a bone-colored sack that shrank and expanded depending on its contents.

She took more time with her makeup than usual, but when a woman reached the age of fifty, it took longer to reach the proper effect. There, she was finished. Maybe she would be lucky enough to avoid everyone if she tiptoed down the stairs.

"Hi, Gran." Nick sat on the landing playing his GameBoy.

Her heart sank. "Hello, sweetheart."

He looked her up and down. "Where are you going?"

"Over to a friend's house for dinner."

"What friend?"

Julianne bit her lip. Ordinarily she delighted in Nick's precociousness. "The man you met the other night—Mr. Gillette."

"Sarah's dad," Nick said matter-of-factly.

"That's right."

"Who's making our dinner?"

"Your mother."

Nick raised his eyebrows. "Can I come with you?"

For a minute Julianne was tempted. Then she laughed. "Shame on you, Nick. She's not that bad."

Jake's voice came from behind her. "I'll cook."

"We can get pizza," Nick suggested.

"Have some faith, kiddo. I'm my mother's son. Our dinner will be spectacular."

"I think I'd rather have Mom cook."

"Your mother's worked hard all day. I'll do the cooking."

Nick recognized the voice of authority and returned to his GameBoy.

Jake opened the door for his mother. "I'll walk you to the car." He waited until they were outside. "So, what's this all about?"

For an instant she considered playing dumb, widening her eyes and asking what it was he referred to. But prevaricating would serve no purpose. Jake was persistent and she had always stressed honesty. "I'm going to Mitch Gillette's house for dinner."

"I heard," Jake said flatly. "What I want to know is *why*."

She frowned. "*Why?* What do you mean by that?"

"Just what I said. *Why?*"

"All right, Jake. I'll tell you *why*. Because he invited me. Because I enjoy his company. Because, sometimes, occasionally, I'd like someone else to do the cooking." She felt the anger rise in her chest. It felt good and right. "Because," she continued, "your mother is not dead yet, nor am I old enough to throw in the towel and resign myself to a single existence for the rest of my life. Because, Jake, Mitch Gillette is the first attractive man to ask me out in ten years." She pulled the keys from her purse. "Is there anything else you'd like to know?"

"I didn't realize you felt so strongly."

"Why should you?" she snapped. "You aren't around very much."

His lips were thin and tight. "That was a low blow."

"*That* was the truth."

Jake leaned against a pillar, his hands balled in his pockets. "What do you want me to do, Mom? I want to come back but Francie won't have me."

"I don't blame her. It makes a woman wonder how she can ever trust a man if he bails when times are tough."

"How do I prove it if she won't give me a chance?"

His mother relented. The sharpness left her voice. "I don't know, love. It looks like you have your work cut out for you." She patted his shoulder. "You've got to get on with your life, Jake. What about your job? You've been here since June."

He looked down at his feet. "I'm not going back to Napa."

Her heart sank. "Why not?"

"I belong here with Francesca and Nick. If I go away again I'll never convince Francie to take me back."

"How will you live?"

"I've got some put away. Quite a bit, actually. Don't worry about that." He attempted a smile. "If I get desperate, I'll bribe Francesca."

"I don't think that's the right approach."

"Have a good time, Mom."

She studied his face. "Do you really mean that?"

This time the smile made it to his eyes. "It's strange for me to see you as anything other than my mother and Nick's grandmother. Give me a little time, okay?"

"Okay. Good luck, Jake, and I'm delighted you've come to your senses. A woman like Francesca doesn't come along every day."

He nodded. "I know that now."

* * *

Francesca smelled the hickory smoke of barbecuing meat well before she entered the courtyard. Her mouth watered. She climbed out of the Jeep and walked around the house to the back patio. Nick sat on the porch, swinging his legs, a soft-drink can in his hand. But it was Jake who had her attention. Shirtless, he stood in front of the brick barbecue, wielding tongs and a spray bottle. Strips of aromatic beef sizzled on the grill. The picnic table was set for three.

She walked slowly over to the table. "What are you cooking?" she asked.

"Tri-tip."

She wasn't sure of her welcome. "It smells delicious."

"Wait till you taste it. I've perfected a barbecue recipe you're gonna love."

She relaxed. "I'll go upstairs and clean up. How long do I have?"

"Twenty minutes or so."

"Can I help with anything?"

He grinned and for a minute her breathing altered. She was sure there were better-looking men than Jake Harris, but not for her.

"I've got it covered. Salad's in the fridge and potatoes are in the oven. I've uncorked the Cabernet. All you have to do is show up."

Francesca raced upstairs and turned on the shower, promising herself that she would do justice to the meal. She would wear something flattering. She would not bring up controversial subjects and she would compliment his cooking. She would even wash the dishes. He would have no reason to find fault with her about anything.

The weather was perfect. A slight breeze floated in from the ocean. It was seven o'clock. They would have the sun for another two hours. Francesa, her hair brushed and shining and swinging against her shoulders, descended the stairs dressed in a sleeveless ivory blouse and beige linen walking shorts.

The table was finished and Jake and Nick were already seated. Jake rose when she walked out of the door and handed her a glass of deep red wine.

She tasted it and held up her glass. "Yum. What is it?"

"Cabernet, 1974."

She looked surprised. "From my dad's private reserve? Is this a special occasion?"

"It was my dad's, too. This is one of my inherited bottles. No occasion. Just an evening at home with my son and his mother." His eyes rested on her hair. "You look beautiful, Francesca."

"Thank you." She sat down.

He passed the salad bowl to her and forked a strip of meat. "Can you cut this up yourself, Nick, or shall I do it for you?"

"Can I eat it with my fingers?"

"Absolutely not," his mother said.

"You can cut it, Dad."

Francesca chewed her meat slowly. "This is wonderful. Thanks so much, Jake."

"My pleasure."

She leaned forward. "I have a favor to ask you."

"Shoot."

"I think the Pinot Noir grapes are ready for harvesting. I need you to taste them and tell me if you agree."

"I'll go out with you in the morning."

"Thanks."

"This is a big deal for you, isn't it?" he asked.

She nodded. "It's something I've wanted for a long time."

"I never really understood why it's so important to you. You've been growing grapes for years. Why is this variety so special?"

She hesitated. Being vulnerable wasn't easy for her, especially with Jake. She poured herself another glass of wine. "I've been growing my father's grapes for years. These are mine. If they're successful, and I can produce a really unique wine, I'll feel as if I've proven myself."

"You've already proven yourself, Francie," he said gently. "You've continued the DeAngelo tradition of producing fine wines. That's a lot harder today than it was when your father took over."

Speechless, she stared at him. He looked sincere. Did he really mean it? She hated the suspicion that rose in her chest whenever it came to Jake, but she couldn't afford to be hurt again. Once it had nearly killed her. Refusing to think about that time after he left, when it had been all she could do to get out of bed, she changed the subject. "You've turned into quite a cook."

He nodded. "Thanks. I guess it's in the blood."

"I'm finished," Nick announced.

Francesca frowned. "Please, eat a little more, sweetheart. You'll be hungry again in an hour."

"No, I won't," he promised. "I'm full."

"We've got dessert coming," Jake promised. "Eat the rest of your meat and two bites of salad and I'll bring on the ice cream."

Resigned, Nick picked up his fork.

Jake turned his attention back to Francesca. "What do you think of Mitch Gillette?"

This was a subject she could tolerate. "Do you mean as a competitor or as your mother's new love interest?"

"Both?"

Francesca sipped at her wine. "He's a workaholic according to Sarah, his daughter, which isn't a bad quality for a vintner. On the other hand, it isn't conducive for a comfortable family life. More than likely, he's a decent enough man. We just happen to be on different sides, that's all."

Jake's eyes were very narrow and blue as they considered her reply. "Do you think he's serious?"

"About what?"

"About Mom?"

Amused, Francesca stared at him. "They just met, Jake. There's a long way between meeting someone and settling down with him."

He relaxed. "What do you say we drive into Santa Ynez for ice cream?"

Nick clapped. "Yes."

Francesca nodded. The night had been perfect. If only she could capture the glow of it, take it out and feel the warmth all over again, whenever she felt low. Suddenly her eyes filled. Quickly she stood and walked toward the door. "I'll get my sweater," she called back.

Jake's eyes followed her exit. He couldn't read her anymore. When had that happened? Four years ago?

Five? He sighed. Francesca was a complicated woman, a blend of sweet and tart, like the wine she was so set on producing.

Nine

Julianne's hand was light on the wheel. She drove a midsize Toyota with leather seats, power windows and an excellent stereo system. She could have afforded more but a car was transportation, nothing more. All she required was reliability and some degree of comfort. A Camry was perfect for a small woman.

She eased the car around the curves of the twisting highway. The Vandenburg estate was off the main road by about ten miles, through a lovely stretch of leaning eucalyptus and spreading oak trees. The house had been uninhabited for a long time. Julianne was curious to see how Mitch had renovated the place.

She pulled into the courtyard and looked around. A surge of pleasure rushed through her. Slate pavers still enclosed the old fountain and lush, red bougainvillea grew in wild abandon over the walls. The house had been improved with a fresh coat of white paint and the windows had been washed, but Mitch had preserved the charm of an old hacienda, complete with outdoor pump, rustic porch furniture and hand-painted tiles. Her estimation of the man, already high, rose.

Slowly, she climbed the porch steps. The door behind the screen was open. She felt awkward, as if she were engaged in something illicit. Her palms felt like ice. Mentally chastising herself for accepting the invitation in the first place, she drew a deep breath and pressed the doorbell. It was too late to back out now.

"I'll get it," Sarah called from another room.

Relief swept through her. She'd forgotten the children. They would not be alone.

Sarah opened the door. "Hi, Mrs. Harris. Come in."

Julianne stepped inside. "Hi, yourself. How are the lessons coming?"

The girl smiled. "Great! As soon as the stable is finished, Dad says I can bring Fairy Light home. I'll miss Francesca, though. She's a terrific teacher. She never gets mad, even when I do something dumb."

Julianne laughed. "That doesn't sound like Francesca. She must like you very much."

"Really?" The child's pleasure was genuine. Julianne resolved to compliment her as often as possible.

"Dad's in the kitchen. May I take your purse and put it in the closet?"

"Please." She slipped out of her sweater. "Take this, too. I've brought a bottle of wine. If you don't think he'll mind, I'll join him in the kitchen."

Sarah opened a closet large enough to be a cloakroom and hung up the sweater and purse. "Trust me, he'll be grateful. Dad's a good cook, but he isn't in your league."

"I've had lots of practice. I don't think I'd be very

good at managing a huge company. Thank goodness we all have our talents."

"I guess so." She looked thoughtful. "I wish I knew what my talent was."

"I can tell you one of them if you'd like," Julianne began conversationally.

"What's that?"

"You're very hospitable. I was feeling uncomfortable standing at your door. I don't know your dad very well and I wondered if maybe he was feeling as if he had to repay me for the times the three of you have stopped in at my house. It wouldn't have been at all necessary, you know."

Sarah's eyebrows rose. "Are you kidding? My dad doesn't do anything he doesn't like to do."

Julianne stared at her. Could she possibly believe that? Mitch Gillette must be very good at hiding his feelings. "Anyway," she continued, "the point is, you've made me feel welcome and wanted. Warmth and hospitality are wonderful gifts. Not everyone has them."

The girl glowed. "Gosh. Thank you."

"You're welcome."

She pointed down a long hall. "The kitchen's this way."

Julianne followed her through the hallway and dining room, admiring the place mats, the table runner and the filmy London shades allowing in the last rays of daylight. Either Mitch had very good taste or he'd hired a decorator. The table was set for four.

The kitchen was equally impressive. A design of black, red and white tiles, dark-wood cabinets, clear glass cupboard doors and copper pots hanging from the ceiling made for an interesting Southwestern look, very functional, very masculine. Mitch was leaning over the center island, the sleeves of his sweater pushed up to his elbows, stirring sauce over a low flame, completely at home. He looked up and grinned at her.

"We're having spaghetti, by request," he said. "Meat sauce for the kids, mariscos for us."

"It sounds wonderful. I love seafood pasta. But I thought you were barbecuing. I brought red wine. I hope it works."

"If it doesn't, we'll dig up something else."

"May I help you with anything?"

He eyed her dress appreciatively. "I don't think so, not when you're wearing white. Why don't you pour us some wine. The glasses are over there." He nodded at a wooden rack over a refrigerated wine bar. "I'm working on a cellar but this will have to do for now." He nodded at his daughter. "Sarah, find the corkscrew for Mrs. Harris and then call your brother. Tell him to come downstairs and say hello to our guest."

Sarah sighed and walked over to a drawer near the wine bar. "I'll try."

"Do better than that," her father said gently.

She handed Julianne the corkscrew, sighed again and left the room.

Julianne looked after her thoughtfully, uncorked her wine and poured two glasses. "A 1987 Syrah. Not the best for seafood," she said, handing it to him, "but wonderful for meat sauce."

He lifted his glass, swirled it slightly and tasted it. Then he picked up the bottle. "Is this one of your estate wines?"

"It is."

"Your daughter-in-law is very talented."

"Thank you. She can't take credit for this wine, however. She was only thirteen years old when it was bottled. This particular blend was one of my husband's projects."

"Tell me about him."

Julianne smiled. "He was a winemaker. We came to the Santa Ynez Valley thirty years ago when Frank DeAngelo hired him. We lived on the estate until he died."

"When was that?"

"Ten years ago."

"Why did you leave?"

Julianne shrugged. "I didn't really, at least not for very long. I had a small house in town until Nick was born and the girls left home. Francesca's father moved into the guesthouse and gave Francie and Jake the house they live in now. They were working long hours and I couldn't bear to have the baby go to someone outside the family. I moved in, renovated the kitchen and worked my schedule around Nick."

"How many children do you have?"

"Three. Two girls and Jake. He's the oldest."

Mitch turned off the heat under the sauce and picked up his wineglass. This was nice, the two of them, just talking. He liked her. She was comfortable and lovely and unpretentious. He hadn't felt so serene and relaxed in a long time. "Were you happily married?" The question came out before he could stop the words. "I beg your pardon," he said, embarrassed. "Please don't feel as if you have to answer that. I don't usually get so personal so quickly."

"My goodness, Mitch," she laughed. "You didn't ask me how much I weigh or if I've had a face-lift. It's a perfectly normal question to ask. Yes, I was happily married, as happy as anyone can be for twenty years."

"You're fortunate."

"Yes, I suppose so, among other things."

"Such as?"

"Tolerant, compromising and I'll even admit to a certain degree of stubbornness."

This time he laughed. "Are you saying those are the qualities necessary for a happy marriage?"

"They're necessary for a long marriage."

"Are you stubborn, Julianne?"

"Very." She set down her glass and changed the subject. "Are you sure I can't help you with anything?"

He shook his head. "Next time. Tonight, I'm cooking for you."

"Your children and me," she corrected him.

"Yes," he said carefully. "My children."

It was an implied, but subtle, invitation. She took a chance. "May I ask you a question?"

He turned up the flame under a large pot of boiling water. "Please."

"How are you getting along with Sarah and Drew?"

He looked surprised. "Why do you ask?"

"That isn't an answer."

"All right. I'll confess. To be completely honest, it's damn difficult," he said ruefully. "Half the time I don't know what I'm doing and the other half I'm sure I'm doing it all wrong."

"Why do you say that? They're lovely children. You must be doing something right."

"If any credit is due, it goes to my late ex-wife. Susan raised them on her own, from the time they were infants.

She wanted it that way and I guess I wanted it, too. It was easier for me to see them once in a while than to share custody. I'm not proud of it and I am certainly paying for my lapse now."

"Why do you say that?" she asked again.

"They don't really know me," Mitch admitted. "Sarah is adjusting but Drew is defiant. I don't know whether to come down hard or ignore him. My instincts aren't particularly good when it comes to children."

Julianne was silent, hoping for inspiration. "Give it time," she said gently, after a minute. "There isn't an easy solution for losing a parent too soon. Your children are at a difficult age. This is the worst thing that could have happened to them right now."

"You're right. I'm trying for patience. Drew's attitude is wearing me down."

"How long ago were you divorced?"

"Thirteen years."

Mentally she did the math. Sarah and Drew were fifteen. "You didn't give it much of a chance."

"I didn't have to," he said grimly. "It was a terrible mistake. I'd do anything to take it back."

She unwrapped the pasta, looked at the label and dropped it into the boiling water. "Good choice," she said approvingly.

"There's a difference?"

"Look at the ridges in the noodles. These will grab the sauce, which makes for more flavorful spaghetti."

"Have you always had a knack for cooking?"

"In a manner of speaking. My family is huge. We would get together on Sundays and argue over traditional Basque recipes."

"Where are you from?"

"South Orange County when it was still ranch land, orange trees and cattle."

"Do you miss your family?"

"They're not that far away. I do miss my daughters, though," she said fervently. "And I miss Jake, although he's been underfoot lately."

"I like him," Mitch said. "And I like Francesca. What happened there?"

She looked pointedly at the pasta. "Be careful. That's cappelletti. You don't want it turning to mush."

"Is that a polite way of telling me to mind my own business?"

"Not at all. But I'm hungry and my priority right now is edible pasta."

Mitch turned off the flame and forked the noodles into a strainer. Then he ran cold water over it.

Julianne bit her tongue. It was his meal after all. Perhaps it would be better to retreat. "Shall I call the children?"

"That would be helpful. Drew might even get to the table some time before dessert."

Ignoring his comment, she left the kitchen and walked upstairs. Experience told her that the twins would be in the room with the pounding bass drum. She didn't bother to knock. The door was ajar and they wouldn't hear her anyway. Instead, she stuck her head in and waved. They were positioned on opposite sides of the room. Drew lay stretched out on the bed, his eyes closed. Sarah sat in a beanbag chair near the window, her legs curled beneath her.

Sarah saw her and smiled. She reached over and

turned off the stereo. Drew's eyes opened. Immediately he sat up, eyeing her nervously. Julianne looked from one to the other. They were very much alike, with the same long limbs, dark hair, fair skin and a mouth full of braces "It's time for dinner," Julianne said.

"What are we having?"

"Spaghetti," said Julianne and Sarah in one breath. Drew groaned.

Julianne's forehead wrinkled. "I've never known anyone who didn't like spaghetti."

"He makes it with meat sauce," Drew explained. "I don't eat meat."

"Do you like seafood?"

"I'm a vegetarian."

"Such as in vegan or will you eat milk and eggs?"

"Those are okay, as long as they're in things," he said.

"So, my chocolate cake isn't completely off your list."

He grinned reluctantly. "I guess not."

"Maybe you can eat around the meat," Julianne suggested.

Drew looked doubtful. "Did you bring a dessert?" he asked hopefully.

"Drew!" Sarah looked shocked.

"I'm sorry, I didn't think of it," said Julianne. "Next time."

"Right." He slid off the bed and stood beside Sarah. "Next time. If there is one."

"If there isn't, I'll invite you to my house and we'll eat it there," she replied cheerfully.

Mitch's voice called from downstairs. "Hey, everybody, come and get it. Dinner is getting cold."

Julianne could see Drew stiffen. Impulsively, she slid one arm through his and another through Sarah's. "Shall we?" she asked.

The staircase was wide enough for the three of them. They descended together, Julianne keeping a firm hold on both their arms. She was very conscious of the look of surprise on Mitch's face and wondered if he'd even thought to make physical contact with his children. "Do you think there might be any plain sauce left over?" she asked.

He looked blank. "Plain?"

"As in meatless."

"Why?"

"Drew doesn't eat meat."

Mitch looked at his son. "Since when?"

"For about eight years now."

"Drew, that's ridiculous," his father protested. "I would have known."

They stared at each other, Drew, bored, defiant, and Mitch, embarrassed.

Mitch rallied sooner. "If there isn't enough sauce, I'll find something else for you to eat. I apologize for my mistake." He looked at Sarah. "What about you? Do you eat meat?"

"Occasionally," she said. "We eat more with you than we ever did before, but it's not too bad."

Mitch looked helplessly at Julianne. "You've been here thirty minutes and already you know what apparently I should have known years ago."

"Don't beat yourself up," Julianne advised. "You're not the only one responsible for communicating. Can we bring anything to the table?"

"Everything's all set except for Drew's meatless sauce."

"Don't worry about it, Dad," the boy said. "I don't need sauce. Some salad and pasta will be fine."

Mitch frowned. "If you're sure—"

Julianne smiled brightly. "Well, that was easily solved." She looked past him into the dining room. "Everything looks wonderful."

Sarah nodded. "It really does, and it smells nice, too."

"Shall we eat?" her father asked.

The children, familiar with the routine, sat down on opposite ends of the table. Julianne took the chair across from Mitch. She looked admiringly at the linen napkins. "These are beautiful."

"They were my mother's," Sarah offered. "She used them on special occasions. I think she would have wanted you to see them."

"I'm flattered," Julianne said softly. "Thank you."

Drew studied her carefully. "You kind of remind me of Mom," he said suddenly, appealing to his sister. "Doesn't she, Sarah?"

"She's nothing like Susan," Mitch began.

Sarah ignored her father, tilting her head to examine Julianne more closely. "She doesn't look like Mom, but I think you're right, Drew. She does remind me of her."

"She was great," Drew explained.

Julianne smiled. "I'm doubly honored. Thank you, again."

"She had this laugh," Sarah chimed in, "that made everyone want to laugh, too, and she was a good cook.

Not great, like you, but really good. Dinner was never a disappointment."

"She would sing in the morning and late at night. It was the first and last thing we heard, her voice singing to us. It was nice," said Drew.

"She liked really sharp pencils when she did the crossword puzzle on Sundays and she'd get mad if we didn't do our best in school," Sarah said.

"Or anywhere," added Drew.

Sarah blinked rapidly. "It's funny what we remember, isn't it?"

Julianne felt her eyelids burn. She wanted to gather these children into her arms and heal them. Willing herself not to cry, she spoke gently. "She sounds very special."

"Did you always do your best in school?" In spite of himself, Mitch was drawn into the conversation.

"No," Drew admitted, "but we knew she wanted us to."

Later, after coffee, Julianne stacked the dishes in the dishwasher while Mitch washed and dried the glasses. "You're awfully quiet," she said after a few minutes. "Is something wrong?"

He dried his hands on a towel, hung it over the back of a chair and looked at her curiously. "Drew said more tonight at dinner than he has since his mother died. How did you manage it?"

Julianne folded her arms. She wouldn't pretend to misunderstand or put him off, but brutal honesty wasn't the answer either. "I think you're all so afraid of stepping on each other's toes that you can't be comfortable together," she said softly. "I said what I wanted to say and asked the questions I wanted answered. The children responded, that's all. Try not to be so careful of their feelings. Be less formal, more human," she urged. "They miss their mother. They want to be comfortable, but it's too soon. Give it time."

"Where did you get to be so wise?"

"Experience. Besides, I'm getting another chance at it with Nick. It's easier because I'm a grandmother this time. It removes me somewhat."

"No one would ever believe you're a grandmother."

Her eyes twinkled. "Thank you. I hoped you would say that."

He moved toward her. "Julianne—"

She stepped back, widening the distance between them. "I think I should be going now. It's late and the roads are dark. Thanks for a wonderful evening. I really enjoyed it."

"Can we do it again?"

"Of course."

"When?"

"I'll let you know," she promised.

He nodded, apparently satisfied.

She hoped he would wait on the porch or at the door rather than walk her to her car. She had no experience with first-date farewells and she didn't want to spoil the evening.

"I'll be right back," he said, sprinting up the stairs. He returned with Sarah and Drew. "They wanted to say goodbye."

Pleased with his tact, she shook hands with them all and walked out to her car alone.

She drove home with the window rolled down, grateful for the cool air on her face. The Gillette family was a mess, as dysfunctional as Jake and Francesca, but Julianne didn't think they were completely hopeless. The children were in pain, and Mitch… Mitch was not quite inept as a parent, but he came close. She was curious to see how it would all turn out.

Ten

At first Francesca thought she was dreaming, but when she heard the roar of falling masonry and collapsing beams, the tearing cracks of splitting trees, the shrieking of the fire alarm and the shrill, musical shattering of glass, followed by a rolling dip and rise like that of a ship caught in a stormy sea, she knew immediately that she was not.

Throwing the covers aside, she jumped out of bed and raced out of her room and down the hall toward Nick's bedroom. On the way she pounded on her mother-in-law's door. Concentrating on her errand, she kept her voice low and calm. "Wake up, Julianne. Earthquake!"

Jake called from the bottom of the stairs. "Is everyone all right up there, Francie?"

She clung to the railing, fighting for balance on the rolling floor. "Yes, except for some broken glass. I'll get Nick."

Julianne ran out of her room. "My God! This one's

strong. Everything is on the floor. Where's Nick? What time is it?"

"Around four, I think." Francesca opened her son's door. He was sitting up in bed, his eyes wide with excitement. "Is it an earthquake?" he asked breathlessly.

"Yes." She grabbed his shoes. "C'mon. We're going downstairs."

He nodded and reached for her outstretched hand. "My teacher said we should stay inside. She said it's safer in the house."

Francesca reassured him. "We'll just go outside for a while until the shaking stops." She wanted to be as far away from the power lines as possible.

He bumped against her. "It's hard to walk, isn't it?"

Julianne waited on the landing. "The shaking isn't as strong. I don't think the stairs will be a problem."

"Hold on anyway," Francesca cautioned.

Gripping Nick's hand tightly, she followed Julianne down the stairs and out into the center of the courtyard. The porch listed, an upstairs balcony sagged in the middle and she saw that several windows had broken in the bunkhouse. Other than that, there appeared to be no other structural damage.

Jake, carrying a flashlight, a cell phone and a battery-operated radio, joined them.

"Hi, Dad," said Nick. "We're having an earthquake."

Jake grinned. "Not anymore, son. The shaking is over." He appeared calm and steady in the artificial light of the torch.

Francesca was reassured just looking at him. "I'm assuming our power's gone," she said.

"I'm not sure," he answered. "I didn't want to turn

anything on yet. After things have settled for a bit, I'll go see if the clocks are affected."

"I've got to check the winery."

"Cyril and Danny will have already gone."

"Thank God we don't have any grapes in the press," she said. "Have you heard anything about the epicenter?"

"The radio stations are reporting that Palmdale is the hardest hit. No one has any numbers yet."

"Palmdale?" Julianne's lips were pale. "If we feel it like this all the way up here, it must have been a very strong quake."

"Has anyone been hurt?" his mother asked.

"It's too soon to tell. Relax, Mom. We've had earthquakes before. As far as I can see, there hasn't been any serious damage."

Headlights flared in the driveway. Collectively, they turned to look. A vineyard Jeep bearing the DeAngelo name pulled into the courtyard and a stocky, dark-complexioned man climbed out. Cyril addressed Francesca. "Other than some bottles, no damage to report at the winery. A few windows shattered and the old fireplace lost its bricks, but that's all. It looks like we pulled this one off, Frances."

She sighed and laughed shakily. "I guess that means we can all go back inside."

Julianne pressed her fingers against her eyelids. "It's time to get up anyway."

"No." Francesca shook her head. "We're all entitled to a little more sleep. I've got to test the sugar content of the grapes. It can't wait any longer. After that, I'll take a nap, too."

"Get some sleep. I'll test them," Jake volunteered. "If they're ready to be harvested, I'll set it up."

Francesca colored. "I'd intended to ask you to test them, but you don't need to do any more than that."

"I don't mind earning my keep."

"Thank you," she muttered, turning away. She didn't want to accept more than she absolutely had to from Jake. "C'mon, Nick. Let's get a few more hours of sleep."

"But I'm not tired anymore," he argued.

"Lie down anyway. If you don't fall asleep you can get up."

"Can I sleep with you?"

"If you promise not to kick."

Francesca pulled the covers around her sleeping son, kissed his forehead and headed downstairs. Julianne was cleaning up the kitchen. The refrigerator had tipped forward and everything not bolted to the walls was on the floor. It was a mess of broken pottery and utensils.

"Oh, Lord," Francesca groaned. "Did you lose anything important?"

"Not enough to put me seriously behind," replied Julianne. "Thank God, I didn't start the food for the Merriman's party last night."

"Do you need help, Julianne?"

She shook her head. "Don't worry about me. You have enough to think about. I think the front pillar cracked down the middle and the support beam is sagging. We'll have to replace that immediately."

"I'll look at it after I check the Pinot Noir vines. Nick's sleeping. I'm going to let him rest for as long as he needs."

Julianne settled a bag of trash on her hip and nodded at the coffeemaker. "Take some coffee with you. It's fresh."

Francesca poured the remaining coffee into her thermos, added milk and sugar and walked out onto the porch. The temperature was warmer than usual and a dense fog had settled over the hills. It made no sense to drive in weather like this. Unzipping her jacket, she slung the thermos strap over her shoulder and started toward the vineyard. She could barely see three feet ahead, but it didn't matter. She could have walked the path in her sleep. The smell of ripening fruit hung in the air. Her feet sank into the loamy soil, the soles of her shoes leaving deep tread marks. Surely the grapes were ready.

She knew immediately when she reached the Pinot Noir vines. The tiny, velvety grape clusters glistened in the morning mist. Kneeling at the base of a vine, Francesca pulled several grapes from a cluster and tasted them. They were incredibly sweet. She spit the seeds into her palm. They were dark, the mark of phenolically ripe fruit.

Strong arms gripped her from behind. "I thought you were going to sleep the morning away," Jake said.

Francesca relaxed. "I tried, but I was nervous. I've got a lot riding on these vines." She eased away from him. "So, what do you think? Are they ready?"

"Yes," he said emphatically. "You can harvest as early as tomorrow if you can get the crew."

"I'll get them," she said fiercely, "no matter what it takes."

He brushed an errant leaf from her shoulder.

"C'mon, Francie. Life doesn't always have to be so intense."

For a minute he thought she would respond. Her mouth quivered and there was a brightness to her eyes. Mustering his courage, he took a step closer.

Like a startled deer, she flung herself back into the trellis, the distress on her face unmistakable. Holding both hands up in the air, he spoke softly. "Relax, Francie. Nothing's happening here."

She thrust the thermos at him. "Your mother sent coffee."

He watched her walk away, determination in every purposeful stride. "You're welcome," he shouted after her.

"I owe you," she called back.

He grinned and shook his head. Francesca was a woman with a mission. He was quite sure he'd never seen anyone as driven in his life. At least she wasn't asking him when he was leaving. Still, she was a long way from wanting him back. His smile faded. Maybe she never would.

True to her word, the very next morning, a predawn crew arrived at the vineyard. Francesca was a fanatic about early-morning harvests. Hot grapes meant spontaneous fermentation and volatile acidity, which negatively impacted the flavor of the wine. Heat eliminated the cold-soak phase, when the native yeasts present in the must began the fermentation process.

Frank DeAngelo had set the standard for a working vineyard years before. Everyone worked, every member of the family, including the owners and their children. From the time she was strong enough to pull a cluster from its vine, Francesca was in the vineyard with the migrant workers and their children. It was a precedent she saw no need to deviate from. No one was exempt, except for Julianne, who provided hot coffee and egg burritos first thing in the morning, cinnamon rolls and more coffee three hours later, and finally, after the grapes were loaded into bins and driven to the crush platform, sandwiches, fruit and lemonade for lunch.

Even Nick, at eight years old, was proficient enough to catch three to four clusters in his hand before placing them in the picking bucket. After the buckets were filled with twenty pounds of fruit, three to five minutes for a good picker, they were dumped into the thousand-pound picking bins towed behind the tractor. Because Francesca insisted on an early-morning harvest, the grapes were still cold by the time they reached the crush platform at the winery.

Jake's job had always been to oversee the bin dumping. Without thinking or asking, he assumed his old position, watching critically, as grapes were slowly and carefully dumped into the crusher-destemmer where the berries and juice, after separation from the stems, dropped into a fermenter. Almost immediately the pinkish hue of the juice began soaking up the color from the skins.

He released his breath, unaware that he'd been anxious. Francesca wanted this very much, but he'd had his doubts. Pinot Noir blends had never been successful in the Santa Ynez Valley. The elegant red wine reached its peak of expression in the centuries-old domains in France's Burgundy region and typically went for over a hundred dollars a bottle. A good California Pinot Noir like Williams Selyem sold for three hundred dollars. Other vintners had tried but, too often, brought forth weedy thin wines that couldn't hold up in competition. Jake respected Francesca for stepping up to the challenge. A good Pinot Noir with its silky texture and powerful flavor was one of the best wines to accompany food.

Two days later, accompanied by Francesca, Jake inspected the bins. The Pinot Noir juice was a dark plum color, smelling of blackberry jam, wild cherries, clean earth and honey sweetness. Jake nodded. "It's perfect. What kind of yeast will you add?"

"The Burgundy RC212 to start with, then the commercial Pinot Noir yeast."

"Be sure to tell Cyril to punch the skins down at least four times a day," he warned. "We want to keep them from oxidizing at the top of the fermenter. Get lazy and you'll have the whole batch smelling like nail polish remover."

She nodded. "I'd planned to press it a little sweet and allow the last bit of fermenting to occur in the barrel. That should protect some of the more delicate fruit aromas."

He raised his eyebrows. "You really have done your homework. I'm impressed."

"You sound surprised. Why would you think I know less than you on the subject?"

"Don't get touchy, Francie," he said gently. "I was complimenting you."

Her color rose. "Sorry. I'm feeling a little sensitive

about these grapes. Pinot Noir is a delicate wine. That's what makes it interesting for me."

They walked in silence down the gravel path to the car. Jake no longer needed crutches but he still sported a slight limp. He climbed into the passenger side, allowing Francesca to drive.

Instead of immediately turning over the engine, she looked around at the hills in the dim, afternoon light. "Dusk is my favorite time of day," she said in a hushed voice. "The workday is finished, but it isn't late enough to turn in for the night. It's really stolen time, the time when life actually begins."

He looked at her for a long minute, wishing he didn't always have to pretend where she was concerned. Then, too soon, he would have to look away. Sometimes she would say something that tore at his heart and made him remember what she was like when they were first married. He wanted to stare at her until he had his fill, but he couldn't and then he would bleed all over again.

"What do you say we look at the Chardonnay vines in the morning?" he asked. "I think they're ready, too."

Francesca turned the key in the ignition and backed out on to the dirt road. "Did he fire you?" she asked suddenly.

"Who?" Jake kept his eyes on the road.

"You know who. Jack Cakebread."

"No," he said evenly. "He didn't fire me."

"You've been gone a long time. A winemaker isn't of much use to a winery if he's never there."

"I'm not much use to them either way."

"C'mon, Jake. Bones heal in half the time you've given them. What's **going** on?"

"Nothing I can't handle. Let's leave it, okay?"

"Why don't you just tell me. I could find out, you know. All I need to do is call Napa. Do you think he won't tell me?"

He shook his head in exasperation. "All right, Francie. You win. I quit. I'm not going back to Napa. I'm staying here."

"Define here."

"In Santa Ynez, or somewhere else in the county."

When she didn't say anything he defended himself. "I grew up here. This is my home."

They pulled into the courtyard in front of the estate house and still she was silent.

"Say something," he said.

"What good will that do?"

"I'd like to know how you feel."

"It has nothing to do with me," she said bluntly.

"It has everything to do with you."

"You have a right to come home. It will be awkward having you here for good, but we'll manage."

"Christ, you're stubborn."

She pointed to a silver-gray Infiniti parked in the courtyard, changing the subject. "Isn't that Mitch Gillette's car?"

"What's he doing here?"

Francesca bit back a smile. "I imagine he's come to see Julianne."

"Why would he do that?"

This time she laughed. "Listen to yourself, Jake. You sound like an outraged father. The man is taken with your mother. You should be grateful that she's enjoying herself."

"I'd be more grateful if he was somebody else. He's years younger than she is and he's affiliated with GGI."

"He's not *years* younger. He's only slightly younger and I think it's marvelous."

"You would," he muttered.

Francesca ignored him. "Let's go in and join them."

"I don't want to interrupt them."

"Don't be ridiculous! What do you think they're doing? Our son is in there."

Julianne opened the door before they climbed the stairs to the porch. "There you are," she said. "I was wondering what happened to you. We have company. I tried to get him to stay for dinner, but Drew and Sarah are at home."

Jake spoke first. "He's right, Mom. It isn't a good idea to leave teenagers to their own devices."

Mitch stepped out from behind her. "I'm sure he's right, Julianne. Thanks for the invitation, but I'll have to take a rain check. Think about this weekend." He nodded at Francesca. "Everyone's invited. Goodbye, now."

He climbed into his car, waved and drove away.

"What did he want?" Jake asked.

"He's hosting a housewarming," said his mother. "He wants me to cater it."

Jake brightened. "That doesn't sound like an invitation to me."

"He wants me to cook, Jake, not serve, and we're all invited. I've told him we'll be there."

"I don't know about that," said Francesca slowly. "It will look like we approve of his being here. I don't want people to think we're accepting the inevitable."

Julianne exploded. "For Pete's sake, Frances, it's a housewarming, not an endorsement of GGI. Lighten up a little. The man's lonely. The kids are lonely. They could use some friends."

Jake and Francesca stared at her in astonishment. Julianne rarely lost her temper.

She looked from one to the other. Finally, she threw up her hands and marched into the house.

Eleven

Mitch looked at his watch. It was nearly eight o'clock. "Drew," he called from the bottom of the stairs. "Sarah. It's time to go." He had an appointment with the board of directors of the Santa Ynez River Water Conservation District at eight-thirty. That allowed him exactly thirty minutes to drop the twins at school and make it down to the boardroom, a tight squeeze under the best of circumstances.

He walked into the kitchen and poured coffee into a travel mug, twisting down the lid securely. Then he sat at the kitchen table and drummed his fingers impatiently. Two minutes. He would allow them two more minutes and then he would personally escort them from their rooms into the car, regardless of their state of undress.

Christ, children were difficult! How had Susan managed it all alone for all those years? If it wasn't one thing, it was another. Registering them for school was a feat he congratulated himself for accomplishing without losing his temper. Untold amounts of paperwork were required, from birth certificates to cumulative records from their previous school, proof of immunizations, sports' disclaimers, credits completed, report cards and test scores verified, to name a few.

Interestingly enough, Drew's scores qualified him as a GATE student, eligible for enrollment in the district's honors' program. Why hadn't he known that until now? The question was a rhetorical one right up there with the way he should have known that Drew was a vegetarian. He blamed himself. The fact of the matter was, he didn't know his children at all. That was his fault as well, and to some degree, Susan's. Upon reflection, she had been perfectly content to relegate him to the status of absentee parent, one who paid the bills while abrogating the bulk of responsibility.

Once again he looked at his watch and stood purposefully. "That's it, kids," he shouted. "I can't wait any longer."

Sarah materialized at the top of the stairs, her midriff bare and her hair in the kind of disarray that, Mitch had recently learned, was intentional. She smiled and floated down to meet him, apparently in no particular hurry.

"Where's your brother?" Mitch asked.

"He's coming."

He handed her a brown bag. "I packed a bagel for you."

She grimaced. "I'm not a breakfast person, Dad. I wish you wouldn't go to the trouble of fixing it."

"It isn't any trouble, Sarah, and you have to eat. You're skin and bones."

She ignored him and stuffed the bag into her backpack. "C'mon, Drew," she yelled up the stairs. "We'll be late."

Drew shuffled down the stairs. At the sight of his son, bleary-eyed and tousled, sporting a wrinkled shirt and pants that barely covered his backside and dragged on the floor, Mitch closed his eyes briefly, reminding himself that every generation had its own form of rebellion and that showers were obviously no longer fashionable. "Good morning" was all he said, handing him a brown bag.

"What is it?" asked Drew.

"Bagel."

Drew nodded, accepted the bag and followed his father and sister out to the car.

"Everything's all taken care of at school," Mitch said.

Neither Sarah nor Drew commented.

"Are you nervous?" their father ventured.

"No," they said in unison.

"Really?" Mitch raised his eyebrows. "I think I'd be nervous if I had to attend a new high school. It's all right to be nervous."

"Cut the therapy," Drew said. "We're not nervous because we don't care what these rednecks think of us."

"Speak for yourself," Sarah reprimanded him sharply. "I, for one, would like to make a few friends."

Drew shrugged. "Suit yourself."

Mitch refrained from saying anything. The fifteen-minute drive was completed in silence. Not until he dropped them off in front of the administration building with an admonition to be outside near the flagpole after school did he breathe a sigh of relief. He didn't envy them. They would be outsiders. High school wasn't the time for a teenager to change schools. Even he knew that. But what choice did he have? He needed to make a living, and GGI had sent him here. He was conscious of a flash of annoyance. Mitch was accustomed to being in control. It was difficult for him to give up something important to someone else. Damn Susan! She'd never done anything convenient in her entire life, not even dying. Immediately he was ashamed of himself. She'd suffered a great deal and must have worried about the future of her children for a long time. The least he could do was respect her memory.

He was almost at Santa Ynez and he'd yet to rehearse his argument. A nagging worry that had nothing to do with grapes crossed his mind. Drew and Sarah were his children and despite their bravado, they were only fifteen and had recently lost their mother. On top of all that, they had been pulled out of their comfort zone and forced to relocate to another home and another school where they knew no one. No wonder Drew needed drugs. Maybe Sarah needed them as well.

Mitch felt his heart pound. He should go back and reassure them that if they weren't happy, they didn't have to stay. He would find them a new school. How much could children their age take without falling apart? Who could he ask? There was no one, except, maybe, Julianne. She had three children who'd lost a father at an early age. Maybe she would have some insights he hadn't thought of. Immediately he felt better.

* * *

Drew slouched against a column near the boys' bathroom, affecting total disinterest in the activity around him. It was lunchtime and he was hungry, but not hungry enough to stand in line in the middle of a bunch of strangers, and certainly not hungry enough to sit alone at one of the tables, an announcement to the world that he was a loser. Where was Sarah? She was supposed to meet him near the flagpole at lunch, but she'd flaked. If he wasn't so irritated and resentful, he'd be concerned. It was out of character for Sarah not to show up. He knew she would have a good reason. She'd probably found a whole new group of friends. Sarah was good at making friends. Whatever, the end result was, he was alone. What if he just walked out of here? What if he told his father he wasn't coming back?

What could he do? Drew rationalized. Mitch Gillette wasn't one to get physical. Drew couldn't remember a time when his father had spanked him or even laid a hand on him for anything at all. His father would be angry. Maybe he would even tighten his curfew, but nothing more serious than that.

"Hey, what's up?" a voice said from behind him.

Drew didn't turn around. The question couldn't possibly be addressed to him. Other than Sarah, he knew no one at Refugio High School. God, what a name! He couldn't even pronounce it.

"Hey, you," the voice said again. "I'm talking to you."

This time Drew managed to swivel around. A boy with a seriously shaved head, a hoop earring in his lip, another in one eyebrow and two in both ears was talking to him. Drew nodded, forcing himself to look at the perforated face.

"You're new here," the kid offered.

Brilliant. How hard was that to figure out? But what could you expect from rednecks who lived in a town without even a movie theater? "Yeah," he replied. "How'd you guess?"

The kid grinned. "What's your name?"

"Drew Gillette."

"Gillette? Like in the razor blades?"

Again Drew nodded. He'd heard that one before.

The boy looked him over and then looked away, apparently satisfied. He leaned against the building across from Drew. "If you're not doing anything after school, me and a couple of friends have a band. You could come along and listen."

Despite himself, Drew was interested. "What do you play?"

"Bass guitar."

"I'll come."

"Cool. I'll meet you in front after school. You got a car?"

Drew shook his head. "Not yet."

"No problem. I'll get you home."

The weight lifted from Drew's shoulders. "Thanks."

Mitch left his sandwich untouched, downed the last of his iced tea and looked around for the waitress. Christ, it was hot, even sitting at a table in the air-conditioned comfort of the Vineyard Café his clothes felt uncomfortably sticky against his skin. The man across from him, Jason Quinn, of the Santa Ynez River Water

Conservation District, had eaten his way through his hamburger and was halfway through his French fries without breaking a sweat.

The waitress refilled Mitch's iced tea. He swallowed his frustration and strove for a pleasant, conversational tone. "Can you give me a date as to when GGI might be able to break ground for the water pipes?"

Quinn wiped his mouth with his napkin, drained his Diet Pepsi and cleared his throat. "Your company has acquired a considerable amount of land that requires laying pipe adjacent to already established waterlines. Some of those are owned privately. You can break ground as soon as you want, but you'll have to decide whether you want public water or private or both. A private well requires permission."

"I told you, the vineyards in question have already been purchased by GGI."

"You haven't done your homework, Mr. Gillette. Buying up a vineyard doesn't give you water rights," Quinn corrected him. "You'll need DeAngelo access for water. Francesca has the closest well and, quite frankly, you don't have a prayer of acquiring it. Francesca DeAngelo's family has been growing grapes in this valley for a hundred years. Her vineyard and winery are profitable corporations. People in this valley have long memories. Don't even begin to think you can push out the small vineyards."

Mitch gritted his teeth. "We have no intentions of *pushing* out family-run vineyards. Those GGI have acquired wanted to sell. They were on the market. The families had other interests and were only too happy to sell to us."

"Which brings us back to my original point. You need water from the DeAngelo well. The Santa Ynez River Water Conservation District doesn't supply water to the area your company will need it supplied to. We no longer get our water from Lake Cachuma. Everything comes from surface waters from the Sierra Nevada watershed. To commit to the amount you need wouldn't make sense for us. We're in the middle of a real estate boom. Single-family homes are our first priority."

"Could we make it worth your while?"

Jason Quinn smiled thinly. "Everything doesn't always come down to money, Mr. Gillette. On this planet, water is limited. We have the same amount of drinking water today as we did when our ancestors' knuckles scraped the ground, only instead of three hundred thousand Homo sapiens walking the earth, we have six and a half billion. Tell me how you can justify tying up the amount of water a vineyard of your company's size will need simply to grow grapes."

Mitch frowned. "You have a point. But this enterprise still needs water and the vineyard and winery will provide jobs and tourists for years to come. Tell me where I should go from here."

Quinn looked at the check, pulled out a ten-dollar bill, and slid both across the table to Mitch. "You're not going to like this."

Mitch picked up the check and left the ten. "Probably not," he agreed.

"Convince Francesca DeAngelo to share her well."

Mitch sighed and leaned back in his chair. "Have you ever had any dealings with her?"

"Francesca is on the board. She's fair and she's loyal." Quinn hesitated.

"Go on."

"She's Frank DeAngelo's daughter. He was an important man here in the valley. Francesca has a great deal to live up to. So far, she's done well. As far as sharing her water, she could go either way. That's up to you. She's not the only one you'll have to convince. Santa Ynez doesn't have a Wal-Mart or a Starbucks or even a Rite Aid. The people here don't have a warehouse mentality." He fixed a level gaze on Mitch. "Personally, I think the odds of your conglomerate making a go of it here in the valley are poor. Why don't you cut your losses and go somewhere else before it's too late to back out?"

Mitch pushed back his chair and stood. "Thanks for your time and the information. Lunch is on me."

The other man looked up at him. "I understand you're in the business of growing grapes yourself?"

Small towns. Mitch wasn't accustomed to having his every move reported before he even made it. "That's right."

"You don't want to step on too many toes if you have a personal investment, Mr. Gillette. People here take care of their own. If you intend to settle here, you want to be part of that."

Mitch didn't offer his hand. "I'll keep that in mind. As I said before, you've been very informative. I appreciate it." He nodded and walked to the cash register where he paid the bill and left the restaurant.

It wasn't until he'd pulled out on to Refugio Road that he remembered he needed groceries. Mitch looked at his watch. His morning errand had taken much longer than expected. He had two hours before he was due at the high school to pick up Drew and Sarah. Then there was her dressage lesson at the equestrian center and he still hadn't visited the construction site. He swore under his breath and turned north onto Highway 154, accelerating to the speed limit. Maybe he could swing grocery shopping with Drew while Sarah took her lesson. Otherwise they would make do with scrambled eggs for dinner.

The road past Los Olivos and the Firestone Vineyard narrowed to one lane in both directions. Once again the natural beauty of the land soothed his spirits and captured his attention. Small creeks, some barely trickles this time of year, gurgled over rocks and the smooth trunks of fallen trees. Rising on either side of the road was a ghostly forest of pin oak in the throes of death, their twisted branches and gnarled trunks strangled by a mesh of delicate sea-foam green, the beautiful but deadly parasitic Spanish moss. A mile down the road, the trees disappeared and soft hills dotted with beef cattle and horses rolled down to the sea. There were vineyards this far inland but no wineries. GGI hoped to change all that. At one time Mitch had enthusiastically supported the project. Now he wasn't so sure. What that meant as far as his career with the company, he could only imagine.

A year ago, even six months ago, temporary unemployment didn't worry him. He had been a free man. Relocation wasn't a drawback. The idea had even been mildly interesting. Now, everything was different. Two teenagers who had just lost their mother couldn't be bouncing around the country, changing schools and friends and neighborhoods. They needed stability. They needed a father who was employed, and there were few employment opportunities in the Santa Ynez Valley.

Mitch drove down the gravel road to the job site. Bulldozers had already leveled the area where construction would begin on the winery. The actual start date was dependent upon the Urban Planning Commission's report forecasting traffic, parking and general pollution problems created by the operation of a winery the size of this one.

Mitch wasn't worried. The site was perfect. He'd looked long and hard for that perfect combination of sloping hills, protective mountains and cool ocean breezes. Already, the ground had been turned on most of the acreage. So far, everything was on schedule, with the exception of the report. But reports were always late. The water factor was crucial. He needed an irrigation source and quickly. Francesca was a possibility, but Mitch hadn't reached his current position by relying on possibilities. GGI would have to dig for its own well. He set the brake, changed into his hiking boots and climbed out of the car. Immediately his feet sank into the mud.

Frowning, he bent down to examine the soil. It was dark and very wet, almost the consistency of swampland. Where was the water coming from? The last rain was nearly two months behind them.

Drew found Sarah near the flagpole. "I waited for you at lunch."

"I'm sorry, Drew. My math teacher had some questions about the math I had last year."

He shrugged and spoke casually. "It doesn't matter. Tell Dad I'll get a ride home later. I've got something going."

Sarah shook her head, dismayed. "Please, Drew. He said to wait here."

He dismissed her with a wave of his hand. "I don't have time for this. I'm outta here."

She watched helplessly as her brother disappeared into the crowd of milling students. "Please, come back," she whispered, knowing the futility of her request. "Please, don't stick me in the middle again."

Twelve

Mitch turned his Infiniti into the school parking lot and pulled up to the curb in front of the flagpole. Sarah sat by herself on a low retaining wall. She stood when she saw him and slowly made her way to the car. "Dad. You're late!"

"I'm sorry, honey. I had a problem at the job site."

She threw her book bag into the back seat and climbed into the car, averting her face. "But you were supposed to be here an hour ago."

"I couldn't, Sarah," he said helplessly. "I'm so sorry." He forced a smile. "How did it go today?"

She shrugged, fighting back tears.

Mitch touched her shoulder. "If there had been any way of letting you know I was going to be late, I would have. Do you believe that?"

"It's okay."

Silently damning the public-school system for their ban on cell phones, he drove out of the lot. It wasn't until he reached the first stop sign that he remembered Drew. "Where's your brother?"

"He met someone. He said to tell you he'd get a ride home later."

Mitch frowned. He opened his mouth to ask if this kind of behavior was normal for Drew and then closed it again without saying anything. Somewhere there was an unwritten rule between siblings about telling tales. Mitch wouldn't put Sarah in that position. "Do you want to know what happened?" he asked instead.

She hesitated and then nodded, trying to appear interested.

Mitch's heart warmed toward her. She really was a trouper. "There's a problem with the water table on the construction site."

"What does that mean?"

"The underground water is so high that the ground is the consistency of sludge. It's impossible to build anything until it's dried out. It sets the project back and it could be expensive. I had to make a conference call to two members of the board of directors. That's why I was late."

She looked at him, concerned. "Are you in trouble?"

He smiled. "No, sweetheart. The project just isn't running smoothly, that's all."

She settled back in her seat.

"Did you happen to meet Drew's new friend?" he asked casually.

"No. He's mad at me. I didn't meet him for lunch because I had to talk to my math teacher." She looked around. "Are we going the right way?"

"Damn. I'm sorry, Sarah." He'd forgotten all about her riding lesson. Mitch had apologized more in the last four months than he had in his entire forty-five years, with the exception of the time he'd lived with Susan.

At the next intersection he made a U-turn and drove back up Refugio Road to the equestrian center. "Do you mind if I shop for groceries while you ride?"

"No. Can you get me some lunch food? I'd like to pack a lunch until I figure things out at school. The cafeteria line is really long."

"What would you like me to buy?"

Her forehead wrinkled. "I don't know, Dad. Just get what looks good. It can't be that hard. You know, chips, fruit, sandwich stuff." Her face lit up. "I know. Ask Julianne. She'll know."

Mitch would like nothing more than to ask Julianne, but he didn't want it to be the sole reason for calling her. She was sensitive and intelligent and very cautious. He didn't want her to think that the primary reason for his interest was his children.

"Maybe I will" was all he said.

Julianne peeked into the convection oven. The cheesecake was perfect, golden on top and firm in the middle. She turned off the timer, pulled on her oven mitts and slid the baking sheet out of the oven to cool.

"Is it done?" her grandson asked, peering over her shoulder.

"Not yet. It has to cool. Then I'll add the topping." She pulled off her mitts and ruffled his hair. "Are you hungry?"

He thought a minute. "Not for real food."

"What then?"

"Something sweet with whipped cream and chocolate."

He'd seen her cream-puff éclairs. She looked at the clock. "We only have about two hours until dinner, Nick. If you eat an éclair now, you won't be hungry, and you know how that upsets your mom."

"What are we having?" he asked.

"Meat loaf."

"I won't be hungry for that anyway, so I might as well have an éclair."

"I thought you liked my meat loaf."

"I like éclairs better."

"I'll tell you what. I really want you to eat dinner. You can have a cookie or a Popsicle now and I'll save you an éclair for dessert."

He considered her proposal. "Who are the rest of the éclairs for?"

"The Gillettes' housewarming tomorrow."

"Am I going?"

"You certainly are. We're all going."

"What are we having tomorrow?"

"Mexican food. Tacos and enchiladas and chili rellenos, rice, beans and tortillas."

"And chips?"

She nodded. "Chips, too."

"All right. I'll eat meat loaf tonight and a Popsicle now."

She pointed to the freezer. "They're in the side compartment. I think there might be some cherry-flavored ones left."

The phone rang. It was her business line. She picked it up. "Julianne Harris."

Mitch Gillette sounded exasperated. "I'm at the grocery store buying lunch food. Can you help me?"

"That depends on what kind of lunch you're serving."

"I won't be serving at all. It's for Sarah and Drew. They want bag lunches and I'm at a loss. Ordinarily I wouldn't bother you with this, but Sarah suggested I call you, and I think it's a damn good idea because I'm hopeless. What do kids eat these days? It can't still be peanut butter and jelly."

"How about some fruit, chips and sandwich stuff? How hard can that be?"

"The variety is ridiculous. What does Nick eat for lunch?"

"I don't think it's the same thing at all," Julianne advised him. "Nick is eight years old. His friends won't think he's odd if he brings lettuce wraps and deviled eggs. That won't do for fifteen-year-olds."

"All right. What do fifteen-year-olds eat?"

"I really think you should let them choose their own food, Mitch. That way you can't lose."

"Sarah's at a dressage lesson and Drew could be anywhere."

"I beg your pardon?"

"A friend is giving him a ride home."

"That isn't what you said."

Mitch sighed. "I didn't like it either, but until he shows up, my hands are tied. Meanwhile, my refrigerator is bare."

"Buy some whole-grain bread, sliced turkey, romaine lettuce, cheddar cheese and a few apples," she suggested. "You can't go wrong with those. Kids usually like anything in small packages. Chips and cookies come that way. You're on your own as far as drinks.

Just don't make the lunches too bulky. They won't eat bulky lunches."

"Thanks," he said. "You're a lifesaver."

"Find your son," she said before hanging up the phone.

Nick's mouth was stained red from the Popsicle. He sat at the table swinging his legs. "I like pudding cups," he confided. "Chocolate ones. You should have told him pudding cups."

"I'll remember next time," Julianne promised.

Drew sniffed at the contents of the plastic bag. "What is this stuff?" he asked.

"What do you think it is?" Jason Saunders flopped down on his water bed. The mattress dipped and rolled with the weight of his body.

The room was dark with olive-green walls and shades pulled down against the afternoon sun. Drew reached into the plastic and pulled out a pinch of fine white powder. "I can't smell anything." He tested it on the tip of his tongue. "I know it isn't cocaine."

"It's heroin. Pure as it comes."

"I've never seen it like this."

"You sniff it instead of injecting. No worry about bad needles with this stuff."

"Is it expensive?"

"Only about four bucks a bag."

Drew looked at the boy lolling on the bed. "Are you high?"

"I don't get high anymore."

"Why not?"

"It doesn't work that way."

"What do you mean?"

"Try it and see."

Drew shook his head. "I don't think so. Pot's one thing, but heroin's bad stuff. You got any weed?"

"Wally does. He's my drummer. He'll be here any minute with the rest of 'em. Come on," Jason coaxed him. "Just once won't hurt. How do you know you don't like it unless you try it?"

"Not this time."

"Why not?"

"I gotta get home. My dad's paranoid. He'll know if I've been doing anything."

"Not with this stuff."

Drew stared into the bag. It was tempting. He'd never done heroin. Maybe just once wouldn't hurt. "How do you do it?"

Jason sat up and reached for the bag. "I'll show you."

Francesca pulled off her gloves and left them on the desk in the entry. Then she went in search of her son. "Nick. I'm home."

"In here, Mom, with Gran," he called from the kitchen.

She stood in the doorway. "Hello, you two," she said. "I'm dirty but I wanted to find out how your spelling test went."

"I only missed two."

"Two? Why? You didn't miss any on the test I gave you last night."

"Miss Keller mixed up the words," he said matter-of-factly. "When the words aren't in order, I don't remember them as well."

"Next time I'll mix up the words," replied his mother.

"I don't have another test until next week," he reminded her.

"How many words are on your test, Nick?" asked his grandmother.

"Twenty."

"Ninety percent is an A, Frances."

"But he had a hundred percent last night." She changed the subject. "What are we having for dinner?"

"Meat loaf."

"Yum." Francesca headed toward the stairs. "I need a shower and then I'll set the table."

"Nick will set the table," said Julianne. She looked at her grandson. "Won't you, Nick?"

The child sighed. "I guess so."

Ten minutes later Jake walked through the back door. "How's my favorite son?"

"I missed two on my spelling test," Nick said immediately.

Jake grinned. "Only two? That's great! You're a genius." He winked at this mother. "He gets it from me."

"Don't let Frances hear you say that," she warned him.

"Gran's letting me have one of Mr. Gillette's éclairs for dessert," Nick announced.

"Excuse me?"

Julianne laughed. "I made éclairs for the party tomorrow."

Jake's smile faded. He avoided his mother's eyes. "I should take a shower. What time is dinner?"

"The same time it's been for thirty years," said Julianne. "Six o'clock."

* * *

Over steaming mouthfuls of meat loaf and baked potatoes, Jake broke down the schedule for the acres not yet harvested. "I think we should be done by the end of next week."

Francesca nodded. "We're on schedule. Did you get a chance to check out the Syrah vines? Cyril thought there might be a problem there."

Jake looked thoughtful. "I thought you discontinued that plot. The vines are gone."

She stared at him. "Gone? They can't be gone. How is that possible?"

"I checked this morning. The ones that are alive are riddled with mold. I assumed you wanted to clear out what was left and start fresh."

"I want no such thing. What's happened to them?"

"There's a leak somewhere," Jake guessed. "It's a big one to have caused that much damage. I'll go over the area tomorrow."

"Take Cyril and Danny with you. Check everything carefully. I'll be at the winery."

"Maybe the earthquake had something to do with it," Julianne suggested.

Jake nodded. "Possibly, although we have safety clips to shut down the system if that happens."

Francesca looked down at her plate. *We.* He said *we* as if he belonged here. Did she want him to belong here again? More to the point, could she trust him to stay? Their relationship was a civil one, sometimes even friendly, but that was all. It was comfortable this way. Comfortable and safe. Safety had taken on new meaning in the last two years. Safety, she'd come to believe, was an acceptable alternative to the pain of loving someone who didn't love you back.

"So, Francie, what do you think?"

"About what?"

"Do you want to go early and help Mom deliver the food to the Gillettes', or shall I?"

"Nick has a soccer game. You take him and I'll help with the food."

Jake nodded at his son. "Did you hear that, big fella? It's you and me at soccer tomorrow."

Nick sighed. "Don't expect a miracle, Dad. I'm not that good."

"Why not?"

"I don't like the clinches. I'm afraid someone will kick me."

"They're supposed to kick you. That's why you wear shin guards."

"It still hurts."

"After dinner we'll go outside and knock the ball around a little," his father suggested. "Would you like that?"

"I guess so." Nick swallowed the last of his potato. "I ate everything." He looked at his grandmother. "May I have my éclair now?"

"Yes," the three adults at the table spoke in unison.

"Yours is on the plate in the refrigerator," said Julianne.

Francesca waited until she was sure Nick was out of the room. "Don't be too hard on him, Jake. Not everyone is an athlete."

"He just needs a little confidence, that's all."

"Maybe it isn't his thing."

"Spelling's not his thing either, but when he works at it he can do it."

"Missing two out of twenty isn't my idea of doing it," she said under her breath.

"For Christ's sake, Francie. What's wrong with ninety percent?"

"It isn't a hundred."

"Come on, you two," Julianne protested. "Call a truce. You both want the best for your son. Ease up on each other a little. This gets exhausting."

Francesca looked embarrassed. "I'm sorry, Julianne."

"Apology accepted." She looked meaningfully at her son. "Well?"

"I'm sorry, too, Mom," he said softly.

"Now," she ordered, "finish your meat loaf, please, and then I could use some help with the dishes."

Thirteen

Jake Harris walked into the tiny building that housed the Santa Ynez River Water Conservation District offices and smiled at the girl seated behind the high counter. "Hi, Cindy."

The girl's brown eyes widened. "Hi, yourself, stranger. It's been a long time. Where have you been?"

"Working in Napa. How about you? I've been home for a while but I haven't seen you."

"I live in Buellton now. I'm filling in for my sister, Isabel. She's on maternity leave." She pronounced the name with a Latin flavor, a sibilant *S* and heavy on the first syllable. Cindy tilted her dark head. "I'm sorry about your divorce, Jake. It surprised everyone. It must be hard for you to come back here. You put your heart and soul into DeAngelo."

Jake shrugged. "That's water under the bridge. Francesca and I are friends now. It works better that way." He grinned. "Especially since that's where I'm living."

"Really?" She looked doubtful. "Whatever suits you

best, I guess. I couldn't live in the same town as my ex. That's why I moved to Buellton."

Jake changed the subject. "I'm looking for Norman Layton. Is he in?"

"I think so." She scooted her chair-on-wheels into the hallway and called out. "Norman? Are you available? You've got company."

"Send 'em back," answered a gruff, tobacco-flavored voice.

"You heard him," said the girl. "It's as close to an invitation as you're ever going to get with old Norman."

Jake laughed and made his way down the hall. He stood for a minute at the entrance of an office that, except for a state-of-the-art computer, looked as if it belonged in another century. A green-shaded banker's lamp sat on a rolltop desk thick with papers stacked on top of each other in no apparent order. Shelves filled with books, pamphlets and periodicals lined the walls. A trash can overflowing with wadded paper, pencil shavings and a banana peel stood near the door, and a cat with a torn ear and orange stripes stretched out on a pillow near the window. Only the computer, blinking blue, green and red lights, gave testimony to the technological age.

Norman Layton, seventy-six years old, diamond-sharp, with no thoughts of retiring, motioned Jake inside. "Come in, come in," he said impatiently. "I shoulda known you'd be here."

Confused, Jake closed the door behind him and pulled up a chair. "I don't remember making an appointment."

"Don't get smart with me, Jake Harris," the old man

warned. "I've known you since you were in short pants. Between you and that wife of yours, I don't have time to do anything other than DeAngelo business."

"Has Francesca been to see you?"

Layton scratched his lined cheek. "When hasn't she? First she pesters me with questions about water rights for GGI until I'm dizzy, and now she's got a notion in her head that there's underground flooding. I told her we'd check it out, but Jake, she wants everything to happen yesterday. There's no satisfying her."

"Francesca has never won awards for patience," Jake admitted, hiding a smile. "But I think she's on to something here, Norm. The water table is higher than I've ever seen it. We've lost some vines. Has anyone else noticed anything?"

Norm sighed and clasped his hands behind his head. "Someone else was in here asking for a map of our local wells. That's about all the company I've had for a week. This time of year everyone's out in the field."

"Who wanted the map?"

"The new GGI man. Gillette is his name."

Jake's forehead wrinkled. "Is he thinking of drilling for his own water?"

"You'll have to ask him. I mind my own business."

"Water *is* your business, Norm," Jake reminded him. "It wouldn't be out of line for you to ask him what's going on."

"Even if I did, it wouldn't be professional for me to tell you, now, would it?"

Jake laughed. "I suppose it wouldn't. We do need someone to check out a potential underground leak. When do you think that'll happen?"

The old man leaned forward, swept aside a stack of papers, picked up his pencil and scribbled something on the desk calendar. "I'll have someone drive out to your place tomorrow. Is that soon enough for you?"

"I couldn't ask for more. Give me a call and let me know how it turns out."

"Carl Harris was a friend of mine."

"Yes, he was," said Jake.

"Say hello to your mother."

"I'll do that."

Jake stood on the steps, squinting against the summer sun, and considered his next move. There was nothing more he could do with regard to the water leak other than scout out other potential problem areas. That would take the rest of the day. What he really wanted to know was why Mitchell Gillette had requested a map of local wells. No one would voluntarily share water with GGI. They might, however, be willing to share it with a local vintner as long as he guaranteed none of that water would be siphoned off to the conglomerate. The amount of water necessary for Mitch's few acres would be negligible, barely noticeable to a vineyard the size of Francesca's, and not nearly enough to irrigate one as large as GGI planned to establish. What the company needed was permission to siphon a number of local wells. Gillette was intelligent enough and persuasive enough, and he had the capital to make sharing their water extremely tempting for local vintners, especially those who had been hit hard by the state's slow economy or by a natural disaster such as a leak that raised the water table enough to destroy premium vines. Not that anyone in the valley would cave in for a quick buck when his future livelihood was at stake, not anyone who wanted to stay in the business.

He checked his watch. Francesca would be at the winery checking the deliveries. She wouldn't be happy with his interruption. The Pinot Noir grapes were at a crucial place. A shipment of barrels had arrived, French oak from the Allier forest. She would be inspecting them carefully to see that one-third of them were new, clean and medium toasted. The barrels would be filled nearly to the top with Pinot Noir until the fermentation slowed, and then they would be topped weekly to eliminate oxidation. After a week or two, the wine would be inoculated, as all red wines were, for malolactic fermentation, making it rich, seamless and more elegant in the palate, satin smooth as only a Pinot Noir can be in the finish.

No, she wouldn't be pleased to have her work interrupted, but she would be more upset by the possibility of GGI's infiltration of local well water. More important, she was a member of the board of directors of the local vintners' association. If Francesca DeAngelo called a meeting, everyone would attend. This time Jake wanted everyone there.

He found her where he least expected, slumped over at her desk, her arms cradling her head, sound asleep. Carefully, so as not to disturb her, Jake sat down, prepared to wait until she woke.

It wasn't often that he found Francesca in a vulnerable position. He didn't think of her as a needy woman. In fact, on a scale that measured capability, she ranked right up there with his mother. Her strength was a shield.

Jake knew that now. For a long time Francesca's pᵉr-ceived strength had kept his tender feelings at bay. He believed she didn't need him. His ego was damaged and their relationship had eroded. Strange what a differ-ence two years could make. Now he recognized his own culpability, the immaturity that caused him to flee instead of staying in the marriage and working through their issues.

Jake's gaze moved over his sleeping ex-wife, her shining hair, the exposed nape of her neck, the thin, muscled strength of her shoulders and back, the curve of her cheek, the tanned skin of her arms. She was beau-tiful. His awareness of her physical attributes struck him almost dispassionately. Francesca had always been beautiful with the kind of looks that made grown men, happily married men, turn and stare. But to him she was much more than just another beautiful woman. Jake was inured to physical beauty. It wasn't important to him. Santa Barbara County had more than its share of lovely women. The combination of money, spas, health clubs and plastic surgeons drew the svelte, the well-heeled, the attractive and those seeking perpetual youth and expensive real estate to its coasts and valleys. No, it wasn't Francesca's looks that attracted him or kept his interest.

Maybe it was the same for everyone who'd been married a long time. Maybe, after a while, every man looked at his wife and saw the person, the entire pack-age, not the outer wrapping. Maybe that was why a woman could gain thirty pounds over thirty years and a man could develop a paunch and lose his hair but, if the marriage was good, neither noticed.

Francesca's beauty was a part of her. Because of it, and because of her intelligence and her sense of who she was, a DeAngelo from a long line of DeAngelos in the community of Santa Ynez, she'd developed confidence. Jake loved her confidence, her enthusiasm for life, her belief that there were no limits to what she wanted to do. She never complained. Nothing was too difficult or too complicated. She was lightning quick when it came to understanding. Frank DeAngelo had never been her match when it came to words. Jake grinned, remembering the heated exchanges between father and daughter and how Frank had often ended an argument he wasn't winning with a roaring, *"Because I said so."*

Jake had learned something in the last two years. He'd learned that family and tradition and loving one woman until he died was how he was made. It was the way he'd been raised, the only role model he had. He didn't have it in him to erase his past, to start again with a new woman who had her own history, her own children, a woman who hadn't shared his youth, or his dream of running his own vineyard, of passing his land and his knowledge down to his own son, to establish a dynasty of vintners in the valley where he'd been raised. It was Francesca's dream, too. He desperately hoped he'd be allowed another chance at getting it right.

A breeze from the window lifted the wisps of hair around her face. Francesca stirred, opened her eyes, a slow butterfly fluttering of her lash-rimmed lids. For an instant after she saw him, she smiled. Then her eyes went wary. She lifted her head.

"What's wrong?" she asked immediately.

"Nothing's wrong."

"Why are you here in the middle of the day?"

"Have you had lunch?" he asked.

She shook her head.

"Why don't we pack up some bread and cheese from the case in the winery and I'll find us a bottle of wine. We can eat at the picnic table, the one with the view of the valley."

"Jake." She stood with her hands on her hips. "Are you sure you don't have something to tell me?"

"I didn't say that. I said nothing was wrong."

She gave in. "All right. Let me make one more phone call and I'll meet you outside."

The western view from the winery was the more dramatic one, with its low hills sweeping toward a diamond-bright sea, brilliantly blue under the late-summer sun. But Jake preferred the other side, the eastern view. The San Rafael mountain range was shadowed, almost blue-gray, a backdrop against the gold and green valley dotted with oak, eucalyptus and olive trees, premium cattle and even more premium horses munching on the last of the season's wild grass.

He'd chosen a sauvignon blanc, a mild white wine, a crusty French loaf, a half pound of sliced salami and wedge of Gruyère for their lunch.

Francesca pulled the blue and yellow French print tautly over the picnic table and, because there was a breeze, secured it with clips. She tucked the napkins under the wineglasses and sat down on the bench. "I'm hungry," she said, reaching for the salami. "Did you bring a knife for the cheese?"

Jake pulled a pocketknife from his jeans and handed it to her. Then he tore two chunks of bread from the loaf and poured the wine while she sliced the cheese.

"I love it here." He waved his arm, encompassing the valley. "I don't know if it's this place in particular or if I'd feel that way about anywhere I'd grown up."

She nodded. "I know what you mean. This is home." She nibbled on a slice of salami and washed it down with a sip of wine. "This is just right," she announced. "I wouldn't have chosen the sauvignon blanc, but it's perfect."

"Thank you."

She drank some more, tilted her head and asked the question he'd been hoping she would ask since he came home.

"Why didn't you make it in Napa, Jake? You're a natural. Any winery would be happy to have you."

He was tempted to swallow the rest of his wine for the temporary glow, the flow of false courage for what might come next. His answer was easy. It was her reaction he was afraid of. "You weren't there."

She stared at him, dark eyes narrow, skeptical, her mouth soft, bare of lipstick, slightly chapped. "You're kidding."

It wasn't a question, just a blunt, matter-of-fact statement. He nearly laughed. Trust Francesca to remove all possibility of romance from the conversation. "No."

"You couldn't wait to get away from me."

He didn't deny it. "I was an idiot."

"I thought you hated me."

"For God's sake, Francie. I never *hated* you. That was never the problem. If I hated you, I wouldn't have been so miserable." This wasn't going the way he'd planned.

"Why are you telling me this?"

He drew a deep breath. "I wanted to tell you the truth. People make mistakes. I made a bad one, possibly an irrevocable one. I shouldn't have left you. I should never have divorced you."

"I divorced you," she reminded him.

He shook his head. "I'm not going to let you make me mad." He looked at her. "Do you know that you're the only person who can make me lose my temper?"

"I'm not sure that's the best qualifier for a marriage."

"Do you want to know what I think it means?"

"Yes."

"I think I care so damn much about what you think, specifically, what you think of me, that I can't see straight. I want you to agree with me. I want you to think like I do. You're important to me." He picked up his glass and set it down again.

Francesca stared out across the mountains, her profile to him. "What do you want?" she asked after a minute.

"I just wanted you to know how I feel," he said. "That's all."

She nodded, picked up the wine bottle and refilled his glass. "This is hard for you, isn't it?"

"Very hard."

"Why?"

"I don't know where I stand with you. You're so damn cool and controlled and I'm losing it."

"I'm sorry," she said, her voice low.

"For what?"

She looked at him this time, with the full effect of her dark brown eyes. "I'm sorry that I don't trust you. I almost died when you left me. I couldn't get up off the floor for three days, not even for Nick. Your mother took care of him. I would hear her telling him stories, singing songs, just talking to him. She told him I was sick." Her mouth trembled. "I *was* sick. I can't risk going through that again."

"You won't have to go through it again. I guarantee it."

"How can you possibly do that, Jake? Are you suggesting a legal contract? Something along the line of, you'll never leave me again?"

"If that's the way you want it."

She smiled. "If only it worked that way. But we both know it doesn't."

He sighed. "What do you want me to do, Francie? This is driving me crazy."

It wasn't nice. She wasn't proud of it. But it gave her the smallest tingle of satisfaction to hear him say it. "I don't want to do anything except grow my grapes and make my wine and watch my son grow."

"What about love, Francie? Aren't you a little young to give up on that part of your life?"

"Love? Is that what we're talking about?" She stared at him incredulously. "Are you saying that you love me?"

"What else?"

She stood and brushed the bread crumbs from her lap. "You'll have to do better than that, Jake." Her smile was brittle. "I have some errands to run. Tell Julianne I'll be home later to help her."

Completely bewildered, he watched her walk away. It wasn't until she'd driven off that he realized he hadn't told her about Mitch Gillette and the local wells.

Fourteen

Julianne loaded the last of the trays into her catering truck and climbed into the driver's seat. She flipped down the shade, checked her hair and lipstick in the mirror, and pulled out onto the service road leading to the main highway. The weather was already changing and it was only September. Deciduous maples were taking on the golden hues of autumn and the air had a crisp spicy smell that signaled the onset of cool weather to come.

The food she'd prepared for Mitch's housewarming was rich, hearty and warm, a perfect foil for the breezy afternoon and chilly evening. The clock on the dashboard said one, and the party was at three, plenty of time to unload, set up for the servers and transform herself from cook to guest.

Mitch had invited everyone in Santa Ynez that he knew, including the local vintners. Despite his GGI affiliation, nearly everyone had accepted, some out of curiosity, some for a free meal, some because they genuinely liked what they'd seen of their new neighbor, a widower with two children, an easy smile and a firm handshake, a man who'd had the sense to leave a historic piece of architecture the way it was meant to be.

Julianne pulled into the courtyard and looked around appreciatively. Colorful paper lanterns hung from the trees and heat lamps were plentiful enough to ensure that every white-clothed table was within proper range for guests to be comfortable after the sun went down. A dark-skinned man in blue jeans and a white apron stood before a large commercial barbecue, smoking pork ribs and chicken. Tubs of ice with beer and soft drinks sat within easy reach of the tables. Julianne had arranged for a cappuccino bar to be set up at one end of the patio. Margaritas and sangria would be mixed at the wine bar on the other side, and long banquet tables had been set out for the food.

She released the latch for the back door and climbed out of the truck. Mitch saw her from the kitchen window and hurried out to greet her. He took the chafing dish from her hands. "Are you always right on schedule?" he asked.

She looked surprised. "Of course. How could I survive in this business if I wasn't?"

"Do you have any idea how unusual you are?" he asked softly.

Julianne shrugged and turned away, slightly embarrassed. She picked up a basket of tortillas and changed the subject. "Did you hire the servers from Manuelos Restaurant?"

He nodded in the direction of the barbecue. "They're already here. Drew and Sarah will be down in a minute to help with whatever you need them for."

As soon as the words were out of his mouth, the children appeared on the doorstep. Julianne waved. Sarah smiled. Drew did not, but they both headed toward the truck.

"What do you want us to do?" Drew asked, his tone just short of what his father called *attitude*.

"You can help unload my cakes," Julianne replied cheerfully.

Sarah peaked into the back of the truck. "What kind are they?"

"Ask Drew. They were his idea."

Puzzled, Sarah lifted the top of one of the containers and assessed the two-layer cake. "It looks like some kind of chocolate only not as dark."

"Whatever it is, it looks great," said Mitch.

"Chocolate-mocha," replied Julianne. "The other one is lemon." She nodded at Drew. "Give one of them to your brother and you can come back for the éclairs."

Sarah handed the lemon cake to Drew and reached in for the chocolate. "How long did it take you to make all this?"

Julianne didn't have to think. "Six hours."

Sarah looked impressed. "*Exactly* six hours?"

"Just about. I have to know exactly how long it takes because that plays a part in how much I charge."

"Did it take a long time to learn everything?"

Julianne laughed. "Are you thinking of going into the catering business, Sarah?"

"Maybe I can work part-time for you?" she suggested.

"That might be a good idea in the summer," said her father, "*if* Julianne needs someone and *if* you can fit it into your schedule. It seems like you're already fairly impacted with what you have already."

"I didn't mean school," Sarah assured him. "I think working with food would be fun."

Drew snorted.

Sarah turned on him, her hands full of cake. "What does that mean?" she demanded.

"You're a lousy cook, Sarah. Even you can't deny that."

"Maybe I'll learn something."

"It'd have to be a whole lot longer than one summer," her brother said under his breath.

"What about you, Drew?" Julianne challenged him. "Is your summer scheduled or could you fit in a part-time job?"

For the space of a heartbeat, he looked interested. Then his eyes glazed over. "I don't think so."

"Why not?"

"I've got other plans."

"What plans are those?" asked Mitch, his voice like steel.

"I might go to summer school and get my math and language requirements out of the way."

"Are you behind in those subjects?" asked his father.

"No, but it would free my schedule for more electives next year if I take the core subjects during the summer."

"You can't—" Sarah began, but Drew's elbow in her back stopped her from continuing.

"That sounds reasonable," said Mitch. "It isn't what I expected, but if that's what you want to do, I suppose we can work out some other way for you to pay for your car insurance."

Julianne looked from Mitch to his son. She was experienced when it came to children. Something wasn't right. She couldn't put her finger on how she knew, but there it was. She smiled brightly, picked up two foil-covered platters and headed toward one of the long white tables. It wasn't her business. No one would appreciate her curiosity or her opinion.

Nick sat in the back seat of his father's car and stared out the window, wishing he had been allowed to stay home and play with Max, Cyril's ten-year-old son. Max came to visit every other week or so. His parents were divorced and his mother lived somewhere to the north. That was all Nick knew except that Max was exciting. He used words Nick wasn't allowed to use. He had a slingshot and he knew the best and most forbidden places to play. A sulk pulled down Nick's mouth. Max would be long gone by the time he got home. There would be no one his age to play with at the party and another weekend would be wasted.

His mother and father were talking in the front seat. At least they weren't yelling at each other anymore. That was a good thing. Maybe, now that his dad had come home, they would be friends. Nick looked at his mother, at her pretty, smiling face, her shiny, smooth hair and the long fingers of her tanned hands moving as she talked. He felt warm all through his middle. It was almost worth it to miss an afternoon playing with Max if it made his mother smile.

His dad looked at him in the rearview mirror. "Are you okay, sport?" he asked.

Nick nodded.

"You're awfully quiet back there."

His mother turned around and looked at him. He felt her eyes flicker across his face and chest. It worried him. She always knew what he was thinking. He didn't want that. His thoughts were private, even if she was his mother.

"Is anything wrong, sweetheart?"

"No."

Her eyes softened. "Max will be back before you know it."

"Why couldn't he come to the party?"

"He wasn't invited," his mother replied.

"I wasn't either."

Francesca sighed. "It's just one afternoon, Nick."

"I know."

He saw his father raise his eyebrows, look at his mother and shake his head slightly. His mother turned away and looked out the window.

He must have dozed off, because the next thing he remembered was his mother's voice saying, "We're here, Nick. Wake up."

He woke to the smell of barbecued meat and the sound of mariachi music. Slowly he opened his eyes. Piñatas and colored lanterns hung from the trees. Men in sombreros with sequins on their pants stood in the corner playing guitars and violins. People stood in groups laughing and talking. The tables were heavy with food. He recognized his grandmother's cakes. She had iced them earlier that day.

He climbed out of the car, saw his grandmother and waved. She waved back. He wandered through the crowd, ending up in front of a large bowl of lime-colored punch.

"Hi, Nick," said a voice behind him. "Are you lost?"

He turned. It was Sarah Gillette. "No."

"Are you hungry?"

He looked at the table groaning with food. "Not really."

"Leave the kid alone, Sarah. Can't you see he's bored to death?"

It was Sarah's brother. His hair was messed up and he wore his pants low on his hips. Nick was flattered that Drew had noticed him.

"I'm not bored," he said quickly, afraid they would think he was rude. "I'm just not hungry."

Sarah looked sympathetic. "Isn't there anyone here your age?"

He shook his head.

"Your name's Nick, isn't it?" Drew asked.

Nick nodded.

"I have some video games in my room, if you want to play," Drew said casually.

Nick was torn. He wanted to play video games, but he wasn't sure he wanted to go anywhere with Drew. He hesitated a bit too long.

Drew shrugged. "Suit yourself," he said and sauntered away.

Sarah smiled but Nick could tell it wasn't a real smile. There was a crease between her eyebrows. "I'll go find my grandma," he said.

Sarah looked relieved. "I'll see you later." She walked away.

Nick wandered toward the food table, took some chips from the bowl and headed toward the group that included Julianne. He leaned into her.

She looked down and immediately her arm circled his shoulders. "There you are." She pulled him in front of her, keeping her arm around his chest. "Say hello to everyone."

"Hello," Nick said dutifully. He knew them all.

Mrs. Monleigh, his grandmother's oldest friend, leaned down and spoke to him. "Cindy's here, Nick. Have you seen her?"

He shook his head. Cindy was Mrs. Monleigh's granddaughter. She was in Nick's class in school. She was also one of those girls the teacher always picked to erase the board and take messages to the office. She had red hair and freckles and when it was hot, her face turned red, too. Nick hated red hair, especially the frizzy, bright orange kind that Cindy had. He didn't like her very much either.

"There she is." Mrs. Monleigh pointed to the porch. "She's sitting on the porch swing reading her book. Look at her, Julianne. I don't know what Cindy would do without a book in her hand. The child is positively antisocial."

"She isn't at all antisocial," said his grandmother. "Be grateful she's interested in books. So many aren't anymore."

"You'll never stop being a teacher, Julianne." She patted Nick on the back. "Go over there, Nick, and ask my granddaughter to play with you before her eyes get so bad she'll be in glasses before she's nine."

Dismayed, Nick looked at his grandmother. Whatever hope he had for the day would be completely destroyed if he had to play with Cindy Monleigh.

Julianne saved him. "There's nothing wrong with

Cindy," she said firmly. "Nick, please ask your mother if she remembered to bring the wine I forgot."

Gratefully, Nick retreated in search of his mother.

Francesca leaned against a centuries-old olive tree. The dark wood and green leaves were a perfect complement for her pale yellow dress and the lightweight cardigan she'd flung over her shoulders. Her legs were very tanned and the combination of shapely calf and red-painted toenails peeking out of strappy sandals was both innocent and seductive at the same time. She was deep in conversation with Mitchell Gillette, but she turned to accept the drink Jake handed her.

Mitch raised his eyebrows. "A margarita instead of wine?"

Francesca shrugged. "I believe in diversifying, and your theme *is* Mexican."

"Does that carry over into areas other than your choice of beverage?"

Francesca sipped her drink. Her eyes met Jake's over the rim of her glass. He winked at her. "That depends."

"On what?"

"On what you're referring to."

"What about a variety of vintners in your valley?"

"If you're referring to small independents, I would say definitely. You're welcome here, Mitch, if you're serious about your own vineyard and winery. That doesn't extend to GGI." She looked around. "This is a lovely party, but it won't change anyone's mind about that company and it won't convince anyone to share their well water with GGI. I'm sorry if that's what you had in mind."

"You are blunt, aren't you?"

Jake hid a smile. Why had he ever thought Francesca couldn't take care of herself?

She sighed. "I suppose I am blunt, although I prefer to call it straightforward honesty. I'm not one for beating around the bush. Now, if you want that well water for yourself, that's another matter entirely."

Nick tapped her on the arm. She turned around, and when she saw who it was her face softened. "Hi, sweetheart," she said in a voice that bore no resemblance at all to the one she used with Mitch.

"Grandma wants to know if you remembered her wine."

Francesca looked bewildered. "Tell her I gave it to her when we first came."

Nick nodded. He had an idea that his grandmother was fibbing. Sometimes a fib was allowed if the reason was good enough. This time he thought it was.

He still wasn't hungry. His mother had given him a directive but he didn't think it was something that needed to be done immediately. Nick walked across the courtyard and stood at the large arched entrance where the pavers ended. He looked back at the mingling guests. Just then Cindy Monleigh looked up from her book. Across the courtyard her eyes met his. Instinctively, Nick stepped behind the stucco wall. His heart pounded in his chest. Without thinking, he began to run up the packed dirt path lined with olive trees, around the bend in the road that hid the house from his view, up the embankment and down toward the sound of water trickling over stones. Only when he'd reached the creek did he stop, his breath coming in great laboring gasps.

His side cramped. He did what his father told him to do, pressed his finger against the stitch and leaned over. After a minute the pain subsided and he sat down.

The water interested him. It was clear, the green furry stones beneath the surface completely visible beneath the tea-colored water. It was higher than usual and appeared to be flowing faster. He stuck his hand in. It was deliciously cold. Pulling off his socks and tennis shoes, he climbed on a large overhanging rock and dipped in one of his feet.

Footsteps sounded behind him. Turning, he lost his balance and plunged into the water. It was deeper than he thought. He found his footing, broke the surface and gulped in a single lungful of air before the current pulled at him again. The water was icy cold as it closed over his shoulders and head. "Help me," he managed before he went under again. His limbs were paralyzed by the cold mountain runoff. His chest hurt. He kicked his legs and forced himself to open his eyes and orient his position. Clawing his way to the surface, he fought to keep the panic from overtaking him.

Then, when he thought he couldn't hold his breath for another instant, strong arms gripped his shoulders and hauled him out of the water and halfway up the embankment.

Sputtering, Nick shook the water from his hair and opened his eyes. Drew Gillette, very pale, soaked to the bone, his chest heaving, sat beside him.

After a minute the older boy looked at him. "Next time, take me up on my offer to play video games. Okay?"

Nick nodded his head.

Fifteen

Francesca set her untouched wineglass on one of the long tables and went in search of Nick. She spotted Julianne seated at a small table with Mitch Gillette. Her mother-in-law was laughing. She looked very young.

Objectively, Francesca was pleased for her. Mitchell Gillette was intelligent, attractive, successful and single, a breed not often found in the small town of Santa Ynez, and Julianne deserved some happiness. If only he wasn't associated with the hated GGI.

Francesca hesitated. She hated to interrupt, but she hadn't seen Nick in quite some time. Maybe he'd told Julianne where he would be. She stood there, unsure of her next move, when Julianne glanced up and spotted her. She smiled and beckoned. Relieved, Francesca approached the table.

"I'm looking for Nick. Have you seen him?"

Julianne thought a minute. "Not for a while. Carol Monleigh was suggesting he play with her granddaughter, so I sent him to ask you a question."

Francesca's forehead cleared. "You asked about the wine?"

Julianne nodded.

Francesca looked at her watch. "That was an hour ago. Do you have any idea where he is?"

Mitch stood and spoke reassuringly. "He's probably somewhere in the house. I'll check for you."

Francesca wasn't listening. She was staring over his shoulder. Drew Gillette stood under the arched entrance to the courtyard with Nick on his back. Her son's head was on the older boy's shoulder and his eyes were closed. Her heart thumped. Something was very wrong.

Somehow, her brain signaled her feet to move and, instantly, she was at Drew's side. "What happened?" she asked as she extricated Nick's long arms and legs from around the teenager.

"He fell into the stream."

"What was he doing there?" Her voice was sharper than she intended.

"I don't know." Drew's voice shook. "I saw him climb on some rocks. Then he fell in."

Nick's clothes were completely soaked and he was shivering.

"What were *you* doing there?" Francesca demanded. Her arms were tight around her son.

"Saving him," the boy replied flippantly.

Nick opened his eyes. "I'm okay, Mom, just a little bit cold."

"Easy does it, Francie." Jake's voice was low and calm. "Let's get him home and into some dry clothes. We'll get the details later." He held out his arms. "Do you want me to take him?"

Fighting back tears, Francesca shook her head.

Jake gathered them both against his chest and spoke soothingly into her ear so that only she could hear. "You're upset and looking for somebody to blame. Let's go home and talk to Nick before you say something you'll regret."

His words penetrated the fear clouding her brain. She swallowed and nodded. Then she looked at Drew. "Thank you," she whispered.

He shoved his hands into his pockets and walked toward the house. Mitch followed him.

"I'll collect our things," Jake said, "while you get him into the car."

Francesca, still clutching her son in a suffocating embrace, stumbled toward the car. His skin was cold. She left him curled up on the front seat to pull a blanket from the back and wrap it around him. Soon, his tremors stopped and he slept.

Mitch caught up with his son on the stairs. "Are you all right?"

"Fine." The boy threw back his head defiantly. "Don't worry about me."

His father reached out and gripped his shoulder. "Look at me, Drew."

The boy's eyes, narrow and skeptical, focused on Mitch.

"I'm proud of you. That child might have died if you hadn't acted quickly. If you want to tell me about it, I'd sure like to hear what happened. If a condition exists on our property that's dangerous, I need to fix it. Do you understand?"

Drew stared at him for a long minute. Finally he nodded. "Can I change first? I'm kind of wet."

Mitch laughed. "Be my guest. I'll wait for you."

"You don't have to do that, Dad," the boy said quickly. "People are still here. A few hours won't make a difference."

"Are you sure? I don't mind."

"Go ahead. I'll be down later."

Mitch nodded. His guests were still downstairs, probably wondering what happened. He watched Drew shut his bedroom door behind him. Why was the boy so reticent to trust him? Had he unintentionally harmed him in some way when he was small? Still deep in thought, he walked down the stairs and out into the courtyard. It was nearly dark. The sky was a dark indigo, edging in on the deep blue typical of country nights. Julianne sat on the bottom stoop. When she looked up it was obvious she'd been waiting for him.

"Hi," he said softly, and sat down beside her. Even without sunlight her eyes were vivid.

"How is Drew?"

"He seems fine. What about Nick?"

"Francesca and Jake will take care of him. He's had a scare but I don't think he'll come to any harm. It won't be the first time a child took a dip in a stream." She tilted her head. "Did you find out what happened?"

"Not yet."

Her gaze was steady, probing.

"Do you know something I don't?" he asked.

"Not really."

"That means something. I can see it in your face."

She lifted her chin. "You don't know me that well."

"Your fault, not mine."

"What does that mean?"

He took her hand. "I've been on my best behavior. How long do you think it'll be before you agree to see me socially?"

She laughed. "That was a mouthful. Does seeing you socially mean dating?"

"If you like."

Julianne sighed. "There are complications."

"Such as?"

"My family and your employer." She smiled at him. "You're very nice and it's flattering to know you're interested. But you may not be here very long and I'm afraid to risk it."

"I like you, Julianne, and I admit I'm very attracted to you. What's wrong with enjoying each other's company for as long as it lasts?"

"In other words, no commitment?"

He stared at her. "If that's what you want."

"Is it what you want?"

"It's what I've wanted in the past," he admitted.

She looked away. "You've never cared enough to remarry?"

He took a minute before answering. "My sojourn in marriage was a disaster. I'm gun-shy. I have Drew and Sarah. The need to remarry and begin again wasn't necessary. Companionship has never been a problem."

"I can imagine," she said dryly. "But what about love and growing old with someone?"

"There are no guarantees."

She sighed and stood, pulling her hand free. "I suppose you're right."

"You never answered my question."

"Which one?"

"Will you go out with me?"

"I'm not sure."

"Why not?"

"I don't know what your motivation is."

"Conversation, good food, companionship."

"I'm not sleeping with you, Mitch."

He didn't flinch. "We're adults, Julianne."

"You're commitment phobic and I'm very much a commitment kind of woman."

"In other words, you want to get married again."

"I haven't given it much thought, but I do know that I don't want to rule it out completely. I'm not about to get emotionally involved with someone who won't consider it."

"Who said anything about emotional involvement?"

"For me, sex is emotional involvement."

He looked surprised. "I see."

"Good."

"All right. No sex."

She laughed. "You look like you're swallowing something very bitter."

"I can't believe I agreed to that."

"I'll hold you to it."

"Does that mean I can call you?"

Her smile faded. She looked pensive, almost sad. "I want you to think about this for a while. I won't be offended if you decide not to call. We can still be friends."

He picked up her hand. It was small and cool in his. "You're a very lovely lady, Julianne Harris."

She shook her head, embarrassed. "Meanwhile, I think your children need you."

"Why do you say that?"

She shrugged. "Something's bothering Sarah. She's very nervous. I don't know her very well and maybe I'm wrong, but—"

"Go on."

"She can't take her eyes off Drew. That isn't normal for siblings. I think she's worried about him."

He nodded. "I'll keep that in mind."

Jake and Francesca did not speak until they reached the house. Jake carried the boy inside and up the stairs to his room. There, he and Francesca removed his damp clothes, dressed him in pajamas and tucked him underneath his comforter. He mumbled, sighed and yawned, but did not awaken.

Francesca felt his forehead. His breathing was even and his skin felt normal. She drew a deep, shaky breath.

Jake slipped his hand under her arm and led her out of the room, leaving the door open. He settled her at the large kitchen table and turned on the flame under the teakettle.

"He's fine, Francie."

"Maybe we should take him to a hospital."

"Let's wait on that. He isn't injured and he doesn't have a temperature. More than likely, he's in shock. A good fright can do that."

"What if he hit his head and has a concussion and we don't know it?"

"We'll wake him in an hour or so and keep watch all night."

Francesca jumped up and began to pace. "I don't trust that boy."

"Drew?"

She nodded. "Isn't it odd that he just happened to be there?"

"Maybe," Jake said slowly. "What are you thinking?"

She rubbed her arms. "I don't know. It doesn't make sense, that's all. The river isn't high enough this time of year to fall in completely. It's no more than a trickle. How could he fall in and completely submerge himself?"

"I'm not sure about that. Something strange is going on with the water table. The ground is muddy and we've had no rain. Some parts of the Santa Ynez River may be higher than normal. Besides, you saw the boy. He looked as bedraggled as Nick. He even carried him all the way back to the house. Besides, he has no motive. He doesn't even know Nick."

Francesca bit her lip. "You're right. I'm not thinking clearly."

"We should be thanking him, Francie. It's possible that he saved Nick's life."

She sank into a chair and buried her head in her arms. Jake attended to the whistling kettle.

Drew never did come downstairs. Mitch checked on him later, after the last guest left, knocking softly on his bedroom door.

"What?" Drew's voice was barely audible over the sound emanating from the stereo speakers.

Mitch cracked the door. "May I come in?"

Drew sat up and threw the covers aside. "I'm kinda tired, Dad."

"You said that you would tell me what happened with Nick."

Drew sighed. "He fell in the creek."

"What was he doing there?"

"You'll have to ask him. He was probably bored. I told him he could play video games in my room, but he didn't want to. I just happened to see him climb onto a rock in the middle of the creek. The water's higher than it was a few days ago. He must have heard me because he turned around, lost his balance and fell in. I pulled him out. End of story."

"What were you doing there?"

"I went for a walk. I'm not much for adult parties."

Mitch tried to piece the scene together in his mind. "You just happened to be there?"

"That's right." His voice raised. "Are you done with the third degree? Next time I'll let the kid drown."

Mitch sighed. "I'm sorry. You're right. Nick was very lucky you were there." He stood. "Good night, son."

Drew pulled the blanket over him and turned to the wall. "Right."

Mitch found his daughter at the kitchen table, drinking a glass of milk and poring over the latest edition of *Equine* magazine.

He sat down across from her.

She looked up. "Hi, Dad."

"Hi."

"What's up?"

"I was going to ask you that."

"I'm fine."

"Are you?"

She frowned. "What's going on?"

"I'm worried about your brother. Are you?"

A red tide washed across her cheeks. She looked away. "I'm always worried about Drew."

"Why?"

"He's my little brother."

"By two minutes. That hardly qualifies as little."

"It's more than that." She shrugged a bony shoulder. "He seems younger and he has such a hard time getting anything right."

Julianne was right about Sarah. Mitch sensed that she was keeping something back. "Let me help you with this, honey. Tell me what's wrong."

Her smile was too wide, too artificial. "Nothing's wrong, Dad. You're imagining things." She pushed back her chair and stood. "It was a nice party. Mom would have liked it."

"You miss her, don't you?"

Sarah's voice choked. She turned to rinse out her glass. "I miss her more than anything. Drew does, too."

Once again Mitch was at a loss.

"Good night, Dad."

She was out the door before he could kiss her good-night.

He stared at the spot where his daughter had last stood. Something had gone amiss and he had no idea what it was.

Mitch wandered out to the courtyard. A bottle of excellent vintage sat on one of the tables, opened but not finished. He considered drinking another glass but decided against it. It would be too easy to anesthetize his problems with alcohol. A drinker did not make a good vintner and Mitch was resolved to become the latter. He looked up at the second-story windows. All were dark. Drew and Sarah were in bed. He hoped Julianne's instincts proved wrong. If something really was wrong, he had no idea how to find out.

Sixteen

The emergency meeting of the vintners' association board of directors took place at the local office on Refugio Street. Simon Reilly of Bridgewood Winery officiated. Francesca refrained from tapping her pencil. Outwardly she was the picture of serenity—cool, unruffled, objective. Even her clothing, a pink, boiled-wool suit with a white linen collar and pearl earrings, gave off an innocent touch-me-not aura that set her apart from the others.

Only one other woman had been elected to the five-person board. Jane Savage, the owner of Cedar Crest Vineyards, a family operation for more than sixty years, sat at the other end of the circle of chairs, deliberately choosing a seat as far away from Francesca as possible. She'd worked hard to acquire her seat on the board and did not want to appear part of a female voting block.

Reilly called the meeting to order. He came right to the point. "The only item on the agenda for this meeting is the request of Grape Growers Incorporated to tap local well water."

"This isn't really a board matter," said John Hume, a quiet man with the smallest vineyard in the valley. "GGI can approach any vintner who has a well for permission. We don't have the authority to speak for individuals."

"In the past when matters such as this have come to the table, we've advised the vintners of our position," said Jane. "No one has ever turned maverick."

"Only out of consideration for everyone else," countered Hume. "That doesn't mean it won't happen."

"In the best interests of the vintners, we can still advise a course of action," said Reilly. "We're all on the same side."

Peter Hartwell, Francesca's neighbor to the south, nodded. "No one in his right mind would sell water to GGI if we came out against it."

Francesca cleared her throat. She was by far the youngest member of the board, but because of her name and her family's standing in the valley, she'd been elected twice. "Two wineries in the valley are for sale," she reminded them. "The asking price for both is more than reasonable. Coincidentally, they're both backed up to land that GGI has already purchased. As you know, Soledad Vineyard has a very large well." She left the obvious unsaid.

"Has GGI made an offer on either one?" asked Reilly.

"No one is saying anything," replied Francesca.

Peter Hartwell exploded. "Let's get Gene in here and put it to him point-blank. He'll tell us if he's selling to the conglomerate."

"Maybe not," Francesca said quietly. "Gene Cappiello has tried to sell Soledad for two years. The vineyard is priced below market value. He's wanted out for a long time and he isn't going to care who buys it."

Jane Savage fixed her protuberant gaze on each of the other board members. "Does anyone know if there are other offers?"

No one answered in the affirmative.

"What about us?" she said after a minute. "Is there anyone in the valley who can afford such a purchase?"

Again there was silence.

"Well, gentlemen, and Francesca, it looks like GGI will be laying down irrigation pipes in the very near future."

"We can still make our position clear," offered Francesca.

John Hume shook his head. "I don't know if we should do that. It might not be a good idea to alienate GGI if we're going to lose anyway."

"GGI is a business, John." Francesca spoke calmly, but inside she was bristling. "No one will blame us for protecting our rights as business competitors. It makes sense for us to object to GGI establishing a foothold in our backyards. We need to do something." She looked around. "I'll talk to Gene Cappiello. The worst that can happen is what we already have, no information."

Reilly nodded. "Can we assume you'll do that and report back to us?"

"Yes."

"Can we call it a night or is there anything else?" he asked.

"We could use a strategy for staying in business if GGI buys up our local vineyards," said Jane sarcastically.

Simon Reilly smiled grimly. "First, let's find out if we have something to worry about."

"There is one more thing," said Francesca. "Has anyone noticed a rise in the water table, unusual flooding, wet ground, anything at all?"

Peter Hartwell shook his head. "Nothing like that where I am."

Hume frowned. "My grapes have been harvested for two weeks now. No one's been out on my land since then. Is there a problem?"

"I'm not sure." Francesca twisted the pencil in her fingers. "I lost some vines to mold in an area where there shouldn't be any water outside of irrigation. The Santa Ynez River near Mitchell Gillette's estate is running twice as high as it normally does this time of year. Norman Layton sent someone out to investigate, but he hasn't found anything yet."

Hume scratched his head. "We had that earthquake not too long ago."

"That was minor," said Savage. "Did anyone hear of increased water levels in the spillovers?"

Her eyes met Francesca's and widened. "Are you thinking what I am?" she asked.

Francesca nodded. "The spillovers work if the dam is functioning properly. If there's a crack somewhere, that could explain the extra water seeping up through the ground."

Reilly spoke up. "How do we get to the bottom of this?"

"I'll start by suggesting the possibility of a crack in the dam to Norman," said Francesca. "Meanwhile, everyone check your own vines. If the ground looks too wet, report it immediately or some of us might not have a season next year."

"We may all have to retire if GGI gets its way," muttered Hartwell.

"You were at the party like everyone else," Jane reminded him.

"We all were," said Hume. "Mitch is a nice enough guy on his own. I wonder if he realizes how hard it'll be to grow grapes and sell wine if GGI gets a toehold in the valley."

Francesca remembered Julianne's suggestion. "Maybe we'll have to offer something that GGI doesn't."

"Like what?"

"Other varietals, premium wines, something that can't be created from mass-production techniques. There will always be a place for specialty wines, John."

"Most people don't know good wine from bad," he returned. "Give them a bottle of six-dollar wine and they're happy."

Francesca laughed. "I refuse to let you depress me. Say no more until I can find out what Gene Cappiello intends to do."

"Do you think he'll tell you?"

"Why not? He has nothing to lose."

Hume shrugged. "Say hello to Julianne for me. Tell her I could use another batch of those chocolate-fudge brownies she sent over when Millie was in the hospital."

"I'll do that," Francesca promised.

Inside her parked car along a tree-lined side street, Francesca looked at her watch. It was only eight o'clock, still early enough to stop in on Gene for a quick visit if she called him now. She reached for her cell phone and punched in the code for Soledad Winery.

Kate Cappiello answered on the second ring. "Hi, Francie. Gene and I are both here. Come on down if you like. If you're hungry, I have some stew simmering on the Bunsen burner."

Francesca laughed. "I'll be right there."

Kate Frasier and Gene Cappiello had been Francesca's classmates all through school. They were high-school sweethearts, but a rift sent them to different colleges where they married other people. Kate came home five years later to find Gene, newly single and working at establishing his own vineyard. They had been married for nearly three years.

Francesca had been meaning to ask Gene why he was selling out ever since she'd learned Soledad was for sale.

The winery was ablaze with light when Francesca pulled up to the door. Kate motioned her inside to a table with three red-checkered place mats, three glasses of ruby-red wine and three bowls of aromatic stew. Gene was at the sink washing his hands. He looked tired. Kate pulled up her chair. "It's great to see you. I don't think we've visited for months."

Gene finished drying his hands. He approached the table with a half smile on his face. "What's going on, Francie?"

"Am I that obvious?"

"You don't show up at eight o'clock at night on the way home from a board meeting just because you've missed us."

Kate touched his arm and spoke gently. "Let her eat before you give her the third degree."

Francesca looked at her stew. "Soledad is for sale. GGI needs a well to become operational. That's a problem for every small vintner in the valley."

Gene's eyes narrowed. "That isn't my problem."

"It's our problem," replied Francesca, "Those of us who are staying need to make a living. We won't if GGI gets in."

"No one was particularly concerned when I wasn't making it," said Gene bluntly.

Francesca left her stew untouched. "What are you talking about?"

"Prices are down. I haven't been in the black for two years now. I don't have a choice. Kate and I would like kids before we're too old. This place is sucking us dry. I'll take any good offer that comes my way."

"What will you do?"

Gene Cappiello, a lean man with Mediterranean dark eyes and a sensitive mouth, lost his temper. "Why does everyone assume I'm helpless outside of a winery? I'll do what everyone else does. I'll learn computers, take up engineering, teach, sell insurance. I'll do whatever I have to do to make a living and support my family."

"You should have told someone if you were in trouble," Francesca said gently. "We all help each other."

The fire died out of his eyes. "Grow up, Francie. We're all in competition with each other. No one cares whether I go out of business. All you care about is that I don't give my water to GGI. I don't blame you. I'm no better than anyone else."

"Has GGI made you an offer?"

"Yes."

"Have you accepted it?"

"Not yet," he replied defiantly.

"Why not?"

"It's not the greatest offer. Quite frankly, I'd hoped for more money."

"Can I ask you a favor?"

"You can ask all you want."

"Will you wait on accepting their offer for another week?"

"Why?"

"I'd like to see if I can get you another one."

Gene looked at his wife. She nodded and squeezed his hand.

"All right, Francie," he said wearily. "I'll see if I can extend the deal. If so, you'll have your week. I don't care who gives me the money. All I want is the best deal for Katie and me. We can't survive another season like this. Bankruptcy isn't an attractive alternative. You'll understand if I don't feel like company tonight."

Kate walked her to the car. "I'm sorry, Francie. Gene is having a bad time right now. It isn't personal."

"Why didn't you say anything?"

Kate shrugged. "What could you have done?"

"Have you tried for a low-interest loan?"

"We're tapped out." Her voice choked. "All we have is Soledad and it's already mortgaged. The proceeds from the sale will see us through until we can find something else to do." She looked back at the brightly lit winery. "I'd better get back. Good seeing you."

Shaken and exhausted, Francesca drove home wondering what DeAngelo's fate would have been if not for Julianne's generosity.

When she arrived, her lower back ached and she was

on the edge of a headache. The kitchen was dark and uncharacteristically empty. She wanted Julianne's sage advice and comforting presence. Normally, at this time, her mother-in-law was puttering around the kitchen, glazing scones, drizzling icing on cinnamon rolls or layering a cheese strata for breakfast.

It was somewhere between the filling of the teakettle and rummaging around in the refrigerator for leftover barbecue chicken pizza that it occurred to Francesca that Julianne was all she'd ever known of a mother. Even as a child she'd taken her scraped knees and bruised elbows to Julianne's nurturing lap. Despite three children of her own, she still had enough love for Frank DeAngelo's motherless son and daughter.

Francesca hadn't always been motherless. She vaguely recalled her own mother, a black-haired, green-eyed Gypsy of a woman with long brown limbs and the graceful hands she'd passed down to her daughter. Lisa DeAngelo had smelled like an exotic flower. Her voice was meltingly seductive, and when she dressed up, with her dark hair piled on top of her head, her thin body wrapped in orange silk and the sparkling drop earrings she favored lighting up her face, she was like something come alive from a fairy tale.

But she wasn't Julianne. She didn't smell like mint and vanilla. She didn't whip up cookies for after-school treats and she didn't drive sleepy-eyed children to school on cold winter mornings when they missed the bus. Lisa DeAngelo had no patience for sticky fingers or runny noses and more often than not she forgot she had given birth to two children who waited in vain for her to walk up the stairs and blow them a kiss from their bedroom doors.

There was something transitory about her. Her children had grown accustomed to her absences and her husband rarely mentioned her, so somewhere around Francesca's sixth birthday, when she left for a weekend in San Francisco and never returned, no one really noticed. It was only occasionally that Francesca wondered about her mother. Where had she gone? Was she still alive? How could someone with two children simply disappear without caring? The pain of abandonment had worn itself out long ago, leaving only a mild curiosity behind. The marriage hadn't survived, but what had caused it to go sour, and was it worth it for a mother to lose her children?

Francesca had eaten most of the pizza and was pouring her second cup of tea in the cozy darkness of the breakfast nook when the kitchen suddenly flooded with light.

She blinked and shaded her eyes. "Please turn that off," she said.

Jake turned off the light. "I thought I heard you down here. How did the meeting go?"

"We adjourned early," she said briefly. "There was no consensus."

"Did you tell them GGI made an offer for Soledad?"

"No. That's not public information yet. Mitch told Julianne and she mentioned it to me. I didn't think it was right to say anything at the meeting."

"Do you think it's wise to protect Gillette at the expense of the small vintners in the valley?"

She could hear the edge in his voice. "I'm not protecting Gillette. I'm honoring your mother's confidence. There's a difference. Besides, it doesn't matter now."

He sat down beside her. "Why not?"

"I stopped to see Gene Cappiello. He told me about the GGI offer. I asked him to give us a week before he accepted it."

"What difference will a week make?"

"I don't know," she confessed. "I wanted time to breathe."

"Did he tell you why he's selling?"

She looked at him. "Why does anybody sell? They're not making it. Kate told me they've considered bankruptcy."

Jake whistled. "Why didn't they tell anyone?"

"Pride, I guess."

"I can understand that. If we're not careful, it might come to that for all of us."

"Why would you say that?"

"Prices are the lowest they've been in twenty years. Orders aren't coming in like they were. This is the third year in a row that you'll be in the red."

Francesca's eyes flashed. "How do you know that? You haven't been here for the last two years. Have you been snooping around in my books?"

She knew she'd overstepped her boundaries the instant the words left her mouth. Before she could take them back, Jake was already on his feet, his hands balled into fists.

"You aren't an island, Francie. All of us are in the same boat. What happens here happens in Napa, too. I was generalizing. I wouldn't look at your precious books even if you asked me to. I guess I've worn out my welcome." He walked away.

"Jake?"

He didn't turn around. "Good night, Francesca."

She buried her head in her arms. Her mind was too full and she was tired. He didn't mean that he was leaving. She couldn't bear it if he left now. Not on top of everything else. Tomorrow she would apologize. Tomorrow she would do whatever it took to convince him to stay.

Seventeen

At first break, Jason Saunders positioned himself on one side of his locker, opened the door, threw in two of his textbooks and pulled out another. Drew walked past him, stopping to talk. The two boys' hands met in what look liked a casual greeting and then Drew walked on. Their entire exchange lasted no more than five seconds.

At lunch the same day Saunders cut into line beside Drew, ignoring the taunts of his classmates behind him. "You're short by a twenty," he said without preamble.

"That's all I have. My dad keeps a pretty tight hand on the money."

"I don't run a charity club, Gillette. Get the twenty or give the stuff back."

Drew gritted his teeth. "I'll get it."

Jason laughed and slapped him on the back. "You need a job."

"I'm fifteen. What kind of job would give me enough money?"

Saunders considered the question. "I could use some help."

"What kind of help?"

"Deliveries. I can't be everywhere at once."

Drew felt the familiar burning in his stomach that inevitably came with indecision. He didn't want any part of Jason Saunders's job, but he did want the weed and it wasn't exactly an expense his dad would spring for. It was easy money as long as he didn't get caught. The penalty for marijuana possession was a citation and the loss of a driver's license. Drug dealing meant jail time. Drew definitely did not want to go to jail.

"I'll think about it," he said.

"Think fast," the boy warned, "or your supply will disappear. Meanwhile, I'll hold what I gave you until I get the cash."

"I don't have it on me. It's in my locker," said Drew.

"You asshole," the boy hissed. "Where do you come from anyway? Haven't you heard of locker searches?"

"You're paranoid. My locker won't be searched."

"You've been here a month and you know everything, is that it?"

"Hi, Drew." His sister's voice interrupted them. "I forgot my lunch money. Can you buy me an ice-cream sandwich?" She glanced at Jason. "Who's your friend?"

"Jason Saunders," Drew muttered.

Jason nodded.

"I'm Sarah Gillette, Drew's sister. I think you're in my biology class."

"Maybe so. I don't remember." He looked at Drew. "Don't do anything I wouldn't do. Okay, buddy?"

Drew lifted his shoulder in a sullen shrug.

Saunders walked off without saying goodbye.

Sarah stared after him. "He's odd."

Drew's nerves, already on edge, cracked. "How do you know that? You've seen him for all of ten seconds and suddenly you're a character expert?"

Sarah frowned. "Relax, Drew. What's the matter?"

He swallowed and shook his head. "Here." He dug two dollars out of his pocket. Get your own ice-cream sandwich."

She watched him walk away. "Where are you going?" she called after him.

He didn't answer.

"He's a druggie," said a voice behind her.

Furious, she whirled around. A tall boy with problem skin and a letterman's jacket stood behind her. "He is not!"

"He's got the look and he hangs with Saunders."

Sarah sputtered. "Lots of people have that look."

"You don't want to get involved with Jason Saunders's crowd. Labels stick around here."

"I'm not involved," Sarah whispered. "He's my brother."

"Oh." The boy blushed an impossible red. "Sorry. I'm probably all wrong."

Sarah nodded miserably. She didn't feel like ice cream anymore, but she didn't want the jock to think he'd driven her away. "Save my place," she said. "I have to use the bathroom."

"Sure. If the bell rings, do you want me to buy something for you?"

"That's okay," she said, relieved at her easy escape. "I'm not that hungry anyway. If I don't make it back in time, don't worry."

Drew sat on a bench in the quad and considered his options. He could walk back to his locker, risk taking out the bag with everyone around and carry it with him all day or he could leave it where it was and take a chance that his locker wouldn't be searched. Who searched lockers anyway? These people were like the Gestapo. High schools in San Francisco weren't searched. It was probably against the Bill of Rights anyway. But maybe kids didn't have rights until they weren't kids anymore, which made absolutely no sense because if anyone needed them it was kids. He leaned his head back against the wall and closed his eyes, his mind blocking out the sounds around him.

The next thing he knew, someone was shaking his arm. "Are you all right, son?"

Drew rubbed his eyes, opened them and met the tennis coach's amused gaze. "What time is it?" he asked.

"Somewhere in the middle of sixth period. You must have dozed off. Is anything wrong? Are you sick?"

Was he sick? For a minute Drew considered the possibility of faking illness. Then he thought of his father coming to get him and decided against it. "No," he said, looking away. "I guess I'm just tired."

"You look hungover," the man said bluntly.

"I haven't had anything to drink."

"I believe you. If I didn't, you'd already be in the dean's office. As it stands right now, I'll send you back to class. You'll have to come with me to the office for a pass."

Drew followed the coach back to the front office, waiting while the man filled out the generic yellow pass used to excuse students from myriad obligations in every high school in every city of the country. "Thanks," he said, pocketing the pass.

"Keep your chin up. You only have one more period to go."

It wasn't until he was inside the back seat of his father's car and halfway home before he remembered the contents of his locker. "Dad, we have to go back to school."

Mitch looked into the rearview mirror. "Why?"

Why? What reason would his father accept? "I forgot one of the books I need for homework."

"Which one?"

Quickly his mind raced through his classes, discarding the ones he shared with Sarah. "Math," he said quickly. "I forgot my math book."

"Sarah," their father asked. "Did you bring your math book home?"

"Yes, but it isn't the same as Drew's. I'm in geometry and he's taking math analysis. I thought I already told you that," she said reproachfully.

"Sorry, honey. I guess we'll have to go back."

Relieved, Drew leaned back against the seat. Then he heard Sarah's next words. "You can't go back now. There's no point. The main buildings close at four. It's a security measure." She looked at her brother. "Isn't there anyone you can call?"

He stared out the window and didn't answer.

"It's only one missed assignment, Drew," his father said. "If you normally turn your homework in on time, your teacher will understand."

Drew nodded, barely hearing the words. He was conscious of Sarah's gaze, troubled, anxious. He closed his eyes, blotting out the image of her face, a feminine version of his own. He heard his father's voice. Was it a question? Was he supposed to answer? Exhaustion claimed him again. Let Sarah answer. She had all the answers anyway. Let them think he was asleep. Let them think whatever they wanted. It just didn't matter anymore.

Norman Layton looked at the geologist's report and stroked his grizzled chin. The dam was fifty years old, built long before the valley's fault lines had become active enough for anyone to pay attention. There was a crack somewhere, a crack large enough to divert thousands of tons of river water into its original tributaries, raise the water table and ruin more than one vintner's next harvest. More than likely the crack was below the dam, near the east end of the valley. He'd stake his professional reputation on it. Not that it mattered anymore. He was well past retirement age and his pension was secure. Still, he'd like to go out with something more than a kick in the pants. Better haul out the big guns and find the leak. Meanwhile, he'd let those who mattered know.

Jake Harris answered the DeAngelo phone line. "I thought so," he said grimly after Norman had explained the situation. "Who else knows?"

"You're the first."

"Who else is involved?"

"Every vintner within twenty miles of Santa Ynez."

Jake spoke calmly. "Start a fire under those civil engineers. I'll tell Gene Cappiello and you call Mitchell Gillette. It's a bad break for Gene, but no one's going to sell any land until we know more."

There was silence on the other end of the phone. Then he heard Norman's voice. "What's going on here, Jake?"

"Gene Cappiello is selling Soledad to GGI," Jake said tersely. "Or, at least he was, until this happened."

"GGI hasn't planted any vines yet. They don't even have water rights."

"Gene's grapes will be affected," Jake cut in. "No one can afford to take on a winery that isn't producing wine."

"That's not for you to say."

"Full disclosure is the law, Norman. I won't complain when it happens to suit my purpose. If Soledad goes, it'll be the first cog in the wheel. I don't want Francesca to be in Gene's position next year."

"Gene and Kate are having a rough time. This sale might pull them out of it."

"No one's stopping the sale if it comes to that," argued Jake. "It can still go through as long as everyone is aware of the facts. You aren't thinking of keeping those from Gillette, are you, Norm? There could be some serious liability in that."

"You know better."

Jake was silent.

"There's one more thing, son."

"What's that, Norm?"

"DeAngelo acreage is right in the middle of the wettest area. You're lucky to have harvested your grapes when you did."

"They're Francesca's grapes," Jake reminded him. "She's been granted a reprieve for this season's harvest, but she's going to lose a lot of vines for the next one unless we find this right away."

"I hear you. I'll have the engineers out here first thing in the morning."

Jake hung up the phone. He didn't really think subterranean flooding would alter GGI's plans to open up a winery in Santa Ynez. They were a long way from planting vines or even constructing an irrigation system. Still, any delay was good news. Maybe it would last long enough for Gene to reconsider the sale of his vineyard. Gene Cappiello didn't need any more bad luck and he deserved more than a phone call. Jake decided to pay him a visit.

Sarah stood in the doorway of her brother's room, an artificial smile on her face. "Mrs. Harris called about the job. She wants us to start on Saturday. I have a dressage lesson. Can you help her?"

Drew lay on the bed, his face turned toward the wall.

"Drew? Did you hear me?"

"Go away, Sarah. Stop bugging me."

Her eyes widened. Why did he always do this to her? All they had of the old days, the time with Mom, was each other. By now she should be used to him and how he went out of his way to hurt her feelings. But each new jab brought a fresh wave of pain. Suddenly she was angry. Crossing the room, she plopped down on the bed and, gripping his arm, pulled him over onto his back. "I bug you because you scare me. Do you think I don't know what you're doing?"

He sighed and sat up. "What am I doing?"

"You're stoned."

"Actually, I'm not. Not at the moment anyway."

"Why can't you just be normal?"

Drew laughed. "Normal? You want me to be *normal?* What's your definition of the word?"

"Normal means someone who doesn't need drugs to go to school, to get up in the morning or to occasionally have a conversation." Sarah was crying now. She knew he thought she was stupid and dramatic, but she couldn't help it. She no longer cared what he thought. She wanted her brother back. "Everything happened to me, too, Drew. I lost my mother and I had to move away from my friends. Do you see me drugging myself?"

"Congratulations," Drew said sarcastically. "Good girl, Sarah."

She threw up her hands. "All right. Have it your way. I have no choice. I'm telling Dad."

"What good do you think that'll do?"

"Anything's better than this."

"You don't know the half of it, Sarah. If you did, you'd think I was a fucking hero."

"I doubt it. You've been at school for a month and you already have a reputation, you and your friend Jason."

"Right. No one even knows I'm there."

"You'd be surprised what people know. You're so out of it you can't see what's around you."

Drew lay back on his pillow and threw his arm across his face. "Go away, Sarah."

"Gladly." She stood looking down at him. "I wonder

if you'd be like this anyway," she said slowly. "Maybe it has nothing to do with Mom or the move. Maybe you're just a loser."

"Fuck you."

Filled with resolve, Sarah slammed the door behind her and walked to the landing. Drew wouldn't listen to her. She needed help, but she wasn't sure her father was the one to ask. He expected perfection. Sometimes she wondered if he'd ever done anything wrong in his life. Secretly, she understood why her parents had divorced. Her mother had been relaxed, loose and available. Sarah couldn't remember a time when her mother hadn't started out trying to scold her only to end up in a fit of giggles. The thing was, she'd been a terrific parent, the kind a kid didn't want to disappoint. What would she think of Drew if she could see him now? "Can you see him, Mom?" Sarah whispered. "If you can, please help him. I don't think I could stand to lose anyone else right now."

Sighing, she turned into her own bedroom. She would think about what to do for a while longer. Meanwhile, Mrs. Harris needed an answer about Saturday. She was a nice lady. If only Sarah knew her better.

The following morning Mitch picked up the phone in his home office on the first ring, expecting to hear Norman Layton corroborate the detailed report he'd received hours earlier from GGI's own internal engineers. Instead, a no-nonsense voice identifying himself as Greg Rivera, dean of students at Refugio High School, asked to speak to Drew Gillette's parent or guardian.

"I'm Mitch Gillette. What can I do for you?"

"Your son is in my office, Mr. Gillette. He was caught carrying a bag of marijuana bud in his pocket. We have a zero-tolerance policy. The police have been notified. We need you to come down here right away."

Mitch's grip tightened on the phone. A thousand questions passed through his mind. Caution warned him to keep his counsel. "I'll be there in fifteen minutes" was all he said.

Eighteen

Drew wasn't scared. He wasn't defiant or emotional either. In fact, all he felt was an absence of feeling as if his nerve endings had been anesthetized and everything around him was happening to someone else. He watched his father walk into the dean's office and assessed him objectively, noting the lean height of him, the impressive shoulders, the thick head of gray-flecked dark hair, the two lines drawn into both cheeks and the firm mouth, tight now with disapproval. He was scary, but interestingly enough, this time, Drew wasn't scared. He wondered if Mr. Rivera, a small man by anyone's standards, was intimidated by the stern, businesslike demeanor of Mitchell Gillette. He noticed the two cops adjust themselves, straightening to their full height.

Just as Drew expected, his father took the offensive. "What's going on here?" he asked.

The younger police officer stepped forward. "Your son was found carrying a bag of marijuana seeds. The street name is *bud*. There's enough here for quite a profit. He's dealing drugs. That's a felony, Mr. Gillette. We have no choice but to take him in."

Mitch's eyebrows rose. "What do you mean *he was found carrying a bag of marijuana seeds?* How exactly was he found?"

"It was in his pocket."

"I see." Mitch chose the older police officer and pinned him with an intense gaze. "Is there a reason you were looking in my son's pockets?"

The man sighed. "Shouldn't you be asking other questions, Mr. Gillette? Questions like, how serious is this offense or does my son have a drug problem? None of us would be here if the kid was clean."

A tick came to life in Mitch's jaw. "I'd like to be completely sure of my facts, Officer. It's possible that this is a misunderstanding. It happens."

Mr. Rivera stood. "With all due respect, Mr. Gillette, it doesn't happen very often. To answer your question, one of our teachers saw Drew exchanging some of his contraband for money. We called your son in and found this." He lifted a plastic bag filled with brown, weedy balls. "So far, he refuses to say where he got it. If he doesn't tell us who supplied him, he may not be released on bail."

"For selling pot?" Mitch looked incredulous. "Isn't that a bit extreme? Should I contact my lawyer?"

"Personal consumption is one thing," said the mature police officer. "But your son is carrying over a thousand dollars' worth of marijuana bud." He shook his head. "We're not the ones you should be arguing with. Drew is under arrest. We won't release him into your custody tonight. He needs to tell us his partner's name and, for the record, it doesn't matter who your lawyer is. The boy will spend the night in juvenile hall. He'll have to go before the judge."

"I see." To everyone in the room, Mitchell Gillette looked to be without expression, but Drew knew his father. He knew what that remote, wintry look meant. The man was furious.

"May I speak to my son alone, please?"

"I'm afraid not," said the officer. "You can take his belongings with you. He'll probably be released sometime between 3:00 and 7:00 a.m., the day after tomorrow, if the judge sees him in the morning. That's usually how it works."

"That's a large window. Can't you do any better than that?"

The young policeman spoke again. "When it comes to the first day of an arrest, we're all equal under the law, even the relatives of law enforcement officers. No one can do any better than that."

For the first time, Mitch looked directly at Drew. "I'll be there to pick you up."

Drew nodded.

Mitch watched as his son was cuffed and taken away. "What will happen as far as school is concerned?" he asked.

Greg Rivera frowned and shook his head. "As I told you, we have a zero-tolerance policy. Possession means automatic expulsion from the district. You'll have to enroll him in a private school, if you can find one that will take him, or he can attend one of our continuation schools…" He hesitated.

"Go on."

"I wouldn't recommend it."

"Why not?"

"He'd be out of his element."

"Meaning?"

"Let's just leave it at that, Mr. Gillette. Trust me on this one. Enroll Drew in the county's independent-study program if a private school won't take him. Obviously, he'll have to give up his bad habits."

Mitch balled his hands and thrust them into his pockets. "Do you get many like Drew?"

"Sad to say, we get enough. Drew is an exception in that his grades are outstanding. There's a great deal of wasted potential in that boy. Has something happened at home to trigger this change from honor student to drug user?"

Mitch's laugh was humorless. "What hasn't happened? Their mother, my ex-wife, died recently. They've come to live with me. It's been a difficult transition for both Drew and his twin sister. Sarah is managing better. I'm not sure why."

Greg Rivera's hands formed a pyramid on his desk. "I didn't realize. Maybe, because of Drew's circumstances, an exception can be made. I'll look into it. It would help if he'd tell the authorities what they want to know. There's a drug ring here at the high school, which, so far, has been impossible to crack."

Mitch sighed. "I'll do my best to convince him. So far, I haven't had much influence on either of my children."

Rivera grinned for the first time that afternoon. "Welcome to parenting teenagers. It's a thankless job until it's over." He hesitated. "If things don't go as planned, will you be taking the children back to the Bay Area?"

"I'm not sure that I understand what you're referring to."

"This is a small town, Mr. Gillette. You can't sneeze without someone handing you a tissue. I've heard that your company doesn't have permission to build a winery."

"We will, Mr. Rivera," Mitch said coolly. "I guarantee it."

Later, in the bar at the Santa Ynez Inn, Mitch was halfway through a very stiff scotch and soda, when he felt a hand on his shoulder.

"I thought that was you," Julianne said. "What are you doing sitting here all alone?"

Mitch looked up and immediately stood, the lie ready on his lips. But he couldn't utter the words.

A worried vee appeared between Julianne's eyebrows. She sat down across from him, keeping her hand on his arm. "Something's wrong. What is it?"

He shook his head and reclaimed his seat. "Nothing at all. What brings you here?"

"I have a contract with the inn." She smiled. "One cake a day. It's quite a feat."

She was lovely, and her smile, warm and sweet and beguiling, tugged at him. "Congratulations."

"Thank you. Now that we're beyond that, tell me what's troubling you."

"You are persistent, aren't you?"

"What are friends for?"

"I don't know," he said, his voice low. "It's been a long time since I've had time for friends."

"That's a shame." She folded her hands in her lap. "Now, go on."

He laughed and something inside him broke free. "Julianne, you have no idea. If you had told me six months ago that I'd be here, confessing this to a woman I'm seriously interested in, I wouldn't have believed it."

The blood rose in her cheeks, but she didn't look away. "Tell me what's wrong, Mitch."

He rubbed his left temple. "It's Drew. He's been arrested for drug dealing."

"Oh, no." Her hand flew to her mouth. "Are you sure? Have you talked to him?"

"They found him with the evidence at school about two hours ago. He hasn't been booked yet. I've called twice. Until he's been through the process I can't speak to him."

"I'm so sorry."

He nodded.

Julianne bit her lip. "I know this isn't much help, but sometimes kids lose their way. It's not the first time something like this has happened. I'm sure he's scared to death. He'll come around."

"You're very sweet, but you've warned me about my lack of parenting skills on more than one occasion. Obviously you were right."

"That's not fair, Mitch," she protested. "Not to me or you. No one could have predicted something like this. The boy lost his mother. He had to move. He hates it here. That much is obvious, and so is your lack of experience when it comes to children. You're not the first man who doesn't relate to teenagers. It's probably more common than not. Rather than wallow in what you *should* have done, why not think about how you can improve the situation?"

He looked at her. "The truth is, I don't know what to do."

"Family counseling is a good place to start. Your children need an outlet. They need to grieve. After that, I don't know, other than be available for them. Talking helps. It may not work, but it's a start. If Drew has an addiction to bring under control, that's an additional problem. Do you think he needs a rehabilitation program?"

Mitch's voice came out sharper than he intended. "He's fifteen years old."

"I know," she said softly.

"Sarah and Drew like you."

"I like them, too."

His eyes were very bright. "Will you help me with them?"

"If I can," she said carefully. "When it's appropriate. The job is still open. I'll talk to Drew about it personally when he's home again."

"It's good of you to trust him."

"For heaven's sake, Mitch. The boy is in jail for pedaling marijuana, not armed robbery. I know a few adults who in the sixties did the very same thing Drew did, only they wouldn't admit it now. We tend to forget our own mistakes."

All at once he felt better. She always made things better. Right from the beginning he knew he liked her. There was something warm and honest and nonjudgmental about her. She looked at both sides of a problem and came up with something positive. He wanted to sink back into the cushions of the lemony couch she kept in the room off her kitchen, drink copious amounts of hot tea and eat her buttery biscuits dripping with local honey. He wanted to feel her cool fingers on his forehead and listen to her sensible advice, no matter if the topic was wine or food or children. He couldn't remember ever feeling this comfortable before in his life. He wanted to sleep with her, as in fall asleep, rest his head on the pillow beside hers, bump against her in the night and wake beside her in the morning. She was the kind of restful woman a man could talk to without the awkwardness such revelations invariably brought with them.

"I think I'm falling in love with you," he said.

Her eyes, impossibly blue, widened. "Don't be ridiculous," she said bluntly. "You're in desperate need of a friend and I'm here. Don't make the mistake of thinking you feel more than you do."

"I don't make those kinds of mistakes."

"Mitch, we aren't—we haven't— " She threw up her hands. "I don't want this."

"What don't you want?"

"We've discussed this before. Saying you're in love is easy. It's the rest that isn't."

"What if I told you I'd changed my mind?"

"Men who've been divorced for as long as you have don't just change their minds. I'm not that naive."

"Why not give it a chance?"

"No."

"Please."

"Why are you doing this? I can't imagine that you have trouble finding female companionship."

His eyes narrowed and twinkled. "Thank you."

"Well?"

"I don't have trouble finding female companionship. But it's your companionship I want. That's worth proving myself."

"Why?"

He looked puzzled.

"Why me?" she said again.

His forehead cleared. "Because you're accomplished and intelligent and lovely. Because your eyes are a blue I've never seen before. Because I love your capable hands and your generous smile. Because being around you feels like coming home."

She released her breath. "That was very nice and I admit, it makes me feel appreciated. Did you just make all that up, or have you been practicing?"

"It came over me." He held up his right hand. "Honestly."

"All right."

"What does that mean?"

"All right. We'll try."

He could feel her embarrassment. How unusual for a woman so attractive to be self-conscious. He took her hand. "Thank you."

Just then his cell phone rang. The display said *private number.* He lifted it to his ear. "Hello."

His face darkened. "All right. I'll wait. Call me no matter what time it is."

Flipping the phone shut, he looked at her. "He won't be processed until after midnight. He didn't want me to worry."

Julianne stood, pulled him to his feet and linked her arm through his. "Pay your bill. You're coming home with me. I'll make coffee and ply you with dessert."

"I can't. I have to pick Sarah up at her dressage lesson."

"Bring her along. She can stay with us when Drew calls. We have extra rooms."

"I don't want to bother you."

"You're not bothering anyone." She slipped her hand inside his. "Really."

Something compelled him. He wanted to wait until she trusted him, but the moment seemed right. Carefully, gently, he bent his head and brushed her lips with his. She did not pull away. "Thank you, Julianne. You've rescued me more than once."

"I'll remind you to make it up to me."

Back in his own car, he recalled their conversation and laughed. Julianne made him laugh. It was amazing, really. An hour ago he thought he would never laugh again.

Sarah kicked the toe of her boot against the ragweed sprouting from the concrete in front of the equestrian center. She'd been waiting for fifteen minutes and she was furious. Why couldn't he be on time for her? He was retentively punctual with everything else.

Ten minutes later she watched her father's silver-gray Infiniti pull into the parking lot. Taking her time, she made her way to the car, opened the door and, without a word, climbed into the back.

"I'm sorry I'm late, honey. Something came up."

"So, what else is new?" she muttered.

He looked at her through the rearview mirror. "Excuse me?"

Sarah exploded. "You're always late picking me up.

What's so hard about getting here on time for a change? If it was the other way around, if I wasn't there when you came, you'd be furious with me."

Mitch was very close to losing control. "Not today, Sarah. I can't take this from you now."

"You never *take* anything from me. You're so busy being polite to everyone else that you've forgotten about me altogether."

Abruptly, he pulled over to the side of the road, turned off the engine and set the brake. Then he turned around. "Your brother is in trouble, serious trouble. I've been waiting all afternoon for him to call me."

"Drew's always in trouble."

"He's in jail, Sarah, for selling drugs. They've arrested him. I'm sorry for being late, but, under the circumstances, maybe you could cut me a little slack."

She stared at him, white-lipped, her face frozen. "Oh, my God. What will happen to him?"

"I don't know. Anything you could tell me would help."

"I knew the kid he was with was trouble."

"What kid?"

"Someone named Jason Saunders. Drew's been tight with him lately."

"I'll make a note of the name. Maybe Drew will tell the police himself if he's frightened enough."

"Or maybe Jason will blame everything on Drew."

"Drew's never been in legal trouble before. According to your dean of students, there's a drug ring that's been operating for some time. Drew is a new student. They'll believe him."

"You hope," she retorted. "Don't count on it."

Mitch started the car again and pulled out on to the road. Were all kids so cynical? Had the world changed that much in thirty years?

Nineteen

Jake found Gene Cappiello squatting on the ground, inspecting the rows of dormant vines along his northern slopes. The Cappiello vineyards were by far the most beautiful in the valley, row after row of thick, woody, twisted trunks reaching toward the sky. Flecks of autumn-colored leaves still remained in the trellises.

"Can't get enough, can you?" he said, coming up behind him. "This is supposed to be the dormant period when you give those vines a rest."

Gene looked up and grinned. "Where did you come from?"

"Kate told me where to find you."

"Why?"

"I wanted to talk about your For Sale sign."

Gene's grin faded. "You, too?"

"I've known you my whole life, buddy. Why didn't you tell me you were leaving?"

"Like you told me two years ago?" Gene challenged him.

Jake reddened. "That was different. Besides, I called you."

"After the fact."

"For Christ's sake, Gene. I was leaving my family. I didn't feel like making the rounds of my neighbors' houses."

Gene stared out over his vineyard. "Then you know how it feels."

Jake frowned. "Look. There must be something we can do."

"There's nothing."

"You don't know that," Jake protested. "We could put our heads together, all of us around here, and come up with something. Anything's better than leaving this." He waved his arm to encompass the cultivated land, the golden hills, the dusty soil and the thick, twisted vines.

Gene shook his head. "What are you gonna do, Jake? You can't ordain a good harvest. This is my last year of ending up in the red. I can't pay anybody and I'm tired of not being able to sleep at night because of what I'm doing to Kate. People around here don't have money to throw away on a losing vineyard."

"It's not a losing vineyard. Your timing was bad, that's all. We've had the roughest three years in two decades."

"The end result is the same."

"What if I figure something out?"

Gene shook his head. "You're not a magician, my friend. I appreciate your enthusiasm, but give it up. It's a lost cause."

"What if someone buys in and takes over as the major partner? What if I found some investors? You would still have an interest in the business. Later, you could buy your vineyard back if it was profitable."

"Who, in their right mind, would do that?"

"Just let me work on it, okay?"

The flash of hope in his friend's eyes was almost too painful to watch. Jake turned away and pretended to scan the horizon.

"I don't know," Gene said at last.

"What would it take to convince you?"

Gene, a man slow to words, took his time finding the right ones. "It takes time to find investors, if you can get them at all. I'll lose the GGI offer."

Jake Harris was born with an innate love of the soil. The genes of his Basque ancestors had predestined him for an affinity with the sun, the seasons, an ability to withstand backbreaking labor and to revel in the giddy, light-headed magic of the harvest. But he was also a man born into the twentieth century, a college graduate with a degree in enology and a shrewd understanding of people. "Give me thirty days. GGI will want your land in a month as much as right now."

It took a full minute for Jake's words to process. Gene raised one eyebrow. "Francesca asked for a week."

Jake grinned. "Francie's a softy."

Gene sighed. "All right. You win. I'll talk to Kate. If she's okay with it, you have your month. How about staying for dinner? She's making spaghetti. It can't compare to you mother's, but it's good."

"I'd be delighted."

It was nearly eleven by the time Jake walked through his own front door. He was mentally exhausted. Drawn by the light and voices, he walked down the hall into the kitchen. Francesca and his mother were lingering over cups of coffee and Julianne's famous molten-chocolate cake.

"Did you save any for me?" he asked.

"As a matter of fact, I did," said his mother. "It's in the ramekin on the stove. Would you like coffee to go with it?"

"I'll get it," he said.

Francesca stirred her dessert absently. "Did you have any luck with Gene?" she asked

Jake sat down at the table. "Temporarily."

Francesca looked up. "What does that mean?"

"We have a month to find a new buyer for Soledad. The catch is, Gene stays on as part owner."

"That's insane. Who would want to do that? The vineyard isn't profitable."

"The wine industry has had a few bad years. I think we could make go of it."

Her eyes widened. "We?"

Jake spooned a healthy portion of chocolate into his mouth and moaned. "Heaven in a ramekin."

Julianne laughed. "Your son said the same thing before he went to bed."

"Jake." Francesca's impatience was obvious. "Who are the *we* you're talking about?"

A minute passed before he answered. "I'm not sure yet."

Her eyes widened. "You can't be serious. You persuaded Gene to hold off on the sale of his bankrupt vineyard and you don't even have an idea?"

"I have an idea, Francie, but I'm not as quick at the

draw as you are. I'm trying to think of the best way to explain what I think is a damn good idea."

"All right." She swallowed another bite of her dessert. "When do you think you'll be ready?"

"Tomorrow." His eyes twinkled wickedly.

She shrugged. "Have it your way. It's not my problem anyway."

"That isn't nice, Frances," Julianne admonished her gently. "Gene is a friend and he's in trouble. Of course it's your problem."

Francesca's cheeks burned. "I wasn't referring to Gene."

Jake looked at her, his voice low. "Francie thinks I've dug myself a grave. Actually, I appreciate the concern."

"Don't take it to the bank," she said under her breath.

Silence settled over the kitchen. Finally, Jake broke it. "So, have I missed any news? How's Nick?"

Julianne sighed. "Nick is fine, but he's only eight years old. I worry about his teenage years. Those are difficult."

"Are you generalizing, or has something specific happened?"

"Mitch and Sarah Gillette left shortly before Frances came in. They stayed for dinner. Drew has been arrested for possession of marijuana."

Francesca sniffed and blew her nose with her napkin. "Possession is a misdemeanor. He won't get more than a fine and a suspended driver's license."

"I'm afraid it's a bit more than that," Julianne said carefully. "The police claim he was selling it."

Jake whistled. "Wow! What's the matter with the

kid? He's got everything, looks, brains and a rich father."

"He doesn't have a mother," Julianne said sharply, "and his father has moved him away from everything familiar. It's no wonder he's looking for acceptance any way he can."

Francesca spoke quietly. "How are you involved in this, Julianne?"

The pink came and went across the fine bones of the older woman's cheeks. "I'm not, really."

"The fact that Mitch would confide in you says something, I think."

Julianne shrugged. "Maybe so. We've become friends. I suggested that I might have work for Drew, something small, on the weekends. It would give him spending money, maybe give him a sense of purpose. The boy is intelligent, and when I talked to him about the business, he appeared genuinely interested."

"Are you still of the same mind?"

Julianne nodded. "Yes."

"You're going to allow a kid who sells drugs around your grandson?" Jake was incredulous.

His mother looked surprised. "I didn't think about it that way."

"Maybe you should."

"Wait a minute, Jake." Francesca's dark eyes pinned him down. "Drew hardly fits the profile of a drug dealer. We all know that. He's a disenfranchised boy who made a bad mistake. Aren't you the one who told me not to jump to conclusions when Nick fell into the creek? I, for one, am grateful to Drew. Maybe we should all give him a chance."

He stared at her, unable to look away, caught by his own words and the wash of guilt he carried around for not wanting his mother to have anything to do with Mitchell Gillette.

"Thank you, Frances," her mother-in-law said softly. "I know you're fond of Sarah. This can't be easy for her. She has a special bond with Drew. I've heard it's that way with twins. I think the move has made their connection even stronger."

Francesca nodded. "I'll see if I can spend some time with her. We really haven't been in touch since she joined the equestrian center."

Jake stood abruptly, rinsed his dishes and stacked them in the dishwasher. Then he sat down again. "I have more bad news, Francie. Norman says the leak in the dam is a huge one. He's calling in a crew of engineers to find it. Until it's corrected, the soil conditions are too wet for vines. We may lose a lot more."

She sighed. "Thank goodness this season's grapes are harvested."

"That's a positive way of looking at it." He yawned. "I'm for bed. Good night."

His mother's eyes followed him until he was out of sight. "I don't know what's going on with Jake," she said thoughtfully. "It isn't like him to be so against someone."

"It's clear as a bell to me," replied Francesca. "He's afraid you and Mitch will become romantically involved."

Julianne blushed. "What's so terrible about that?"

"A number of things." Francesca ticked them off on her fingers. "Mitch works for GGI, which means he isn't here permanently. One of two things could happen. You could be hurt or, you could pack up and go with him. Then there's the obvious. Jake is your only son. In typical male fashion, he's not used to sharing the lime-light."

"He already shares it with Nick."

"Nick is Jake's child. In his mind, that's acceptable."

Julianne frowned. "How do you know all this? Has he told you or is it all speculation?"

"Jake doesn't tell me anything, but therapy does have certain advantages. I've been going long enough. I should be getting something out of it."

Julianne reached across the table and covered Francesca's hand with her own. "Why haven't you told me about this?"

Francesca blushed. "It's not something I wanted to advertise."

"Which part, Francie, the therapy or the fact that you still love Jake?"

Francesca was silent. "Both," she admitted after a minute.

"What are you going to do?"

"Keep going the way I've been going."

Julianne smiled. "I'm talking about Jake."

"I'm doing all that I can right now."

"He loves you, too. Surely you know that."

Francesca nodded. "He says he does, but—"

"What?"

The hurt in her eyes broke Julianne's heart.

"What's different?" Francesca asked. "How do I know it will work this time? I can't go through another breakup. I won't make it. I'm not an easy-come-easy-go kind of person. I can't love Jake like I did because I can't trust him."

Julianne wanted to cry. There were so many things she wanted to say. She wanted to take the girl by the shoulders and shake her into sensibility. She wanted to say, *You'll figure it out,* the way she did with her own daughters. But she was very afraid that Francesca *wouldn't* figure it out. When would she realize that sharing life with someone who cared whether or not you came home at night and whether or not your children came home at night with a similar intense passion was more important than anything else?

"Oh, Francie," she said helplessly, trying to explain. "There are no guarantees, but there won't be with anyone else, either. Are you planning to spend your life alone? Because, unless you are, why not try again with Jake? You share a history. It's always better to try and work things out with the father of your child. Have you thought of the whole new set of problems you'll face with someone new? Even if you meet a man who doesn't have an ex-wife and children, think of how it will be sending Nick away to wherever Jake is. You can't possibly think he'll be able to come and go the way he does now?"

"You've married me off already. I haven't even met anyone."

"I'm trying to open your eyes, my love. I wouldn't have said anything if you'd told me you had no feelings for Jake, or if he had none for you." She kissed Francesca's cheek, gathered the dishes and set them in the sink. "I'm completely drained. It's been quite a day."

Francesca nodded. "Good night."

"Will you think about what I said, Frances?"

"I always do."

Jake knew he was dreaming. It was the same dream he always had: he would be sleeping and she would come to him, a tall, slender woman with hair the color of ripe honey, dark in the shadows, roan-brown and shiny in the sunlight. Her shoulders were slender and summer-tanned, her hands long and brown and callused. She wore something white that floated when she moved. Her eyes were dark with flecks of gold and her bones were strong and defined under her smooth olive skin.

He was unable to move, his will suspended under the massage of her hands, the lave of her tongue, the wet heat of her mouth. He lay still, absorbing the richness of her skin, the pulsing in her throat, the strands of her hair swimming into his mouth, tickling the back of his throat. She moved against him and over him, the gauzy floating material no longer between them. He felt the throb of his blood, the call of her rhythms. His body rose to meet her, and then, she would leave.

He would wake instantly, his body wet and heaving, a mess on the sheets, an ache in his chest. If only he could keep her there, long enough to tell her he wanted it all, much more than this. If she would stay, he would make her understand the wanting. If only he could move and speak in her presence.

He heard the click of the door. He stared at the ceiling. Soon, in less than a minute, she would be with him. Inside him the wanting roared. It was too much to hide, or pretend otherwise. He turned and watched her walk toward him with an extra–slow moving grace. Their eyes met.

She stood by the bed looking down at him. Her long fall of hair hung over her bare shoulder. She wore something shimmery and short, not white at all. Her legs were shapely and brown all the way up.

This time he found his voice. "You came."

She nodded, and when she spoke he realized this was no dream. She was real and she was here.

She nodded. "Your mother said I should."

Perhaps he would live after all. "I didn't think you would."

"I know."

He picked up her hand and pressed his mouth to her palm. He felt her tremble, saw her close her eyes, lean her head back, exposing the long, lovely line of her throat. He filled his hands with her hair and pulled her down beside him. Then he looked at her, at the bones at the base of her neck, the scoop of her nose, the blades of her cheeks, the smooth line of her forehead, the small, perfect breasts, all the parts of her that had the power to send him over the edge.

Incredibly, she spoke. "I want you to kiss me. That's what I missed the most, the way you kiss. The way your lips fit my mouth."

He laughed exultantly and then he began, softly at first, gently, until his control broke and the part of him that didn't think beyond the now reared up, hard and dangerous and desperate. He hadn't had a woman in a long time and the only one he wanted, Francie, his friend, his love, his wife, was here and willing, wanting him.

He murmured against her throat. "Ride with me."

She said something, but Jake was beyond hearing. For the first time in two years, he felt a woman's flesh close around him and he came inside her, explosively.

Minutes passed. Maybe he dozed. He opened his eyes. She leaned on one elbow, her eyes dark on his face. "Do it again," she whispered.

And he did, and then once again.

When he woke it was still night, but she'd gone. The only evidence she left was the soreness between his legs and the sheets, stained from what they'd done together.

The smile started somewhere in his middle and made its way to his mouth. It wasn't a done deal, but it was a start, a very good start.

Twenty

Francesca tied the laces of her shoes, tucked her blouse into her jeans, grabbed her hat and sunglasses and ran down the stairs. She heard Julianne in the kitchen with Nick, smelled the sweet, cinnamon smell of her apple pancakes, heard the soothing tones of her voice in conversation with her grandson, but decided against stopping. She couldn't face Julianne just now. She couldn't face anyone. Time was what she needed. Time and peace and a place to think.

The vines in their dormant stage called to her. She stopped at the shed to pick up her pruning shears, threw everything into the Jeep and set off over the hills toward the Chardonnay acres at the southern end of the vineyard. The dirt road narrowed near her destination. Parking the Jeep, she grabbed the shears, climbed out, tied the wide-brimmed hat under her chin, pulled on her gloves, hiked into the rows and bent over the woody canes.

The buds, sensors of light, temperature and humidity were fleshy, red-colored, thorny. She attacked them with a vengeance, working carefully, cutting away all but two twenty-four-inch canes per vine, using year-old wood the way her father had taught her. Then she tied them down with wire and paper twists. In spring, the buds would break, producing a shoot tip that wrapped a tendril around the upper wires before shooting up in a vertical direction, seeking the sun. These two tendrils would fill out to a veritable wall of foliage with pounds of fruit hanging from the bottom sections.

In order to produce superior grapes with intense varietal characteristics, sixty to ninety percent of DeAngelo's dormant canes would be pruned, reducing the yield by over half and allowing the clusters to hang long enough to develop complex flavors. It was a back-breaking job requiring the hiring of outside labor for two weeks in late fall.

Several hours later, despite the chilly air, she was soaked with perspiration. Her shoulders ached, she was thirsty and she still hadn't resolved Jake's place in her life. The bottom line was, Francesca wasn't a risk taker. She wanted guarantees, and even if Jake gave her his solemn word, she knew it meant nothing if at some point in the future they weren't right together. Not that she wanted someone to stay with her because of a promise. But she wanted him to *say* he would anyway. She wanted him to think, here and now, he would never leave again. They didn't speak of the two years he'd lived in Napa. She didn't know if there had been anyone else. All at once it became very important that she know.

Her water bottle was in the car. Removing her gloves, Francesca wiped her forehead with the back of her hand and started walking through the even rows toward the Jeep.

A late-model SUV was parked behind it and a man stepped out. At first she didn't recognize Mitch Gillette behind the dark glasses and baseball cap. "Hello," she said surprised.

He walked toward her. "Julianne thought you might be here. I took a chance."

She reached into the Jeep for water, unscrewed the cap and drank deeply. "What can I do for you?"

"I have a grape question."

She kept her eyes on his face. "Are you asking as a local vintner or as the vice president of GGI?"

"Local vintner," he said immediately.

She smiled. "It must be an important question."

"I didn't want to wait."

"Fire away."

"I'm interested in planting dormant vines."

She nodded.

"How do I do it?"

Her eyebrows rose. "You're kidding, Mitch. Tell me where to start."

"From the beginning."

"You can't possibly expect me to go over the entire process of planting dormant vines while we stand here on the hillside. There's more to it than can be explained in a single afternoon. Besides, you can hire people to plant them for you."

"They're already planted, but they're not taking root," he said grimly. "I want to know why."

She folded her arms against her chest and leaned back against the Jeep. "First I need to ask you a question."

"Go ahead."

"Why are you asking *me?* We're not exactly the best of friends."

"Because your family has been good to mine. Because I don't think it's me you object to, not personally. No matter what our differences are, I believe you'll give me an honest answer."

Francesca chewed her lip. "All right. Fair enough, but only because I'm flattered. Let's start at the beginning. What kind of rootstock are you using?"

"American 5C."

"That's good," she said approvingly. "What about scion wood?"

"Dijon 76."

"Still good. Your soil should be loose at the bottom with no compaction on the sides."

He nodded, listening intently.

"Snipping the root ends guarantees vigorous root tissue at the top. When you drop the vine into the hole, the roots should be spread out, then covered with loose soil and tapped down."

"I've done all that."

"Are your vines close to the stake and your graft union a few inches from the ground?"

"Yes, to both of those."

"What's the soil like?"

"What do you mean?"

"That could be the problem. I'll show you." She gestured toward the Jeep. "You can ride with me."

Francesca climbed into the vehicle and waited for Mitch to settle himself beside her.

"Where are we going?" he asked.

"I've lost vines, too. I want to show you the ones still in the ground and see if we're talking about the same problem."

"If you're referring to the crack in the dam and an excess of water, it isn't that. My soil isn't wet."

"It doesn't have to be. The water may have already receded. New vines need optimal conditions. If chemicals or an excess of minerals have leached into the fields, the balance might be off."

The Syrah vines were located along the eastern border of the vineyard, in the bosom of two hills. Francesca killed the engine and pointed to the valley. "That's where the damage is. Come and look."

Mitch followed her. She dropped to her knees beside a row of gray, wilted vines and pulled lightly on the trunk. It came out easily. "Normally, when vines come out this way, I'd say it's due to rodents, phylloxera or nematodes. But not this time." She held the root close to his face. "These haven't been nibbled. This is root failure due to chemical damage." She dropped the root and dusted her hands on her pants. "What do you think? Does any of this look familiar to you?"

"I think you're damn smart, Francesca DeAngelo," he said slowly. "And, yes, these roots look like mine."

"We're in good company. Every vineyard in the valley has it, too, some more than others." She looked around. "Thank goodness we can stand the loss. Syrah doesn't account for a large portion of our harvest."

His mouth went tight. "I can't say the same for me. I'm only interested in Pinot Noir. I was counting on the new vines. It sets me back a year, at least."

Francesca stood. She was tall enough that their eyes

were nearly on a level. "The winery isn't your liveli-hood, Mitch," she reminded him gently. "You have an-other job. Others are in a much more difficult position. I'd say you have bigger fish to fry."

"I assume you're referring to Drew."

She nodded. "Julianne told me. Is there anything I can do?"

"Thank you, no," he said briefly.

"Is he home?"

Mitch nodded. "He'll appear before a judge in three weeks."

She changed the subject. "How is Sarah holding up?"

He looked surprised. "She's fine. Nothing's wrong with Sarah."

"You aren't finding her more irritable, sensitive, more emotional?" Francesca probed.

"No."

"Good." She was surprised that he hadn't told her to mind her own business. "Shall I drive you back to your car?"

"Thanks."

The ride back was silent. Behind the dark glasses, Mitch's eyes were focused on something outside the windshield. Francesca left him alone.

"I hope I helped," she said before dropping him off.

"Yes, thank you." Mitch hesitated. "Sarah likes you."

"I like her, too," Francesca said warmly. "Very much."

"She hasn't made many friends."

"Give her time. She's personable."

"She's also very busy."

Francesca smiled. "It's a very good thing for a teenager to be busy."

He opened the door and climbed out of the car. Keeping his arms on the edge of the window, he leaned in. "I know this is an imposition, Francesca, but maybe you could spend some time with her."

"I'd love to."

"I'm not doing a very good job in the raising-my-children department."

All at once she realized that Mitchell Gillette was quite likable. Despite his arrogance and his GGI affiliation, he was a good man, not afraid to ask questions or to admit when he was wrong. "Sometimes even the best of intentions go wrong. Ask Julianne about her daughter Kinley Rose. She was a wild child. I don't think drugs were a problem, but she certainly was defiant. Julianne managed her all alone, too. Carl was gone by then."

"She never mentioned anything to me."

Francesca nodded. "Julianne is a private person. Don't give up."

Mitch grinned. "I don't intend to. Thanks for the vote of confidence."

Jake drove into the courtyard at the same time she did. Anticipating their first meeting after the night before, Francesca had prepared for it, talking to herself on the way home, perfecting just the right air-light tone, the pleasant, neutral smile, commanding by sheer will the telltale color to disappear from her neck and cheeks.

They met at the porch stairs. Playfully, he tugged her braid. "How are you?" he asked softly.

Calling up what she hoped was a convincing smile, she answered him. "Fine, thanks. I've been pruning Syrah vines."

His eyes moved over her face, lingering on her mouth. Despite her intentions, Francesca blushed.

He looked away. "I have a business proposition for you."

"Can we talk about it over lunch?"

"Sounds good. I'm hoping to interest my mother as well."

She followed him into the kitchen. Julianne had already set their places and was dishing out healthy portions of ginger-carrot soup. Fat Reuben sandwiches, stuffed with corned beef, sauerkraut and Swiss cheese, dripping with her secret sauce, sat on a serving plate in the middle of the table. There was milk for Francesca and lemonade for Jake.

Julianne needed no reminders of who preferred what when it came to food. She never failed to remember that Jake drank his coffee black and unflavored, while Francesca liked whole milk, not cream, and coffee that was flavored with cinnamon, pecan or hazelnut. Both loved mushrooms, but Jake preferred his raw while Francesca wouldn't eat them unless they were sautéed in butter and garlic. Francesca drank milk with her meals. Jake hadn't touched a glass of milk since he was fifteen years old.

Jake rubbed his hands together. "The food looks great, Mom."

She smiled at him. "Thanks. Wash your hands and sit down. I don't want the soup to get cold."

They sat together at the end of the long wooden table

that fed a dozen or more men around pruning and harvest seasons. No one spoke for several minutes, savoring the meal, the warmth and the combination of unusual spices.

"I don't know if I ever appreciated this growing up," Jake said.

"You didn't." His mother sent him a fond glance.

"I didn't either," admitted Francesca, "until I went to someone else's house for dinner. The food was never as good."

"Amen," Jake said reverently.

Francesca swallowed the last of her sandwich. "Are you going to tell us about this business proposition?"

"I want to buy Soledad Vineyard."

Both pairs of eyes, brown and blue, stared at him.

"Can you afford it?" Francesca asked.

"Not without help. That's where you and Mom come in."

"Jake, Soledad is worth millions," his mother protested. "We don't have that kind of money."

"You have collateral."

Francesca's heart was in her throat. "You want me to put up the winery."

He nodded.

"The answer is no," she said shortly. "I won't risk Nick's inheritance."

"Hear me out, Francie."

"I don't need to. I'm not changing my mind."

Julianne's cool blue eyes darkened. "I'm not saying it's a good idea, Frances, but it doesn't hurt to listen. I helped you when you needed it."

Francesca bit her lip. Julianne had a point.

"I've looked at the books and the numbers," Jake went on. "With the three of us going in together, we can swing it."

"Would we be equal partners?" Julianne asked.

"Yes."

Francesca frowned. "Where's your share coming from?"

"I have stock options I can cash in from Napa as well as some real estate that's appreciated. My dad left money that I invested and I've saved every penny for the last two years. I don't need much capital from either of you for a down payment. All I need is DeAngelo Winery on paper. I've already talked to Marvin Roach at the bank. We can do it without the vineyard or the house."

"I have money, Jake," his mother said slowly. "You don't have to tap yourself completely."

"Who will work the vineyard?" asked Francesca.

"Gene and Kate, with my help."

"They aren't doing a very good job right now," she reminded him.

"They bought at a bad time and expanded too soon. We can remedy that." He looked at Francesca. "What do you say, Francie?"

She felt herself wavering. It sounded as if Jake had done his homework. "I want to see the books before I decide anything."

"That isn't a problem." He turned to Julianne, his excitement barely contained. "What about you, Mom?"

"I'd like you to have something that's yours." She avoided Francesca's eyes. "Your father never did. I think he would approve. But, first, I agree with Frances.

I'd like to have a professional check the books and figure out where the Cappiellos made their mistakes."

Jake appeared lit from within. He pushed himself
away from the table. "I'll get on it right away."

Francesca exhaled. She'd been temporarily re-
prieved, but not for long. She knew Jake. He wouldn't
allow them to pretend last night never happened.

Twenty-One

Francesca parked near the elementary-school flagpole, checked her watch and decided to leave the car in idle. The bell would ring in another minute and Nick would be out for the weekend.

She spotted him immediately, her gangly, towheaded son, his legs so long and deer-thin and awkward it looked as if he would never grow into them. Her heart swelled with love. He waved and ran toward the car. She waved back and reached across the seat to open the door for him.

"Hi, Mom."

"Hello, love." She stopped herself from asking how he'd done on his spelling test. The moment was too sweet. "Are you hungry?"

"Not yet."

Nick was never hungry. Food was nothing more than fuel to him. If he never had to eat again he would be delighted.

She checked to make sure his seat belt was clasped.

"How about if we stop in at the bakery for hot chocolate and a brownie?"

"Is Max at home?"

"I think so."

"Can we just go straight there?"

Francesca was disappointed. "I thought we'd spend a little time together. I've been pretty busy lately."

"Max doesn't come very often and besides, Gran's brownies are better."

Francesca relented. "All right. We'll go straight home to Max, but don't blame me if Grandma hasn't made brownies today."

"She has," Nick said confidently. "It's Friday."

Not only had Julianne whipped up a batch of brownies, she'd also wrapped one for Max. "Sit down and drink a glass of milk first," she said, setting a tall glass in front of Nick. "Max isn't going anywhere."

Nick sat. "I got a hundred on my spelling test," he announced.

Julianne's eyes widened and Francesca clapped. "I knew you could do it."

"The words were hard, too. We had to hear them in sentences or we wouldn't know which way to spell them."

Francesca nodded her head and leaned one hip against the counter. "Homophones. I'm so proud of you, Nick."

"Can I have another brownie?"

"No," the two women said in unison.

Nick grinned. Chocolate covered his front teeth. "Just checking."

Francesca laughed. "Brush your teeth and then you can go. Say hi to Max for us."

They watched him race out of the room and up the stairs.

"My goodness." Julianne yawned. "All that energy makes me tired."

"He's growing up," observed Francesca. "I remember when I was his whole world. Now I have to make an appointment."

"I know. I remember. But, in the long run, independence is a good thing. It's what we all want for our children."

Francesca opened the refrigerator and poured herself a glass of milk. She sipped it standing up. "I'm at loose ends. I think I'll have one of those brownies, too."

Julianne set a brownie on a plate and handed it to Francesca. "I have a suggestion for you, but first sit down and eat."

Francesca sat. "What is it?"

Julianne pulled up a chair and sat across from her. "Sarah Gillette has her dressage lesson this afternoon. Why don't you go and watch?"

"You have Sarah's schedule *memorized?*"

"Not exactly."

"What does that mean?"

"Mitch mentioned to me that his daughter could use a mentor and you said you would help."

Francesca looked at her mother-in-law. She didn't look thirty but she definitely didn't look fifty. "Why aren't *you* volunteering?"

"She likes you and you have the horses in common. I'll tackle Drew."

"Is this getting personal for you?" Francesca asked casually.

Her forehead wrinkled. "I'm not sure," she said after a minute. "I know the children need help and it takes so little effort on our part."

"All right." Francesca reached for another brownie. "I'll wrap this up for her. No one can resist your brownies."

Julianne smiled. "I know she's not Nick, but she's still not much more than a little girl. I think you could help her."

"I'll give it my best." She didn't get up.

A minute passed. Francesca turned her empty glass around on the tabletop.

"Is something on your mind, Frances?"

Her voice was warm and low, inviting confidences. Francesca swallowed. "You want Jake to have Soledad, don't you?"

Julianne sighed. "Yes, I do. And I want Gene and Kate to have a reason to stay. They're good people, but most of all, I want Jake to have something of his own." She looked down at her hands, and when she spoke again, her voice was full of emotion. "You don't really understand that, Francie, because you've always had it all. Your legacy was right here in the land from the day you were born. Jake gave that up when he married you. He put all his energy into this vineyard, but it was still all yours."

"I shared everything with him," Francesa said, stung by her mother-in-law's words.

"As long as he stayed with you. But he left and nothing was his. Soledad will be his."

Francesca's eyes were very bright. "Do you blame me for not giving him anything?"

"Oh, Francie, of course not. DeAngelo Vineyards is yours. It came to you intact from your father and his before him. It'll be Nick's after you. That's the whole point. Jake needs something of his own, something apart from what you can give him. I've always felt that was a huge part of the problem between you. You're a strong woman and you bring a great deal to the table, not the least of which is a profitable vineyard and winery. Jake's ego couldn't take that. I don't know many men who could. This venture will be good for him. It will be good for both of you."

She strove for a light tone. "I guess that means you think I should mortgage the vineyard."

"No, I don't." Julianne sifted her hair with her fingers. "I'm not explaining myself very well. DeAngelo Vineyards has been in your family for a hundred years and your father would be turning over in his grave if you risked it. But the winery is different. You and Jake worked together to build it from scratch. He gave up all interest in it to you when he left for Napa. He didn't have to do that. I think it's time to return the favor."

Francesca's eyes burned. She looked down at the brownie in her hand. What she was feeling needed to be said. "I'm not over what he did to me, you know. No matter what I feel or what I want, there is still that. If you think I've forgiven and forgotten, you're wrong." Her voice broke and the tears spilled over. "Maybe it's selfish of me, but that's the way it is. If I do let him have the winery, it will be because of you, Julianne, not because of anything I owe Jake. Because you've always been there for me."

Julianne was out of her chair, her arms wound tightly around Francesca's shoulders before she could draw another breath. "Oh, my darling," she murmured against the younger woman's silky hair. "If only you wouldn't struggle so. No one would ever call you selfish. You're wonderful and loyal and dearly loved by all of us, including my son. If he weren't such an idiot, he would have realized that long before he made the dreadful mistake he did. I only hope and pray you'll forgive him, for all our sakes. But I certainly don't expect it, Francie. Whatever you do will be the right thing."

The words, validating and conciliatory, cooled the fire in Francesca's chest. She'd often wondered how Julianne felt about her, especially after Jake left. As a child, she knew that Julianne had been fond of her. But Francesca wanted more. More than anything, she wanted to be Julianne's daughter. In many a juvenile diary she'd created her own imaginary story, the one that ended with the unveiling of a document proving she was really a Harris. Her head told her that Julianne would always love Jake best. After all, he was her son. But Francesca, a little girl without a mother of her own, wanted Julianne to love her, too. It was good to know, after all these years, that she did.

The School of Dressage on Refugio Road was a low white structure with the inevitable Spanish red tile roof typical of public buildings in the Santa Ynez Valley. A split-rail fence, also white, circled the ring where the art of dressage was taught and the paddock where horses grazed.

Francesca walked into the office, waved at the

woman on the phone behind the desk, passed through the double doors and out to the ring. Sarah Gillette was finishing her lesson. Hooking her arms over the top rail of the fence, Francesca relaxed and watched the trainer lead the girl through the finer points of the canter.

Sarah looked the part, fine-boned and lean with a straight back, strong hands and a face made for the small-brimmed, velvet hat on top of hair skinned back into a bun. She was completely intent on her task, which, at the moment, was maneuvering Fairy Light into the high-stepping strut necessary for parading in front of a panel of judges.

Francesca watched approvingly. Sarah was good and, from the satisfied expression on the trainer's face, she followed directions. Not wanting to distract her, Francesca walked back to the stables to look at the horses. She didn't have long to wait. Ten minutes later, Sarah, hatless now, led Fairy Light into the barn. She grinned when she saw Francesca.

"What are you doing here?" she asked.

"I came by to see if you needed a ride home."

"Really?" Sarah looked skeptical.

Francesca laughed. "Really. I haven't seen you in a while and I wanted to know how the lessons were coming."

"I love them. If it weren't for coming here, I don't know what I'd do with myself."

Francesca clucked softly and moved toward Fairy Light. Gently, she stroked her nose and head. "How are you, girl? Are they treating you the way you deserve?"

The horse nickered and blew into Francesca's cupped hand.

"Do you miss her?" Sarah asked, handing the horse off to the small, wiry man who'd followed her into the barn.

"You bet I do." Francesca nodded at the man. "How are you, Juan?"

The man's grin was very white in his brown face. "Very well, thank you. It's good to see you again, Francesca."

"You can ride her if you want," Sarah offered.

"That's okay." Francesca backed away. "She belongs to you now. From the looks of it you've been doing a wonderful job with her. I knew you two would be good for each other."

"She's my best friend," Sarah said softly. "I think I'd run away if it wasn't for Fairy Light."

Alarm bells rang in Francesca's brain. "Do you want to go for a soda and talk for a while? I brought you one of Julianne's brownies, but maybe you'd like to go somewhere and save it for later."

"My dad is coming for me," Sarah said regretfully.

"Why don't you call him and see if it's okay? I'll drive you home later."

"Do you mean it? You're always so busy."

She reached into her pocket. "Use my cell phone. I'll wait outside until you're done."

Francesca waved goodbye to the groom and headed toward the exit. Before she was halfway there, Sarah caught up with her. "Dad says it's fine. I thought he would. It's a huge pain for him to come out here and pick me up three times a week."

Francesca's eyebrows rose. "Three times a week is a lot of expensive dressage. I hope you're grateful. Most kids are lucky to get one lesson a week."

"It's the least he can do," Sarah muttered.

"I heard that." Francesca unlocked the car door.
"I wanted you to."

"Why?"

Sarah shrugged. "Giving your kids *things* isn't the best way to do it."

"Do what?"

"Be a dad."

Pulling out on to the road, Francesca drove toward the center of town. "Maybe it's a start for a person who's as unfamiliar with the territory as he is. Obviously, your dad wants you to be happy or he wouldn't do things for you."

"It would be a lot nicer if he did some things *with* us instead of for us."

"I can't argue with that," Francesca agreed. "But what if he doesn't know how to do that?"

"Dads are supposed to know those things." Sarah looked out the window. "My mom did."

"Well, that's the thing." Francesca was beginning to feel sorry for Mitch. His daughter's expectations were tough to live up to. "Moms are different, Sarah, not necessarily better, just different." She changed the subject. "How's your brother?"

Sarah kept her face averted. "He's fine."

"I heard otherwise."

Sarah groaned. "I guess the whole town knows."

"Look at it this way. If Drew was selling drugs, others were buying them."

"It's just so seedy and embarrassing."

"Don't take it so personally. You're not your brother's keeper. People know you for yourself."

"That's the problem. No one knows us at all. How do they know I'm different?"

"By the way you behave," Francesca said reasonably. "You can't worry about what people think of other members of your family. Be yourself. You're a very nice person. People will see that."

"Drew's a nice person, too," Sarah whispered. "At least he used to be."

"He's a good person. Whenever I think of Drew I get a warm feeling inside."

Sarah looked surprised. "Why?"

"I remember the barbecue when Nick fell into the river. He might have drowned if Drew hadn't fished him out and carried him home. I'll always be grateful to him for that."

This time Sarah's flush was from pleasure. "He did do that, didn't he?"

"He certainly did."

"Drew's changed," the girl confided. "He wasn't like this at home before Mom died. He was funny and smart. He told the best jokes."

"Did he?"

Sarah nodded. "Mom and Drew had a terrific relationship. They played off each other like a comic routine." She drew a deep breath. "Sometimes I felt left out, almost as if I was from a different family. I'm more like my dad, I think."

"That's not a bad thing."

"No. I guess not." Sarah did not appear convinced.

Francesca took the exit leading away from town.

"Where are we going?" Sarah asked.

"I thought we'd go into Solvang. They have a great

ice-cream parlor and the shops are quaint. Do you mind?"

"No. I'd like that."

Later, fortified with double-dip ice-cream cones, they wandered through the Danish village. Francesca stopped in front of a window filled with clocks. "I've always wanted a cuckoo clock."

"Why don't you have one?"

"They're expensive and I don't really need it. Besides, there's always a better reason to spend my money."

"Like ice cream."

Francesca laughed. "Exactly."

Sarah smiled sunnily. "This was really nice of you, Francie. I was feeling sort of down, but you perked me up. Thanks."

Francesca melted. She was sweet and vulnerable with those big blue eyes and the spray of freckles across her nose. "You're very welcome. I'm glad I helped."

"Maybe we can do this again some time."

"I'm counting on it. I'd like you to be happy here."

"I thought you wanted us to leave."

Francesca's smile faded. "Why on earth would you think that?"

"Because of the winery my dad's company is building."

Francesca sat down on a bench and motioned for Sarah to join her. "How much do you know about that, Sarah?"

"Only what I've heard from other people. My dad doesn't really talk about it with us."

"What have you heard?"

Sarah's lower lip trembled and she looked away. "Some of the girls at school said that the winery GGI is building would take business away from the local people. They'll lose their jobs."

Francesca sighed. "I guess that's kind of hard to hear when you're fifteen and hoping to make friends."

"Is it true?"

"Yes and no. But either way, it has nothing to do with you personally."

"I don't understand."

"A few people will lose their jobs, but more people will get new ones. Those who will lose are the local growers, like me. There aren't more than fifteen working vineyards with wineries in the whole valley, so the losers don't make up a large part of the population. The people who work for us will be absorbed by GGI. It's that simple."

"It doesn't sound simple to me."

"The bottom line is that I have as much to lose as anyone in this valley if GGI gets its winery. But that doesn't mean I want you to leave Santa Ynez or that we can't be friends. Please believe me."

Sarah tilted her head. Her blue eyes, intense and considering, met Francesca's. Then she smiled. "I believe you."

"Thank you." Francesca stood. "It's time to go home. Your dad will be worried."

"My dad doesn't worry about me, but I do have homework."

Francesca maintained her smile. Mitch Gillette was an intelligent man and he loved his children. That was clear to everyone who knew him. What a shame that his son and daughter didn't know it, too.

Twenty-Two

Mitch slid the knot of his tie close to his throat, shrugged into the jacket of his charcoal-gray suit and checked out the final results in the mirror. He felt off, somehow, and slightly uncomfortable. It had been quite a while since he'd worn a tie. He hadn't missed it but, on the other hand, he didn't want to get too comfortable with the lifestyle in Santa Ynez. Once the winery was built, he would be sent somewhere else. Hopefully, for the sake of his children, that was still a few years away.

"Drew," he called down the hall. "Let's go."

"I'm down here," the boy called back.

Mitch met his son at the foot of the stairs and looked him over. Drew looked good. His hair, combed back from his face, was still damp from the shower and his clothes, although still baggy in the loose style teenagers preferred, actually fit. He was nearly as tall as Mitch. He nodded. "Good for you."

A wave of red spread across the boy's face. *Embar-*

rassment or pleasure? Mitch didn't know. "Are you looking forward to the new job?"

"Actually, I am," Drew said, surprising him. "I think I'll like it."

"Well, then, shall we say goodbye to Sarah and go?"

"She's sleeping. If I were you, I'd let her. She doesn't get much time to relax."

Mitch bit back a comment. In his opinion, teenagers had too much time to relax. "All right," he said instead. "I'll take your advice."

Drew climbed into the car beside his father. "So, Dad. Where are you off to on a Saturday morning?"

"I have to meet with a real estate broker. GGI is buying two local vineyards with water rights. I have to sign some papers."

"I heard that you don't have permission to build yet."

Mitch looked sideways at his son. "I didn't know you were paying attention. Who told you that?"

"It's big news at school."

Mitch turned back to the road. "It's true. We don't have the results of the traffic and pollution report yet."

"Are you worried?"

"No. We'll get it. If not, we'll have a general election. The town will benefit from this winery. The opposition is mostly local vintners. There aren't many of those, not enough to make a difference if it comes to a vote."

Drew looked out the window. "It's a little tough for Sarah and me."

Mitch frowned. "How?"

"Popular opinion is with the local growers. Every-one knows we're on the other side. This place—" he waved his arm "—is the back of beyond. It doesn't even have a Starbucks. They have a different mentality here. I feel like I'm in Montana."

"They'll adjust," Mitch said grimly.

"I hope it's worth it," Drew replied under his breath.

Mitch pulled into the DeAngelo courtyard. "I could use a cup of coffee. Do you mind if I come in with you?"

Drew shrugged. "Suit yourself."

The camaraderie of the morning was gone. Mitch wanted nothing more than to be rid of his sullen teenager and move into areas where he was confident of success. Mustering his resolve once again to involve himself in the lives of his children, he followed Drew up to the house.

Julianne opened the door. "Hi. Come in. Mitch, how about a cup of coffee?"

"I was hoping you'd say that."

"Drew, would you like anything before we start?"

"No, thanks."

"All right." She picked up a card from the counter. "You'll be working on cream puffs. Study the recipe for a minute and then assemble the ingredients. You'll find everything in the pantry and the refrigerator."

"Are you using whipped cream or custard?" Drew asked.

"Whipped cream."

Drew grinned. "My favorite."

Julianne laughed. "I'm glad you approve. Maybe, if you're very good, I'll let you sample a few."

Mitch listened to their banter in disbelief. A hot pool of jealousy rose in his chest. His son was practically comatose around him. All Julianne did was point him in the direction of the refrigerator, bribe him with cream puffs, and the boy was actually smiling. He couldn't remember when he'd last seen Drew's teeth. "Maybe I should be going," he said. "I'm in your way."

"Nonsense." Julianne was already pouring the coffee. "I've been up for quite a while and could use a break. I'll meet you in the breakfast nook."

Gratefully, he walked into the other room. She joined him in a matter of minutes.

"Thanks for taking him on," he said, accepting the cup she held out to him.

"I could use the help and Drew has some talent when it comes to food."

"How did that come about? I wonder."

Julianne smiled. "Don't ask. Just appreciate it."

Mitch's smile didn't reach his eyes.

"What's the matter?" she asked.

"You're very good at assessing my mood."

"Am I prying?"

He shook his head. "Actually, your interest is flattering and—" he grinned "—to a small degree, comforting."

She sipped her coffee. Her eyes were an exotic Siamese blue above the rim of her cup. They distracted him. "Susan's eyes were dark brown," he said. "It's odd that her children have such blue eyes."

"Not really. Yours are very light and she obviously carried a recessive gene. Biology 1–A."

"Sometimes I forget that you were a teacher."

"Those were good years, but I'm glad they're over. Working for myself suits me better."

"I imagine it would suit anyone better."

"Why not try it?" she suggested.

"And do what?"

"Do what you know. Be a vintner. Your background in business is strong enough to allow you to manage your own vineyard. You could hire a winemaker and learn the specifics. It might be rough for a few years, but starting out usually is. We've all been there. You'd have help when you needed it."

It was the edge of an idea, a dream, that would semiform in his consciousness only to be promptly shut out. "It's tempting."

"Think about it."

"It's a risk."

"Yes, but if it worked…" She let the sentence hang.

He stood. "I should go. I have a meeting."

"I'll drive Drew home. There's no need for you to come out of your way."

"Thanks. I'll pick you up tomorrow. Is six all right?"

"Where are we going?"

"The Old Stagecoach Inn. Do you approve?"

Her eyes sparkled. "I love it."

Julianne watched him drive away from the kitchen window. Drew, his cheeks flushed, his forehead wrinkled, was bent over a saucepan gradually adding flour to a butter and sugar mixture. She liked his intensity and the fact that he didn't try to make conversation. All his attention was focused on his task.

"I'm not sure this is working," he said. "Can you come and look?"

Julianne peeked over his shoulder. "It's perfect," she pronounced. "The batter is supposed to seize up just like that. The secret to perfect cream puffs is temperature control. At the exact moment they puff and set, they should be removed from the oven. The recipe has been perfected. As long as you follow it, you'll be safe."

He nodded.

Her carrot cake, due at the Santa Ynez Inn late in the morning, needed icing. She unwrapped two packages of cream cheese, measured sugar, vanilla and a drop of kirsch into a bowl and plugged in her mixer. The whir of the appliance and the faintly sweet smell of vanilla and sugar that permeated her kitchen during baking soothed her, lifted her spirits.

Out of the corner of her eye, she saw Drew drop spoonfuls of dough on a cookie sheet. She smiled. At the same age, Jake wouldn't have been caught dead in a kitchen baking cream puffs. Either Drew was very secure and didn't care what other people thought, or cooking was no longer perceived as a solely feminine accomplishment.

"How are you coming over there?" she asked.

Drew slid two pans of cream-puff dough into the preheated convection oven. His clothes were dusted with white flour and the satisfied expression on his face was an answer in itself.

He nodded. "I like this."

"Good. Keep an eye on those puffs. A minute or two can ruin a whole batch."

"That cake looks great."

"Thanks. It's a cake day today. I have to make a mocha-chocolate for a birthday party. I'll start the layers. While they're cooling, I'll deliver this one. Then I'll make us lunch. Now that you're an expert on cream puffs, do you think you can handle éclairs?"

Drew grinned. "I'll try."

"They're almost the same as cream puffs, but they have chocolate drizzled across the top. The chocolate requires a thermometer. Otherwise it won't have that nice glossy look that good bittersweet chocolate is sup-- posed to have."

"Where did you learn to do all this?" Drew asked, waving his hand to encompass the kitchen.

"I've always loved to read recipes." Julianne began assembling the ingredients for her mocha-chocolate cake, pulling eggs and butter from the refrigerator, and chocolate, flour and baking powder from the pantry. "First, I started experimenting. Finally, one day, my husband asked me why I hadn't served the same meal to my family twice in the last year."

"Was he complaining?" Drew asked incredulously.

Julianne tilted her head, trying to remember. "I think so," she said at last. "Carl was a creature of habit. He didn't like anything to upset his routine. You can imagine what it must have been like for him to have a different meal every night, especially something he'd never heard of."

"I think it sounds great. My mom was a health nut. She made soy burgers and tofu scrambled eggs." He blinked, passed his hand over his eyes and bent down to check the cream puffs through the oven window.

"And your dad?" Julianne asked gently.

"He's limited to steak, salmon and spaghetti. Other-wise, we order in. We do eat together, though," he said after a pause.

The oven timer beeped. Drew pulled the cookie sheets out of the oven and set them on the counter. The cream puffs were a delicate golden brown.

Julianne's eyes widened. "Oh, my," she exclaimed. "These are truly culinary masterpieces."

Drew reddened. "They did turn out all right, didn't they?"

"All right?" She took him by the shoulders and looked up at him. "That's the understatement of the year. Drew, you really have talent. Have you thought of culinary school?"

"Not until I met you."

"I think you're a natural."

"Tell that to my dad."

Julianne returned to her cake. "I intend to do just that."

Mitch ordered a glass of iced tea and a sandwich. He sat at a well-lit corner table at Andersen's Pea Soup Restaurant. It was far enough away from Santa Ynez to guarantee him enough anonymity to meet with the broker and finalize the closing documents for the two vineyards he'd purchased for GGI.

The broker was late. Mitch pulled out the pollution report he'd picked up this morning and began reading it carefully line by line. The first paragraph, highlighted in bold print, was impossible to misinterpret. GGI had been denied permission to build its winery. The negative effects of increased tourism, the additional strain of providing utilities, parking and shelter for those employed by and visiting a vineyard and winery the size of the one GGI proposed had been weighed against the benefits of future employment opportunities in the community. The committee had arrived at the resulting decision only after careful consideration. GGI could appeal this decision by providing new information.

Mitch's disappointment was fleeting. He'd expected and planned for just such a contingency. GGI would appeal, of course. But he wouldn't leave it at that. The next step was to override the committee with an emergency general election, one that could be organized with voting taking place as early as six weeks from now. People needed jobs. The economy wasn't good. He had every confidence that in a general election, GGI would prevail. He would pick up the paperwork after lunch and see about renting an office in Santa Ynez. There were petitions to print, signatures to collect and an advertising campaign to organize. It would be best to hire a local person, someone who could command support from the community. He pulled out a pen and began making notes on the back of the report.

Rick Lane, the commercial-property broker, sat down across from Mitch and apologized profusely. "I came from Santa Barbara. The traffic was a bear."

"No problem," Mitch said coolly. "I've already ordered."

"Is the deal still on?"

"Why do you ask?"

"I heard about the pollution report."

"The deal is still on."

Lane frowned. "As much as I want this sale, it's my professional responsibility to warn you that GGI's winery has a very good chance of not being built."

"I'll handle it."

Lane shook his head. "I'm going to say this one more time. I might even write it into the contract. Then you can't complain that I didn't warn you. Santa Barbara County is a world apart. People who have power are old and they have money. They won't widen freeways or approve of new construction. They live behind the walls of their Montecito estates and work very hard to keep everything the way it is. Change isn't in their vocabulary. They don't think anything new is an improvement."

"I appreciate your honesty. But Santa Barbara County also has a large and resentful minority population. The public schools are largely second- and third-generation Hispanic. These people deserve jobs, housing and opportunities. Their votes will outnumber the wealthy. They're the ones this winery will appeal to."

The broker lifted one hand to signal the waitress. "You're the boss."

Twenty-Three

Julianne opened the door and Mitch's eyes widened with pleasure. "You look beautiful."

She smiled. Compliments were difficult for her but he sounded so genuine she believed him. Besides, she knew she looked good. She'd gone to considerable effort to look exactly right this evening, sophisticated enough, but not too dressy, for the old roadhouse-turned-restaurant located on a remote back road east of Santa Barbara. Her skirt, fitted at the waist and hips and cut in the new flirty style around the hem, hit the top of her knee. A clingy, scoop-necked sweater with three-quarter sleeves in the same raspberry color complemented her hair and skin. She felt attractive and feminine and more nervous than a fifty-year-old widow with three grown children and one grandchild had a right to be.

In the car the silence between them was distracting. She waited for Mitch to turn on the radio. When he didn't, she searched her mind for a topic of conversation. *The children*. That was it. Children were always safe. "How is Sarah?" she asked politely.

"Sarah's doing well. By the way, I really appreciate the time Francesca took with her the other day. Sarah hasn't stopped talking about it."

"I'll tell Francie you said that. She'll be pleased."

Silence again.

"I think Drew is happy working with me. Has he said anything to you?"

"Drew rarely says anything to me. But it's obvious that he adores you. I'm pleased that he has a healthy interest, thanks to you."

"You're welcome."

Mitch looked at her. "I have a great deal to thank your family for. You've been kind to us."

"It's nothing, really. People here help each other. When does Drew have to appear in court?"

"Next Thursday."

"I can be there, if you'd like," she offered. "It might help if I showed up as a character witness."

"Would you do that?"

"Of course, but you should ask Drew if it's all right with him. We haven't talked about what happened. He might be embarrassed."

"I'll do that."

The conversation died again. Julianne's heart raced. They were still twenty miles away from the restaurant. What was the matter with him? Finally, she couldn't stand it any longer. Tucking her hair behind her ear, she spoke up. "You're quiet tonight."

"Am I?"

"Yes. In fact, I'm wondering if you wouldn't rather be somewhere else. You're awfully preoccupied."

Unbelievably, his cheek, the one visible to her, darkened. Could he be embarrassed?

"I'm sorry, Julianne. I'll try to be better company. I've hit a glitch in the construction of the winery and a million thoughts are racing through my head."

"Is there anything you'd like to bounce off me?"

"That question is almost risqué."

She laughed the first genuine laugh of the night. "I didn't mean it that way at all."

He turned the wheel to the right suddenly and the car swerved. Before she had time to ask what he was doing, he'd set the brake and released his seat belt. Then he lifted her chin and kissed her.

For Julianne, everything stopped, her senses aware of nothing but the kiss. She hadn't been kissed by a man in ten years. No, that wasn't completely true. She hadn't *welcomed* a kiss by a man in ten years. And before that there was only Carl. The sensation of firm lips on her mouth, warm hands stroking her throat and the steady beat of a heart that wasn't hers was soothing, exhilarating and deliciously forbidden at the same time. She leaned into the kiss for what seemed like a long time.

Finally he pulled away.

"My goodness," she breathed, her voice shaky, airfilled. "Why now?"

"I wanted it out of the way. The tension was thick."

"For you, too?"

He nodded. "For me, too."

"That's a relief." Julianne leaned back in her seat. "I thought I was boring you."

"Never that."

"Are we finished?"

He laughed. "For now."

She leaned back against the headrest, her confidence restored. "Are you going to tell me what's causing you to be so preoccupied, other than my presence?"

He pulled out into the flow of traffic. "The pollution report came back. GGI doesn't have approval to build."

Julianne stared at him. "What does that mean for you?"

"I have to find an alternative to approval by the county board of supervisors."

"What kind of alternative?"

"Popular vote. I think there are enough people in this valley who need jobs and would like to see a large winery built."

Julianne didn't think so at all, but she wanted to hear him out. "Are you thinking of putting some kind of initiative on the ballot for the next election?"

"I can't wait that long. I'm thinking of holding a special election."

"Can you do that?"

"It's been done before. I have no choice. The company has gone out on a limb for this property. The loss would be significant. It wouldn't look good for me."

Julianne's forehead wrinkled. "I'm sorry, Mitch. I don't know what to say, other than I hope you have an alternate plan if it doesn't work. The people here are set in their ways."

"Unemployment is a powerful factor, Julianne. The timing is good for another winery."

The turnoff leading to the restaurant loomed ahead.

Thankful to be changing the subject, Julianne pointed it out.

"It's crowded for such an out-of-the-way place," he observed.

"Have you been here before?"

"No. I chose it based on a recommendation."

"It's a good choice. The menu is unique. They serve ostrich, buffalo and venison."

"Good Lord! I hope they offer something else as well." He pulled into an empty parking space.

"Not feeling adventurous?"

"Not particularly."

"I'm sure they'll have something you'll like."

To Julianne's surprise and pleasure, the old inn hadn't changed much since she'd seen it last. Smoke-stained beams and white-stuccoed walls decorated with branding irons and horseshoes gave the rooms a warm, Old West feel. Jam jars served as vases for Mexican sage and California poppies, centerpieces for the scrubbed oak tables and spindle-backed chairs. Baskets of wild mustard, sorrel and rosemary brought color to the white walls, dark wood and rag throw rugs scattered across the floors. Gleaming copper bowls heaped with wood, dry twigs and lavender sat near each of the glowing fireplaces.

A young woman in a long black skirt and tailored white blouse seated them in a cozy corner near the fire. There were four other tables in the small room, all of them filled, all of them lit by the soft glow of slender wax candles.

"This is incredible," Mitch said after she'd left them with menus and a wine list. "Who would have thought a place like this existed way out here?"

"Wait until you taste the food."

"That's definitely a recommendation coming from you."

"I appreciate a good restaurant as much as anyone else," she said. "I don't go out as much as I'd like."

He looked up from the wine list. "Why not?"

"I'm not sure." She frowned. "Maybe people think that because of what I do, I'll be critical. Actually, I'm rather easy to please."

"Does that apply to everything, or just food?"

Her eyes sparkled. "I'd say everything. Life is too short to be terribly particular."

"I agree. Would you like a drink before dinner?"

She shook her head. "Wine with dinner is all I need."

He set the list aside. "Tell me you're enjoying yourself."

"Very much."

"I wondered for a minute there in the car."

"I was nervous."

"Me, too. It's odd."

"What is?"

"This feeling I have when I'm with you. It's different somehow. New. Comfortable and yet exciting. It's odd, but I can't remember what I felt for Susan, my ex-wife. I must have felt something or I wouldn't have asked her to marry me." He signaled the waiter. "I don't know why I brought that up. I'm not making sense. Let's order our wine and then I'll have an excuse. Is the Pinot Noir all right with you? It's a Sterling label and a year I've wanted to taste."

"Yes. I'd like that, too.

"I don't think what you're feeling is odd at all," she

said, continuing the conversation. "People's feelings change and fade daily. If not, we'd all be miserable about something that happened years after it was over. It's a defense mechanism programmed into all of us. I know that I loved my husband. I know that I was grief-stricken when he died. But I no longer cry myself to sleep at night because he's gone. Thank goodness. Otherwise, how could anyone continue living?"

His gaze was steady, unblinking. She blushed. "What are you thinking?"

"That I'm going to order the venison after all."

"What made you change your mind?"

"This is a night of firsts and I've never had venison before."

Francesca twisted her hair into a knot at the back of her head, retied the sash of her sarong skirt and slipped her feet into sandals. Julianne was out and the kitchen was hers. She couldn't compete with her mother-in-law when it came to cooking, but she still enjoyed the process and ritual of preparing a meal for her family, even more so when Julianne wasn't there to oversee her mistakes.

Tonight she was trying a bread-salad recipe from the culinary school in Napa. She'd picked up fresh shrimp, French bread and sweet corn at the grocery store. Jake had been recruited to choose the wine and later, to do the dishes. Nick would shuck corn and set the table. A delicious shiver of contentment radiated from her center. They would be alone, the three of them. The occasion was something to celebrate. Glowing, she ran downstairs.

There was no worry about ingredients. Julianne's spice and condiment cupboard was a virtual library of both the exotic and mundane, from imported cooking oils to the rarest of spices, all arranged in alphabetical order. She found the avocado oil immediately, then the cumin, red pepper and oregano. The shrimp was already peeled and deveined. After patting them dry, she sprinkled sugar and salt over the entire batch, filled a pot of salted water to boil for the corn and pressed the speaker button to activate the intercom. "Nick, wherever you are. It's time to shuck."

"Can I finish my computer game?" he asked.

"How long will it take?"

"Ten minutes."

"Set the timer and be down here in exactly ten minutes."

"Okay."

She chose a serrated knife and began dicing the French bread. It was toasting on a cooking sheet in the oven when Jake walked through the door carrying a bottle of wine.

"Need any help?" he asked.

"No, thanks. I have everything under control."

He leaned against the counter, arms crossed, and watched her, a thoughtful expression on his face.

After a minute or so, she began to feel self-conscious. "Did you want something?" she asked pointedly.

"No. Just enjoying the view."

She rubbed her arms. "You're embarrassing me."

"Sorry." He didn't move.

"What's going on, Jake?"

"You're good at this."

"So?"

"You don't get to do it often, do you?"

"No, I don't. But I can't do everything, can I?"

"No," he said slowly. "I guess not. But, maybe—" He stopped.

She waited.

"Maybe we could arrange things differently."

Francesca chose four tomatoes, two red, one orange and one yellow and began dicing. "I don't understand."

Jake found a corkscrew, opened a bottle of Chardonnay and poured it into two glasses. He handed one to Francesca. "What if we ask my mother to move back to the small house?"

She gasped and set down the glass. "Are you serious?"

"Yes."

"Jake, you can't mean it. Can you imagine how your mother would feel if, after all she's done for us, we threw her out of her home?"

"We're not throwing her out, Francie. We're suggesting that she might like some privacy by offering an alternative. The house isn't more than a quarter of a mile away."

"What about Nick? Who will he come home to? Who will cook if I'm away until ten or eleven at night?"

"I will," he said evenly.

She closed her eyes. He was going to ruin their evening. He was going to bring up a subject they couldn't finish before Nick interrupted them, one that would hang over them through the entire meal. The enjoyment would be ruined for her. "Don't do this now, Jake. Please. Can't we just enjoy the evening?"

"I want to enjoy this evening. I want to enjoy every evening with you and my son."

"Do we have to discuss this now?"

"Damn it, Francie. When do we discuss it? How long are you going to run away from me?"

Her hands shook. "I'm not running away. I'm just not ready. I don't want to commit to something I'm not sure of. On the other hand, I don't want to say there's no chance when there might be. Please understand. Give me some time."

"Two years is a long time."

"That's right. But it wasn't until two weeks ago that I had any idea you'd considered coming back. Maybe we could take one step at a time. You're living here. We could—" She looked down at her hands.

"What? Just say it."

"You could share my room."

"I want to marry you, Francie, not just sleep with you. I want to start over. This is more than sex. I want a marriage and all that it means."

"That didn't work out very well the first time."

"Sarcasm doesn't help."

"All right. Exactly what *does* marriage mean to you, Jake? Maybe we should clear that up first. Obviously we have different definitions."

A thin white line appeared around his lips and his eyes blazed. "You don't want this to work."

"That isn't true."

"I don't know what else to do to show you that I'm serious. I work until I'm so tired I can't even stand and, in case you haven't noticed, I'm not on the payroll. I try to lighten your load every way I can. I've listened to you, made suggestions, offered to do the grunt work and I've yet to hear a thank-you. I love you. For some strange, and I'm beginning to think tragic, reason I've been programmed to have that feeling for one woman and she's you. For some people there's only one person, Francie. Maybe it's that way for you, too. It's been two years and you haven't even gone out on a date. For someone else, that might not be so unusual, but you're drop-dead beautiful. So, if you don't want to spend the rest of your life alone, maybe we should give this another shot."

"Have *you* gone out on a date, Jake?"

"I might have known you would bring it back to that."

A small voice piped up from behind them. "Are you fighting?"

Francesca froze.

Jake walked to where his son balanced first on one foot and then the other. He lifted him into his arms as if he were no more than a toddler. "We're discussing, Nick. That's all. Sometimes people need to discuss."

Nick's lower lip quivered. "You were yelling."

"I suppose we were." Jake offered no apology. "Sometimes people yell. It means they care."

"I came down to do the corn."

"Where is that corn? I'll help you."

Nick pointed to a basket on the counter.

"C'mon, buddy. I can eat two pieces. How about you?"

"That depends on dessert."

Jake laughed. It irritated Francesca that his mood could change so easily, or even that he could pretend so easily. If in this, why not in other things?

"What's for dessert, Francie?"

"Ice-cream sundaes," she said defiantly. "I'm not Julianne."

Both blond heads turned to look at her. "No one expects you to be," Jake said gently.

"Gosh, Mom. What would we do with two grans and no mom?"

Francesca's eyes filled. "I love you, Nick."

"Dad, too. Say you love Dad, too."

She was crying in earnest now, fat salty tears that found their way into the corners of her mouth. "He already knows that."

"Say it anyway," Nick insisted. "He likes it."

"I don't think—"

"C'mon, Mom."

"Stop it!" She threw up her hands. "All right, Nick. Give me a break. I love Dad, too."

Jake smiled broadly. "Thanks. I needed that."

In spite of herself, Francesca laughed, tore off a paper towel from the roll, wiped her eyes and blew her nose. "Please, finish the corn, or we won't eat until midnight."

Jake crossed the space between them and, with Nick still in his arms, kissed her soundly. "You have only to ask and all will be yours."

"I'm asking now and all I want is the corn shucked and boiling in ten minutes."

Jake bent his forehead to Nick's. "She means us."

Nick nodded. "I guess we'll have to do it."

Francesca turned away, hiding a smile. She picked up the knife to resume her dicing. Ten minutes ago she didn't think it was possible to redeem the evening. Now— Well, maybe things weren't as black and white as she thought.

Twenty-Four

An older-model Lincoln rolled slowly into the DeAngelo driveway and stopped in front of the porch. A woman stepped out and looked at the house. She didn't bother to close the car door. A full minute passed before she turned a quarter turn to the right and looked out over the hills. She turned again to look, for the same amount of time, over the dormant fields and then back again at the house, a three-hundred-sixty-degree sweep.

Jake, on his way from the winery to the house to grab a late lunch, sat in his Jeep jotting down notes when her car pulled in. He was sure he'd seen her somewhere before and equally as sure that if he had he wouldn't have forgotten. She wasn't the kind of woman a man forgot. Coffee-dark hair was pulled back into a casual bun under a wide-brimmed straw hat. She had the kind of willowy, magazine-cover body that most women wanted and few had. Her white dress was sleeveless and slit to midthigh, high enough to show her legs. They were spectacular. Her features were exotic and her skin was good, although at second glance she was older than she first appeared, somewhere in her late forties, maybe even older.

He knew she'd seen him but she didn't react. He climbed out of the Jeep and met her on the porch. She removed her sunglasses. Under the brim of her hat, bottle-green eyes surveyed him coolly. He caught his breath. Suddenly he knew who she was. The resemblance was undeniable. He held out his hand. "Hello, Mrs. DeAngelo. I'm Jake Harris."

Her carmine lips parted, and her words, whiskey-soft, rolled off her tongue. "Well, well, well. Little Jake Harris." She took his hand while her eyes flickered across his face. "You certainly turned out to be a gorgeous man."

He nodded, barely acknowledging the compliment. "What brings you to Santa Ynez?"

She shrugged and dropped her hand to her side. "Curiosity and motherly instinct. Apparently I have a grandson, although I wouldn't admit it to any passing stranger. What do you think, Jake? Do I look like a grandma?"

He ignored the question. "You're a little late. He was born eight years ago."

"I'm not going to apologize."

"Even if you were, it's not me you owe."

She smiled seductively. "No? Maybe not. I'm sorry about your father."

"Thank you."

"Are you going to invite me in?"

Jake opened the door and waited for her to pass in front of him. "Francie is working at the winery," he said pointedly.

"I guess that's supposed to remind me that I haven't asked about her."

"Take it any way you like."

Lisa DeAngelo tilted her head back to look up at him. "You don't like me, do you?"

"I don't know you, Mrs. DeAngelo. The last time I saw you I was in first grade."

"I must have made quite an impression. You remember me."

He shook his head. "Not really. You resemble Francie. That's how I knew you."

"Really?" She looked surprised as if the thought that she could have a daughter with similar features had never occurred to her. "I'm almost curious."

"My mother lives here now. She runs a catering business from the kitchen."

"How quaint."

Jake's mouth twitched. The kitchen door was closed, a sure sign that his mother was cooking. He opened it, blocking the entrance and Lisa from view.

His mother was pulling puff pastries from the oven.

"Any chance I can get a quick bite to eat before going back out?"

She blew a wisp of hair from her forehead. "I can't stop to make anything now. But help yourself. There are plenty of leftovers in the refrigerator."

"We have a visitor."

Julianne straightened. "How nice. Who is it?"

Lisa slipped out from behind Jake and stood in front of him. "It's me, Julianne. The prodigal daughter returned to the fold."

For a long minute the two women, of similar age and

yet so different, stared at each other. Lisa looked like a naughty child caught in the middle of a prank. But it was his mother's reaction that worried Jake. Julianne's hands shook. Her cheeks were very pale and the puff pastries were definitely in danger of sliding off the tray.

Jake grabbed a towel and reached for them, taking the tray from his mother's hands and setting it on the counter. "Are you all right?" he asked his mother.

"Yes."

"Of course she's all right," Lisa purred. "We're old friends, aren't we, Julianne?"

Julianne recovered. "I don't remember. Did it seem that way to you?"

"You haven't carried a grudge all this time, have you? I certainly haven't."

Julianne's eyes flashed blue fire. "I'm sure you're a true role model, Lisa. To answer your question, I put you out of my mind completely. As for your being the prodigal daughter, aren't you a bit long in the tooth for that?"

"I believe we're the same age," said Lisa.

"Only if you had Chris when you were fifteen. You remember him, don't you? Chris, your thirty-five-year-old son?"

Jake stared at his mother. He couldn't remember a time when she wasn't warm and gracious, a soft touch for every child selling cookies and magazine subscriptions, every Salvation Army Santa Claus with a bell, every homeless man or woman in need of a day's work, a shower or a decent meal.

"Never mind." Lisa said quickly, turning to look at the kitchen. "My goodness, what have you done to this place? It doesn't look anything like it used to."

"How would you know?" replied Julianne. "You never cooked a meal in your life."

Jake couldn't help himself. "Jesus, Mom, c'mon. She's Francie's mother."

Julianne crossed her arms. "It takes more than biology to be a mother. Francesca will agree with me."

Jake watched the high color flame across Lisa's cheekbones. He frowned. "Why don't we call a truce and tell Francie she has company?"

Julianne turned back to the stove. "You be the bearer of bad news. I'd rather not."

Jake was shaken. Whatever had happened between these two women was personal. His mother was acting like a stranger. Normally, she wasn't prone to snap decisions or poor judgment. Impulse control was something she'd drummed into her children at every relevant occasion. What was the matter with her? What had Lisa DeAngelo done to bring out such a vitriolic reaction after more than twenty years? Not for a minute did he believe his mother was the source. It just wasn't possible.

"I think I'll stay a while if you don't mind," said Lisa. She smiled at Jake. "Is there a guest room?"

Jake looked at his mother. She was removing the puff pastries from the tray, her entire focus on the food. "I'll see what I can do," he said.

At the winery, Francesca was working the Cabernet must, punching down the skins to mix with the juice. Concentrating on her task, she didn't hear the door open or the sound of footsteps on the concrete floor of the cave. It wasn't until Jake stepped into her line of vision that she realized she wasn't alone.

"Hi," she said, looking up. "I thought you were pulling up the dead Syrah vines."

"I was. It's four o'clock."

"Are you finished already?"

"Not quite. I came home for a late lunch. Need any help?"

She shook her head, turned off the paddle and smiled at him. He looked so earnest and familiar and comfortable. Objectively, Francesca knew that Jake was a good-looking man. Sometimes it hit her when she was least expecting it, just how handsome he was. But that wasn't what she thought of when he came to mind. The essence of Jake wasn't his looks. It was his intensity that had attracted her, his focus, his desire to stretch farther than the last time, to break his own record. Jake didn't recognize limitations. He was quite simply the most exciting person she'd ever met. He was funny and wise, shamelessly happy and had been since kindergarten. The realization that there wasn't anyone as interesting or attractive as her ex-husband could also be a drawback. "And you couldn't stay away?" she asked.

"Not exactly."

Something was wrong. He was definitely uncomfortable. She straightened her shoulders. "What is it, Jake?"

He took her hand and, leaning against the long bench that ran along the walls of the wine cave, pulled her toward him until she stood between the vee of his legs. "I don't know how to tell you this."

"You're making me nervous. Just say it."

"All right. Francie." He spoke slowly, without

expression. "Your mother is here. She's at the house now."

She stared at him. "My mother?"

"Yes."

"That's impossible," she said flatly.

"I know, but it's true."

"Why is she here?"

"I'm not sure. She didn't volunteer a reason. It's possible that she wanted to see you."

"After twenty-four years?" Francesca's eyes were very bright. "I don't think so."

"People change, Francie. Especially when they get older. They realize how important family is."

"Not my mother."

Jake sighed. "This is going to be a difficult evening. My mother hates her and apparently you aren't going to make it any easier. I guess Nick and I will have to hold down the fort."

"I don't want Nick to have anything to do with her."

"He's going to be polite. She's a guest in his home. You wouldn't want him to behave any other way."

Francesca shivered. "I know this sounds strange, but if it were anyone else I'd agree with you. She's different."

"You've only heard that from others. You haven't experienced it yourself. Give her a chance. Maybe you only got one side of the story."

"I haven't heard from her in twenty-four years, Jake. What kind of mother would absent herself from her children's lives for that long?"

"Maybe she was driven away. You haven't heard her side."

"Are you on her side?"

"I'm on your side, Francie," he said softly. "Don't you think I know what it was like for you not to have a mother?"

"I had your mother."

"It's not the same. You know it's not the same. You should have had your own."

"Whose fault is it that I didn't?" she countered.

He sighed. "All right. Have it your way."

She ground her fists into her hip bones. "Why are you championing her cause?"

"I told you. I want you to have your mother."

"There's more to it. Tell me. What's your stake in this?"

He looked at her. "You really have no idea, do you?"

"No."

His words came out in a rush of embarrassed logic. "Maybe if you could forgive your mother, it would be easier for you to forgive me."

She stared at him. "How I feel about you has nothing to do with how I feel about my mother."

"Maybe not," he admitted. "But think about it. Two very important people in your life, your mother and your husband, bailed on you. It's no wonder you're afraid to trust anyone. I wouldn't either."

"I'm not afraid," she said slowly, "but I'm not gullible either. My mother has made no effort to contact me, not ever. She's never been a part of my life. Our situation, yours and mine, is different. People divorce, Jake. That's sad, but not unusual. Our relationship is conditional upon certain behaviors. A mother leaving her children *is* unusual, as well as tragic, because her love for them should be unconditional. Do you see the difference?"

"Yes," he said after a minute. "When you put it that way, I do."

"I could never leave Nick or stop loving him, no matter what he did."

"But you could stop loving me."

"Yes," she said, looking away from the pain in his face. "People do it all the time. They grow apart. They fall out of love. They meet someone else. Once, you were my husband. Now, you're not. We can both marry again and someone else would be your wife and my husband. With children it's different. I'm the only mother Nick will ever have. That relationship is unique to the two of us."

"You've thought about this, haven't you?" he asked. "It isn't something you just came up with."

She shrugged. "I've been seeing a therapist for about two years. I think I'm finally making a breakthrough."

"Where does that leave us?" he asked softly.

She smiled. "Exactly where we were before this conversation began. We're reevaluating. I'm talking longer than you, that's all."

"Why is that?"

"Maybe because I didn't start thinking we could ever get back together until you came back with your broken bone. You dumped me, remember? I didn't think I had a choice. You always had one. For a long time I wanted you to come back. You knew that."

"When did you change your mind?"

"After the divorce was final. I was miserable. I'd never gone through anything so painful in my life."

"I don't know what to say. 'I'm sorry' seems like such an understatement."

It wasn't what she wanted to hear. He was so bad with cues. She wanted reassurance and promises and most of all, she didn't want to always tell him what she wanted. "It *is* an understatement, a pathetic one," she agreed.

"What do you want from me, Francie?"

"I don't know."

He reached for her, but she stepped back. "I can't give you the magic words that will put us back together, minus the problems we had. I'll know when I hear them. That's the best I can do."

Jake chose his words carefully. "I want to ask you a question, but I don't want you to lose your temper. Can we agree on that?"

"Go ahead."

"Are you holding off because you want to do to me what I did to you?"

She thought a minute before answering. "I don't think so. If I am, it isn't intentional. Life's too short for vengeful paybacks. I don't want to keep score anymore. I don't think a marriage benefits from that kind of mentality." She hesitated. "I've decided that the next time I marry, if there is a next time, I'm going to be a completely different kind of wife. I'm not there yet, Jake. I don't blame you if you don't want to wait for me, especially when there are no guarantees. That's up to you."

"Can you at least tell me if I have the inside track?"

She smiled. "Of course you have the inside track. You have the entire track."

He reached out and gently tugged her braid. "Then, I'll wait."

A rush of relief, so intense that she swayed on her feet, swept through her. She nodded and would have turned away, but he pulled her back into his arms and tucked her head under his chin. "Whatever happens," he said gruffly, "you're my best friend, Francie. That won't change."

Twenty-Five

Francesca climbed the front porch slowly. At the door she hesitated. How many times had she anticipated her mother's homecoming? Too many to count. Why, then, was she dreading their inevitable first meeting? Twisting the knob, she opened the door and listened. Nothing. Careful to make as little noise as possible, she crept down the hall and peeked into the living room. Still nothing. Both the dining room and the large family room were also empty. Could Lisa be in the kitchen with Julianne? She highly doubted it.

"Hello," she called out. "Is anyone home?"

Julianne's voice called from the kitchen. "In here. I'm just finishing up."

Francesca walked into the kitchen.

Her mother-in-law sat at the table holding a mug, staring out the window. Her apron hung over a chair. The collar of her white, button-down shirt was pristine. Her sleeves were rolled up to the elbow and her capri pants still had their early-morning crease. Julianne always looked tidy no matter what time it was.

Francesca sat down across from her. "Are you done for the day?"

Julianne continued to stare out the window. "Yes."

"I don't think I've ever seen you just *sitting* during a workday. Is something wrong?"

"Something is very wrong, Frances." Julianne met the younger woman's worried gaze. "I know it sounds ridiculous because it's been such a long time, but I honestly thought I'd never see your mother again. Now that I have, everything's come back and I don't quite know how to handle it."

Francesca's eyebrows lifted. "That was a mouthful. I know what she's done to Chris and me, but what has she done to you?"

"Why don't you ask her?"

"Because I don't know her. Because I'll get the truth from you."

Julianne's jaw relaxed. She reached across the table and squeezed Francesca's hand. "Bless you for that. This isn't your fault. I'm not upset with you. It all happened a long time ago. Better to let it rest."

"Where is she?"

"Doing what she does best." Julianne couldn't keep the bitterness from her voice. "Resting in the blue guest room."

Francesca looked at her watch. "It's science-club night for Nick. That gives me about an hour before he gets home." Sighing, she stood. "I'd like to get this over with before he shows up."

Julianne's jaw was tight again. "I don't want her to stay, Frances."

"For the night or permanently?"

"Neither, but one night is negotiable."

Francesca bent to kiss her mother-in-law's cheek. "I'll tell her. Don't worry about dinner. I can cook, or would you rather we go out?"

Julianne nodded. "Take her out. That would be best for all of us."

Francesca passed the door to the guest room and climbed the stairs to her own bedroom. She showered quickly, changed into fitted navy slacks and a white sweater, brushed out her hair, swiped lip gloss across her lips, replaced her small gold hoops with pearl studs, glanced in the mirror and pronounced herself ready. With her shoulders back, she descended the stairs and knocked firmly on the door to her mother's room.

At first there was no answer. She lifted her fist to knock again, when the door opened and Francesca looked at her mother's face for the first time in twenty-four years. The shock of recognition startled her. She was a little girl when Lisa disappeared from her life, and her father tolerated no pictures, but still Francesca would have known her anywhere.

"Hello," she said softly. "I'm Francesca."

Lisa, her hand at her throat, nodded and stepped aside. "Would you like to come in?"

Francesca hesitated, noting the gauzy shift her mother wore that couldn't be anything else but sleep-wear, the bed-tousled hair and dilated pupils, the pulled draperies. "I woke you. I'm sorry. I'll come back later."

Lisa shook her head. "No. Come in, please. I was

hoping you'd come. There are a few things we should clear up and it's better that we do it without an audience."

She waited until Francesca was seated in one of the wingback chairs near the window. Then she pulled the drapes aside and sat down across from her. "Let me look at you."

Francesca blushed, but allowed the inspection. She was doing the same. After a long minute, Lisa sat back in her chair. "My goodness. We're a great deal alike. I didn't expect that. Your brother is all Frank."

"You've seen Chris?"

"We've communicated occasionally over the years."

"How is he?"

"Managing, Francesca, just managing. Your father left him money, not a lot, but enough to get by." She laughed bitterly. "Certainly it's more than he left me."

Francesca, familiar with the provisions of her father's estate, kept silent.

Lisa reached for her purse and pulled out a pack of cigarettes. It was empty. "Damn." She looked at Francesca hopefully. "Do you smoke?"

"No."

Lisa sighed. "I should have known you wouldn't have vices."

Francesca ignored the comment. "What made you decide to come back?"

The green eyes flickered and lowered. Francesca noticed that her mother's nails were ragged and bitten.

"I won't insult you by saying I've had an attack of nostalgia," Lisa began. "Frankly, I was miserable here. I left with nothing. If I'd had more than a suitcase of clothes, I would have done more for you and your brother, but your father wouldn't allow it. He wanted me out of your lives, permanently." Again, she fixed her glass-green eyes on her daughter's face. "Money is power, Francesca. He had the power and I didn't. I'm back because he's gone."

"He's been gone for quite some time."

The corners of Lisa's mouth lifted. "You're no shrinking violet, are you?"

Francesca didn't answer.

"I've had some bad luck," Lisa admitted. "I'm between things right now. I was hoping you'd take me in and I could catch my breath."

"You want to stay here at the house with us?" There was no mistaking the dismay in Francesca's voice.

"Not for long, a week, maybe two."

Francesca lifted her hands to her cheeks. Her skin felt hot. "I don't know," she said slowly. "It's not up to me."

Lisa's back straightened. "Why not? Didn't Frank leave the house to you?"

"We had some bad years," Francesca explained. "There was a glut of grapes and no buyers. Jake and I expanded the winery to produce more of our own wines. Julianne gave us money, remodeled the kitchen and started her catering business. I'm the sole owner of the vineyard, but that's all." She saw no need to tell her mother that she had agreed to mortgage the winery.

"In other words, Julianne needs to give her permission."

"Julianne and Jake," Francesca amended.

"Somehow, I don't think Jake will be a problem," Lisa said dryly. She leaned forward. "Do *you* want me to stay?"

Francesca looked into her mother's beautiful face, at the arched eyebrows and the faint age lines radiating from her eyes, at the sharply defined bones, thick hair and olive skin. This was her mother, the woman who'd given her life. Would there ever be another chance to know her? "Yes," she said. "I do."

Lisa's eyes gleamed. She sat back in her chair. "Well, then. We'll just have to convince Julianne, won't we?"

"It might be difficult."

A slight, satisfied smile flickered across Lisa's face. "Leave it to me."

Julianne zipped her boots, dabbed perfume behind her ears, grabbed her jacket from the closet and ran downstairs. Jake was just coming in.

"Whoa," he said; reaching out to clasp her shoulders. "Where are you going?"

"Out for dinner."

"What about us?"

"You're grown-ups, Jake," she said sharply. "I work a full day, too. You can make your own dinner on occasion."

"Jeez, Ma, don't bite my head off. I didn't mean anything by it."

Julianne softened. "I believe Francesca is taking Nick and her mother out. You'll have to ask if you're included."

Jake studied his mother's face. "Why aren't you included?"

"I chose not to be. Obviously, as you've probably noticed, there's no love lost between Lisa and me."

"I noticed. I'd like to know why."

Julianne shook her head. "I'd rather not rehash all that again. It was a long time ago."

"It's affecting you now."

She looked at her watch. "I'm late, Jake."

He looked at his mother's face. It was a youthful face, fine-boned, exotic, filled with purpose, dignity and character, nothing like the seductive and slightly dissipated beauty of Lisa DeAngelo, a brunette whose eyes and legs never gave out. He stepped aside. "Drive carefully."

Mitch leaned over his daughter's shoulder as she entered the amount of the invoice into the accounting-software program he'd installed. "How does it look?" he asked.

She nodded. "So far, we're under budget. Things don't cost as much here as they do in San Francisco."

Mitch squeezed her shoulder. "You've been a tremendous help, Sarah. I don't know what I would do without you."

She beamed. "Thanks, Dad. It's been fun." She looked around at the furnished space, the three desks, chairs, phones and computers. "Do you think I'll still be able to help after you've hired people?"

"You can count on it. I want Drew to join us, too."

Sarah's smile faded. She drew a deep breath and formed the words she'd waited for an opportunity to voice. "I'm not sure Drew is ever going to be what you want him to be, Dad."

Mitch looked surprised. "I don't have a plan for Drew. I'd like him to use his potential, but that's about it. Most of all, I want him to be happy. I want that for both of you."

"Do you really mean that?"

"I do," her father said emphatically.

"He doesn't support what you're doing here," Sarah confessed. "He thinks GGI will ruin the smaller vineyards and bring a warehouse mentality to the valley."

Mitch nodded. "I gathered that. When did he become so concerned about Santa Ynez? As far as I know, he'd like to pack up and move back to San Francisco."

"He'd still like to do that," Sarah agreed, "but down deep he's an environmentalist. He believes in recycling and conserving fossil fuels and he won't step into a Wal-Mart. He's always been that way. When the migrant workers went on strike, he wouldn't eat grapes or lettuce. Neither would Mom," she added. "They were alike that way."

"What about you, sweetheart? Do you have an opinion on any of this?"

Sarah tilted her head. "I'm not as smart as Drew," she said finally. "I think I'm more like you than Mom."

Mitch grinned. "I'm taking that as a compliment."

"I think people are confused about what's important."

"How so?" It was odd having an intellectual conversation with his daughter. Mitch was enjoying it.

"It's easy to believe in causes when you're comfortable," she explained. "It's not so easy to be principled if you're out of work and your family can't afford to buy things." She smiled at her father. "In other words, I think there's a place for Wal-Mart. Not everyone can afford Saks or Nordstrom."

"You know what, Sarah. I think you're every bit as smart as Drew, and in some ways, maybe you're smarter."

"Don't tell him that," she warned. "He likes to have everyone think he's the brilliant one."

All at once Mitch felt weak with love for this sensitive, worried child. Impulsively he kissed the part on Sarah's head. "Don't worry so much," he said. "You're not responsible for all of us."

Sarah's eyes widened. "Maybe not *all* of us, but I am for Drew. Mom made me promise before she died."

He stared at his daughter. "Explain that, Sarah."

"Mom told me to take care of Drew. She said I would be all he had after she was gone."

Summoning all of his discipline, Mitch worked to keep his anger from showing. "She was wrong, sweetheart. People who are in the last throes of illness often say things they don't mean. You don't need to take care of Drew. What he can't manage on his own, I'll handle. You've got plenty on your shoulders just being you."

She looked unconvinced.

Mitch took her hands in his. "I'll tell you what. We'll compromise. If you think Drew is having trouble with something, let me know. Okay?"

She hesitated. "I'll try."

"That's good enough for me."

Drew rummaged through the cabinet for a nonstick pan, set it over a low flame and tossed in a pat of butter and two cloves of chopped garlic. Then he added three tofu patties and set the timer. The table was already set for three and the salad was mixed. All he had to do was reduce the sauce and steam the broccoli.

He heard the front door open, followed by his father's voice. "Something smells delicious."

Sarah called out, "Hi, Drew. We're home."

"I'm in the kitchen. Dinner's in ten minutes." He turned up the heat under the broccoli.

Ten minutes later, they were seated around the table. Mitch bit into his tofu patty carefully. He was pleasantly surprised. "This is incredible. I'm appointing you chief cook."

Drew's skin pinkened with pleasure. "Thanks."

"How's the job going?"

"Great. I'm learning a lot. It's fun. Mrs. Harris is a nice lady."

"Any calls while I was out?" Mitch asked.

The boy's flush deepened. "There's a message reminding you about my hearing on Thursday."

"Three days from now," his father said. "It's on the calendar."

"Today is Tuesday, Dad. There's another message, too. I think it's from your boss."

"My boss?"

"Yeah." Drew avoided his father's eyes. "You can listen to them if you want. I saved them both."

"I'll do that, but not until I finish this excellent meal."

Drew relaxed. "It is good, isn't it?"

The phone rang. Drew tensed while Sarah eyed her father nervously.

"Let it ring," said Mitch. "We're important, too."

Four rings later, Julianne's voice sounded from the speaker. "Hi, Mitch. Did I get the time wrong? I'll go ahead and order and try you later."

Mitch froze. Sarah clapped a hand over her mouth and Drew shook his head. "Good goin', Dad."

Mitch crushed his napkin and stood. "I'll be right

back." He walked into the den, picked up the phone and closed the door. The last several months had been nothing short of a nightmare. For the first time in his life, Mitch felt overwhelmed. The possibility of failure was very real. It served him right that the only woman he'd seriously considered in terms of forever should come into his life at the same time he'd taken on his children and a resistant community.

Quickly he punched in the numbers of Julianne's cell phone. She answered immediately. "I'm sorry, Julianne." It didn't occur to him to lie. "I got the days mixed up. I didn't realize it was Tuesday. I'm a day behind because I worked most of the weekend. Please, forgive me."

"Don't worry about it," she said too quickly. "I'll just have a quick bite to eat and go home."

Something wasn't right. "Is anything wrong, other than my lapse?"

Her silence was answer enough.

"Come over," he said.

"It's all right, Mitch. Don't worry."

"Please. Drew made dinner. I can't leave now, but I want to see you. Say you'll come."

"When?"

"Now."

She laughed and his heart lifted. "I've already ordered. I'll eat first and then I'll come."

"I'll be waiting."

He hung up the phone and took several deep restorative breaths. One hurdle passed. The others would, too. He punched the playback button and listened to his two remaining messages. The board of directors' meeting he remembered. Drew's hearing he had not. Once more he was in the position of having to choose between his children and his job.

Twenty-Six

Julianne stood in front of Mitch's front door berating herself for involving him in her personal history. She should have eaten her dinner and visited a friend, gone to the bookstore or to a movie. When was the last time she'd seen a movie? The last thing she wanted was a mercy invitation from Mitch Gillette. Contempt so often followed pity. She did not want Mitchell Gillette to feel sorry for her.

Acknowledging that the damage was already done, she raised the ring on the brass knocker. Before she let it fall, the door opened. Mitch stood there, backlit by the warm glow of a chandelier. Without speaking he held out his arms and, as naturally as if she did it every day of her life, Julianne walked into them. They closed around her. Pressing her head into his shoulder, she stood there, lapping up the comfort he offered.

"Thanks," she said shakily, pulling away. "I needed that."

"Do you want to talk about it?"

"No," she said quickly, then, "Yes." She rubbed her temples. "I don't know."

He took her hand. "Come on. We'll be more comfortable in the living room."

He led her into a comfortable room with deep couches, low tables and dim light. He poured brandy into two snifters. Gratefully, she accepted one of them. "Thank you."

He nodded and sat down beside her. "Can I help?"

"I don't think so," she began. "It's nothing really. I don't know what's wrong with me. It happened so very long ago that it shouldn't matter anyway."

"I don't know if time has anything to do with it," he said slowly. "Sometimes, things don't get resolved and we carry them around until they do."

She looked at him hopefully. "Do you have something like that, too?"

"Lord, yes. There were so many things I wanted to say to Susan and never got the chance. I used to have imaginary conversations with her where she'd actually listen and, finally, understand."

Julianne leaned forward, her expressive eyes on his face. "What went wrong between you, Mitch?"

He grimaced. "I don't know where to start. She wanted someone I wasn't. We didn't share any of the same goals. She wanted children immediately. I wanted to sock some money away first. She spent as if we had unlimited funds. The word *budget* terrified her. I suppose it didn't matter anyway, because we had a different vision for our future. In a nutshell, I was immature, she was dishonest and we were both selfish." He rotated the glass in his hand. "Not a pretty picture. I hope I'm not scaring you away."

"How old were you?"

"We married when I was twenty-seven. The kids were born three years later and we divorced two years after that."

"What did she do?"

"Whatever she pleased. She had a trust fund."

"Did you resent that?"

He leaned his head back on the cushion and stared at the ceiling. "I don't think it was the money I resented. But her money had a great deal to do with the contempt I came to feel for her. She had no goals. She never finished anything. I realized after a while that she had nothing to talk about."

"The children see her differently."

"Of course they do. And they should. Other than being a terrible role model, she was good to them."

"Is she why you never remarried?"

"A psychologist would probably say yes," he admitted.

"What about your mother? Is she still alive?"

Mitch laughed. "No, you don't. You came here because you were upset and you've got us talking about nothing but me. Tell me what's bothering *you.*"

Julianne swallowed the last of her brandy and held out her glass for more. Mitch refilled it.

"Be careful," he warned. "You're not very big."

"Francesca's mother is here," she said.

He waited.

"She left Santa Ynez when Francesca was six years old. This is the first time she's come back."

"Is there more?" he asked gently.

Julianne nodded. She swirled the amber liquid and,

tilting her head back, drained it in one gulp. Liquid fire filled her throat. Her eyes filled. She waved her hand in front of her face, momentarily diverted by an inability to utter more than a feeble rasp. "Water," she gasped.

Mitch left the couch, returning immediately with a tall glass of ice water. Julianne drank it quickly. Relief was immediate. "Thanks," she said.

"You're welcome." He grinned. "I think we should stick to wine."

She nodded, embarrassed.

"Now, what were you going to tell me?"

She knew that saying the words wouldn't make a difference. It happened. Keeping it inside had no effect on the present. Breathing deeply, she concentrated on keeping her voice steady. "Lisa DeAngelo had an affair with my husband."

He didn't react. It gave her confidence to continue. "When I found out I made him choose. The job at DeAngelo or me."

She was silent for a long time.

"And?" he probed.

Julianne lifted her chin. "Frank chose for him. *He* made her leave."

"Are you saying that Frank DeAngelo sent his wife away to keep his winemaker?"

"No." Julianne wet her lips, choosing her words carefully. Her mind was thick from the alcohol and the words were difficult to form. "Frank sent his wife away to keep his winemaker's wife."

It was well after midnight when Julianne pulled into her own driveway. She unlocked the door and tiptoed down the hall to her room. A light flicked on in the kitchen. She froze, every nerve on edge. Then, with a sense of inevitable doom, she moved toward the source.

Lisa DeAngelo sat at the small table, her long ragged fingers stroking the stem of a wine goblet. A half-empty bottle of Syrah sat in front of her. "I waited for you," she said. "I even saved some wine. Big of me, wasn't it?"

Julianne, caught up in the dreamlike fiction of the moment, floated toward her. "You shouldn't have bothered. I don't want any."

"What do you want?"

Julianne sat down and leaned her chin on her hand. "I want you to go away."

Lisa lifted one eyebrow. It emphasized the widow's peak marking the center of her forehead. "None of it was personal, you know. Neither of us thought of you."

"Obviously not."

Lisa leaned forward, her lizard-green eyes fixed on Julianne's face. "If you think about it, I should be the one hating you."

"I don't care if you hate me or not, Lisa," Julianne said calmly. "All I hoped for was to never see you again, but now that you mention it, I am curious. What have I ever done to you?"

"You made my husband fall in love with you."

Julianne moved her hand, a quick sweeping gesture, brushing away the words. "Frank was old enough to be my father. Nothing ever came of it. You know that, and yet you deliberately set out to seduce Carl. Why?"

"I wanted him," she said simply. "Frank was older and so inflexible it was hard to breathe. I couldn't live up to his expectations. Carl was impressionable, adoring. I was flattered."

She lifted one shoulder, a fluid, graceful gesture of a movement, the kind Julianne was incapable of, the kind that had ensnared Carl Harris.

"I couldn't resist."

"That's your excuse?" Julianne felt the rage boil up inside her. "That's enough to destroy two marriages?"

"The only marriage that was destroyed was mine," Lisa said evenly. "I'm the one who was forced to leave. Frank chose you over me, his *wife*. I'm the one who had to leave my home and children."

"You'll get no sympathy for me. You were to blame."

Lisa's eyes narrowed to thin glittering slits of color. "Do you think they'll canonize you, Julianne? Long-suffering wife, devoted mother. Don't you ever get tired of being perfect? Haven't you ever been tempted to do anything outside of the box you've created?"

"Unlike you, I have a conscience. Someone else's husband would be off limits."

"Why did you stay with him?"

"He was my husband, my children's father."

Lisa shook her head. "You'll have to do better than that."

Julianne rested her hands on the table. They were steady without the slightest hint of tremor. Lisa DeAngelo no longer intimidated her. She was just a woman, sad, homeless, a failure, without children or grandchildren to insulate her old age. "I would have left him if he had been with anyone else. You were different. You were evil. I knew it and Frank knew it. Carl was an innocent, completely incapable of resisting you. You were clever, more than he ever was. He was simply no match for you. I knew that if you were gone, it would never happen again. Carl loved me. You were a diversion to the dark side."

"So, that's how you justified asking Frank to send me away."

Julianne shook her head. "He came up with that one on his own. I offered to leave. He wanted Carl to stay."

"Carl Harris was an average winemaker at best," Lisa said bitterly. "You were the one Frank wanted. Admit it, Julianne."

Memories assailed her, the sharp, feral scent of her instincts before Lisa's banishment, and later, when all she'd imagined proved to be true, when the stabbing ache of her husband's betrayal was so severe she couldn't think of anything else had dulled to a bone-deep ache, Frank had been there, the port in her storm. "What are you doing here, Lisa?" she asked wearily. "Surely you can't imagine there's anything for you here."

"I wanted to see Francesca and my grandson."

"You don't care about Francesca and it would surprise me if you remember the boy's name."

"Of course I do."

Julianne was finished. She stood. "Good night, Lisa. You've had your visit. Please be gone by the time I'm up. It's late and I think I'll sleep in. Nine o'clock sounds like a reasonable time for you to leave."

Lisa pushed herself away from the table. "It's not that easy. Do you think you can send me on my way and waltz up the stairs of this house that was once mine? Think again, Julianne. You've had your nice little ordered life all these years while I've had nothing. I'm not going to fade into the woodwork so easily."

"As usual, you refuse to take responsibility for your own actions. I'm sure you'll do what you want. You always do. But this house is mine, too, and I say you go."

"Francesca wants me to stay."

Julianne felt a fist close over her heart. She pushed the doubt away. Francesca wouldn't do that to her. "I'll have to change her mind."

"Jake wants me to stay, too."

Julianne turned on her. Rage, white hot and consuming, began in the pit of her stomach. "Jake wants no such thing," she said carefully. "You leave him out of this. Do you think you can twist every man around your little finger? He's your daughter's husband, for God's sake. Have you no shame at all?"

"My, my." Lisa's eyes widened. "I think I've just found your Achilles' heel. Be careful. I might use it against you."

"I wouldn't put it past you." Julianne folded her arms. "Have you considered how your daughter would feel if you attempted to work your wiles on my son?"

"Jake and Francesca are divorced. What difference would it make to her?"

"You really are an idiot, Lisa. You never could see beyond yourself." Julianne turned to leave. "I don't want to deal with you anymore."

"See you in the morning, Julianne," the woman called after her.

The heat woke her, that and the sensation of another body occupying well over half the bed. Francesca lay

still for a minute, orienting herself to the darkness and
the unfamiliar arrangement of furniture and windows.
For an instant she was confused. This wasn't her room.
Then she remembered. It was Jake's room and something had awakened her. She turned over and looked at
the clock. It was nearly one o'clock in the morning. Jake
was deep in sleep, his breathing even and slow. He'd put
in a long day at the winery and, later at the restaurant
where they'd taken her mother, he'd played the perfect
host, unfailingly polite, slightly reserved.

Francesca was pleased with her mother. Lisa DeAngelo had exhibited just the right amount of interest and
humility for a woman who'd voluntarily been out of
touch with her family for twenty-four years. She hadn't
pretended that her behavior was normal or even acceptable and she hadn't avoided the questions, not Francesca's unspoken queries nor Nick's blunt demands.
She wouldn't mind if Lisa stayed longer. If only Julianne wasn't so adamant about having her gone. Francesca would talk to her in the morning. Maybe she
would change her mind.

Silvery fingers of moonlight parted the drapes, illu-
minating the bedposts and half the bed. Jake's twisting
had pulled the sheet loose from the end of the mattress,
leaving Francesca without enough to cover herself. She
gripped a corner and gave it a gentle tug. It was firmly
wedged under Jake's body. Rising on one elbow, she
pushed him from his side to his stomach, pulling free
the sheet as he rolled. She attempted to turn over, only
to find that her hair was caught under his chest.

Frustrated, she lay on her side, mustering the energy
to free her hair. Jake's back shook. He was laughing.

"Slide over," she hissed. "When did you get to be such a bed hog?"

He lifted his head. There was enough moonlight to see his eyes twinkle. "Since I've been sleeping alone."

"You're pulling my hair."

He sat up and she moved her head, smoothing her hair behind her back.

"How long have you been awake?" he asked.

"Not very long. I thought I heard voices. Maybe it was a dream."

"It wasn't a dream. I was on my way to the kitchen when my mother came home. Yours was in the kitchen and I don't think it was coincidental. I considered eavesdropping but my better instincts prevailed."

"I wish you had," Francesca said bluntly.

"Oh? Why is that?"

"I haven't had a mother in more than two decades. I'd like to get to know her."

"Ask her to stay."

"Julianne would have a fit. She told me Lisa could stay for the night and that was it."

Jake frowned. "It's good of you to be so considerate of my mother, Francie, but you have some say in this, too. If you want Lisa to stay, then say so."

"Do you mean that?"

"I do."

Francesca smiled into the darkness. "All right. I will."

Jake reached out to stroke her arm. She shivered.

He leaned over her, his head silhouetted by the bright moon. "Maybe I've had a memory lapse, but I don't remember doing anything more than falling into bed tonight. Am I right?"

"Yes," she said, suddenly breathless.

"I could remedy that, if you're agreeable."

"Why do you think I woke you?"

The chuckle came from deep in his throat.

Filling her hands with his hair, she pulled his head down and offered up her lips to his kiss.

Twenty-Seven

Julianne was in the middle of dusting a cinnamon-sugar mixture over her apple pastries. "Life has a way of reminding us that we shouldn't get too comfortable," was all she said when Francesca told her she'd like to extend her mother's visit by a few more days.

Francesca pulled at a corner of the dough and nibbled it absentmindedly. "She's my mother and I don't even know her," she explained. "You wouldn't want me to lose this chance, would you?"

Julianne's chin-length hair was tied back with a hot-pink bandanna knotted on top of her head. Her flushed cheeks were almost the same color and her eyes glittered with an emotion that Francesca was sure she had never seen before.

"The very idea that you have only one chance to know your mother says a great deal about your mother," Julianne answered. "I don't want her here. I've made that clear. But, this house is, for the most part, yours. My only request is that I have nothing to do with her. I can't imagine her voluntarily seeking me out, so that shouldn't be much of a problem. But I do work here."

"You really hate her, don't you?"

"Yes," said Julianne. She patted down her phyllo dough without looking up.

"What has she done to you?"

Julianne slid the tarts into the oven. "I don't want to discuss it."

Francesca picked off more dough. "Have you heard that Mitch Gillette is forcing a general election?"

"He mentioned it."

"Why would he do that?"

"I should think that would be obvious. The ecological survey came back negative. He wants to build a winery."

"Is that okay with you?"

"Of course not."

"You could use your influence, Julianne. He listens to what you say."

"That's because I don't try to tell him what to do. Mitch is my friend. I like him. I'm not going to hold that friendship over his head. It isn't fair. If a giant winery isn't what people here want, they won't vote for it."

"And if they do?"

Julianne's gaze was level, unwavering. "Then you'll have to figure something out, won't you?"

Francesca bit her lip. "It won't be easy for a new winery to compete."

"If you're referring to Soledad, I know that. I want the very best for Jake and for Soledad, but not at the expense of the people of this community, and I mean all the people, not just the fifteen families whose incomes allow them to shelter most of their profits."

"It sounds to me as if you're going to vote for GGI's winery."

Julianne sighed. "No, Frances. I'm not going to vote for the winery. But my decision is based on the county report's statistics regarding traffic and pollution and the destruction of a way of life that is specific to this valley. In the long run, I believe protecting our environment is more important than the short-term gains of minimum-wage unemployment." She washed her hands and pulled a towel off the rack to dry them. "I suggest you figure out some way of entertaining your mother while she's here. I've never known Lisa to get out of bed before noon, so your workday won't be affected all that much."

Francesca gasped. It was difficult to believe it was Julianne talking. For as long as she could remember, her mother-in-law's sweetness had soothed the tempers of all who moved within her sphere.

She decided not to respond. Grabbing her gloves, she walked out of the kitchen and nearly ran into Nick on his way to the kitchen. "Hi," she said, grabbing his shoulders to steady him. "What are you doing up so early?"

"It isn't early," he replied. "It's Tuesday and I'm late for school. How come nobody woke me up?"

Francesca's hand flew to her mouth. "Oh, no. I didn't think—Gran always—" She stopped. Why *did* she always assume that it would be Julianne who woke Nick and fed him breakfast? "I'm sorry, Nick. I'll take you to school. We'll grab something to eat on the way."

In the kitchen, Julianne sat at the table, her hands pressed against her cheeks, listening to the conversation between Francesca and Nick. How could she have forgotten to wake her grandson? She'd done it every school day of his life. Lisa's coming had rattled her more than she cared to admit. She had to get back on track no matter where Lisa DeAngelo decided to spend her time.

Change was difficult for Julianne. She wasn't afraid of it, but she didn't welcome it either. The emotion she felt when her world tipped was somewhere between acceptance and fear. *Tolerance* was the right word. She'd learned to tolerate.

Long ago, after Carl died, after the Rosary, when the mourners had gone and she was alone in the dark church, she'd come to realize that change and life were synonymous. She couldn't have one without the other and she very much wanted to hold on to life. From that moment she resolved to tolerate the unexpected as graciously as possible. And, for the most part, she had. But gracious tolerance and a passionate lust for the unusual were two very different reactions.

Much as Julianne would have liked to be the kind of woman who pulled her blouse off her shoulders and danced to Gypsy music on tabletops in a skirt slit to her hips, a woman whose chunky, silver bracelets jingled while her hands moved in symbiotic harmony with her mouth and whose hair fell to her waist in long spiral curls, she simply wasn't. Her tastes ran to pearls and fine gold chains and cashmere sweaters. Her neat, bobbed hair and petite figure inspired words like *tailored* and *classic* and *trim.* She was Melanie Wilkes to Lisa's Scarlett O'Hara and, if she were completely honest with herself, she was more than a little jealous of the Scarletts of the world.

Mitch turned down Sagunto Street and pulled into the only available parking space along the boardwalk. Santa Ynez was crowded for a Tuesday morning. The office space he'd rented for the election-campaign headquarters hummed with activity. Every desk, with the exception of his own, was occupied, mostly with professionals from out of town, flown in by the company. He hadn't had much luck recruiting the locals, but he refused to admit defeat. People who were reluctant to take a public stand still voted. Mitch was counting on those votes. His future depended on it.

He greeted the woman at the front desk, nodded at someone whose name he couldn't remember and sat down in the cubicle he'd designated for himself. His cell phone rang. He looked at the number in the window identifying the caller, spent exactly three seconds debating whether to answer it and pressed the call button.

"Hello," he said tersely. Then, "Yes, the meeting is on my calendar, but as I explained in my memo, I'm not able to attend." Another minute passed. "I'm sorry, but it's a personal issue." His jaw tensed. "I'm aware of that. Under normal circumstances, I wouldn't hesitate to change the appointment, but this time it isn't possible. No. I don't believe so. Of course, I'll try," he said impatiently, "but it's highly unlikely. Please convey my apologies to the board."

Pressing the call button, he cut off the chairman of GGI's board of directors, turned off the power on the cell phone and stared, unseeing, at the portable wall in front of him. Drew's court date and GGI's board meeting conflicted and he wasn't about to send his son to appear before a judge with only his lawyer in attendance. He swore under his breath. In every aspect of his life the deck appeared to be stacked against him. Never had he wanted out of the corporate world more than he did right now.

Mitch was feeling very unlike himself. Normally, he welcomed a challenge, and constructing a new winery in the Santa Ynez Valley was definitely that. Maybe he should take Julianne's advice and give self-employment a shot. Get out while he was still on top. Soon, he might not have a choice.

"Mitch?" Leanne Houston, a staff worker from northern California, peered over the wall. "I think we have our first recruit," she whispered. "Do you want to meet her?"

"Why not?" He rose and walked around the cubicle partition. The woman stood silhouetted in front of the window with the morning sun behind her. He couldn't see her face, but the body and stance he recognized immediately. Francesca DeAngelo was no recruit.

It took no more than an instant and a few more steps in the woman's direction for him to realize that she wasn't Francesca. She was older by twenty years, leaner and harder, with skin more olive than gold and very dark hair. Still, the resemblance was remarkable. He would have known Lisa DeAngelo without the introduction.

"Good morning," he said. "I'm Mitch Gillette. How can I help you?"

She looked around. "I want to volunteer. Tell me what to do."

His eyes flickered over her short khaki skirt and crocheted vest. She wore high-heeled sandals and silver earrings that swept her shoulders when she moved. Her hair was pulled away from her face and held back with a bananna clip. But whatever she wore wouldn't have mattered. She was a woman worth a second look.

Mitch cleared his throat. "Are you sure you're up for this, Mrs. DeAngelo?"

She turned the full effect of her moss-green eyes on his face. "How do you know my name?"

"You look like your daughter."

The corners of her mouth turned up. "I'd rather not admit to that. I don't feel nearly that old."

"You do know that Francesca is against us."

"What does that have to do with me?"

Mitch studied her for a minute. "I'm sure we can figure out something for you to do. There's a chair in my office. Will you join me?"

"That's the best offer I've had all day," she purred, preceding him down the aisle to his cubicle.

Leanne Houston, typing away on her computer, raised her eyebrows. Mitch struggled to control his laughter. He hadn't been on the receiving end of such blatant flirtation in years.

Lisa sat down opposite his desk and crossed her legs. Mitch leaned against his desk, arms folded, and tried, unsuccessfully, not to notice. "What are you doing here?" he asked bluntly.

"I told you. I came to volunteer."

"Surely you know that Francesca and every other vintner in the valley are opposed to this election. She won't be pleased."

"I gathered that."

"And you still want to volunteer?"

"Yes."

"Why?"

"Does it matter?"

He considered her question. "I think so."

Beneath the khaki skirt, one leg swung back and forth. "Let's just say I'd like to repay old debts."

"How will your presence here do that?"

She shrugged. "The DeAngelo name stands for something in this valley. A DeAngelo campaigning for the winery wields some influence. You won't be sorry."

"Is this a vendetta for past slights?"

She laughed. "Where would you get an idea like that?"

"I imagine you already have the answer to that question."

"Ah." The syllable came from deep down in her throat. "The estimable Julianne Changala Harris."

"Well?" Mitch asked.

"I'm trying to follow my daughter's advice and make myself useful away from the house. Julianne and I don't see eye to eye. The more I'm out from under her feet, the better it will be for the entire family."

"Why did you come back?"

She arched one eyebrow. "Honestly?"

"Honestly."

Her smile faded and all traces of the coquette disappeared. "I had nowhere left to go," she said softly. "This is my last shot."

He frowned. "Are you saying you're destitute?"

She lifted her chin. "Hardly that, but I'm out of choices."

He held her gaze until she looked away. Finally, he nodded. "All right. I'll put you on the phones two afternoons a week."

"Is that all?"

He stood. The interview was over. "If you really want to make yourself useful, Mrs. DeAngelo, you might help Jake and Francesca in the vineyard. They have their plates full right now. An extra pair of hands would be appreciated."

"I doubt that Julianne would approve."

"You'll have to change her mind, won't you?"

Lisa tilted her head. "May I ask you a personal question?"

"Go ahead."

"How well do you know Julianne Harris?"

He grinned. "Not nearly as well as I'd like to."

"So, that's the way it is."

"Yes."

"Too bad." Lisa stood and walked toward him. She trailed a finger down his arm. "Is she playing hard to get?"

He backed away. "She thinks highly of herself. I think she's worth the wait."

"Maybe I could fill in while you're waiting."

Mitch laughed. "You're an interesting woman, Lisa DeAngelo, but I don't think so."

Her cheeks flamed. "Why not?"

"You're not my type."

Her facade vanished. "I'm not asking you to marry me, for God's sake. I could use a friend around here, that's all."

"I've found people here to be quite friendly."

"Present company excepted," she muttered.

He laughed. "I know your number and I'm not biting. If you really intend to fit in, you'll have to go about it a different way. Try making yourself useful."

Lisa stared at him. "She told you, didn't she?"

Mitch ignored her question and stepped aside. "You can start tomorrow if you're still willing to help out. Leanne will show you the ropes. Do you mind knocking on doors or would you rather make phone calls?"

"I'm definitely more of an answering phones kind of person."

"Really?" His eyebrows lifted. "I would have thought you'd prefer a more public presence."

"Screw you!" she said sweetly and walked past him out the door.

"Not anytime soon," he said under his breath and sat down again.

Twenty-Eight

On Wednesday, Julianne drove down the highway toward the town center of Santa Ynez deep in conversation with herself. Francesca had a right to come to her own conclusions about her mother. Most people had family members they would rather not have. Mothers weren't all cut from the same cloth. Some women looked to their mothers for everything, called them daily for advice, dropped in for coffee, scheduled shopping trips. Others made the obligatory phone call once a week, sent a Mothers' Day card in May and that was it. Francesca had the choice taken from her too early and by the one person whose love was supposed to be unconditional. But she was intelligent. She wouldn't be taken in by the likes of Lisa DeAngelo.

"Stop trying to control everything," Julianne said out loud. "Let the girl come to her own conclusions."

The thing of it was, Julianne considered herself to be Francesca's mother figure. Over the years, she'd grown protective of Frank DeAngelo's discarded daughter. As a little girl, all dark eyes and long legs, abandoned by her mother, disregarded by her father, Francesca had pulled at Julianne's heart. That hadn't changed in thirty years. Jake's defection hadn't helped Francesca's confidence either. And now Lisa was back and, because she was Lisa, more damage was inevitable.

Julianne didn't usually spend time agonizing over what she couldn't change. Deliberately, she forced herself to think of something else. Drew's hearing was tomorrow and he'd specifically asked for her to be there. She pulled into a parking spot down the street from Mitch's campaign headquarters and reached into the back for the bag of muffins she'd made earlier. It was as good an excuse as any for a visit.

It was the first time Julianne had been to the campaign office. She pushed open the door and looked around. A woman draped in an oversize green T-shirt with the words *Save a Tree* was seated behind a desk staring at a computer screen. A young man barely out of his teens, with an intense look on his face, was arguing with someone over the phone. She spotted Mitch immediately. His back was to the door, and looking up at him as if every word was gospel to live by was Lisa DeAngelo.

"May I help you?" the T-shirted woman asked.

Julianne's smile was brilliant and unnatural. "I'm Julianne Harris." She held up her bag. "I've brought muffins."

"I don't think anyone ordered any muffins."

"No one did. They're my treat."

"Oh." The woman looked surprised. "Thank you. Would you care to meet Mr. Gillette? He's in charge."

"That won't be necessary," Julianne said. Mitch had turned around and, over Lisa's head, their eyes met and held.

Julianne set the bag down on the front desk. "Enjoy the muffins." She turned and walked quickly out the door. The burn in her stomach intensified. She rifled through her purse for her keys. Where were they? Her heart pounded and her chest felt tight. She pulled at the car door. It was locked. Her tears were very close to the surface. Soon, very soon, she would lose control. She left the car and walked down the street, blind to everything around her. Where could she go?

She heard Mitch shout her name. Ignoring him, she quickened her pace. Across the street, Marcy Goodman waved to her from the bakery. She liked Marcy even though her bakery was Julianne's competition. She forced herself to wave back. She needed to find a private place, somewhere safe without people, to find her keys, collect her thoughts, corral her emotions. But where?

Footsteps sounded behind her. A hand reached out and gripped her arm, swinging her around. Mitch looked down at her, a concerned frown marring the space between his eyebrows. "What's the matter? Didn't you hear me call you?"

She blinked her eyes against the tears threatening to spill over. "No," she lied.

He searched her face. "You're angry."

"I'm furious."

"Why?"

She jerked her arm away. "Don't be ridiculous."

"I suggested she help Francesca at the winery. She said you wanted her out of the way."

"I want her gone."

"That's unrealistic, Julianne," he said gently. "She's Francesca's mother."

"That didn't stop her from running away twenty-four years ago. She wasn't here for Francie's graduation from high school or college. She wasn't here for her wedding or when she had Nick. As far as I'm concerned, she's abrogated all rights to motherhood."

"Shouldn't that be Francesca's call?"

"Maybe," Julianne conceded, "but it certainly shouldn't be yours."

"What are you talking about?"

"You're giving her a reason to stay."

"I did it for you," he protested. "For your family."

Scorn laced every syllable. "I doubt that very much."

His jaw clenched. "Are you suggesting I have another motive?"

Julianne's anger had faded to resigned contempt. Her mind was sharp again. "Lisa DeAngelo is a magnet for any man between fifteen and seventy. She can't help herself. She's completely without morals. She's beautiful, which helps, and very sexy, and you've bought into it. She's no more interested in helping your cause than I am. I suppose I should be grateful she's taken with you. That way maybe she'll leave my son alone, although I doubt it. I only pray that Jake, at least, is smart enough to see through her, even if he is his father's son."

"You're not being objective, Julianne. The woman is working in my office. Eight other people also work there. I have no interest in Mrs. DeAngelo. Even if you hadn't told me what transpired between you, I wouldn't be interested. Yes, she's attractive. I'll even admit that she's beautiful. But so is Francesca and I'm not the slightest bit interested in her, either."

Julianne swallowed. The steel-wool feeling in her throat wouldn't go away. "You don't understand. Carl wasn't *interested* in her either, not seriously. He loved me. He was terrified of losing me. When it came to a choice between us, she lost. But it doesn't take away the pain of knowing that my husband was unfaithful because he couldn't help himself. Our life, our family, *I* wasn't enough beside the temptation of a woman who refused to lift a finger in the operation of the vineyard, who spent her days watching soap operas while waiting for the socially correct time to start mixing martinis, a woman who never read a book or a newspaper and who thought that Zimbabwe was an exotic perfume. Lisa is potent. She's also relentless. She made a shambles of my life for a very long time. I can't risk it again." She threw down the gauntlet. "I won't see you or allow myself to care for you if you have anything to do with her."

Mitch shook his head. "I'm an adult, Julianne. I made an enormous and regrettable relationship mistake once in my life. I won't be making another. I'm sorry your husband hurt you. But it isn't sound or fair for you to blame me, or any other man, for his mistake. Frankly, it doesn't sound to me that you married a man worthy of you. You've done much better for yourself now that you're alone. I've fallen in love with you. It's taken me a long time to say that to a woman. You're spunky and intelligent and classy, and so sexy I have a hard time keeping my hands off you, except that I know you're not ready for that. I can wait because I'm in for the duration. It isn't likely I'm going to be diverted by anyone as transient or as obvious as Lisa DeAngelo."

She crossed her arms, fighting the urge to fling herself against his chest and cling to him, crying out, *I'm ready. I'm ready.* Instead, she said, "Why won't you tell her to go?"

"Because that's nothing more than offering an aspirin to heal your cancer. You've been living with this for nearly thirty years without resolution because she's been out of the picture. You've convinced yourself you can't compete with her at the most basic level. I'm telling you you're wrong and I'll prove it. Lisa DeAngelo can move into my back bedroom for all I care and it won't matter because all I see is you. As for Jake, he's in love with Francesca. He won't be making his father's mistake."

Julianne stared at him, emotions roiling through her. She'd listened to him, but she was far from convinced. The bottom line was that Lisa was staying. Because of Mitch, she had an excuse to stay. "I've got work to do," she said woodenly. "Tell Drew I haven't forgotten about tomorrow. I'll be there."

"Julianne." He held her shoulders. His lips brushed the top of her head. "Don't go like this."

"I'm no good right now," she explained, pulling away. "You said things I've never considered before. Now I need to think, not talk. Please don't try to stop me."

He watched her walk away, worried but slightly reassured by her words. One of the qualities he most admired in her was her ability to step back and analyze.

Today was an aberration. Normally she wasn't impulsive, or temperamental, or over-the-top emotional. He liked her evenness, her grounded common sense. She would come around. She wouldn't be Julianne if she didn't.

Nick tiptoed to the kitchen door and looked around. His excuse was a cookie and a glass of milk. What he really wanted was his grandmother back. She was the constant in Nick's short life, always ready with something delicious to eat, a ready smile and a word of praise. Unlike his parents, she had time to listen to him talk. His friends liked her, too. She knew when to ask questions and when to nod her head and say nothing. Nick loved her. She was tied with his mother for favorite-person-in-his-life status. He'd never heard her raise her voice except to call him in for dinner and yet, yesterday, he heard her yell at his other grandmother, the new one, the one he'd never seen before.

As far as Nick was concerned, if Gran didn't like his new grandmother, the one who told him to call her Lisa, he didn't like her either. Today, while he was at school listening to his teacher read from *Stuart Little,* he decided to tell her. Maybe she would smile again. Maybe she would even laugh.

Filled with a sense of purpose, he called out from the door. "Hi, Gran."

She looked up and immediately smiled. "Hi, sweetie. Is it that time already?"

He nodded.

"Are you hungry?"

He wasn't, but refusing food wouldn't get him anywhere. "Yes."

"Really?" She looked surprised. "For real food or something sweet?"

"A cookie and milk."

Again she smiled. "I have just the thing." She unwrapped a plate arranged with an array of supersize cookies and offered it to Nick along with a napkin. "Help yourself."

He chose a chocolate chunk, set it and the napkin on the table and poured himself a glass of milk. "Do you want any?" he asked.

She thought a minute. "I do. Pour a glass for me. I'll have a cookie, too."

"Choose peanut butter and we can share," Nick suggested. He poured a glass of milk for Julianne and left the carton on the table.

She laughed and he felt better.

"So," she began when they were seated across from each other at the small table. "Don't you have practice tonight?"

"I didn't go," he informed her.

She bit into her cookie. "Why not?"

"Mom couldn't pick me up and Dad said he'd be working late."

Julianne frowned. "No one asked me. I could have picked you up."

"Mom said not to bother you."

Julianne's cheeks flamed. "Next time ask me anyway."

"It's okay," he reassured her. "I haven't missed any other practices. I won't get in trouble."

"I'm relieved to hear that. But, next time, I still want you to ask me. Okay?"

"Okay." He swung his legs back and forth under the table. "Is Lisa still here?"

"I think so."

"I don't like her very much. Do you?" he asked innocently.

Her answer would influence Nick. She knew that. "Why don't you like her?" she hedged.

He shrugged. "She talks too much and she laughs too loud."

"Those aren't reasons to dislike someone, Nick." She refilled his glass. "I'd wait until you know her better before you make any judgments."

"You don't like her," he observed.

"No," Julianne said honestly. "But I knew her a long time ago. Maybe she's changed. Anyway, she isn't *my* grandmother. She's yours."

"How long is she staying?"

"I don't know." She brushed the hair away from his forehead. Such a solemn little boy with Francie's big brown eyes. "Why?"

"Mom said she was making dinner until Lisa left."

"She misunderstood. I'll make dinner just like I always do."

He nodded. "Good."

She laughed. "Any preferences?"

"Hamburgers."

"With French fries?"

"And ice cream," he added. "Peppermint-stick."

"We'd better go to the store. I don't think we have peppermint-stick ice cream."

* * *

Four hours later a serene Julianne presided over a meal of hamburgers, French fries, sweet corn and peppermint-stick ice cream.

Jake licked the back of his spoon. "Great food, Mom," he said, flashing her a genuine smile. "Not your usual gourmet spread, but a nice change."

Nick piped up. "I picked the ice cream."

"Thank you, buddy. It's my favorite." His father winked at him. "There was a time when peppermint only came out at Christmas time."

"What a shame," murmured Lisa.

"You're not eating your dessert," Francesca said to her mother.

"It's not my favorite."

"Oh." Francesca looked worried. "Can I get you anything else?"

"No, thank you. I don't eat dessert." She rested her hand on her concave stomach. "After a certain age, a woman needs to be careful of her figure."

Jake's eyebrows lifted. "You're kidding! You could stand to eat dessert now and then, Lisa."

"I'll take that into consideration," Lisa replied sweetly.

Julianne reached across the table for Lisa's ice cream and set it in front of Nick. "You know what they say," she said to her grandson.

"What?"

"One man's misfortune is another's gain. Live it up."

He beamed. *"Two* ice creams in one day?"

Not once did she look at Francesca. "Only on very special days."

He dug into the ice cream. "My project is due tomorrow," he announced.

"Are you finished?" his mother asked.

"I need help with the map and I need to bring in Indian corn bread."

"What kind of map? Jake asked.

"It's a relief map. I have to make it with flour and water."

Francesca looked alarmed. "How long have you known about this map?"

"Since the beginning. I told you a long time ago."

"And you waited until tonight to remind us? I have a board meeting." She looked at Jake. "What about you?"

He shook his head slowly. "I told you I have to present papers to the loan rep tonight. I'll try to get back as early as I can, but I can't cancel. What if we do it after I get back?"

"It'll be too late. Nick will be in bed."

Julianne spoke up. "I'll help him. We'll make the corn bread and put together the map at the same time."

"Don't you have food to get ready for tomorrow?" Francesca asked.

"I'll do that after Nick goes to bed, unless—" Julianne looked at Lisa. "Maybe you could help him."

"That's okay, Mom," Nick said quickly. "I'll figure it out."

"I'm sure you will, Nick?" Lisa's voice fluttered. "I wouldn't know the first thing about it. Besides, I've worked all afternoon at the campaign office. I'm exhausted."

The silence was difficult.

Finally Julianne spoke. "We've all worked today."

"Maybe Nick needs to learn not to leave his homework until the last minute," Lisa suggested. "Let it be a lesson for him."

"I didn't leave it," Nick protested.

"Give the kid a break," said Jake. "He's eight years old."

Francesca spoke carefully, directing the full force of her words at her mother. "He didn't leave it until the last minute. The rest of the project is done. He forgot to remind us. There's a difference. Nick is not irresponsible."

"It's all beside the point anyway. Julianne can help him."

Francesca folded and refolded the napkin in her lap. Her cheeks burned and it was an effort to keep her voice level. "Julianne is busy." She smiled at her son. "I'll help you, sweetheart, and next time, I'll put the date your project is due on the calendar."

"Well." Lisa affected a yawn. "Now that it's all settled, I think I'll turn in." She stood. "Good night."

They watched her leave. Silence, thick as syrup, settled over the table.

Jake rubbed his chin. "She's an original. I'll give you that."

Francesca's cheeks were very red.

Julianne smiled at Nick. He smiled back.

Twenty-Nine

The following morning, Mitch waited at the foot of the stairs for Drew. The boy's pants fit and his shirt was tucked in, but those were the only concessions he'd made for his court appearance.

"A suit and tie would be better," his father said.

"I don't have a suit."

"You had one for your mother's funeral."

"It doesn't fit anymore. I'm three inches taller."

Once again Mitch was conscious of a sense of failure where his children were concerned. He didn't even notice that Drew had outgrown his clothes. And what of Sarah? Girls always needed clothes. They loved to shop. And yet Sarah had never once asked him for money for clothing. "I'm sorry, Drew. The next time you need something, let me know."

"Hey, Dad, it's okay. No one wears suits anyway, except to—" He stopped before voicing it, the only time he'd needed a suit.

Mitch cleared his throat. "Are you up for something to eat?"

"Maybe later, when it's over."

"Okay." He held the door open. "Shall we?"

The courthouse located in the downtown beach community of Santa Barbara was a white, Spanish-style building, with red tiles and thick walls, its courtyard surrounding a sea of green grass and lush foliage. The interior was cool and dim. The doors were wood and so low that a man six feet or taller had to bend his head to step into the various rooms lining the corridor. People gathered in small groups, lawyers clutching briefcases dressed in expensive suits, their clients wary, nervous, arms crossed protectively against their chests, all speaking in hushed voices. Mitch looked around for Drew's attorney. He hadn't yet arrived.

"Do you think I'll go to jail?" Drew asked.

"Of course not." Mitch's voice was sharp.

Drew released his breath. "Good."

"Have you been worrying?"

The boy nodded.

"I told you it wouldn't come to that. Yours is a first offense. You've never been in trouble before and you're fifteen years old. All of that will be taken into consideration."

Drew decided not to tell his father that he'd never told him any such thing. They'd never discussed what might happen or even the circumstances of the crime. Beyond a terse "This will never happen again," Drew's dabble in the drug trade was a taboo subject. As far as he knew there was a chance he could be led away in handcuffs.

A large man in a rumpled suit with a swath of hair combed over his freckled head sat down on the bench beside them. He was breathing heavily. "Hello, Mitch." He held out his hand.

Mitch shook it. "This is Drew."

"A pleasure." The man pumped Drew's hand and smiled so that his eyes disappeared in folds of skin. "I'm Declan O'Shea. I'll be representing you in court."

"Nice to meet you," Drew mumbled.

He spoke directly to Drew. "Let's get down to business. It's an open-and-shut case if you plead guilty. You'll be released, put on probation and assigned community service. If you're not guilty, there will be a trial and we'll have to prove your innocence. The judge won't like that."

"I thought I was innocent until proven guilty."

"Nice idealistic principle. But not in juvenile court." Again the attorney's eyes disappeared with his smile. "Actually, not in any court I've ever been in. The truth is, here in California, if you're white, rich, can post bail and are represented by an outside attorney, you'll probably walk. Small brown people who come before the judge in handcuffs and orange jumpsuits serve time. So, what's it gonna be?"

Did he really need a lawyer for this? Was this a real lawyer? He looked at his father. "Dad?"

Mitch frowned. "Mr. O'Shea has been practicing law here for a long time, Drew. You were caught with a large amount of marijuana, more than you could possibly use yourself. The charges could be very serious. The choice is yours, but the evidence is against you. I suggest you plead guilty and accept the consequences.

You're a minor. You can have your record sealed when you're eighteen."

"Or, you could leave it as is," said O'Shea. "Sometimes a minor drug conviction isn't as much of a deterrent to a future employer as a sealed record. It's up to you."

Drew hung his head. "I'll plead guilty."

"Hey." The lawyer held up his hands. "If you're not guilty, just say so. If you're up front with me and you're really innocent, I'll get you off. If not, a plea is the way to go." Suddenly the folksy accent disappeared altogether. "Are you innocent, Drew?"

The boy shook his head. "No."

O'Shea sighed. "No. I didn't think so. You guys never are. It's a good thing you spilled the beans on your friend, Saunders, and that his story agreed with yours. That will go in your favor. So will the fact that your involvement was minor. I understand you're an honors student. Does that still stand?"

"Yes."

"Is there anyone who can vouch for your character, teachers, family friends?"

"I work for Julianne Harris at DeAngelo Vineyards. She said she'd be here."

Mitch cleared his throat. "We can't assume that, Drew. Something might have come up. Let's just go with what we have now."

O'Shea nodded. "Fine by me." He looked at his watch. "It's time to go in."

He led the way down an aisle flanked by auditorium seats. Drew and Mitch followed him to the first row of seats. They watched as their lawyer and the prosecuting attorney conferred. After several minutes, O'Shea sat down beside Drew.

After a minute, the flutterings in Drew's stomach settled and he looked around as the courtroom slowly filled from back to front. Nearly everyone his own age was accompanied by parents, work-weary mothers and fathers, more shabbily dressed than not, who looked as if they would rather be anywhere else than here. His father's dark suit and crisp tie stood out.

Drew was cold, with an empty, barren, bone-aching cold. It was the uncomfortable kind that no amount of heat from the outside, no warm jacket or hot drink could change. It began at the base of his spine and radiated up and outward to his fingers and toes, his ears and the tip of his nose. Gingerly he touched his nose. It didn't feel cold.

Someone slid into the seat beside him. He glanced sideways. Julianne Harris caught his eye and smiled at him. He smiled back. The cold receded.

"Sorry I'm late," she whispered. "I couldn't find a parking space."

"It's okay," Drew whispered back. "Nothing's started yet."

The bailiff turned to the courtroom. "All rise for The Honorable Susannah Merriman."

Collectively, everyone stood.

"Raise your right hands," the bailiff intoned. "Do you swear to tell the truth, the whole truth and nothing but the truth? Answer I do."

"I do." The chant filled the high-ceilinged room.

"Please be seated."

One by one the accused stood before the judge. After

a while, Drew relaxed and listened, drawn into the personal dramas around him.

Judge Merriman was fair. She listened, asked questions and meted out sentences with a calculated impartiality that could only have been learned through long years on the bench.

Finally it was Drew's turn. The bailiff called his name. Slowly, he walked to the front of the courtroom. Declan O'Shea stood on one side of him, his father on the other.

The judge read the charges. Then she looked at him over the rim of her glasses. "Do you understand the charges?"

Drew nodded.

"Answer the question for the court reporter," the bailiff ordered.

"Yes."

"Your Honor," O'Shea whispered.

"Yes, Your Honor," Drew repeated.

"How do you plead?"

"My client pleads guilty, Your Honor. This is Drew Gillette's first offense. There are mitigating circumstances, which have been discussed with the prosecution. They have agreed to community service and probation. In addition, his high school has allowed him to return in good standing."

Judge Merriman fixed her gaze on the young female prosecutor. "Is that correct, Miss Shaw?"

"Yes, Your Honor."

"I'm inclined to agree except for the amount of the goods he was carrying." She looked at Drew. "I'm concerned about that."

Julianne stood. She looked very crisp and sincere in

her white suit and pearl earrings. "Your Honor, I'd like to say something."

"State your name."

"Julianne Harris."

The judge smiled. "I thought I recognized you. Do you remember me, Mrs. Harris?"

"I do, Your Honor."

"Are you still teaching?"

"No. I'm in the catering business."

"I'll tell my daughter. She still talks about you."

Julianne laughed. "Oh, dear."

Judge Merriman returned her smile. "How do you know Drew Gillette, Mrs. Harris?"

"He works for me. He's conscientious and intelligent. I think he had a difficult time when he first came. He recently lost his mother to cancer. To move away from everything familiar was difficult for him. Please take that into consideration."

The judge was silent for a minute. "Very well," she said. "So ruled, with the added stipulation that the boy's driver's license be suspended for an additional year." She looked at Drew. "That means you won't be able to apply for a license or drive alone until your seventeenth birthday, even with drivers' training. Do you understand that, Drew?"

Relief left him weak. "Yes, Your Honor."

Outside, Mitch, Drew, Julianne and Declan O'Shea gathered at the bottom of the steps. Drew shook his lawyer's hand. "Thanks."

"Don't thank me. You got lucky with this lady." He nodded at Julianne. "How often do you find a character witness who taught the judge's daughter?" He grinned. "I'll be on my way. Don't get into any more trouble. You won't be so lucky next time."

Julianne kissed Drew on the cheek. "I'm happy for you. It could have been much worse."

"Thanks to you, it wasn't," said Mitch. "Can we take you to lunch?"

"No, thanks. I've got things to do at home. Will I see you tomorrow, Drew?"

The boy nodded. "Right after school."

Man and boy watched her walk away. "She's a nice lady," Drew said.

Mitch nodded. Then he looked at his son. "There isn't much point into driving back to school today. How about choosing a restaurant for lunch? There's got to be something vegetarian around here."

"You choose. I can get a salad anywhere."

Mitch checked his watch. "Let's leave a message for Sarah. She's worried sick about you."

"She's at school."

"I told her to check in with the office."

Drew looked skeptical.

"I won't be specific, Drew," his father reassured him, pulling out his cell phone. "I'll just say everything worked out well."

Drew waited for his father to fill Sarah in on the morning. Then they walked side by side down State Street, Santa Barbara's trendy shopping district. Drew looked at the menu of an outdoor café and pronounced it acceptable.

They ordered and had made serious inroads on the bread and butter, when Drew cleared his throat. "I don't think I thanked you, Dad."

Mitch smiled. "No. You didn't."

"This hasn't been easy for you either, has it?"

"It's been hell." He shook his head. "My hat's off to your mother. I had no idea raising children could be such an emotional roller coaster. She did most of it alone and I'm sorry for that."

"I guess I didn't think you cared all that much."

Mitch's eyes were very bright. "You're damn right I care. I couldn't sleep last night worrying about the worst that could happen to you. Why did you do it, Drew?"

Drew shrugged. "I don't know, really. Nothing seemed to matter." He looked at his father. "It's hard to explain. I wasn't feeling anything anymore. At first, that was okay. I didn't want to feel. When Mom died it hurt so much, all I wanted was to sleep everything away. Then, things changed. I couldn't feel even when I wanted to. I guess I wanted something bad to happen to me, just to see if I could care about anything."

"What have you learned from this?"

Drew returned his father's look steadily. "I've learned that what I do affects other people, good people. Sarah and you and Mrs. Harris, even the teachers at school. I won't be doing anything stupid again."

Mitch's eyes twinkled. "Let's not go that far. After all, you *are* a teenager."

It was good to see his father smile. "All right. Stupid, maybe. Illegal, no."

"That's good enough for me."

Jake hung up the phone and stared glumly at the desk calendar. He'd asked Gene Cappiello to wait thirty days before accepting GGI's offer, hoping he could get loan approval in plenty of time. Now that the news about the valley's water-table problems and the crack in the dam was out, property values had dropped. DeAngelo Winery's appraisal had come in too low, even though the damage had been isolated and repairs on the dam were in progress. He would need more collateral to purchase Soledad, and all he had was two weeks before his thirty days were up. If he didn't find more money immediately, Gene would sell to GGI.

Francesca walked into the office from the cave. She rubbed her arms. "I'm freezing."

He pulled off his sweatshirt and threw it at her. She tugged it over her head and thrust her arms through the sleeves. "Mmm. It's warm and it smells like you. Thanks."

"No problem."

His tone gave his mood away. She frowned. "What's the matter?"

He looked at her, torn between working it through himself or telling her and allowing her to rescue him. More than anything, he wanted to tell her what was on his mind. She was great when the chips were down. Francesca was smart, with an analytical mind designed for problem solving. She was also his best friend, all of which should have had him spilling his worries. Two years ago he wouldn't have hesitated. But this time he held back. This time he wanted to rise to the occasion, handle it himself, make her proud. Francesca loved him. He knew that. He also knew that she wasn't sold on him. He had the feeling that if he didn't manage this one on his own, she would forever find him wanting.

She stood there, long hair falling over her shoulders, Bambi eyes, dark and watchful, filling up her face. She was so beautiful his heart hurt.

His forehead cleared. "I'm thinking that we should lock the door, spread a blanket on the floor and make love until we're dizzy."

She blushed. "All right."

"I'm serious."

"So am I."

He pushed the chair away from the desk and walked toward her slowly, a smile starting in his eyes. The winery could wait. Everything could wait but this moment and this feeling with this woman, his woman.

She met him halfway, clasping her arms around his neck, pulling his head down to meet her lips. Her cheeks were cold from the cave and her mouth tasted like blackberries. "Have you been sampling the must?" he asked, coming out of the kiss.

She nodded. Her eyes were closed. Tenderly, he kissed both eyelids, her cheeks and her nose. "There's only one thing I want more than this."

Francesca pulled back to look at him. "What's that?"

"I want you to tell me we'll always have this, whenever we want, when we're old and shriveled."

"I'll never be shriveled," she teased him.

"I won't care if you are."

She searched his face and her arms dropped to her sides. "We're not going to do this, are we?"

"No."

"Why not?"

"Because it isn't enough. Not without the rest of it. Because if we keep doing this and then you decide it's over for good, I won't be able to stand it."

"I thought men were different."

"How so?"

"I thought sex and love were two different things for a man."

"Not this one. Not with you."

Then she asked the question she'd wanted to ask for two long years. "Has there been anyone else, Jake?"

He opened his mouth to speak, but she stopped him, her fingers against his lips. "Please tell me the truth. I can take the truth, but I can't take a lie if I found out later."

"There's been no one else, Francie. There never has been. Not for me."

She looked into his eyes. They were blue and clear and serious. She believed him.

"Thank you. I needed to hear that."

He nodded.

"Aren't you going to ask me the same question?"

"No."

"Why not?"

"Because if there has been someone else, I don't want to know. I don't think I could take it."

"Would you still want me if there had been?"

His eyes clouded. "Yes. I'd still want you. I know you, Francie. If you commit, it means forever. If it's me you want, there won't be anyone else."

"I wanted there to be," she confessed. "I wanted to forget all about you and find someone wonderful."

"I deserved that."

"But it never happened. No one appealed to me."

He grinned. "I'm flattered and more than a little relieved."

She looked at her watch. "Nick will be out of school soon. Shall we pick him up together?"

"How about the three of us grabbing a bite to eat in town?"

"What about our mothers?"

"Now that you mention it, I was hoping to avoid them."

Francesca frowned. "It's not going very well, is it?"

"No."

"Shall I ask mine to leave?"

"Is that what you want, Francie?"

"I don't know," she said truthfully. "She isn't what I expected."

"Don't do anything until you know for sure what you want. It'll come to you."

"Meanwhile, what do we do?"

"We collect our son and eat in town."

Francesca picked up the desk phone. "I'll relay the news."

Thirty

Mitch stared in disbelief at the television screen. Voting results were in and GGI's winery had gone down two to one. The citizens of the Santa Ynez Valley had chosen no growth over jobs. Who would have thought such a thing would happen? Mitch was stunned. He'd never judged a situation so poorly. There would be no conglomerate vineyard and winery in Santa Ynez. All the blueprints, the land purchases, the contractors waiting to break ground were moot. For the first time in his career, he'd been dead wrong.

The telephone rang. He looked at the clock. It was after 11:00 p.m. Using the remote, he turned off the television and glanced at the caller-ID screen. Then he answered the phone.

Leland Hawkins, chairman of the board, didn't bother to identify himself. "What happened, Mitch?"

"We lost."

"Obviously. The question is *why?*"

Answers, glib and conciliatory, passed through

Mitch's mind. He could prevaricate, ask for more time to get the message out. He could request additional money and staff. He could say that the vote was close enough to warrant another go at it next time around. But he did none of those things. "This is a different kind of community, Leland. People like things the way they are. They see no need for a massive winery."

The silence on the other end of the line was a long one. Finally, Hawkins spoke. "That's your final assessment?"

"I'm afraid so."

"I assume the water problems in the area still exist."

"The crack in the dam has been repaired. There's nothing wrong with the acreage. It could be ready for planting next year. However, the site isn't far from a fault line and buyers could be skittish. It could take some time to sell."

"All right. Wrap it up as quickly as possible. There's a site in Washington State that looks promising. I'll be in touch next week."

Mitch replaced the phone and turned off the light. He walked through the kitchen and opened the door to his recently installed wine closet. Selecting a bottle Julianne had given him, he found a glass and returned to the living room. The setting was dreamlike. A soft autumn rain drummed against the windowpanes. In the fireplace, flames leaped and hissed, throwing an arc of light against the back wall. Upstairs, his children slept contentedly in their beds. Here, in the living room, he sipped a world-class Pinot Noir/Grenache blend.

If only his mood matched the comfort of his surroundings. If only he could chalk this failure up and go forward without the complications that moving his family would bring. Drew and Sarah had finally settled in. He balked at the idea of telling them that once again they would be uprooted, to another home, another school.

In his worst moments, Mitch had considered boarding school. There, at least, they would have stability. It wouldn't be as important for him to establish a base if they were only home on holidays. But as soon as the idea formed in his mind, he'd discarded it. He'd spent a lifetime without his children. They were nearly adults and he barely knew them. If he was ever to establish a relationship with them it was now. Besides, now that most of the kinks had been ironed out, they were comfortable with one another. He liked them. He enjoyed their individual personalities. He looked forward to their being here in the house with him.

He leaned back against the couch cushions and closed his eyes. His options were clear: stay with GGI for a regular paycheck, benefits and stock options, or strike out on his own. What would be best for the kids? They would be leaving for college in less than three years. He wasn't poor by any means, but if he stayed and tried to make a go of it as a vintner, most of the capital from the sale of his Tiburon property would be used up starting a business. Then there was his personal life to consider. But not now. He wasn't up to it.

At first, he thought the tapping at the door was more rain, but when it stopped and then started again, he realized that someone was knocking. He frowned. It was nearly midnight. Setting his glass on the table, he walked across the room and opened the door.

Julianne, the collar of her trench coat standing up against the downpour, stood on his porch, empty-handed and smiling. "Is it too late to come in?"

Surprise and pleasure left him momentarily speechless.

"If it is, I can go."

"No, no." He took her hand and gently pulled her into the house. "I could use a friend."

"I'm sorry about the election, Mitch."

"Thank you." He smiled. "I've opened a bottle of wine. Will you join me?"

"Yes."

Together they walked into the warm living room. He held out his hand. "Let me take your coat."

She shook her head and sat down on the couch. "Not yet. I'm still cold." She picked up the bottle of wine and looked at the label. "It's one of ours."

"Yes. It's exceptional. Warm up near the fire and I'll be right back with your glass."

When he returned, she was staring into the flames, a delicate flush coloring her cheeks. He poured her wine and handed her the glass.

"I really am sorry about the election."

"Are you?" He stood across from her near the fire, his eyes level and steady on her face. "I would have thought otherwise."

"I voted against you."

"That doesn't surprise me."

"It wasn't easy, you know."

"Why is that?"

"Because I knew what it meant while I was doing it."

"What does it mean, Julianne?"

She spoke quickly. "That you'll go away and I'll never see you again."

He nodded. "That's one possibility."

"So, you're really leaving?"

He looked at her, his gaze moving over the petite strength of her small figure, at the blue, blue eyes and the sharp bones of her cheeks and the way the firelight danced over her nose and lips. "I don't think so," he said slowly.

She caught her breath.

"I think I'll stay here, raise my children and see if I've got what it takes to grow grapes and make wine."

Her hand flew up and stopped halfway to her mouth. "Are you sure? Really sure?"

"Yes."

She leaned back against the cushions, pressing her palms against her hot cheeks. "I was so afraid."

He went completely still. "Why?"

She shook her head.

"Why, Julianne?"

She couldn't speak, couldn't tell him what she wanted, what she'd always wanted since the very beginning, when he'd knocked on her door and asked if she had a horse for sale. He was the reason her hands shook when she marked the ballot against the development of the land GGI had purchased for their winery. She'd done what was right for the land and for Francesca and Jake and Nick. But it wasn't right for her. It couldn't be right to send him away, not when she felt this feeling every time she was with him.

Desire was a complicated emotion. She desired Mitchell Gillette, but it was much more complicated than mere wanting. She knew it had to do with the way he felt about her. When a man says he's falling in love, a woman sits up and takes notice. She can't help wondering what it would be like to love him back. Julianne hadn't loved for a very long time, not since Carl had helped Lisa DeAngelo with her buttons. Funny, how that seemed so unimportant now. Time was the balm to all wounds.

She drew a deep breath and then exhaled. She reached for her wine and in a single gulp downed a glass of three-hundred-dollar Pinot Noir without tasting it. Then she stood and untied her belt. "I have stretch marks," she said. "My price for three children."

"Is that what you're hiding under that coat?"

The amusement in his voice gave her courage.

She unbuttoned the top button. "I'm five years older than you."

"I don't believe you."

"You're teasing me."

He nodded. "Under the circumstances, it's allowed."

The middle button was next. "I haven't done this in a long time."

"Actually, I'm relieved to hear it. I don't do well with competition."

The last button slid out of its hole. "I'm scared to death."

The coat dropped to the floor. She stepped away from it. With the exception of a pair of knee-high boots, she was naked.

His eyes widened. "You are full of surprises, aren't you?"

She lifted her chin. "Good ones, I hope."

He set his wineglass on the mantel and walked toward her. "Very good ones."

She met him halfway. Her arms locked behind his neck. "Shall I keep the boots?"

"Definitely keep the boots." His voice thickened. "Christ, you're lovely." He traced the silvery marks spidering across her stomach. "Stretch marks and all."

He bent his head to her mouth. She wrapped one leg around his and slid her hands under his shirt, pulling it up and away from his skin. Then she pressed herself against his chest, gratified to hear his sudden intake of breath. Without taking his mouth away, he muttered something she couldn't hear. It didn't matter.

Julianne felt her other foot leave the floor as he lifted her into his arms for the brief moment it took to move her to the couch. Somehow, his clothes disappeared and his body, warm arms and long legs and hair-rough chest, settled over her. "What about Sarah and Drew?" she whispered.

"Don't worry. Teenagers sleep like the dead."

He touched her in places she'd forgotten could feel. He touched her until she was dizzy and trembling and weak. He kissed her lips and her throat and her shoulders and her breasts, and when her back arched and her head fell backward and her eyes closed, he moved over and into her, in and out, again and again until the firelight and the shadows and the heat coursing through her peaked. She bit into his shoulder and scored his back with her nails and murmured his name against the bulge of his arm, repeating it until it rang like a drum in her mind, and this moment, this memory, lodged in her brain never to be diminished, lost or forgotten.

He said the words, low and muffled against her throat. "I love you, Julianne Harris."

She pushed against his shoulders, but he was too heavy for her to move. "Please, look at me. Look at me when you say that."

He braced himself on both arms and smiled down at her. "I'm looking and I'm saying it again. I love you, Julianne. I'd ask you to marry me but I'm unemployed."

She laughed. Tears of relief brimmed. "Six months is a bit soon to ask someone to marry you."

He shook his head. "Not when we're as advanced in years as we are."

"Speak for yourself. I've never been younger."

"Will you consider it?"

"I'll do more than that. I'll consider myself promised."

His eyes darkened. "I won't let you down, Julianne. You won't be sorry."

"Will Sarah and Drew be pleased?"

"They'll be thrilled. Their biggest concern was that this election would turn you against me."

"It wasn't the election I was worried about."

Mitch kissed her nose and then her mouth. "Lisa was never in the picture, not for a minute, certainly not for me." He sat up and pulled her with him. "What about *your* children?"

Julianne hedged. "What about them?" She reached for her coat, sliding her arms into the sleeves.

"Will they be happy for us?"

"The girls will be excited. They thought I was buried alive."

"And Jake?"

"Jake will be a harder sell. It's nothing personal." Julianne said quickly. "It's just that he was very close to his father and he's never considered the possibility of me with anyone else. It's my fault, really. I didn't do anything to make him think differently."

"What about Francesca?"

Julianne bit her lip. "That depends."

"On what?"

"On whether she allows Jake back into her life. She won't need me anymore if she does."

"Have you come to terms with her mother?"

Julianne lifted her chin. "I've allowed Lisa far too much power in my life. That's over now. She can go or stay. I'd rather she go, but that's not up to me. Although, I have a feeling she won't be staying for long. She's not a woman who needs roots."

"Good for you. It sounds as if the only obstacles in our path are Jake and Francesca."

"Which is why it's better to wait a bit before we talk about marriage."

He drew her back into his arms and settled her head against his shoulder. "You're a smart woman, Julianne Harris. I can learn from you."

Francesca walked the last row of Chardonnay vines inspecting their dormant trunks. She loved this time of year when the sun was pale, the air chilled, and barren stalks stood in rhythmic rows of dark relief against butter-gold hills. Sage, mint, lavender, horses, dried grass and gravid earth, valley scents, were swept into fragrant flurries by a soft but persistent wind blowing in from the west. The sun draped the hills like a blanket of melted copper, and a pair of red-tailed hawks soared in perfect harmony over the horizon.

She made the last of her notes in the margin of the legal pad she carried with her and started back toward the house. Lisa, dressed in a flowing kimono with white hibiscus flowers splashed randomly across a red background, met her on the porch.

"Can we talk alone for a minute, Francesca?"

Francesca experienced a rush of pleasure. "Of course."

Lisa crossed her arms against her chest. "I'm leaving," she said bluntly.

Francesca felt light-headed. She sat down on the step. "When?"

"Tomorrow."

"You haven't been here very long."

"Long enough, I think."

"What does that mean?"

Lisa sighed and sat down beside her daughter. "I don't belong. That should be obvious to you. I'm useless here. I always was."

"It doesn't have to be that way."

Lisa shook her head. "It wouldn't work."

"You could stay a little longer," Francesca said stubbornly. "Nick doesn't even know you."

"You don't get it, do you?" Her laugh was brittle. "I'm not interested in all this." She waved her arm to encompass the vineyard. "Nick will get along fine without me. He has you and Jake and Julianne."

"I'd like him to have you, too."

"No, thank you." Lisa laughed shortly. "I'm not very good with children, not even my own."

"Don't say that." Francesca's lip was trembling. She felt like a little girl again, a little girl whose mother didn't want her.

"It's true, darling. There's no point in crying. I'm not the motherly type and I definitely am not ready to be a grandmother."

"Whether you're ready or not doesn't matter. You *are* a grandmother. I want you to stay."

Lisa stood. "I can't. A friend is coming for me tomorrow."

"A friend?"

"Someone I've known over the years. He's in between things right now. We're going to see if it works out."

"Congratulations," Francesca said woodenly.

"Don't look like that, sweetie," her mother coaxed. "Be happy for me."

Francesca lifted her chin. "This time *you* don't get it. I've waited my whole life for you to come back." Her voice choked. "And now you're leaving again. Doesn't any of it matter to you? How can a mother disappear for a lifetime?"

"It is odd, isn't it?" said Lisa, as if they were discussing the outcome of a recipe that didn't turn out the way it was supposed to in the picture. "I'm sorry."

Francesca stared straight ahead. "No, you're not."

"Yes, I really am. I'm sorry I'm not the person you would like me to be. I'm sorry I wasn't the wife Frank wanted or the mother you and Chris deserved. Especially you, Francesca. You've turned out remarkably well, considering your parents. It's probably due to Julianne."

"Why do you hate Julianne?"

"I don't hate anyone. It's the other way around. Julianne hates me."

"Why?"

"I'd rather not say. She wouldn't appreciate it."

"She said to ask you."

Lisa's mouth twisted and for the first time, Francesca did not think she was beautiful.

"All right. Carl Harris and I were involved."

"How involved?"

Lisa's hands clenched. "We had an affair," she said defiantly. "It lasted for quite some time. He was the reason I left."

Francesca shook her head. "I don't understand."

"When Julianne found out, she was going to leave Santa Ynez. Frank suggested that I go instead." She lifted one shoulder in a careless shrug and looked away.

Francesa sat for a minute, allowing the information to sink in. She waited for the rise of a recognizable emotion, compassion, pity, even contempt. There was nothing except a small, secret kernel of gratitude for her father's wisdom.

She stood and dusted off the seat of her pants. "Good luck, Mother. I hope everything works out for you. Don't be such a stranger. Stop in and visit now and then. There might be a time when flesh and blood is more important to you."

"Ouch." Lisa grimaced. "My goodness. You can scratch."

"I can bite, too, but I'd rather not. You're my mother."

"I'm not a very good one," Lisa confessed. "I wish I was different."

"I do, too." Francesca sighed. "But I guess we'll have to make the best of it. Do you want me to see you off tomorrow?"

"That won't be necessary. I know you have to be up early."

Francesca nodded. "Send me an address when you're settled."

"Of course, darling."

Thirty-One

Francesca sat in the idling Jeep in front of Ralph's supermarket and pressed the phone-book button on her cell phone, scrolling through the numbers. Where could Jake be? She'd tried the winery, the office, the private line at home and his cell phone, only to hear her own recorded voice and then his, telling her to leave her name and number. She didn't bother. Francesca wanted a real person, someone to answer back, to respond, to tell her why her long-lost mother found it too boring and inconvenient to stay long enough to establish a relationship with her daughter and grandson.

Julianne would listen. She always listened. But this wasn't the time to involve her mother-in-law. She had her own reasons for wanting Lisa DeAngelo out of the way. Francesca pulled out of the parking lot and drove down the highway toward home. At the intersection of Refugio and Edison, she waited for the light. Glancing into the rearview mirror she spotted Jake's car parked in front of the Red Lyon Inn. Quickly, she turned right, drove around the block and pulled into the hotel parking lot.

Jake sat at the bar, nursing a tall, untouched glass of golden ale. "Hi," she said, scooting into the seat beside him.

He forced a smile. "What are you doing here?"

"Looking for you."

"I'm popular all of a sudden?"

Francesca frowned. Something wasn't right. "Are you okay?"

"I'm fine," he said. "What's going on?"

"My mother's leaving."

The blue eyes clouded. "I'm sorry, Francie. I know you didn't want it this way." He looked genuinely concerned.

"The thing is, I was hurt at first, but now I don't really mind all that much. Isn't that strange?"

"I don't think so," he said slowly. "It would be strange if you were really broken up. She hasn't ever been a part of your life."

"I thought she'd changed. I wanted her to know Nick."

He took her hand, lifted it to his lips and kissed it. "She wasn't particularly maternal."

"That's what she said." Francesca's laugh was brief and bitter. "She said I turned out well despite my parents. She said it was probably because of Julianne. She said—" Francesca stopped. Jake had worshipped Carl Harris. Maybe it wasn't fair to tell him about his father. Julianne would have told him if she wanted him to know. "Never mind," she said. "It doesn't matter now."

He wasn't paying attention.

"Jake, something's wrong. Tell me, please."

He looked down at this drink. "The Soledad purchase fell through. I have to tell Gene and Kate today."

Francesca's stomach burned. "Why? How?"

He shrugged. "It doesn't matter."

"Of course it does."

"Property values are unstable because of the dam."

"But the crack has been repaired and the entire dam is being inspected for reconstruction. That can't be the only reason."

"I don't have enough money up front, Francie. Soledad is on the other side of the valley. It's still worth full value. Other properties haven't fared as well. DeAngelo Winery's profits are based on its vineyard's harvest. The vineyard lost acreage. Next year's harvest won't be what it was this year."

"We've had low harvests before and come back just fine the following year. That's the nature of the wine business."

"I can't make them give me the loan," he said impatiently. "Those are the committee's reasons for refusing the money. It probably has something to do with GGI's interest in the area as well."

"GGI's bid went down in the election."

"For now. That doesn't mean it won't come up again. Banks are conservative."

She bit her lip. "Surely we can do something."

"This isn't a *we* thing, Francie. You can't control everything. This was my project, and every argument you've given me is one I've already thought of. The outcome is disappointing, but I'll get over it."

Francesca's chest hurt deep inside, as if her heart

were being squeezed dry. She couldn't concentrate long enough to figure out what it all meant. "What happens now?" she asked, her voice low.

"What do you mean?"

She swallowed and forced herself to ask the question. "What are you going to do?"

He grinned. "I'm going to stay here, work for my ex-wife and convince her to marry me again." His arms closed around her. "Is that all right with you?"

Too relieved to answer, she leaned against him.

"I love you, Francie. I'm not going anywhere. I thought I'd made that clear."

She straightened and reached for his glass. "Do you mind?"

"Help yourself."

She sipped at the ale until her insides warmed and the shaking in her hands stopped. "How much more money do you need?"

"I'm not taking your reserves, Francie."

"What if we mortgage the vineyard, too?"

He shook his head firmly. "I appreciate the offer, more than you know. But I'm not taking it."

"Will you think about it?" she pleaded.

"Not this time."

"Why not?"

"Because it isn't a fair exchange. That didn't work for us the first time. I don't want to risk us again. There will be other deals. Now isn't the right time. Trust me." He kissed her briefly on the lips. "Let's go home."

She followed him back to the house and they pulled into the courtyard together. She recognized Mitch's parked car. Nick was outside shooting balls into a net with a hockey stick. He waved and ran up the steps to wait for them at the door.

"Hi, buddy," his father said, ruffling his hair. "How's the practice going?"

"It's okay. Where were you?"

"I met your mom in town and we came in together."

Francesca leaned over to kiss his cheek. "How was school, sweetheart?"

"Good. My special day is tomorrow. I need a poster with pictures of me as a baby and special awards on it."

Francesca groaned. "How long did you know about this, Nick?"

"It came home on the Monday worksheet."

Jake cut in smoothly. "I'll help him with it, Francie. I've got nothing going on tonight."

"We'll both help," she said. "It'll be fun if we do it together."

"Lisa left," Nick announced, "and we're having company for dinner."

"She didn't waste any time," Jake said.

Francesca refused to think about her mother and what could have been.

"It's Mr. Gillette and Sarah and Drew," said Nick, continuing his train of thought.

"My goodness." Francesca's eyes widened. "That's quite a crowd for a weeknight."

Jake held the door while Francesca and Nick walked into the house. He followed them into the kitchen. Drew and Sarah were chopping vegetables. Julianne was standing over the stove, stirring something in a pot, and Mitch was seated on a bar stool opening wine.

Julianne greeted them. "Just the people we wanted to see."

"What's the occasion?" asked Jake.

"We're celebrating," Mitch informed them. "I've resigned from GGI."

"You're kidding." Francesca accepted the glass of wine he held out.

Mitch shook his head. "Not this time. We're staying. I'm going to try to make a go of the vineyard."

"Congratulations." Francesca looked at Sarah. "How do you kids feel about all this?"

Sarah's blue eyes sparkled. "I'm excited. I really didn't want to move again now that we're all settled. The company was sending him to Washington."

"Nobody wanted to move again," Drew added. "Besides, where would I find another job like this one?"

"What are your plans, Mitch?" Jake asked casually.

"I'll learn as much as I can about growing grapes and make do on what I've got until my first harvest."

"Three years is a long time."

"I've planted Pinot Noir. The rest will have to come later."

"Pinot Noir isn't a sure thing," offered Jake. "You won't make a living on that variety, not here in the valley."

"Do you have another suggestion?"

Jake grinned. "As a matter of fact, I do." He stood. "How long until dinner, Mom?"

Julianne looked bewildered. "A half hour or so."

"Give us forty-five minutes."

"I can do that."

Jake nodded at Mitch. "Will you join me in the office? I have a proposition for you."

Julianne waited until they left the room. "What's going on?" she asked Francesca.

"I think Jake is offering Mitch a share of Soledad. He needs more capital and he won't take it from me."

"You don't have more capital."

"I have the vineyard."

Across the space of the kitchen, their eyes met. "You offered him the vineyard?" Julianne's voice sounded different.

"Yes. But he refused."

Julianne smiled. "Good for him."

Drew and Sarah looked at each other and shrugged. Nick, not understanding but wanting to be included, shrugged, too. For some reason the adults around them were charged with positive energy. It flowed through the warm room surrounding them until they were caught up in its rhythm.

Dinner was even more celebratory. Julianne's carrot soup, delicious and nourishing and tasting nothing like carrots, accompanied grilled chicken, sun-dried tomato, cheese and portobello mushroom sandwiches. A pear salad finished off the meal.

Mitch waited until every last spoonful of Nick's favorite, peppermint-stick ice cream, had been consumed before he stood and held up his wineglass. "I'd like to offer a toast," he said. "To a successful future partnership."

Julianne poured sparkling cider into the children's glasses. "Everyone stand and hold up your glasses. You're part of this, too."

Chairs scraped the wood floors, glasses clinked and warm wishes were exchanged.

"My goodness," Julianne said when they were seated again. "That was fast."

"Jake did his homework," Mitch explained. "All the documents were there, with facts in place. It's a great investment and it will give me an income until my own grapes come in."

Francesca looked across the table. Her eyes met Jake's and held. "Jake and I have an announcement, too." She laughed out loud. "We're getting married. Again."

For an instant there was silence and then everyone spoke at once.

Julianne leaned back in her chair and closed her eyes. "Thank goodness."

"Wow!" said the twins.

Nick clapped his hands.

Again, Mitch stood. He looked at Julianne. She shook her head slightly.

"This calls for another toast," he said lifting his glass. Everyone did the same. "To marriage," he said, "and family, and the future."

"To good friends," Francesca added, winking at Sarah.

Drew whispered something to Nick. The two held up their glasses. "To dads," they said in unison.

Julianne laughed at the expression on Mitch's face. "I'll call my daughters and tell them the news. They'll be thrilled." She picked up an empty serving bowl and, on her way to the kitchen, briefly rested her hand on Mitch's shoulder.

Across the table, her son noticed the caress. And then he smiled.

The latest novel from
New York Times bestselling author

ERICA SPINDLER

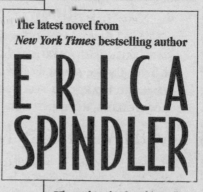

"Spindler's latest moves fast and takes no prisoners. An intriguing look into the twisted mind of someone for whom murder is simply a business."

—*Publishers Weekly* on *Cause for Alarm*

When a friend is found brutally murdered in her New Orleans apartment, former homicide detective Stacy Killian has reason to believe her death is related to the cultish fantasy role-playing game White Rabbit. The game is dark, violent—and addictive. As the bodies mount and the game is taken to the next level, Stacy sees cryptic notes that foretell the next victim and no one—no one—is safe. Because White Rabbit is more than a game—it's life and death. And anyone can die before the game is over…and the killer takes all.

KILLER TAKES ALL

MIRA®

Available the first week of June 2005, wherever books are sold!

www.MIRABooks.com

MES2186

NEW YORK TIMES BESTSELLING AUTHOR
MARY ALICE MONROE RETURNS TO THE
CAPTIVATING AND MYSTICAL SOUTH CAROLINA
LOWCOUNTRY, A PLACE OF WILD BEAUTY AND
UNTAMED HEARTS, TO TELL THE MOVING STORY
OF HEALING, HOPE AND NEW BEGINNINGS....

Mary Alice Monroe

E.R. nurse Ella Majors has seen all the misery that she can handle. Burned-out and unsure of her next step, she accepts the temporary position as caregiver to Marion, a frightened five-year-old who suffers from juvenile diabetes. There is more sorrow in the isolated home than the little girl's illness, and the bond that is formed between Ella and Marion reveals the inherent risks and exhilarating beauty of flying free.

skyward

"A devoted naturalist and native of South Carolina's Low Country, Monroe is in her element when describing the wonders of nature and the ways people relate to it.... Hauntingly beautiful relationships between birds and people add texture to the story.... Monroe successfully combines elements of women's fiction and romance in this lyrical tale."

—*Publishers Weekly*

Available the first week of June 2005, wherever books are sold!

MIRA®

A quiet Amish community...a terrifying threat

KAREN HARPER

One morning Leah Kurtz wakes her infant daughter and immediately knows something is wrong. Very wrong. She is convinced that her baby has been switched with another child. When no one believes her, Leah turns to an unlikely ally—an outsider—despite the fact that her Amish community frowns on its members seeking help in the outside world. Leah is only concerned with the truth. But sometimes, finding the truth may have deadly consequences.

"The book is strongest in its loving depiction of Amish life, its creation of a dark mood and its development of the central romance."

—*Publishers Weekly* on *Dark Road Home*

DARK ANGEL

Available the first week of June 2005, wherever paperbacks are sold!

MIRA®

www.MIRABooks.com

MKH2179

There is no statute of limitations on murder....

Laura Caldwell

"There is no statute of limitations on murder. Look closely." That's all the anonymous letter said, but attorney Hailey Sutter understands the meaning behind the well-chosen words. Someone wants her to investigate what happened to her mother, who died when Hailey was only seven. The death was ruled accidental, but Hailey begins having flashbacks that tell a different story....

Obsessed with uncovering the truth, it's soon clear that the answer is right in front of her—all she has to do is find the courage to look closely....

Look Closely

"This fast read has a thought-provoking theme and an interesting medical angle."
—*Romantic Times* on *A Clean Slate*

Available the first week of June 2005, wherever paperbacks are sold!

MIRA®

www.MIRABooks.com

MLC2183

In July, receive a
FREE copy of
Jan Coffey's

**TRUST ME
ONCE**

when you purchase
her latest romantic
suspense novel,

**FIVE IN
A ROW.**

*For full details,
look inside
FIVE IN A ROW,
the July 2005 title
by Jan Coffey.*

MIRA®

www.MIRABooks.com

MJCPOP0705

If you enjoyed what you just read,
then we've got an offer you can't resist!

Take 2 bestselling novels FREE!
Plus get a FREE surprise gift!

Clip this page and mail it to MIRA®

IN U.S.A.
3010 Walden Ave.
P.O. Box 1867
Buffalo, N.Y. 14240-1867

IN CANADA
P.O. Box 609
Fort Erie, Ontario
L2A 5X3

YES! Please send me 2 free MIRA® novels and my free surprise gift. After receiving them, if I don't wish to receive anymore, I can return the shipping statement marked cancel. If I don't cancel, I will receive 4 brand-new novels every month, before they're available in stores! In the U.S.A., bill me at the bargain price of $4.99 plus 25¢ shipping and handling per book and applicable sales tax, if any*. In Canada, bill me at the bargain price of $5.49 plus 25¢ shipping and handling per book and applicable taxes**. That's the complete price and a savings of over 20% off the cover prices—what a great deal! I understand that accepting the 2 free books and gift places me under no obligation ever to buy any books. I can always return a shipment and cancel at any time. Even if I never buy another The Best of the Best™ book, the 2 free books and gift are mine to keep forever.

185 MDN DZ7J
385 MDN DZ7K

Name	(PLEASE PRINT)	
Address	Apt.#	
City	State/Prov.	Zip/Postal Code

*Not valid to current The Best of the Best™, Mira®,
suspense and romance subscribers.*

Want to try two free books from another series?
Call 1-800-873-8635 or visit www.morefreebooks.com.

* Terms and prices subject to change without notice. Sales tax applicable in N.Y.
** Canadian residents will be charged applicable provincial taxes and GST.
 All orders subject to approval. Offer limited to one per household.
® and ™are registered trademarks owned and used by the trademark owner and or its licensee.

BOB04R   ©2004 Harlequin Enterprises Limited

MIRABooks.com

We've got the lowdown on your favorite author!

☆ Read an excerpt of your favorite author's newest book

☆ Check out her bio

☆ Talk to her in our Discussion Forums

☆ Read interviews, diaries, and more

☆ Find her current bestseller, and even her backlist titles

All this and more available at

www.MiraBooks.com

MEAUT1R3

JEANETTE
BAKER

66910	BLOOD ROSES	___ $6.50 U.S.	___ $7.99 CAN.
66696	THE DELANEY WOMAN	___ $6.50 U.S.	___ $7.99 CAN.

(limited quantities available)

TOTAL AMOUNT	$_____
POSTAGE & HANDLING	$_____
($1.00 for one book; 50¢ for each additional)	
APPLICABLE TAXES*	$_____
TOTAL PAYABLE	$_____

(check or money order—please do not send cash)

To order, complete this form and send it, along with a check or money order for the total above, payable to MIRA Books, to: **In the U.S.:** 3010 Walden Avenue, P.O. Box 9077, Buffalo, NY 14269-9077; **In Canada:** P.O. Box 636, Fort Erie, Ontario L2A 5X3.

Name:_____
Address:_____ City:_____
State/Prov.:_____ Zip/Postal Code:_____
Account Number (if applicable):_____
075 CSAS

*New York residents remit applicable sales taxes.
Canadian residents remit applicable GST and provincial taxes.

MIRA®

www.MIRABooks.com

MJB0605BL